THE BOOKWORM
PAPERBACK EXCHANGE & GIFTS
1625 WEST 7800 SOUTH
WEST JORDAN, UT. 84084

He Was The Strongest Man of His Time—Until She Became His Weakness . . .

Beautiful, devout, young Tara, a novice in a country abbey, finds her cloistered life suddenly destroyed when Viking invaders burn the convent and take her prisoner. Wedded against her will to the pagan chieftain Rorik, Tara slowly overcomes her fear as Rorik introduces her to the joy of passionate love.

Then a vicious abduction separates the lovers—and their search to be reunited takes them from the dramatic northern fjords to the shores of the Black Sea, from Arabian domed palaces and the slave marts of Constantinople to an isolated Greek island. For the love of Tara and Rorik must survive the ravages of war, the cruel twists of treachery, and the challenge of a vast continent . . .

Other Avon Books by:
Barbara Ferry Johnson

DELTA BLOOD	32664	$1.95
LIONORS	36111	1.95

Tara's Song

BARBARA FERRY JOHNSON

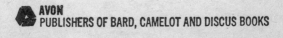
AVON
PUBLISHERS OF BARD, CAMELOT AND DISCUS BOOKS

TARA'S SONG is an original publication of Avon Books. This work has never before appeared in book form.

AVON BOOKS
a division of
The Hearst Corporation
959 Eighth Avenue
New York, New York 10019

Copyright © 1978 by Barbara Ferry Johnson
Published by arrangement with the author.
Library of Congress Catalog Card Number: 78-58903
ISBN: 0-380-39123-6

All rights reserved, which includes the right
to reproduce this book or portions thereof in
any form whatsoever. For information address
Writers House, 132 West 31 Street,
New York, New York 10001

First Avon Printing, September, 1978

AVON TRADEMARK REG. U.S. PAT. OFF. AND IN
OTHER COUNTRIES, MARCA REGISTRADA,
HECHO EN U.S.A.

Printed in the U.S.A.

For my two mothers:
ANNA HEYRON FERRY and
GLADYS HEARON JOHNSON

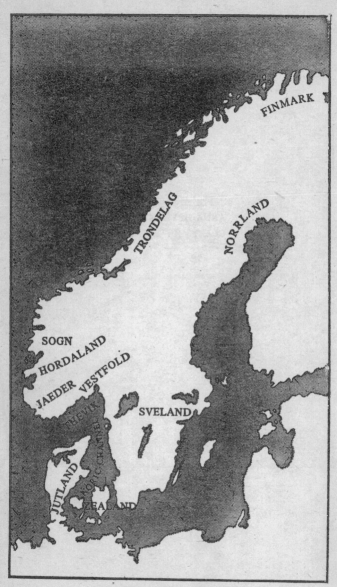

VIKING SCANDINAVIA

TENTH-CENTURY EUROPE

Western wind, when wilt thou blow,
The small rain down can rain?
Christ, if my love were in my arms,
And I in my bed again!

—ANONYMOUS

Chapter One

LESS THAN AN HOUR BEFORE DAWN I heard the first scream.

My immediate reaction was one of irritation. Someone had dared to disturb the hour of quiet between morning prayers and breakfast. Offended at the sacrilege, I felt merely an urge to hush the thoughtless person. Only when the sound finally registered as a scream did an icy shiver, more chilling than the cold stone floor of the chapel I'd been kneeling on, pierce me from head to foot.

After the early-morning service of Matins, the other women in the abbey had walked silently from the chapel to their cell-like rooms for private prayer before the bell announcing breakfast and the beginning of our busy routine.

It was not my usual custom to remain behind after this service, but the abbess had taken to her bed a few days earlier with a mild fever, and she had delegated to me the responsibility of overseeing the daily routine. Young though I was, not yet twenty-one, I often assisted her in this way.

On this first frost-tinged autumn morning, I had awakened to the acrid odors of peat fires in nearby cottages, the heady aroma of fresh rain on new-fallen leaves, and the earthy smells from the abbey community's one chicken coop and small byre of ewes and lambs. Old one-eyed Cock-a-doodle-doo, our chanticleer who had long since learned to crow by abbey time rather than sun time, had roused me in his impudent, no-nonsense way to inform me it was time to ring the bell for Matins. Sleepy-eyed nuns and scurrying novices shivered in the clammy atmosphere of the chapel, and they chanted the service at an almost blasphemously fast pace. Their minds, I was sure, were dwelling more on the hot porridge and herb tea awaiting them in the big kitchen-refectory than on their breveries.

From the chapel I had planned to go to the infirmary to

1

look in on Berthe, the infirmarian, and sit with the patients while she breakfasted. Intense pity overwhelmed me when I thought of the two patients in the infirmary, and I always said an extra prayer of thanksgiving that I was young and still had a long, peaceful, if uneventful, future ahead of me. Sister Ilsa was dying from a fiery lump that grew like a child in her belly while slowly consuming all flesh from her body. A stiffening of Sister Sarah's joints had progressed so far as to render her completely immobile, and she had to be turned frequently to prevent the eruption of festering sores on her back. None of our herb poultices or hot tisanes could do more than ease their misery for short periods of time. Death had been cruelly biding his time to bring both of them release from pain, but on this morning as I prayed for them he was hovering nearer than I realized.

The first scream was followed immediately by a second and then a third, all coming from the sleeping quarters. A brief hope that a sleeping nun was having a nightmare was immediately dispelled by more outcries. Shrouded in pre-dawn darkness, I moved to the door of the chapel, drawn and yet repelled by the sound of bodies being dragged helplessly across the stone floors, while rough masculine voices shouted obscenities and made lewd demands.

Terrified, I wanted to stay hidden, yet I knew I should run out and help. We had been invaded, but by whom? Who would dare to violate our sanctuary? Once more I started to leave the chapel, only to stand transfixed with fear when I realized the attackers were within a few feet of me. I was helpless to act; my legs would not move, and I leaned, gasping for breath, against the door jamb as I became more aware of what was taking place.

"Here's a saucy wench to stir a man's blood!"

"No—no!" I recognized the terrified voice of a novice. "Please, sir, no!" Oh God, I thought, not that, and my stomach churned as I visualized what was happening to her.

"Come, come, lass. Lift your skirts and we'll have a bit o' fun. 'Tis certain I am you'll like it."

In spite of his coarse, guttural accent, I understood every word. The voice sounded like that of a large man, and I knew the girl would be helpless to resist.

I tried to close my ears to the long, agonized shriek that followed. Pains like those she was enduring shot through me; my flesh crawled with the agony of what she was suf-

2

fering. I could not breathe, and I was choking on the phlegm in my throat.

Surrounding me now was a horrid cacophony of sound: boisterous laughter and victorious shouts from our assailants; the desperate pleas and low moans of the women. Then came a long, ear-splitting yell that froze the blood in my veins.

"To O—O—Odin!"

We were the victims of an attack by the Vikings, the most dreaded of all the invaders along the coast. From childhood I had heard stories of their ravages, how they burned and looted, how they captured and raped the women. No one was spared when they raided the countryside. I had to do something, yet I was weak with indecision. I could run and hope to avoid being caught, but that was a desperate thought. I dared not hide in the chapel for long. They would soon be looting it, knowing it was filled with priceless objects. There must be some way to get help.

I ventured out a little way into the arched cloister and took a moment to look at our attackers. The courtyard was filled with a horde of rowdy, uncouth, rough-looking men. Their hair was long and shaggy; their beards, unkempt and filthy. They were dressed in dun-colored woolen blouses; loose, baggy trousers wrapped around their calves with leather thongs; and rough, sleeveless leather jerkins.

Numb with shock, unable either to move or to turn my eyes away, I watched as some dragged their victims, screaming and pleading, into the courtyard. I was fascinated yet repelled, as if watching a scene I was not really part of. A few had already lowered their trousers and were assaulting their captives in full view of all, laughing with hideous delight when the women clawed at their faces or tried to resist. There was no escaping these huge men from the North. More powerful-looking than any bred on Britain's shores, they were as massive and fearsome as the heathen gods they worshipped.

One of the novices was trying to fend off her attacker by gouging his eyes. I watched, horrified, as he quickly raised his knife and stabbed her in the throat. My hand went to my own throat, and I swallowed quickly, forcing back the bile that rose unbidden at the sight. From the novice's still-pulsating vein, blood spurted everywhere, covering her gown and the man's clothes. He swore loudly and then turned to find a new victim. Watching her endure several

3

seconds of agony before she died, I felt another hot rush of liquid in my throat; and before I could stop it, I was retching uncontrollably. Finally, after spewing up nothing but gall, the spasms ceased.

Weakened by nausea and my abject helplessness to aid those being attacked, I clutched the wall to keep from fainting. Somehow I had failed in my duty to protect the women the abbess had put in my care. Now the shouts and screams had been replaced by heavy breathing and whimpering cries. The women who had already endured brutal rape lay huddled in their torn and bloodied robes, afraid to move for fear of further attacks. Many, I knew, had passed out; others pretended unconsciousness to prevent repeated abuse.

Having taken vows of chastity, my gentle sisters in God were suffering the torments of the damned as both body and soul were violated by the lust of the heathen invaders. These were women who had patiently served our Lord by aiding the sick, the needy, weary travelers, and those set upon by forest marauders. Now they were victims of a rapacious cruelty far more evil than most of the sufferings they had been called upon to ease.

Although my heart was still beating wildly from fear, I finally decided what I must do. So far I had not been seen, and there was one way I might yet escape from the chapel and seek help. As quietly as possible, I made my way back into the darkened building and thence to a narrow rear hall leading to the kitchen.

In the near dark, I stumbled over two bodies, and I gasped before I could catch myself. The man was panting, and I moved quickly to avoid the heavy hand that reached up and touched the skirt of my robe. The girl underneath him was quiet, and I hoped she had fainted before feeling the painful thrust of his body.

Once in the kitchen, I looked and called softly for Sister Mara. There was no answer. The porridge was cooking over the fire, but either she had fled from an attacker or been dragged outside. From the bits of broken crockery beneath my feet and on the long table, I knew she had not gone willingly.

I heard the heavy breathing behind my back a scant second before a rough hand grabbed me and began pulling at my robe. It did not tear under his frantic clawing, but it did give him the leverage he needed to spin me around.

4

Before I could get away, I found myself clutched against his chest while his brawny arms squeezed the breath out of me. His fat lips began slobbering kisses over my face and neck. His rough beard scratched my skin, and his hands bruised my arms and shoulders.

When he tried to kiss my mouth, I reeled from his odious mead-sodden breath and sweaty stench. Suddenly, as if I'd had cold water dashed over me, I recovered from the first shock of attack and found the courage to fight. Wildly I reached around for something to fend him off. If he intended to rape me, he would succeed only after he knew he had been in a fight. My hand finally touched the table, and I felt myself clutching a large crockery pot. Without stopping to think or aim, I began swinging and hitting until I heard a sickening crunch and a loud moan. He fell heavily forward, forcing me to the floor with him and pinning me helpless under his huge, inert body. While I struggled to free myself I heard voices at the door, and as I realized my safety depended on playing out our little charade, for a moment fear was replaced by cold, calculating thought. Although sickened by having to do it, I guided my would-be rapist's limp hand with my own and made it look as if he were forcing up the skirts of my robe. To add a touch of realism, I moaned and whimpered pleadingly.

The two intruders did not leave as I hoped, and I prayed they wouldn't notice my assailant's lack of movement—or the blood dripping from his temple down the side of my neck. I was slowly suffocating under the man's dead weight; but if I made one false move and the others came to investigate, I would be completely at their mercy. To continue the dangerous game I was playing, I moved just enough to budge the man slightly. My legs began to cramp, and I couldn't suppress a cry when I tried to change position. But it seemed to convince the men their friend was too busy to be disturbed, and after a few obscene remarks they left.

I waited agonizing minutes, fearful someone else would appear. My terror increased when I realized the man on top of me was dying. I had to get out of the kitchen as soon as possible, and to that end I pushed and heaved until I was finally able to crawl out from under the unbearable weight. With both legs still numb, I half-crawled, half-slid across the floor, pushing broken crockery out of my way as I moved along.

5

I dreaded what I might find in the infirmary, and I almost turned back when I saw the door to it open. All around me was silence, the silence of death. The smell of fresh blood pervaded the room, mingling with the noxious odor of the fluid that drained constantly from Sister Ilsa's diseased body. I recoiled instinctively and wanted to flee from the horror I knew awaited me, but the thought that someone might be alive and needing help urged me forward.

Cautiously I made my way across the short distance to the two beds, guided by the light from a single sputtering candle. Sister Sarah lay immobile as always, but her knees were drawn up, and she had flung her arms across her face as if to protect herself from an attacker. I could not keep from weeping; the pain those movements caused her must have been excruciating. Warm blood from a single wound in her chest seeped onto her already cold skin.

On the other bed, Berthe lay in a macabre position over the body of Sister Ilsa, where apparently she had flung herself across the elderly nun in an effort to protect her. Berthe's long braids, usually wound around her head, were soaked with blood and hanging down her back. I could not determine where she had been struck until I lifted the braids and saw the ugly gash in her throat. Choking with grief, I visualized what had probably happened. One of the Vikings, laughing at her feeble attempt to save Sister Ilsa, had jerked her head back by her hair and slashed her throat. In an unknowingly ironic jest of a hideous fiend, Sister Ilsa had been killed by having her belly ripped open.

In spite of the danger, in spite of the threat to my own life, I had to take a few moments to cleanse the bodies and lay them out in quiet repose, to restore to the room some semblance of propriety. All the while I wept, wept at the indecencies and impious acts of the invaders as well as for those who had suffered at their hands. Somehow the act of caring for these dead calmed me, and when I finished I was better able to think about what I should do next. I dreaded entering the courtyard, but I knew I must see how the abbess had fared. I took one last look at the infirmary, a place of healing now become a charnel house, and headed for the small cottage where the abbess lived somewhat apart from the rest of the community.

Even as I clung to the safety of the outer wall, I had time to think about the attack. Viking raids along the western coast of Britain, around the shores of Ireland where they had established strongholds, and into the interior of the Outer Isles were no novelty. But never to my knowledge had they ventured this far inland in our section of the Southwest. Something—or someone—had led them here.

I reached the rear door of the small cottage nestled comfortably in the corner formed by two of the community's main outer walls and partially protected on the outer sides by a low wall of random-piled rocks. The sun would soon appear above the trees; but I stayed close in the shadow of the wall and was not stopped. Though I moved at a sure, steady pace, inwardly I was quivering with fear at the sound of raucous laughter, quiet sobs, scuffling feet, and the sight of upraised mead horns, torn garments, and the pitiful attempts of victims to drag their mutilated bodies across the courtyard.

Cautiously, fearing I might find the same death and destruction I'd seen in the infirmary, I opened the rear door of the two-room cottage which was the abbess's private domain. It contained her simple bedroom in which I now stood and a small reception room where she often greeted visitors from outside the abbey. Once inside, I heard her speaking with an emphatically severe edge to her usually well-modulated voice.

"Did you hear me? I said get out!"

Thank God! Lady Anna was still alive. So far she had not been harmed, but she would not be safe for long if someone were threatening her. Although she was absolutely fearless in the face of danger, Christian courage would not protect her against these heathens. I waited a moment, thinking it wiser to learn what was happening before entering. If she could handle the situation herself, my entrance would only endanger her.

The only answer to her command was the sound of someone moving heavily across the floor. Was the Viking leaving or attacking? I dared wait no longer to see what was taking place. As quietly as possible I opened the connecting door. A huge man stood a few feet from Lady Anna, a menacing scowl on his face. Something in her defiant manner had made him stop in his approach, but I feared his hesitation was only momentary. He moved again, away from her and out of my range of vision. For a second I relaxed, thinking he had left. I stiffened again when I

7

saw the abbess striding furiously toward him. Oh, no, Lady Anna, don't do anything to rile him, I thought.

"Don't you dare touch that!" She ordered in a threatening tone. Oh God, I prayed again, don't make him mad. Let him take what he wants and leave. "Put it down, you heathen," she stormed. "Here, take these and these, but you cannot have that."

I could not see what the Viking had picked up, but now I feared Lady Anna was really in danger. No words of hers, no matter how insistent, would stop him from taking what he wanted. I was far less concerned about the loss of a valuable object than the prospect of her being harmed. There was no question now of not going to her aid. I had to go in and protect her from her own foolish actions or she would surely be killed. Yet, to my shame, for a brief moment I hesitated, fearful of the danger to myself if I intervened. Certain he would turn from her to me, preferring a young victim to one of her advanced age, I swallowed hard while summoning up the courage to enter the room. That one instant of selfish hesitation on my part would haunt me for the rest of my life.

I was finally stirred to action when the man struck her, and I saw her fall to the floor, moaning from the heavy blow. No longer caring what might happen to me, I rushed in, fully expecting him to turn and attack me. To my amazement, he stared transfixed at Lady Anna and then ran from the cottage. Although surprised, I cared not why he had fled but was only grateful that I could devote all my attention to the abbess.

"Lady Anna! Let me help you." I bent down to raise her head off the floor.

"Oh God, Tara, is that you? Are you all right?" As was her wont, her first concern was for me rather than herself. Although nearly seventy, she ran the community with almost ceaseless energy. Her frail-looking body belied the strength and endurance that shamed those much younger.

"I'm fine," I assured her, "but I fear you've been hurt."

"Not badly, but you can help me onto the bed. I've just had the breath knocked out of me." For her even to admit she needed assistance was a sign she was more badly injured than I first thought.

Lying awkwardly on the floor, she was finally able to raise up enough to put one of her arms across my shoulders while I supported her at the waist. I knew from her

8

short, gasping breaths and pale face she was in more pain than she wanted me to know.

"Lady Anna, you're seriously hurt. You need real care."

"Just to lie down. I shall be all right." But her voice had become so faint that I knew it was difficult for her to talk.

My hand slid up from her waist, and I first felt and then saw the blood draining from a wound in her side. Dear God! What had he done to her? By this time I had led her into the bedroom and was easing her onto the bed.

"What did he hit you with? No fist could have done this."

"No. The side—of—of—his broadax." She was now straining for every breath.

"Just lie still. Don't try to say any more."

I ripped away the already torn gown until I located the open gash. What could I do to save her? There was no way to get help from another of the women. Feeling as gently as possible with my fingertips, I tried to determine if any bones were broken. Although the wound was long, it did not seem very deep; but from the profuse bleeding, I feared she might have ruptured something. Reaching up and pulling off my white linen undergown, I tore it into squares to make pads to stanch the blood.

"He—wanted—the silver crucifix." Her voice was barely a whisper now, each word uttered painfully. I had often seen the cross she spoke of. It was covered with jewels and worth a king's ransom, but its real value to her was that it had been blessed by the Pope.

"Tara." Now she spoke so softly I could hardly hear her. "Someone has to go for help. Is there anyone?"

Surely she knew what had taken place in the rest of the abbey, but if she didn't, how could I be the one to tell her? I hesitated too long in answering. My momentary silence told her what my voice could not.

"They are all dead, aren't they?" The sigh escaped her as if it were the very breath of life.

"Oh, no," I hastened to assure her. "But they're being held by the Vikings." She would learn of the deaths soon enough.

"Oh, Holy Mother! Then you must go." Some inner need to protect those in her charge gave added strength to her voice.

"Pray, Lady Anna, do not ask me to go. I'll not leave you like this."

"We need help, Tara."

All my thoughts were concentrated on her. The time to worry about the others could come later. This was my mother lying on the bed. My real mother. Not the one who had given me birth, but the one who had shown me unselfish love and concern. I could not leave her to die or to be further endangered by the Vikings. Terrified after what I had already witnessed, the easiest thing for me to do was to flee right then, to go for help and perhaps save myself. I had no illusions that we would be left alone in the cottage. Only after struggling with these thoughts did I acknowledge to myself that her needs were greater than my fears. "Your wound must be tended to immediately. You need someone to stay here and care for you."

"Do what you can for the wound," she agreed, "but then you must go. There are others to think of, too. Rouse the villagers and serfs. They may be able to prevent the Vikings from taking the women captive."

Captives! That was a danger I had not considered. In my innocence, I thought the heathens would loot the abbey but leave the women behind once their lust was sated. Lady Anna's concern for the others was, as always, more urgent than her own pain.

"If you wish," I said. "Just as soon as I know you are as comfortable as I can make you." I eased her into a position that seemed to lessen the pain. "But you must promise not to move."

"I will stay right here on the bed. I do not think I will be bothered again. They will be looting the chapel. But you must leave immediately."

She spoke with an urgency I knew had been evoked by a deep-seated fear that she was dying, a fear she was trying her best to conceal from me. I did not think the wound was fatal, but I could best console her by doing exactly what she wanted.

"Just as soon as I cover the wound."

I found a sheet and tore it into strips. The bleeding had lessened considerably, but it had taken all of the pads made from my undergown. Now I was able to bathe the area and make certain it was completely clean. I fashioned more thick squares, pressed them hard against the open gash, and bound them as tightly as I could. For the moment there

10

was nothing more to be done. I watched closely and sighed with some relief when no blood seeped through the bandage. Lady Anna needed only to lie quietly.

"I'll go now," I said, "and return just as soon as possible."

"God be with you, Tara. Before you go, take these." She opened the palm of my hand and placed a few flat stones on it.

I tried to pull my hand back. "No, Lady Anna, I do not want them."

"I insist." Once more that determination in her voice that could not be denied. "You know their meaning, and they saved me."

"Saved you!" I couldn't keep the fury from my voice. "From what? Not that wound in your side."

"No, but once the Viking had me down, he was threatening to kill me. He fled when he saw these in my hand, terrified at what he had already done. No Viking will intentionally harm someone who has the runes. So keep them close to you."

The seven flat stones she handed me were crudely incised with strange designs. There were those who believed they were magic stones, dropped from the heavens or scattered by the Druids said to have built the great circle of cairns called Stonehenge.

Although I considered the stones no more than interesting curios, there was something eerie about them. I was well aware they were not without value and significance to the Vikings. The different signs or runes carved on them were said to have been the creation of the ancient Norse gods. When given by the gods to the Norsemen, the runes continued to carry secret powers which could be interpreted or released only by those initiated into the great mysteries. To one who could read the runes was ascribed the vision to see through the fog obscuring the future and foretell coming events.

Sometime in the past, so the tale went, these particular rune stones had been brought to the abbey by the daughter of the great King Arthur; and through the years, in spite of their being pagan objects, one nun in each generation had been taught to read and understand their meanings. Lady Anna had learned from the previous abbess, and she in turn had taught me. Yet I feared them. No one knew why the heathen relics had not been destroyed; perhaps it was because they had become one of our abbey's traditions. Now Lady Anna wanted me to take them. Although they might save me from harm by the Vikings, I cringed at the thought of carrying them.

"My crucifix is all the protection I need." I fingered the heavy silver chain. "Have you forgotten it contains a piece of the true cross?"

"And you think that means anything to those heathens? Did crosses protect the other women? Do not scoff at the runes, Tara. We may never know what secrets they hold, but they have a power all Norsemen venerate."

To appease the abbess, now terribly weakened by pain and loss of blood, I slipped the rune stones into the deep pocket of my robe. I could not know how dramatically that simple act would affect the course my life was going to take.

There was a small gate by the back door of the cottage, hidden from unknowing eyes by a tangled cluster of berry bushes. In less than a minute I was on the other side of the wall and had reached the edge of the forest. The abbey was set well back from the road, once an important Roman highway, and it was surrounded on three sides by a thickly wooded forest which, at various times, had offered both protection and danger.

I approached the first of the "marked trees," so called because of a short iron spike embedded waist high in each. Running in a straight line from the wall toward the path leading to a group of cottages, they indicated the boundary of abbey property on which novices were allowed to walk. In their wisdom, the early church fathers had known that newcomers to the community would find life within the walls confining, and they gave permission for the novices to walk along the trees as far as the path.

As I made my way to the second tree, I remembered my own first days of preparation to enter the religious life. Each tree had been watered with my tears as I despaired of ever knowing real happiness again without marriage to the man I had loved since we were children. With Ian by my side, I had learned to ride, to fish, and to discover the beauty of the world around me. Then fate intervened, and all thoughts of marriage to him came to an abrupt end.

There was no time now to remember. I was in the midst of a new and more violent tragedy, and I had to keep

12

moving until I reached the first cottage and sounded the alarm.

In spite of the morning chill, I was perspiring heavily, and my face felt hot. As I moved steadily on, a cautious step at a time, dry twigs crackled beneath my feet. Feeling suddenly faint from all I'd been through and flushed as if with fever, I stopped. Something seemed wrong, but I couldn't tell what it was. Then I listened. All was not as quiet as it should be. The air carried a strange sound. I turned around and then I knew.

The Vikings had fired the abbey!

The horror of it engulfed me and I began shaking in a cold sweat. The heathen bastards! Had they not done enough without this? Not knowing whether I should start running to the cottages for help or return to the abbey, I remained rooted to the spot.

Already the flames were lighting up the sky, and the glow from the burning buildings silhouetted the trees between us. Smoke and ashes blew toward me, stinging my eyes and surrounding me with a hot, gray, acrid fog.

From the direction the smoke was coming, I knew they had first ignited the small barnyard and byre. Suddenly, a huge bonfire was visible through the trees. The hay and fodder had caught, and I thought of the animals trapped within the walls like living sacrifices. The rickety wooden buildings would burn in seconds, and my heart pounded with pity for the ewes and lambs, penned in the service yard by the very stone walls meant to protect them.

Much as I suffered for them, I could not think long about the animals. If the flames spread or more fires were started, all of the women might be trapped within the holocaust. Thinking of Lady Anna lying helpless on her bed, I became terrified at the danger I had left her in. No time now to go for help. I had to return and rescue her. It was my fault she had been harmed, my moment of indecision that had allowed the Viking to attack her. No more feeling my cautious way through the underbrush. I turned and ran toward the road which would get me there more quickly.

Too late I heard the rattle of cartwheels, the pawing of horses' hooves, and the frightening sounds of harsh, masculine and pleading, feminine voices.

"Lie down, I said." The voice was cold and cruel, and I instinctively receded among the trees.

13

"Please sir, not again." I cringed at the helplessness of the whimper.

"Leave her alone, Guthorm. Haven't you had enough?"

There was a harsh laugh. "When does a man have enough?"

While I crouched behind a tree, praying the Vikings would pass so I could get back to Lady Anna, one question kept nagging at me: where had they gotten carts and horses?

The small wagons moved so close to me I could see the grizzled faces of the men driving them as well as those riding inside. At least ten nuns—their faces streaked with dirt and tears, their robes torn—sat huddled on piles of straw. They seemed shrunken into terrified, almost lifeless images of their former selves. Through the slotted sides of a haywain, I saw one of them lying down, and I watched her body heaving with sobs. A man kneeling astride her slapped her across the face and then stood up, cursing sullenly.

Every part of me longed to help them, yet common sense told me I could do nothing against so overwhelming an adversary, and the wisest course was to return to Lady Anna and rescue her from the burning abbey. To that end I remained frozen behind the tree, waiting for them to pass. Much to my dismay, something caught the eye of one man, and he turned his glance directly on me.

"Oh ho, look what we have here. Stop the carts. Such beauty should not be left behind."

It was the man of the cruel voice, the one called Guthorm. I shrank inside myself, remembering what he had been demanding of Faeve, the young novice in the cart. In that instant Lady Anna was forgotten. All I could think about was the brutal treatment that lay ahead for me; the clawing, the struggling, the ultimate submission to his vile body, and the searing pain I must endure. I fought to keep back the tears. Above all, I would not let them know I was afraid.

"With that golden hair she could be the Goddess Freya herself. Beautiful and filled with love just ready to share."

The second man, though sounding less heartless, inspired as much fear as the first. I did not realize until then that my head was uncovered. I must have lost my wimple during the scuffle in the kitchen.

Guthorm leapt from the cart and swaggered toward me.

14

No, I would not be taken that easily. I started to run, hoping to lose him among the trees; but in two long strides he was beside me, pulling my hair and clutching my shoulder.

"Thought you'd escape, did you? Most unwise. Come, see what we do to comely wenches who try to run away."

"Remember, Guthorm," a third man spoke, "Freya is also Goddess of Death. Be careful how you request her favors."

From the time the man Guthorm captured me, I neither moved nor spoke. Their references to the goddess gave me an idea which might save all of us from further harassment. For the moment I was drained of emotion, and an amazing coolness took over. When I refused their invitation to climb into the cart, maintaining the stance and pose I thought a goddess come to earth would assume, I was grabbed roughly by two of the men. I did not resist but let them drag me the short distance to the haywain and throw me down beside Faeve. Then I determinedly sat up, holding the rune stones in the palms of my hands. When I saw the startled looks on the men's faces, I knew my ploy had worked. We would not be harmed any further, at least for the time being.

"Treat her gently, Harek," one man said. "We'll take her to Rorik."

"Aye, Sigurd, she looks like one to please him."

These words immediately obliterated the momentary sense of security I had been enjoying. I liked not the sound of the name Rorik; it boded a ruthlessness more deadly than what I had already seen. How soon, I wondered, would we meet up with this as yet unknown menace?

We left the main road and began bumping over a rutted path through the woods, a path no stranger to our lands would know. The riddle was getting more involved. First the carts and horses, now the obscure roadway. But all riddles have answers when one locates the right key. But no time to concern myself with that now. Better I should rest and try to prepare myself for whatever confrontation lay ahead.

I do not know how long we rode. There were several carts in our caravan as well as a number of horses. Years' accumulation of dead leaves and matted undergrowth muted the sound of hooves and wheels, and all around me

15

seemed asleep after the morning's orgy. I hoped the hostage nuns were finding some peace.

For me it was difficult because of memories. I knew these woods well, having roamed them since I was a child. We were not many leagues from my home, and I prayed that my father or Ian would be near. Two or three men were not enough to halt the Vikings; but if they saw us, they could round up a force large enough to stand them off. It was a futile prayer. We moved along unseen by any but a few rabbits and a fox that scurried out of our way.

Several leagues below the abbey we reached a river and were transferred to shallow barges. This meant we were nearing the coast, and I thought about the stories I'd heard of women being taken captive to the Northlands, never to be seen or heard from again. This new threat was far worse than being raped or brutalized, and I could not keep from weeping. Even as the barges rode smoothly atop the placid water and the sibilant, rhythmic swish of the oars marked the passing minutes, all I could think about was being forced aboard a strange ship and taken to an even stranger land. Neither the warmth of the sun nor the gentle breezes could ease the pain strangling my heart. The willows on the shore, their branches sweeping the water, seemed to weep with me; and the song of the birds was like the haunting refrain of a funeral dirge. I cannot bear it, I thought; I would rather die than go to live among heathens.

My ears were almost constantly battered by the harsh voices of the Vikings. When giving orders to us, they spoke in words we could understand. Now they had lapsed into the coarse, unpleasant, guttural dialect of the North, reinforcing the horror I felt at the thought of being carried off by them. To keep from giving in to complete despair, I concentrated on the flat stones in my hands and the inscriptions carved on them.

Sometime late in the afternoon, we neared the mouth of the river. Several Vikings had riden along the river bank in a course roughly parallel to that of the barges. Amid shouts of success, they sped up to ride on ahead. Over and over I heard references to Rorik, whom I inferred was a leader they both feared and admired.

The men slowed the barges and guided them through the reeds along the shore and then pulled them better than halfway up the gently sloping banks. We were ordered to alight, but some inner sense told me not to obey; as if in a trance, I remained seated in the boat with Faeve still huddled, ill with fright, at my feet. I was as terrified as she, but by taking several deep breaths, I was able to regain my composure and appear outwardly calm and indifferent to what was going on.

"Where in the name of Thor have you been!"

The deep, authoritative voice demanded an immediate answer yet contained a hint of mocking laughter. The man who had spoken was taller and more powerfully built than the others, who had seemed immense up until now.

"Just a little foraging, Rorik. You were not here, so—"

"So you thought to assume command. Hoping my ship would be blown off course? Or Thor would send me to the bottom of the sea?"

"No, no, sire. But with so many places nearby begging to be looted. No lookouts. No guards."

Guthorm began with an air of braggadocio, but his last words carried an unmistakably conciliatory tone. If he were afraid of this man Rorik, what could we, unwilling captives, hope from him? The future looked bleak indeed.

"Looting!" His anger surprised me. I should have thought he would be pleased. "We came here to establish a base from which to trade. You should have been studying the lay of the land, the best places for vantage points and landing sites. And what do you do?" His voice was getting louder and more stern. "Go rampaging through the woods, bringing back a bunch of mewling, feeble women who faint if you touch them."

"And all this, sire." Several men had begun unloading sacks from the barges, and now they tipped them up, spreading before Rorik the precious gold and silver crosses, candlesticks, chalices, patens, and small bejeweled caskets so greedily snatched from the abbey. "Feast your eyes on this and say you are not pleased."

Rorik picked up one of the more ornate chalices, studied it for a moment, and then dashed it to the ground. I was more shaken at that sacrilegious act than at the objects being stolen in the first place.

"By Odin!" he yelled. "A church! You looted a church. Now every Christian in the countryside will be after us. And I had planned to take over and settle here, after persuading the people it would be to their advantage not to

17

oppose us. We would have had the local villages cowed in a few days, but not now."

"What are your orders, sire?"

I scarcely recognized in the contrite Guthorm the man who had dragged me out of the woods. I had been right in thinking the leader Rorik was not one to oppose with impunity.

"Stow it all quickly. In *my* ship." He then called all the men around him. "You disobeyed orders. You know what happens next."

I waited with both curiosity and trepidation to see how he would punish his men for blatantly going against his wishes. It seemed most unusual for a Viking leader to disapprove of his men looting a church; and after what he had done with the chalice, I knew it was not from pious convictions. I could hardly believe he really wanted to establish a peaceful settlement on our shores; but then this man was obviously quite unlike the rest of his crew. How much different, I wondered. So far he had ignored the women, except for his disparaging comments, and that too was interesting. Yes, in spite of my loathing for Vikings, this man fascinated me.

The men began whooping and hollering, slapping leather and placing bets. Strange and more strange, I thought. I expected the men to be whipped, at the very least.

"The battle-axes," they called. "Bring the battle-axes and the spears."

"Clear the ground."

"Get the women out of the way."

"Now you will see something, my good Briton." Guthorm spoke to another man standing near the boats. A Briton? I had assumed they were all Vikings. The riddle might be slowly revealing its own clues.

The men formed an irregular circle, all save Rorik. While he waited for his cohorts to group themselves, I studied him more closely. He was not only taller, but finer featured and fairer than any of the others. Full mustaches covered his mouth and reached below his chin on either side. Otherwise he was clean-shaven. Under other circumstances I would have considered him attractive. Over garments similar to his men's he wore a long woolen cape, its twin points front and back barely touching the ground. Elaborately decorated with heavy braid, it was open on one side to free his fighting arm, and it was pinned to-

18

gether at the shoulder with a large silver clasp. His stance, his manner, and his garb left no doubt he was a chieftain. If he really was disturbed at what his men had done, he might not be averse to setting us free. *Not* out of compassion—I saw none in his deep-set, piercing eyes—but to thwart the desires of his men.

Rorik now stood in the center of the circle and began brandishing a long spear, swinging it round and round while the men jumped over it. With each sweep around the circle, the spear rose higher and higher, reaching first knees and then hips. One man fell. Others tripped or were struck on shoulders or head. But they were all laughing as they slapped each other and pummeled those on the ground.

It was meant as punishment, and they were making sport of it. I could not believe what I was seeing. What kind of people were these Vikings?

Next they picked up their broad axes. As they began throwing them at one another, I stared in horror, expecting any minute to see crushed heads and shattered bodies. But no bloody mayhem ensued. Now I dared look more closely. They were aiming above or to one side of each other, hitting the trees they stood under just above or next to their heads. I wished they would split their skulls; then I crossed myself hastily for having such sinful thoughts.

In a few minutes they stopped and began drinking.

"All right now, the fun is over." Rorik strode among his men. "Get ready to sail. High tide in less than an hour." He then walked to the edge of the riverbank. "Who is this?" He stared as if he'd not seen me before.

I looked into the face of this man Rorik, and I was suddenly afraid. More afraid than at any time during the long nightmare that began before dawn. Shock, terror, horror—all these I had experienced as I moved from one part of the abbey to another, witnessed the rape and carnage, and finally been taken captive. But it was nothing compared to the fear that took hold of me now, a dread of the unknown made even more fearful by memories of childhood superstitions. As I looked at the Viking leader, I relived the terrifying nights when, as a little girl, I snuggled deep under the feather bed after being sent to my room for misbehaving.

Children in Britain were deterred from disobeying their

elders by threats that the double-horned ogres from the North would whisk them away across the cold sea. No other bogeymen filled us with quite the same fear. Satan had horns, so we knew the Vikings must be devils sent to do his bidding, and the frozen Northlands seemed to us an especially terrifying form of hell.

Rorik was not a fairy-tale ogre but a real flesh-and-blood man. If the dual horns on his helmet were those of a pagan barbarian rather than of a devil, he was no less frightening. As he spoke, he threw back his cape, brushed his long, reddish-blond hair off his shoulders, and raised one eyebrow. He stared intently at my face, and slowly a wicked grin spread under his mustaches. God's blood! He thinks me to fall under his spell. Submit to him if I must, but only as an unwilling captive.

"Who is this?" he asked again.

"We brought her for you, sire—untouched and unharmed."

So I was to be a gift, was I, a peace offering to soften the ire of the chieftain. Fear was replaced by fury, a fury that again strengthened my determination to fight for my freedom as long as I could.

Rorik nodded to his companion. "You are a man of superior judgment and excellent taste, Sigurd."

"She is beautiful, is she not, sire?"

Rorik wrinkled his forehead quizzically but did not answer the question. "She reminds me of someone."

"The Goddess Freya, perhaps?"

"I have not had that privilege, Sigurd. Have you?"

During this mild bantering, it occurred to me I might have the solution to my dilemma right in my hands. The rune stones. I had forgotten about them since we landed.

"Have I what?" Sigurd asked, looking dumbfounded.

"Seen the goddess?" Rorik's eyes gleamed with laughter.

"Oh, no, Rorik. We only thought . . ." He seemed not frightened, but a little overawed.

A deep, booming laugh greeted this response. "You thought well, Sigurd. She could be a vision of Freya, but I'm more inclined to see her as a very desirable young woman. Do you know her name?"

"I think it is Tara, sire."

This second comparison to Freya, the heathen goddess, was disturbing. However, it might abet the power of the runes I held.

He walked to the side of the boat. "Come here, Tara."

His tone was surprisingly kindly and cajoling, but I wondered what he would do when I did not respond. I merely opened my palms so he could see the flat stones. Obviously startled, he jumped back a foot or two.

"Where did you get those?" he asked.

I did not answer but only stared back at him.

"Can you read them? Do you understand their meaning?"

"Yes."

My hopes that the stones would send him running for his ship or cause him to order our release were instantly dashed; the sight of them had just the opposite effect.

"Then it is fated by the gods that you should belong to me. The wisdom of the runes is all I need to become the most powerful chieftain in all of Norvegia. I have waited a long time for you to appear, Tara."

It occurred to me that had I kept the rune stones hidden, I might have been able to elude his grasp in some way; instead I had delivered myself right into his hands. But still I did not move.

"Come, come, Tara, give me your hand. Do not fear. I'll not hurt you. You are too beautiful, and you hold my destiny within your hands."

I sat up straighter. Was he saying all this to weaken my resolve or did he speak true? I looked at the other women huddled together under the trees, and I saw their tear-streaked faces and torn garments. They were cowering with fear at the thought of what lay ahead for them. They had suffered greatly, and now that the drunken Vikings were again approaching them, their piteous cries tore me apart. I thought of Lady Anna, and how my one moment of cowardice had resulted in her being brutally wounded and unable to escape from the burning abbey. I was no martyr, but if saving these women from further degradation would atone even a little for what I had done, I could endure the embraces of a Viking.

In a challenging tone that belied the rapid beating of my heart and the icy lump in my throat, I answered him: "Not unless you promise to let the other women return to the abbey, under safe escort."

Rorik looked startled, but he could not hide a certain admiration for my audacity. "Oh no, so the goddess is

21

going to make demands." Now he looked almost amused. "But the men say they burned the abbey."

"And the women will rebuild it, with help from God and our friends."

Close behind me I heard a high-pitched laugh, so evil I knew it would haunt me for the rest of my life. "Beware of her, Rorik. She is her own father's daughter."

The riddle was solved. I had heard that laugh when my father turned one of our serfs off the estate for stealing. So he had led the Vikings to the abbey, undoubtedly for a share of the vast treasure it contained.

Only one thing obsessed me now. No matter what was done to me or where I was taken, I swore I would return to avenge the deaths at the abbey.

"Well," Rorik said, "the men have had their fun. If I let the women go, you will come with me?"

Suddenly I wanted to forswear my offer, and I wondered why I had been so foolish as to present myself in place of the women. Going with him could mean a hasty coupling before he sailed or, more likely, becoming his slave and going with him to the Northlands. I shuddered at the thought of what such a life would be like. Better I did not know. Awaiting my answer, Rorik frowned and his eyes grew cold and stern. The women looked at me pleadingly. The choice was no longer mine.

"Yes," I said quietly.

"Willingly?"

I hesitated only a moment. "Yes."

"And do whatever I say?"

"If you so desire." I would be an obedient captive, but only so long as it took me to find a way to flee from him. It might be days or it might be months, but I would find a way to escape.

"Then give me your hand," he commanded.

I held out my arm in such a way that he had to come forward into the boat and lead me out of it. Once on shore, he gathered me into his arms.

"You are indeed beautiful, and now you are mine." He cupped my chin with his hand. "Look at me, Tara." I am not short, but he stood a good head taller than I, and I had to tip my head back to look up at his face. "Are you afraid to look into my eyes, Tara? Afraid of the desire you see there?"

"No, sire." I stared into clear, blue eyes—so pale they

22

seemed almost transparent—as if by doing so I could peer into his very soul. "I see only a ruthless desire for power and one who is willing to utilize all the forces of evil to gain that end."

He threw back his head and released a long, spine-chilling howl that echoed to the skies. "O—O—Odin! What a trickster you are. You send me not a beautiful, hot-blooded goddess of love but a willful and virginal saint! What shall we do with her, Odin?"

Now that there was no turning back, all strength left me, and I slumped in his arms. I felt completely drained of fear or hate or despair, and I waited numbly, uncaring, for him to have his way with me.

Chapter Two

IN THE NARROW BOW OF THE DRAGON SHIP I curled up on the thick pile of warm furs and pulled another up close enough under my chin to set its fine hairs atremble with my breath. The sun had long since set, and I could not stop shivering. The wind blasting down on us from the great ice floes north of the Western Isles was cold, but no colder than the icy block of fear that encased my heart.

Above me rose the S-shaped prow, sweeping the skies and plowing a path among the stars. To take advantage of the evening tide, the single, square, red-and-white-striped sail had been unfurled. Four other ships, with their dragon-headed prows and striped sails, followed closely in our wake. It was, indeed, a formidable flotilla that Rorik led. To the power of the wind had been added the rhythmic sweep of the long oars, the men pulling to some ancient melodic chant. I tried to close my ears to the sound, aware that each stroke was taking me farther and farther from home and nearer to the land of the hated heathens whose captive I was. I longed for sleep, but the events of the day persisted in flitting through my mind like hideous ghouls that taunted with assurances I would never be able to forget what I had seen and experienced.

After his wild cry to Odin, I had been sure the Viking leader would go back on his word to return the other nuns to the abbey under safe conduct. But, true to his promise, he ordered their release and then gathered me once more into his arms.

"The men have called you a goddess," he said, "and truly you do carry in the rune stones a gift from the gods. Do you know who Freya is?"

"I heard them talking about her," I whispered, feeling uncomfortable and yet strangely moved at being held by a man again. Not just any man but a heathen whose followers raided and killed and desecrated the Lord's house.

"She is our goddess of love who brings pleasure to the hearts of men and dispenses her favors with joy."

No, I told myself, I will not allow myself to feel anything for him, to let his touch disturb me. Throwing my head back, I said furiously, "And the goddess of death for Viking warriors"

"By Thor, you are lovely when your eyes spark like that."

"But not a heathen goddess."

"No, a most desirable woman."

He drew me close to his chest, and I felt his heart beating rapidly. When he kissed me full on the mouth, I neither resisted nor responded.

"Ah, Tara, you are as beautiful and cold as snow on my mountains and the glistening ice crystals on their fir trees. But snow and ice melt under the gentle fires of the spring sun, and so will you."

With that he lifted me up and carried me like a child to his ship. I knew it would be futile to resist, but he was wrong if he thought I would melt. Some might call him handsome, but no disarming smile could belie the evil I saw in his eyes or charm me into succumbing to his wiles. So I was as beautiful as the snow and ice crystals on his mountains. All right, I would be just as frigid as they. He would find that instead of thawing me with the heat of his passion, I would freeze him with my hate.

He set me down on the stern deck, and I remained immobile, waiting for him to make the first move. Would he rip the clothes off me or would he try to woo me now that I was his captive? Much to my surprise, he did neither, but turned and strode off the ship. In a few minutes he returned with a plate of flat oaten cakes and a mug of wine. I wanted to refuse, but I had not eaten all day, and going hungry would hurt no one but myself. The simple cakes were delicious, and I found myself swallowing them greedily. Rorik said nothing while he alternated between watching me and directing the men who were loading the ships and preparing to sail. Even when I finished, he neither said anything nor made any move to leave, and I found the silence oppressive.

"The women are safe?" I asked, feeling the need to say something.

"On their way back, escorted by three of my best men who'll not touch them. They'll feel my spear if they do. We meet them later off the Cornish coast. I have kept my part of the bargain."

"And I'll keep mine. But I promise you this: no matter how long it takes, I will avenge the destruction your men wrought. A Briton led them there, and such treachery cannot go unpunished."

"Are you so sure you will be back? 'Tis more certain time will ease the pain."

"By all that's holy, I give you my word."

Enraged at his complacent assurance that I might forget what had happened, I seethed inside. For too long I had placidly accepted or fled from things that hurt. Now all the love I felt for Lady Anna and the abbey turned to hate for this heathen monster. By all the powers within me, I would find a way to avenge the destruction and suffering I had witnessed that day. Devising a way to do it was a challenge that would keep me from dwelling on my own misery.

"Well, you are free to do as you please while on the ship. I have to get her underway now."

Again he strode off, and I made my way toward the prow, away from the tiller where I knew he would be sitting.

Sometime later, Rorik came to stand beside me where I grasped the rail in an effort to keep from becoming sick from the unaccustomed heaving and rolling of the ship. I had been watching one of the Vikings clamber up the prow to reset the fearsome dragon head—anything to keep from giving way to despair. Rorik, too, watched until the man completed the task.

"It was removed earlier, Tara, when we approached the coast, to keep from frightening the land spirits."

If he hoped for a comment from me, he would be disappointed. Captive though I might be, I did not intend to engage in idle conversation. He kept on talking, as if unaware of my attempts to ignore him. The men were now hoisting the sail.

"It is a glorious sight, Tara, the raising of the sail on your own ship. I have seen it hundreds of times since I was a child and stood by my father on board, but I never cease to thrill to it. Those sails have made us masters of the seas."

26

"And its most hated tyrants," I threw back, forgetting I didn't want to talk to him.

"You must try to forget what happened earlier today."

"Forget!" Did he think I was like a child who could be appeased with a piece of candy after a slight hurt? "I agreed to come with you, but do not expect me to forget why. Never! By the Holy Mother of God, never!"

Recognizing I was in no mood for a reconciliation of any kind, Rorik said nothing more, but showed me the pile of furs on which I was to sleep.

"I shall be at the tiller all night, and the men asleep," he said, "so you will not be disturbed."

In spite of his reassuring words, I could not sleep. I was on a ship with the same lusty, cruel Vikings who had ravaged the abbey, and I was none too sure I was safe. True, most of them were wrapped in their long cloaks and asleep on their benches, waiting only for daybreak to begin rowing again. But what if one of them woke up, saw me lying helpless in the prow, and decided to sate his lust with me. I had only Rorik's word that none of the men would touch me, and he was at the tiller, the length of the darkened ship away. I snuggled deeper among the furs, squeezing my eyes tightly shut in the hopes of being lulled into blessed forgetfulness.

The ship sped easily along, its slim prow gently skimming the waves and finally rocking me in and out of a restless sleep.

In my waking moments I was haunted by one question: Why was I on this ship? Because of Ian and Deirdre? Or my own hurt? When I closed my eyes I was back on a hill covered with buttercups and blue cornflowers, the very air around me bursting with spring. Hand in hand, Ian and I walked among the blooms, glorying in the beauty of the day and our love for each other. I had loved Ian, the son of a neighboring lord, for as long as I could remember. Four years older than I, he had taught me to fish, to hunt, to hawk, and to ride bareback—activities frowned upon by my mother as unsuitable for a young lady who was the daughter of an earl. Ladyhood, however, was not among my plans until I suddenly realized I was no longer a child. Before that, Ian was my favorite companion, someone to tease and try to beat at games. All too soon, he became a young man whose nearness started my heart fluttering and my hands perspiring.

Then came the afternoon on the hill. Under a whispering aspen tree and amid the buttercups and cornflowers, he made love to me and opened up a whole new world of beauty. His mouth on mine had been hard and demanding, and my body welcomed him eagerly. For years he had been my hero; now he was my lover. My heart sang when he smiled down on me, and under his touch I knew greater delights than I had ever dared dream about.

At fifteen one does not die of heartbreak; but emotions, set afire and then thwarted, shrivel up and atrophy. At a gala dinner the following week, preceding a three-day hunt to which lords and ladies for miles around had been invited, my father was honored to announce the betrothal of my older sister, Deirdre, to Ian, son of his long-standing friend, Lord Balan.

As the beautiful daughter of Lord Graymount, my sister Deirdre always carried herself with the proud hauteur and grace of one born to the purple and gold. Although we were the same height, her regal bearing made her appear taller, and her gowns hung in graceful folds from high, proud breasts while my dresses always bunched in the wrong places. When she gathered up her burnished-gold hair into a chignon or wrapped it around her head in thick braids, it remained meticulously in place; whereas loose strands of mischievous pale blonde curls escaped unbidden from mine. So it had become my habit to wear it long or pulled back with a ribbon. As a little girl and a young woman, Deirdre was the epitome of the lady my mother wanted me to be.

But Deirdre was no fun. When Ian and I went fishing, she shuddered at the thought of getting her feet wet and returned to her embroidery. She would go hawking with us, but she always looked the other way when a bird returned with its prey. An excellent rider, she often condescended to join us, cantering sedately along, while Ian and I raced the wind or each other or chased a fox over hedges and through briars. When we returned to the stable, Deirdre's riding dress was as immaculate as when we rode out.

It was not surprising that my parents arranged for Deirdre's betrothal before mine. She was the elder, and it was proper she should marry first. But of all the sons of their friends, why Ian? It was true the estates joined, and a merger of the two would strengthen their defenses and increase their wealth, but my marriage to Ian would have accomplished the same end. I knew Father was disappointed at having no living sons—two had died at birth—and was concerned with arranging worthy marriages for four daughters; but it seemed so unfair of him to enter into an agreement without considering our wishes.

I looked at Deirdre as my father made the announcement. Blushing modestly, she stood next to Ian and was as poised and calm as ever, even though I was certain the announcement was a complete surprise to her. It was not Father's wont to inform his children about what he considered adult matters, and Mother merely obeyed his wishes. Since Deirdre would have married the man in the moon if they ordered it, she looked neither pleased nor dismayed. Would anything ever ruffle her, I wondered. I thought of her lying cool and unmoved in Ian's arms and remembered my own eager response to his touch. Was he as shattered as I by the announcement, or was he pleased to be marrying a beautiful heiress? Had he known when he made love to me that our days together were coming to an end?

I tried to avoid looking at Ian, fearing our glances would reveal to everyone our love for each other. I need not have worried. Never taking his eyes off Deirdre, he looked as if marriage to her was the fulfillment of a lifelong dream. If I had not willed my body to be stronger than my emotions, I would have fainted. Instead, I spent the rest of the evening flirting with all the other young swains who clustered about, knowing I would be the next daughter offered up on the marriage market. Even the second daughter of Lord Graymount would bring with her a substantial dowry and eventually inherit a generous portion of his estate.

I never learned whether Ian had known of the betrothal when he declared his undying love for me. I was less concerned with having given up my maidenhead to him than with his having dishonored me by playing me false. I did not want to know the truth.

The day after the announcement, I fled to the abbey where I knelt before the altar and declared it was my desire to enter the religious life. Within two hours I was wearing the simple habit and short veil of a novice.

As I expected, my father learned where I was and sent a peremptory order for me to return home immediately.

The messenger was sent back with word I was in seclusion and would not be permitted to speak to anyone outside the abbey for six weeks. A powerful man in the secular world, my father had little influence in the sacred one. He would be allowed to visit me at the end of the six weeks, and if I had changed my mind, I would be permitted to return home with him.

I was delighted at the thought of the confusion my flight must have engendered at home. Although my father was strict and my mother meekly acquiesced to his wishes, I knew they loved me and were undoubtedly distraught at my actions. Unless my flight forced a change of plans, Deirdre and Ian would be married before the six weeks had passed. I was impish enough to savor the idea that all the while my mother was overseeing preparations for the wedding and advising Deirdre in her role as a wife, she would be worrying about me. I could not stop the wedding, but I could certainly give them all something else to think about.

In fleeing to the abbey, I ran away from heartbreak and what I thought was insurmountable tragedy. I gave no thought to what lay ahead, to what life as a postulant would be like. The first days passed in a cloudy haze, partly from the shock I was still experiencing and partly from the strangeness of it all. Having been brought up under my father's strict discipline, the rules of the abbey held no fears for me. When at last my parents were allowed to visit, I had made my choice. I would stay at the abbey. Although my days of hawking and riding were brought abruptly to an end with my decision, there was a calm security in the abbey which I craved.

The years sped by swiftly, their passage marked by such events as the births of Deirdre and Ian's three children, the death of my mother, and my final vows. I cannot deny I longed for the worldly joys during the first months of the austerity of life in the abbey. But I was not entirely unhappy. Never, however, had I thought my early decision would result in my being captured by Vikings.

I was awakened by the morning sun shining full in my face. Inhaling deeply, I knew why the roughest sailors waxed eloquent about the smell of fresh sea air in their nostrils and the sting of salt spray against their cheeks. For just the briefest moment I forgot where I was and why I was there. All too soon I remembered I was a prisoner, sailing to a strange land with a man I loathed.

When Ian and I had rowed lazily down the river, he often spoke of sailing across the Channel. I would have gone with him to the ends of the earth, to the great dropping-off place inhabited by huge monsters that sucked up the waters and spewed them out again twice a day to cause the ever-shifting tides. Some said gigantic sea serpents coiled themselves around ships, pulling them down into the depths; others averred that gigantic fish lured men off the edge and they fell forever through nothingness. One or two minds, laughed at by most, insisted the world was round like a ball. I knew not what to believe, but I had the strangest feeling that on this day I would like to sail on and on to discover the truth for myself. It could be no more terrifying than the mysterious land to which I was being taken.

Suddenly I was frightened, not so much of what lay ahead but of strange feelings stirring inside me, emotions I had long kept imprisoned and thought to be dead. Something kept whispering, "You're free, you're free." It was as if I, too, had been released from a prison of my own making. I should be horrified at facing a future I knew would violate all the vows I had taken, but instead I was enveloped within a peaceful calm. At the same time, I experienced an exhilaration I had not felt since before I entered the abbey. Like a child seeking a quiet corner into which to crawl, I had made the mistake of walling myself into that corner. Now the walls had crumbled. I would not forget I was an unwilling captive, but I could now see the future as a challenge to grasp hold of and conquer in my own way rather than a chimera that would subdue my will.

"Aren't you tired of lying down?" Rorik seated himself beside me on the pile of furs. "Wouldn't you like to stand by the rail?"

"No, thank you. I am fine," I said, forcing back a desire to do what he suggested. Yes, I would love to stand by the rail, but he would not know that.

"Just as you wish. I thought you might like to discover what a morning at sea is really like."

"If you command me." Do command me, I thought.

Make me get up. Don't make it look as if I'm giving in easily to what I really want to do. "Otherwise I prefer to remain here." I waited for his orders, but none came.

"Tara, I do not intend to issue commands. Here on the ship you are free to do as you please."

Damn you, I thought, and my whole mood changed. I wanted nothing more than to be left alone in my misery. I snuggled back down among the furs, maddened at hearing the sound of the Viking's soft boots moving toward the farther end of the ship.

I had never hated before, never before experienced the actual physical torment I suffered because of my loathing for these Vikings. The hatred aroused a passion far greater than any I thought myself capable of. My body burned with the energy of that pent-up passion, and I felt as if my head, my chest, my arms—all of me—would explode from keeping it contained. It was an uncontrollable desire to destroy those who had wantonly destroyed everything I loved. I felt as if I would explode from the energy created by my hatred which had built up until every nerve and muscle tensed with the need for release in action of some kind. One time in a fit of temper, I had held my breath until I thought my lungs would burst from the pain and my eyeballs pop from their sockets. I was experiencing the same agony again.

Then I heard one of the men laugh, and I was suddenly as frigid and stiff as an icicle. All the while I had to force back the bile that filled my throat and threatened to choke me. I no longer feared the Vikings or what they might do to me. They could touch me only superficially. I did not fear, but I hated. It was then I determined to devote all my thought and strength to finding a means of escape and revenge at the first possible moment.

I was left alone for the remainder of the day and the night that followed. One of the crew raised a piece of striped wool across the prow, giving me some much-welcomed privacy. Twice I was given something to eat: a tasty meat stew around noon and more oat cakes sometime after dark. I seldom shifted position, preferring to remain locked in my shell of defiance. Rorik seemed intent on leaving me alone, which suited me just fine, and my fear of being harmed by the others lessened as each hour passed. I slept more easily the second night, lulled by the steady rhythm of the waves breaking against the hull.

"Get up!"

Still half asleep, I saw the figure of Rorik looming above me. He had assumed a wide-legged stance to brace himself against the rolling of the ship, and his arms akimbo with fists on hips enhanced the domineering pose.

"What?" I asked groggily. His voice was muffled by the fur around my head.

"I said get up and stop feeling sorry for yourself. You ought to be horsewhipped for wallowing in self-pity on a beautiful day like this."

On one hand I was furious at being disturbed; on the other, strangely pleased that he was at last paying some attention to me.

"You said you would never command me to do anything."

"I changed my mind." His grin was something between a smile of delight that he had aroused my anger and an undisguised leer that frightened me.

I stood up as best I could, feeling I would be safer from him on my feet than lying on the pallet. Reeling with the movement of the ship, I grabbed for an edge of the prow but only succeeded in tumbling myself right into Rorik's arms.

"Now that is what I call a proper response," he said, "immediate and to the point."

"Not the point I intended, I assure you," I said, trying to sound superior to my awkward position. Flushed with embarrassment, I nonetheless began to shake from the cold.

"Here," he said, "put this around you." He wrapped me in one of the furs I'd been sleeping under. "Only a ninny would stand against this breeze without some protection."

I noticed he now wore a heavy, fur-lined jerkin under his long woolen cape.

The sun was warm on my face, but the wind blowing from the Irish Sea was bitterly chill. I shivered. Rorik put his arm around me, and in spite of my dread of what might come next, I was grateful for his supportive strength. I looked toward shore. Less than a league off the the coast, we were just far enough out to avoid the rocky shoals which took so many seamen to their deaths but

33

close enough to keep land ever in sight. My land. Would I ever see it again? I closed my eyes, trying to dispel the longing that was tearing my very soul apart.

"Ever been at sea before, Tara?"

"No, nor ever saw it." I had to keep the conversation light, not let him know what I was suffering. He must not have a hold of any kind over me, not even one of pity. "I've always lived inland, but I'm finding the sound of the sea as magnificent as the sight of it."

"You are not afraid?"

"Of being at sea? No. I've learned to conquer fear of things over which I have no control." Let him make of that what he would. "Where are we now?"

"There's a good southwest wind blowing, and we are sailing along the coast of Cornwall. Much too dangerous to try a landing yet."

I looked at the immense rocky cliffs, the surf pounding at their bases, the dangerous whirlpools caused by the tide ebbing from deep caves, and I was relieved we sailed no closer to land.

"How will you find your men?"

"There's a deep bay many hours north of here. We should reach it early tomorrow morning. My men will meet us there."

We stood silently by the rail for a few minutes until Rorik said he had to issue orders to the steersman about changing course.

Still afraid of being close to the men who had wrought such destruction at the abbey, I made my way nearer the prow. From that vantage point I gazed along the full length of the dragon ship and looked more closely at what had become my prison. It was of an impressive size, some seventy feet long and at least eighteen feet wide.

While I looked at the ship, I studied each aspect of it with an eye to how I might best escape when the right time came. A single bank of rowers on each side pulled with steady, even strokes on the long oars that glistened and swept the sea in such perfect unison they looked moved by a single hand. Under each man's bench was a large sack or length of rolled-up leather which I'd seen them use as sleeping bags. If at any time they landed and I were left alone on the ship, the benches would be an easy means of getting off. Near at hand to each man were his weapons—knives, axes, and spears. Although I knew that a Viking always kept his weapons with him—they were as much a part of his dress as his wrapped leggings and leather jerkin—I might be able to lay hands on a knife. I would have to have some protection if I hoped to reach help unharmed. A lone woman was not safe roaming the countryside.

Shields, each lapped halfway over the next one like thatch on a roof, were securely adjusted in slots beside the men. Although gaily painted in a variety of colors and designs, so as to impress anyone viewing the ship from a distance, the shields presented as formidable a defense as armor plate. They were interesting but could be of little use to me, unless as foot- and handholds if I needed to climb off the ship. I was really hoping that, when the ship landed to take on the men who had gone with the women to the abbey, I would be allowed ashore and be able to make my escape from there.

Putting to the back of my mind the thoughts of getting away, I concentrated on the activities around me. A burly Viking, not nearly as tall as Rorik but broader in the chest and with legs like sturdy oaks and arms that could no doubt crush a bear, steered with a tiller fastened to the port side and near the stern of the ship. He handled it as easily as a child twirling a top. Another man stood on the narrow deck across the stern and roared out a lusty song extolling the pride and courage of the Vikings. From time to time the rowers responded with a rhythmic, repetitive chorus which always ended in a wild yell to Odin or Thor. The men's chests swelled, their mouths grimaced, and their arms bulged with the effort of pulling on the oars in a steady, unbroken cadence. They must have been rowing thus for several hours, and yet there was no faltering, no slowing down of the fast-paced rhythm. Finally, after almost another hour, the wind freshened, and the men could cease their labors. With the strong breeze billowing out the huge sail, we continued to move across the water at a rapid pace.

I gazed up at the sail, full and taut as it caught the wind. Made of some heavy wool-like material, its bold stripes were embroidered in vibrant colors with strange-looking animals, created by imagination rather than nature, and serpentine figures. I wondered if they were part of their religion or if they came from the seaman's superstitious lore. Either way, they were unlike anything I had seen before. One, with a grotesquely smiling face and several hands, looked as if it were excitedly hugging itself. Well, I thought, I wish I were as overjoyed, little fellow, as you seem to be at the way we are sailing steadily northward.

Four other ships followed in tight formation in our wake. They, too, were large and formidable, but I knew instinctively the one I sailed on belonged to a far from ordinary Viking raider. It was longer by some ten feet than those in its train, and its carved dragon head was more intricately detailed and painted in gleaming purple and gold. I had known from our first meeting that Rorik wielded unquestionable power. Now I wondered from whence that power came.

Rorik once more came alongside me at the rail. Something about his smiling but imperious attitude cautioned me that I would be better off pleasing him than angering him in any way. The more I learned about him, the easier it might be for me to escape from him.

"Your name—Tara—is most unusual." He looked out over the waves rather than at me when he spoke.

"My father's pride in his Irish heritage."

"Irish? That explains the fire in your eyes."

"Yes." I went on, as if I'd not heard his last remark, "Tara was the home of the ancient Irish kings. I am not fond of the name, but I do not really hate it. It seems strange to be a place rather than a person."

"I know it well. I have been there. We have settlements nearby. 'Tis very beautiful. Almost as beautiful as you. Yes, 'tis a fitting name for you."

No, Rorik, I thought, you are wrong if you think to win me over with compliments. I'm not so easily beguiled. Yet, perhaps I should flatter him so that he would begin to trust me enough to let down his guard.

"I do not know why you let the women go," I said, "but I cannot deny it was a gallant act on your part."

"I let them go because I never intended taking them."

"What!" I was furious and chagrined at the same time.

He laughed. "You think I wanted a gaggle of whimpering women on board ship. Where would I put them?"

"You mean—you mean you planned to send them back all along?"

"No, I meant just to leave them. You assumed I was taking them with us."

"You—you tricked me." I wanted to cry, to scream, to beat on him, anything to release the fury building up inside me. What a loathsome bastard he was! I had been stupid to fall into his trap. No, not stupid, just arrogant enough to assume I was so desirable Rorik would release the women just to possess me. If there had been a trap, I'd made it myself. "You did not tell me you were letting them go."

"Why should I? You were so eager to become my captive, I was loath to disappoint you."

"Believe me," I stuttered, trying to keep my voice calm while inside, all of me was in turmoil, "I would not have been disappointed. If that was your only reason, I don't know why you bothered with me."

"By Thor!" he shouted, hitting the rail with his fist, "I don't know why I did either. I saw you and wanted you. It was as simple as that. Also," he added more quietly, "I admired your spunk when you offered yourself in place of the women. I liked the way you challenged me, not knowing I wasn't taking the women. I knew I could possess you only on your own terms."

"Possess me? No. I'm your captive and I'll keep my part of the bargain, but you will never possess me."

I cringed at his laughing response. "You are mighty independent for a captive."

I was still seething with hatred for him, but I was not going to let him know it. " 'Twill take more than enslavement to humble me. Only you know your plans for me, but do not expect me to crawl to you on hands and knees pleading for mercy. I cannot say I look forward to being a slave, but I can learn to tolerate it."

Having turned my back on him, I didn't see his change of expression until he put both hands on my shoulders and turned me around. His voice was no longer gruff and mocking but strangely gentle, and there was a softness about his eyes.

"Tara, my dear, you are not going to my home in Hordaland as a slave. You are going as my wife."

His words shocked me more than any of the atrocities I had seen or obscene words I had heard, and I struck out at him ferociously. "Marriage to a heathen? Never!"

He grasped my flailing hands in his and forced them down to my side. "Ah, my little she-bear, pull back those claws. Do you think you have a choice?"

Locked rigidly against his chest, I could no longer fight him, but it did not mean I had to acquiesce. "Do what you wish with me, but I will never marry you."

"Consider this well, Tara. The men were most unhappy when I sent the women back. It was part of their punishment for disobeying my orders. We could easily have stayed another two or three days and let my crew have their fill of your friends. They might cease grumbling, however, if I gave you to them. See, they look this way now."

Their faces were turned toward me and I saw them as I had seen them at the abbey, grinning with savage lust, raping the women, and I cringed at the thought of being passed from one to the next, crushed in their brawny arms and violated over and over.

"Your rather loud cries of protest," Rorik continued, "have aroused their violent passions. If you think you will enjoy their caresses more than mine, so be it."

"How soon do I have to choose?"

"You have until the day before we are due to arrive."

It was like listening to my death sentence for a crime I had not committed. I had heard men scream out their innocence before being hanged, and I was now suffering the same agony. At least I had time. How much I did not know, but it strengthened my resolve to escape at the first possible opportunity.

Chapter Three

SHAKEN TO THE VERY DEPTHS BY RORIK'S WORDS, I had to get as far away from him as possible. When he released his grip on me, I moved swiftly toward the prow. The thought of becoming wife to a pagan Viking was so loathsome, I felt as if I had been infected with a foul disease. I lay sobbing on my pallet until I was too exhausted even to think about escape. I remembered how I'd felt standing at the rail, looking at the wild and incredibly beautiful world on shore but feeling separated from it by more than the physical barriers of the ship and the sea. Every minute the view of the coast changed: from rough, rocky cliffs to small, placid bays; from large areas of uninhabited dense forest to clusters of thatched cottages emerging through a faint mist. It was a scene that constantly receded from me as we sailed along the coast, and I felt again the longing for the land I might never see again.

I had watched the sea birds sweep and soar through the sky as if with no destination in mind, and I envied them the freedom that was denied me. Would I ever be really free again? Then suddenly a gull wheeled around, dove straight down, and came up with its helpless prey. I was a fish in the viselike talons of the Viking, completely helpless and vulnerable.

The bitter realities of the situation I was in overwhelmed me. I was the prisoner of a man who could hand me over to be raped by each of his crew in turn with as little concern as he would toss a scrap of meat to a pack of wolves. He was a monster, as evil and brutal as any of his men. I had a choice, yet what difference did it make if I were raped once by many men or repeatedly by one man under the mockery of being married to him. The idea of being passed from man to man revolted all my senses; yet marriage to a heathen was not to be endured. It was a sin, only slightly less damnable than heresy.

I had accepted the idea of being a slave because that would be forced upon me against my will. There was no sin in that. To submit to this marriage was to damn myself to the eternal fires of hell, the end I had been taught all my life to fear. I tossed and turned on the pallet, bathed in sweat and then shaking with cold. When I slept, Rorik's face weaved in and out of my dreams; when I awoke, his voice was constantly audible all over the ship.

Rorik. What kind of a man was this Viking chieftain? When his men disobeyed him by looting the abbey, he punished them by playing games. He was willing to give me to the men, yet when one of them had approached me on the ship and put his hands on my shoulders, he went livid with rage. Rorik had the man tied up and tossed overboard, to be pulled alongside the ship, gasping and gagging in the turbulent waves. And despite the fate he threatened me with, his manner toward me had been gentle and considerate for the most part.

I could think no longer. My head ached and I felt sick to my stomach. I needed to stand by the rail and feel a fresh breeze on my face. Rorik said I had time. And once again I realized time might bring me the opportunity to escape. Meanwhile I would forget I had a decision to make and try to enjoy the days on board ship. If I were patient, perhaps I would be guided in some way toward the path I should take.

As yet unwilling to move much beyond the small area of the ship where I felt reasonably safe, I began thinking about myself, trying to sort out my feelings. From the time I was old enough to sense that my parents neither loved nor understood me as much as they did Deirdre, I had learned to move with an air of independence and self-sufficiency. In truth, I was a shy, dependent person who desperately longed for love and security. I neded to be sustained by someone else's strength. When I did not find it within my family, I turned to Ian and showered him with every ounce of love I possessed. With his engagement to Deirdre, I felt wretchedly betrayed; and I ran to the security of the abbey and the much-needed affection of Lady Anna.

Now I was alone once again, drowning in a sea of despair and unable to sustain myself in spite of the strong-minded exterior I presented to Rorik. He was a powerful personality. If anything about him ultimately drew me to him, it would be his ability to fulfill that need in me for someone strong; with that, more than physical attraction, he might be able to seduce me. I would need to be cautious. Nor would I let pass a chance to escape. The fear of my unknown future in the mysterious Northland was as terrifying as marriage to a pagan.

Yes, I would try to escape at the earliest opportunity. That was my first choice. If I were unsuccessful, I would not let regret ruin my life. I would live with Rorik as his wife, heathen though he was, and try to reconcile my religious beliefs with a situation over which I had no control. Perhaps it would help if I learned what life as a Viking wife would mean. It would also be wiser for me to get to know him, to talk to him rather than remain aloof and ignore him. Not only to learn how best to escape from him, but to be prepared for what lay ahead if escape were denied me.

Through all this I tried to subdue the real fear that haunted me. The fear that if once I were forced to submit to Rorik, I would become dependent upon his strength and then be abandoned again. That was the thought that tormented me most as I lay contemplating my situation. Better to watch what was happening on the ship and forget about myself.

Rorik was standing in the stern, urging on the rowers with stirring songs and taking his turn at the tiller. After a while the wind freshened, the sail billowed out, and the crew lay down their oars. Then I watched with interest as some of the Vikings dropped lines overboard to catch large fish while others hauled in nets full of smaller ones. I was amazed at their agility in handling the nets in the rough waves that the ship breasted like a wild stallion jumping hedges.

When it came time to prepare the evening meal, I saw the crew spreading large squares of thick leather on a platform. I was eager to move closer, to see just what was going on, but I was still too afraid of being near the men, who eyed me as much with hatred as with lust. Cautiously I moved forward a few feet, and saw two men drag out tremendous brass cauldrons and layer chunks of peat inside. With all of them seeming to ignore my presence, I allowed curiosity to overcome fear, and I walked between the benches to the middle of the ship. When I saw a hand reaching toward me, I instinctively recoiled. In another moment I was blushing with mortification. The man I remembered as Sigurd was merely reaching for a brass pot on the bench beside me. The peat in the cauldrons burned down to hot, glowing coals, and he immediately nestled the smaller pot inside one of them.

Aware that Rorik had been watching me the whole time, I was not surprised when he called out, "Tara, come up here beside me."

For the briefest moment I hesitated, then realized I would look like a fool if I refused and he had to make it a command.

"Glad to see you showing signs of life," he said, after I sat down beside him. "Want to know what they're doing?"

I nodded.

"The cauldrons are on leather to prevent what sailors dread more than a storm: fire at sea. With good seamanship, we can maneuver through the most violent gales, but we'd be helplessly trapped on a burning ship. Hungry?"

"Yes," I said under my breath.

"Then watch closely and you'll see how your supper is prepared."

While several men filled the pots with water drawn from the sea, others cut up the fish they had caught. From knobby sacks came cabbages and onions which were sliced and added to the stew along with crushed, dried leaves. It was this last—herbs unknown to me—that sent a delicious, mouth-watering aroma throughout the ship.

Within a few minutes, the Vikings were ladling the savory stew into deep wooden bowls. Some ate it with wooden spoons; others scooped it up with hard chunks of dark rye bread. Rorik filled a bowl for me and then continued to steer with one elbow while he ate.

Remembering my determination to be less haughty and try to find out more about him, I said, "This is very good."

"My men are good cooks. Spending weeks at a time at sea, they have to be."

This was just the opening I had been looking for. "And at home?"

"There the women tend the fires and cookpots."

"And?" Was I going to have to pry the information I wanted out of him? And at the same time not let him think I was considering his proposal.

"What do you mean?" His almost naive, quizzical tone was exasperating.

"What else are the women expected to do?" I meant what chores or tasks were allotted to them, but that was not the way he took it.

"To please their masters at all times." Rorik threw back his head and laughed, but I was fuming inside. He had guessed the intent of my questions and was taunting me. "Is that not the answer you expected?" I forced myself to smile. "But, my timid seabird, they are the real rulers of the home."

Somehow that made me more uncomfortable than if he said the men beat their wives every day. I wanted to keep on hating the Vikings and this chieftain in particular, who thought he could win me over with kindness. I wanted to hate them as one hates a killer wolf. I did not want to find out anything that would make them seem human.

"I cannot believe that," I said, "after seeing how ruthless you are with the innocent women you capture."

"You do not know men very well, Tara."

"Yes, I do," I said quietly, thinking of the afternoon on the hill and Ian's expression when he looked at Deirdre the following week. Which was the lie? His declaration of love for me or his apparent admiration of her? I had given myself to him physically, but I had been raped spiritually. No, Ian's actions, though less violent, were no different from those of the Vikings.

In the autumn twilight, a few stars began to appear, and Rorik became silent while he studied the sky.

"You know why we rule the sea, Tara?"

"Because you are ruthless marauders who strike fear into the hearts of other seamen."

"Ah, that bitter tone again. I must find a way to cure you of that. No, it is partly because we know how to sail by night as well as by day. Someday I will show you how to read the stars. But the real reason is our ships. To those who never raised a sail or handled the tiller, a ship is oaken planks and a pine mast. To me she is a living thing."

In spite of myself, I was touched by his feelings for his ship. For the first time, despite my hatred for him, I saw him as something other than a monster who wanted to possess me. As he spoke, he seemed almost unaware of me sitting next to him.

"In heavy seas," he continued, "she heaves and bends, but she never breaks. Sometimes if you look closely

43

enough, you will see the bottom planks expand and contract—like she was breathing. My *Raven of the Wind* I call her, and she wears her sail, the Cloak of the Wind, like a queen. I designed her myself and oversaw every board while she was being built. Then I polished and rubbed her down until she gleamed like a jewel."

With each poetic word he spoke in describing his feeling about the *Raven,* I found myself more moved by this man.

"Her?" I had been intrigued by his use of the feminine in every sentence.

"A ship is always 'her.' Like a woman she responds best to gentle handling, but rough or tender, she always obeys. She cradles me in her arms when I am tired, but she is ready to take the wind in her sail and race the waves with real spirit when I give the command."

My first reaction was that no man who spoke thus could be intentionally cruel to anyone. Then I caught myself. I dared not let myself be drawn toward him. Even if forced to become his wife, I must never allow myself to feel anything for him. To quell the emotions rising in me, I determined to keep him at arm's length. "And I assume you expect a woman to be just as obedient," I said matter-of-factly.

"If I show her as much love as I do the *Raven,* she will want to. As for others, 'tis their duty to obey."

I was not about to ask him which category he put me in. If he said the first, I would not believe him, and the second would only make me angry. I did not intend ever again to have my life ruled by the word "duty," in spite of my agreement with him. If I could not escape, if I had to belong to him, I would do everything in my power to avoid being mastered by him. I was not going to be enslaved either emotionally or physically.

Into the midst of my thoughts came Rorik's voice. "You have seen the dragon head." He pointed to the prow where the intricately carved image rode, a proud vanguard.

" 'Tis very beautiful." Although hating what it represented and the fear it inspired in all who saw it appear over the horizon, I could not deny I was impressed.

"I carved it myself and painted every brush stroke. I worked on it at night after supervising construction on the ship all day."

Darkness had fallen and the ship was illuminated only

by the glowing coals in the cauldrons and two pine-knot torches fore and aft the mast, but I could recall every detail of the dragon's red mouth filled with fanglike teeth, the gold-feathered crest that looked as if it were ruffled by the wind, and the overlapping scales of purple outlined in gold. Its beauty was terrifying yet majestic.

"It must have taken hours," I said. "All the carving and painting. You must have great patience." Slowly I was seeing more facets to this man's character, sides of him that made him seem quite different from those in his crew. Yet I had to keep in mind that he was a Viking, a heathen I had vowed to hate.

"Patience!" he laughed. "You'd not say that if you heard me curse the gods each time I broke a knife blade. I started the day we laid the keel and finished in time to set it aloft the day the *Raven* first touched the sea. The dragon has led us safely home many a time when I thought we'd not make it."

"I cannot believe you could ever be lost," I said in mock horror in order to conceal the growing admiration I had for the way he spoke about his ship.

"Lost? Never! Rorik does not get lost at sea. But there are storms as well as other rovers of the whale road who would like to capture me or see me go to the bottom."

He turned abruptly, as if he regretted mentioning the threats to him. After studying the night sky intently for a few minutes, he adjusted the direction of the tiller. "Some night I will show you how I steer by the stars. For now I think you had better return to the prow. The men are beginning to get surly. Too much to drink and too long a confinement on the ship."

After those words I was ready to get behind my woolen shelter and crawl between the layers of furs. The night was bitter cold, and a strong wind had blown up. I could not stop shivering, but more with fear of what Rorik had said about the danger from storms than from the cold wind that whipped the woolen hanging unmercifully and threatened to blow my coverings away. So far I had not felt many ill effects from the motion of the ship, but I was uncertain how I would fare if we encountered rough seas. The thought of drowning during a storm, however, was no less fearful than the dread of having some of the crew, now drunk and restless; attack me during the night. If more than one decided I was fair game for their lust,

Rorik alone would not be able to stop them. Awake, I listened to wild talk and drunken outcries; asleep, I relived the attack on the abbey in one nightmare after another, only now I was one of the victims; and it was Rorik who leered threateningly down at me. Each time I awoke just before he touched me. Finally—mercifully—I fell into a deep, dreamless sleep.

In the morning I awoke to Rorik's sharp, rapid commands and the exuberant answering shouts of the men. When I peered around the shelter, I saw that the ship was heading slowly into a large bay, a natural harbor bulwarked by rock formations jutting out from shore. This must be where Rorik will meet his men, I thought. More important, it could be the perfect place for me to escape. We were many leagues from home; but if I took time to study the area, I might see places where I could seek refuge. First of all, however, I had to get off the ship, either by invitation or by stealth. While I waited to see if Rorik would suggest I go ashore, I'd take the opportunity to scrutinize the lay of the land and the best way to get off the ship if he were not of a mind to take me with him.

As the ship was steered into the harbor and alongside one of the elongated rock formations, I waited to see how close they would come to this natural jetty, which might prove to be an excellent access to shore. Because of their design, the Vikings' serpent ships could not be easily beached, and the water here was deep almost to the base of a low, sloping bluff—too deep for one to wade ashore. So I had to forego any idea of jumping overboard and trying to swim, something I had dared only a few times in the stream near home. No, the rocks would be the most obvious means of escape.

The *Raven* slowed down and finally paused with the prow no more than several yards from land. Then, three of the oars were placed so as to form a bridge between the ship and the rocks; and men were soon across them with ropes to secure her fore and aft. Immediately this was done, the rest of the Vikings raced across the oars and along the rock ledge to shore. The air was filled with the sound of their fists beating against their leather-covered chests and howls that always sent anyone in earshot scurrying for the safety of homes or nearby woods.

46

I looked at the oars and wondered if I had the courage to imitate the crew. I doubted I was either agile or experienced enough to keep my footing, and the ship was too far from the rocks to jump, so that route of escape seemed closed to me. That meant one thing. Rorik had to be encouraged to take me ashore. Perhaps if I merely assumed I was to leave the ship, he would not think twice about helping me off the ship. I waited impatiently for him to leave the tiller and come to where I stood at the rail.

"Good morning, Tara. You see, we found the bay just when I said we would."

"I never denied you were a skillful sailor," I smiled, intent on being as pleasant as possible. " 'Tis a pity you don't rule the sea as traders rather than marauders."

"Oh, but we do—trade, that is—and very successfully, too. We go Viking for pleasure as much as for the rewards it brings. You see my men now? They are a lusty crew. Do you think they would be content to live a life with no excitement, no threat of danger?"

I saw the crew, racing up and down the shore like children on holiday. But they were not children; they were cruel, vicious monsters who would soon be terrorizing any who lived nearby. No, I would not think about them but concentrate on my own immediate problem.

"Do you think you could help me ashore?" I asked. "I don't think I can manage the oars by myself." Let him think I am completely helpless and he would be persuaded I dare not try to escape. "I do look forward to being on land again. Perhaps you know of a stream where I could bathe and wash my hair." I hoped he would be gentleman enough to leave me alone; and if I couldn't get away during that time, I could at least discover a route for making my escape later.

His words came as a chilling shock of disappointment. "No, Tara, you stay on the ship."

"Afraid I'll run away?" I taunted, and then I could have bitten my tongue for putting the idea into his head. "Please let me go with you." I tried a more conciliatory tone. "I'm not used to being confined like this. Closed in one corner like a dog in a hovel."

"The confinement is your idea, Tara. You've been free to walk the entire ship."

"Among those rough, uncouth men of yours? No, thank you." God's blood! This conversation wasn't going at all

47

the way I wanted it to. Every time I tried to be pleasant, he'd say something to make me angry all over again.

"All the more reason to stay on board. They have been confined, too, so once on land they will be drinking—and —and celebrating and—"

"Wenching, you mean?" If I were to be denied my wish to go ashore, there seemed no reason to be polite. "You can speak frankly. I am not naive, though I wear the garb of a nun." I looked down at the ragged, filthy robe that had been neat and clean on the fateful morning I donned it. With all that had happened, I had almost forgotten I was a nun. And if—if I did not succeed in escaping, there would be no point in remembering, living as I would be among heathens.

"You will be alone here," Rorik said, as he prepared to leave, "so feel free to walk the ship. Just don't try to sail her away. I do not think you have the strength for it," he laughed, and I could cheerfully have strangled him right then and there. "I will return with something to eat and drink." He turned on his heels and ran nimbly across the oars and along the rocks.

How I envied him his freedom to come and go. Dared I try walking the oars just to see if I could do it? No, I would either be seen or—more likely—fall off and have to scream for help or drown. But there had to be a way, and I would find it. Once off the ship and away from the harbor, I was certain to come across cottages or even a village where people would offer refuge and guide me to a road leading southward.

Rorik had said he would return with food. That meant waiting until I was completely assured he would not be back again until morning. It did not bother me to remain on board alone, and during the interim I took Rorik's suggestion and walked from one end of the ship to the other. Not just to stretch my legs, but to see if there were anything on board that might aid me either in getting off or making my way inland later. I doubted that any of the crew left knives behind, but I searched diligently under each bench and also in the storage area under the stern deck just to make sure. All of the weapons had been taken; but much to my delight, I found a small knife stashed among the sacks of vegetables. It had a ring on the handle as if meant to be attached to a chain. Knowing it might be invaluable to me while I made my way alone through the countryside, I tore strips from a sack, knotted them together to make a belt, slid the knife on, and tied it around my waist under my robe. Now at least I had some protection.

Looking at the potatoes I had dumped out of the sack, I realized I might not always be able to find food along the way, but all of the sacks were too large to carry. Remembering that I had seen a small leather bag during my earlier search of the ship, I again scrounged under all of the benches until I found just what I needed to carry a few provisions with me. The bag was drawn together at the neck with leather thongs which I could sling over my shoulder as I walked.

With the knife safely around my waist and the leather bag stowed in the prow, I had plenty of time to walk along the rail and look carefully at the countryside beyond the harbor. I paused first to look across the bay in the direction opposite the rock formation where we were tied up. In the distance I saw several spirals of smoke, close enough together to indicate a small village or at least a cluster of cottages. Surely someone there would offer sanctuary and maybe even find a carter traveling along the road who would take me some leagues on my journey. I was beginning to feel very optimistic about my chances of getting far enough away before my absence was detected to make it impossible for Rorik to follow me.

Then I remembered. The Vikings would have seen the smoke, too, or perhaps even known in advance that the cottages were there; and they would never miss the opportunity to raid. Had the looting begun? Were women screaming in terror at being dragged off or raped in their homes? There might be men there to protect them; but they could be taken by surprise, and probably even killed as they tried to defend their women and property. All my previous hatred for the Vikings welled up in me, and I felt my hopes shriveling to nothing. I found myself reliving those moments of terror at the abbey. There seemed to be no escape from the hideous fiends, but escape I would, even if I could not count on help from those cottagers.

In order to calm the fear that clawed at me like some grotesque animal, I tried to concentrate on the countryside to the cottages. We had seen the last of summer, but much of the land was still green, accented by the gold and red of leaves already touched by frost. I caught glimpses of several patches of wild flowers—brilliant sparks of blue and yellow and orange; and I felt buoyed up again by the thought I would soon be running through them.

Then I returned to watching anxiously the spot where I had seen the smoke. Any minute now I expected to see flames, like those that burned the abbey. When, after some time, there was no sign of fire, I considered that perhaps the Vikings had met no resistance or simply had lost their lust for burning. So there was a chance, even a slim chance, I might yet find help in that quarter.

Lost in my reverie, I didn't hear Rorik approach until he came up behind me.

"Tara, I've brought food and a small jug of elderberry wine."

I didn't turn around. I was afraid he would be able to read my plans in my face. "Just put them down," I said. "I'm not hungry right now." In truth I was famished, but I didn't want to be drawn into a conversation with him just then. I had more important things on my mind.

"There are apples and grapes, not two weeks picked. And bread hot from the ovens."

My mouth watered for the fresh fruit, but went dry again when I wondered whose ovens had been robbed and what had happened to the housewife tending them.

"I'm really not hungry, I'll get them in a bit."

"As you like. I'll be back again later."

Holy Mother! Why didn't he leave me alone and romp on the shore with his crew? How could I get away if he kept coming back? I had to find some way either to get ashore with him, and then away from him, or make myself unpleasant enough that he wouldn't want to return.

Meanwhile I had to conjure with the biggest problem of all—how to get off the ship without being seen. One thing for certain, I would have to wait for it to become dark. Many of the Vikings had returned to the bluff, within sight of the ship, where they were constructing rude shelters and building fires. I could discern several women among them, and it was not difficult to imagine what was taking place when some of them disappeared into the shelters. But that was not my concern. I had to work out a safe plan for leaving the ship.

Once more I leaned over the rail and looked closely at the long rock jetty. Somehow I had to get over to it. Then if I could crawl across the top without being seen and down the other side, I should have no trouble making my way to land, there to lose myself in the woods at the top of the bluff. It would put the Vikings between me and the cottages; but once there I would have plenty of time to decide my next move, either around behind the crew or off in the opposite direction if I saw a road or habitation of some kind.

I looked at the oars. There seemed no way I could walk across them without being seen or falling into the water. I had once been adept at climbing trees, another trick Ian had taught me and at which my mother frowned. Perhaps if I lowered myself under one of the oars, I could maneuver along it, hand before hand. The distance seemed no more than ten feet, but it had been a long time since I'd swung from a limb. Just thinking about it made my arms ache, and the dread of falling into the cold, dark water turned my insides to jelly. But it was the only way. I'd use the time until dark to work up my courage rather than succumb to fear. Rorik had said he would return, so I knew I'd best wait until after his next visit. I could also judge what kind of mood he was in.

Soon after twilight, Rorik came back on board with two plates of food, and we ate in silence after he refused a second time to let me go ashore. That meant that I definitely had to try getting away across the oars and the rocks. I was too furious to indulge in polite conversation, but he had different ideas.

"This is as clear a night as I have seen on the voyage, Tara. Would you like me to show you how we steer by the stars?"

"I am not interested." Let him talk. Maybe if I was unpleasant enough he would leave again for the rest of the night. What I needed to do was make him mad enough that he would not want to return. "Thank you for the food. You can go now. No need to worry about me. I am sure you want to return to—to the celebrating."

"What makes you think that?"

"Your cohorts are enjoying themselves so much, I cannot imagine your wanting to miss any of it. It must be such fun—drinking until you are sick, tearing clothes off the women, and then mauling them. You are all just—just a herd of wild, vicious animals."

I thought surely that would send him away; but I'd not

realized how loud and more hysterical my voice had become until Rorik grabbed me by the shoulders and began shaking me.

"Quiet! I like my women to have sweet, soft voices. You sound like a shrieking crone."

"Good. Then you'll not want me near you."

"Wrong. I want you very much. 'Tis why I brought you this." He handed me a comb, crudely carved from bone. "Your hair is a mess, and it was shining and beautiful when I first saw you. Use it. I'll help you with the tangles in back."

"Never mind. I can reach them myself."

I didn't want to take the comb, but oh, it would feel good to have my hair unmatted and smooth again. Not for Rorik. Never for him, but for my own pleasure. I began working out the tangles. With those at the front and sides, I did fine, even when pulling the comb through them brought tears to my eyes; but no matter how hard I strained, I could not manage the back.

"Here, give me that." Rorik took the comb from my hand. "You're only making it worse, and you're going to break my gift."

He worked the comb through the strands. "There now," he said, "it looks more like it should." He handed me the comb but continued running his hand over my head and curling strands of hair around his fingers. "Tara, look at me." I kept staring out across the harbor, now completely enveloped in darkness. Why wouldn't he go and leave me alone? "All right, don't," he said. "I can talk to your back. Do you know why I brought you the comb?"

I shook my head.

"Because when I found it, I remembered how beautiful your hair looked in the late-afternoon sun, silver like the crest of a wave or the shimmer of a fish just under the surface."

"My, you talk as if you're trying to sound like a bard," I said rudely, but I remembered how he had waxed eloquent about his ship. He did have a touch of the poet in him, and once more I had to fight to keep from being moved by his words.

"Not a bard, Tara. Just trying to show you I am not what you seem to imagine Vikings are like. As for my men, I am their chieftain; and to keep them loyal, I have to give them their freedom from time to time. How long do you think I could control them if I did not? 'Tis in our blood to go wild, as you put it, when we are aroused. If you were not here, I'd be back on shore with my men and the women from the village."

" 'Tis what I thought. Well, go back. I'll not keep you here." Maybe that would send him scurrying for shore.

"By Odin, Tara, you're impossible. I am trying to tell you I want to be here with you."

"Why? Because there are scarce enough women to go around? Or is it my sparkling conversation?" I was taking a chance in irritating him to the point of making him really angry; but instead of arousing his fury, my words had just the opposite effect.

Before I knew what was happening, Rorik had pulled me into his arms and crushed me until I thought I would break in two. His mouth was forceful and demanding on mine. Though it was impossible for me to protest, I was screaming inside, *I won't, I won't give in to him*.

"There," he said hoarsely, "that seems to be the only way I can hush you up long enough to say what I really want."

He leaned back against the rail, still holding me lightly, but quite securely, in his arms. I was seething inwardly, furious at his actions but more upset at the feelings he stirred up when he touched me. I was too unnerved to speak. I would not give him the satisfaction of either fighting him or letting him know that he could move me to an emotion of any kind.

Calmly, as if he had not just left me gasping at his actions, he said, "Since you have let me know what you think of Vikings, you will now listen to what I have to say. With no interruptions! The raid on the abbey was wrong. Not because we don't make a practice of raiding, but because this time it was against orders. We came here with one purpose—to find a good site in the south of Britain from which to trade along the western coast of Europe. We have other settlements in Ireland and the Outer Isles, but for reasons not important now, we need more. As to the ravages you think are taking place up there on shore. If you would take time to look closely, you'd see everyone— everyone!—enjoying themselves."

"I do not believe you. The men, yes; but I hardly think the women are."

I thought about the nuns at the abbey, and I stiffened

in his grasp. He had not come back on board just to talk to me or to bring me a comb. In another minute I'd find myself grappling with him and trying to fend off his attack. If he thought to win me by kind gestures and foolish explanations, he was very much in error. If I had to fight him, I'd not have the strength left to escape. Somehow I had to drive him away, to make him prefer the women on shore to me.

"Don't be a silly goose," he laughed, and I hated him for laughing. "These peasant women like variety. It gives excitement to their otherwise drab lives. They'll have a little fun, then go home, innocent of any intentional wrongdoing. As victims of the evil Vikings, they will be called martyrs and have something to talk about the rest of their lives. How horrible it was. How terrible to be captured and forced to submit. But when they tell their grandchildren how the wicked men from the North set upon them, all the while they'll be licking their lips over the memory."

"You are horrible!" No longer could I conceal how I loathed him and his attitude toward women. "No woman feels that way."

"You think not? Faugh! What do you know? You've spent too much time on your knees and none on your back. How do you know what a normal woman wants?"

"You're vile!" I spat at him. But I am a normal woman, I thought, and I do know what it is like to desire a man. But only someone I loved and who—no, I couldn't say that. I could never know whether Ian had loved me or merely used me, as these men used the women they captured. "No woman wants to be forced against her will, and by rough savages."

"And who says they are being forced? If you listen, you'll hear laughter. No woman who is forced will laugh like that. Nor did they resist overmuch when the crew captured them after their men went to the fields."

I could scarce believe what he was saying. "Drunken laughter is what I hear. You make them drunk so they cannot resist. Or they are afraid of being killed. Strength breeds terror."

And at that very moment I was as terrified as I thought them to be. From the crazed look about Rorik's eyes, I knew I had maddened him all right, but not the way I'd

54

hoped. Then he dropped his arms, releasing me from his hold.

"I'll not argue with you now, Tara. I came up here to keep you company. I thought to have a pleasant time together, but as you suggested, I think I'll go back where there is more congenial company and everyone is enjoying themselves. 'Tis no mood I'm in for a moral lecture. So stay by yourself and brood over these supposed insults to chaste womanhood. Women who were probably tumbled in the hay or on a grassy meadow many a time before they wed."

His last words were like a knife in my heart, but in another moment I knew only relief that he was at last leaving. He strode off, running the length of the oars as if as glad to be away from me as I was to have him gone.

Now I was sure he would be occupied for some time, I could begin to carry out my plan of escape. I looked again at the rock formation to which we'd tied up and the oars leading from the boat over to it. The rocks jutted out from a high, sheer cliff on the other side; but earlier in the day I had been able to make out a narrow, sandy beach at its base. Once on the rocks, I could lower myself down the other side and onto the beach. The entire coast was honeycombed with caves, and I counted on taking refuge in one, free from prying eyes, until I recovered enough to climb up to the woods on top. If I could do all this before daylight, I might be well away from the harbor before Rorik knew I was gone. The knife was still tied securely around my waist. Thank God, he had not felt it when he held me in his arms. I went to get the small sack of vegetables. It was heavier than I remembered, but I slung it over one shoulder.

A full moon had come out, so that ended any thought of even trying to walk across the oars. I would be seen immediately. Cautiously I lowered myself over the side of the serpent ship and grasped one oar from the underside. For a moment I hung over the dark water, letting my arms get accustomed to the weight of my body. Then I carefully put one hand in front of the other, and so began my slow progress.

Less than halfway across I had to stop; my muscles had cramped with pain, and I could not control my breathing. My bloody fingers were full of splinters from the rough wood of the oar, and my heart beat so rapidly, I was sure it was tearing apart. I felt as if I couldn't hold on a second longer, yet fear of falling into the water urged me on. When I started up again, my right hand slipped, and I was left dangling precariously by only the other. I managed to regain my hold, but I lost the leather bag of provisions. I wanted to cry when I heard it splash into the water, but I consoled myself that at least it was not I sinking into the black depths.

Getting a new grip on the oar, in spite of the blood that now made it slippery, I moved ahead. There was no pain I could not bear if it meant being free from the Vikings. I simply closed my eyes and willed my hands to move. I thought of pleasant things, like getting back to the abbey and being once more in my own bed. Even restoring a burned abbey and mourning the dead would be preferable to what I would have to endure as a captive wife.

Suddenly my legs, swinging free, hit rock, and I knew I had reached the ledge. For a moment I merely leaned against it, still clutching the oar. The next problem was to get over or around the rocks. Climbing on top would again put me in danger of being seen. The ledge was actually an extension of the cliff, an outcropping of large boulders, formed over the centuries by wind, water, and time into a natural breakwater. They should offer a good footing if I stepped carefully from one to another. Once more I wrapped my skirts around my waist. I had to keep my hands free and check each rock before I put my foot down. One misstep and I would be in the water. Waves washed the lowest rocks, but the tide was still out, giving me ample time to get around the end. Once on the other side, I would be in less danger of discovery.

I wanted to hurry, but I dared not. I had to take my time and trust that Rorik would remain on shore. Before I took each step, I made certain I had secured a good handhold. Only then did I move forward. It seemed like hours but was probably only minutes when I finally rounded the narrow tip of the ledge and was able to see the other side.

It was then I almost gave up. Ahead of me lay not the narrow beach I had seen in the distance, but the cliff rising sheer out of the water. At its base were jagged rocks against which the waves rushed and pounded. I lay gasping on one boulder, fearing to go on, yet dreading to go back. It was true there was a large, flat rock just ahead

56

and above me. If I reached that, I could lie there out of sight. Perhaps until the ship left. But that was dreaming. Once Rorik missed me, he would order a search, and in daylight I would be spotted immediately.

The melody of the waves, their steady, rhythmic movement in and out, almost put me to sleep. I roused myself enough to notice that at one point their regular pattern broke. Then I saw why. There was a place where they didn't stop at the base of the cliff, but swirled into it. There was an opening. It was one of the caves I'd hoped to find. It would mean getting wet, but once deeper inside, I was certain to find a dry place.

I had paused long enough. It was time to go on. Once more I moved from boulder to boulder. The going was much easier than it would be when I reached the cliff from which the long mass of rocks curved out. Once I gained the spot where the cliff began, I thought about climbing it rather than trying for the cave. With rocky outcroppings at irregular intervals, it seemed to offer enough hand- and footholds to make the climb look easy. Once on top, I could lie under one of the gnarled trees that clung near the edge, undaunted by the wind blowing off the sea. An hour's rest and I would be ready to move on, through the woods that came almost to the bay, and around to the village.

Buoyed up by being so near to freedom, I got careless. My hand reached for a rock that came loose, and in my desperate attempt to grab for another, I lost my balance. Cold, dark water swirled above and around me. In a panic, I began flailing my arms around, not knowing which way to the surface. My lungs were bursting with the effort to keep from breathing. Finally one wave swept me toward shore, and my head came out of the water. A second wave pounded me against one of the tall rocks, and I reached out for it. Before I could get a grasp on it, the undertow pulled me back. But I knew if I could remain afloat, another wave would carry me toward shore again. I waited and let the natural motion of the sea propel me forward. When I finally had my arms around the rock, I was able to hang on.

The question now was where to go from there. The cave was some distance away, but if I moved carefully along the protruding rocks, waiting each time until the waves had receded, I could do it. I merely had to be more cautious.

My arms were numb but no longer sore, so I lay where I was, waiting for some strength to return before venturing forth. The one real danger in my path was a small whirlpool just outside the entrance to the cave, formed by the waters rushing in and out. I closed my eyes again, forcing myself to breathe calmly and trying to relax all my muscles.

"You need any help?"

The taunting voice—the voice I knew so well—came from the ledge right above me. For a moment I came very close to letting go and allowing the waves to take me where they would. Yet I did not want to die. Being once more his captive was like being captured by the devil, but death would be worse.

"I said, do you need any help?"

Now I could see Rorik standing on a boulder right near me. Legs apart, hands on hips, he threw back his head and laughed. Yes, he was a devil, a grinning imp of Satan.

I was furious with him! I had almost made it. Just a few minutes more and I would have reached a safe hiding place in the cave. My muscles were screaming with pain, but I could have willed them to exert the additional effort. After a short rest, I would have been ready to go on. I wanted to scream, to reach up and scratch out his eyes. With most of his face in shadow, the moon highlighted the smug, self-satisfied grin under his drooping mustache, and he reminded me of a leering satyr. I was sorely tempted to continue struggling along from rock to rock and force him to come down into the water after me if he was that determined to recapture me. I might not get away, but I would know the pleasure of seeing him as soaking wet and shivering as I was. Then with his next words all strength left me; and for the moment, there seemed no point in trying to defy him.

"You look a sight. For God's sake, give me your hand and let me get you out of there."

I was now too tired and disheartened not to obey. He lay face down on the rock and reached for the arm I held out. Then he pulled me roughly through the water. Half-dragging, half-carrying, he got us both to the top of the ledge. There I collapsed in his arms.

"I ought to spank you, you know that?" he growled. "Scaring me half out of my mind, trying to run off like that."

Instead he gathered me up like a child and carried me to the ship.

"Now, take off those wet clothes," he ordered.

"No, I—"

"I said, take them off. You'll freeze to death if you don't. If you won't, I will." He reached over to carry out his threat.

"All—all right," I said between chattering teeth. "I'll do it."

"Stand there by the cauldron. The coals will blaze up in a minute. I'll get some furs."

Even standing by the brazier, I began shivering so violently I couldn't manage the water-soaked garments. My fingers were numb with cold; and when I held them over the fire to warm them, the pain was so intense, I wanted to scream. In spite of my feeble protests, Rorik unfastened and pulled off my robe and undergarments. I was too miserable to care that I stood before him absolutely naked.

Immediately he wrapped me in a rough woolen blanket and began toweling me down with it. His strong hands were surprisingly gentle as they moved the prickly cloth unceasingly over every part of my body to first dry and then restore warmth and color to my chilled skin. At first I tensed under his touch, certain he would try to seduce me now that I was so completely vulnerable. Then I realized he was caring for me as he would a baby rather than an object of desire, and I began to relax. My body tingled all over; was it from the stimulation of the rough blanket or the touch of his hands? His gentle treatment surprised me, and I began to feel a new warmth spreading through me that came from more than the fire and the blanket. Then I looked at Rorik and realized I was beginning to fall under his spell just as he'd said I would. Oh, no, I thought, you might have rescued me from an icy death, but I've not weakened that much.

"I'm fine now," I said, struggling to pull the damp blanket closer around me.

"Good. I don't think you'll catch a chill now, but you need more than that blanket."

Before I could stop him, he had pulled off the blanket and had me wrapped in furs. Then he sat me down—hard—on the deck and began stirring up the embers in the cauldron. Treat me like a child, would he? Well, he'd find he had more to reckon with than a disobedient little

59

girl. He'd tricked me again by returning to the ship, and I meant to find out why.

"How—how did you find me? How long were you standing there?"

"Long enough to watch you climbing along the rocks."

"You mean you stood there and let me struggle?" What a loathsome human being he was! No, not human. An animal. "You saw me fall in the water and made no move to stop me, or—or help me?"

"I rescued you, didn't I? You'd scarce have lasted much longer in that icy water. You thought you were resting. What you were getting ready to do was slip back in the water and drown."

"Never!"

"Oh, yes, just as easy as that."

I stared into the glowing coals, refusing to say anything more. So I was not dead, but I was still a captive. I had lost one chance but there would be others. I might even be forced to become his wife, but someday I would be free from him forever.

"I am really disappointed in you, Tara. I thought I could trust you. Now I daren't let you out of my sight for even a minute."

If he thought that would elicit a response, he was wrong. I merely glared at him.

"I was more than disappointed that you would run away, Tara. I was deeply hurt."

Hurt? Why should he be hurt? He knew how much I despised him.

"You see," he continued, "I have another gift for you. Hold out your arm."

I didn't want any more gifts. I wanted nothing that would make me beholden to him, but I could not resist looking at what he held in his hands. It was an exquisite bracelet fashioned from numerous strands of gold as fine as human hair, which had been intricately braided into an open circle. At each end was a detailed dragon's head, and when brought together, they locked to form the clasp. In truth, it was magnificent, the finest I'd ever seen. What would it mean if I did accept it? Would I be any less his slave if I refused it? Any chance of getting away from the ship now was hopeless since he'd said he would stay right by my side from now on. That meant agreeing to become his wife before we reached his home. How many days more of freedom I had, I did not know, but I could at least have that time to myself.

Rorik was frowning and I knew I had made him angry by not immediately holding out my arm. If I let him put it on, I knew it was tantamount to accepting his proposal, yet it seemed pointless to delay the inevitable. While I wrestled with these thoughts, Rorik quietly reached for my hand and slipped the bracelet onto my arm. When I looked at it, I thought only that now I was truly manacled like a slave. The metal circlet was cold but it burned into my skin like molten ore from the devil's forge. A ring of fire. It was heavy, the weight of his claim on me. When I slid it down to my wrist, there were fine, serpentine lines engraved in my flesh, the stigmata of my bondage. Intuitively I sensed that now, somehow, there was no turning back. He had made the decision for me; but by not immediately removing the bracelet, had I not willingly accepted it? For good or evil, had I chosen a path which, like a rushing stream, carried me ever forward.

"Do you like it, Tara?"

" 'Tis very beautiful." He would not know that I was afraid or that the sight of it was abhorrent to me. "But I do not want it. Please take it off." It was a daring request; but if I ultimately had to marry him, I was determined there would be no ties until the last possible moment.

As if he had not heard me, he ignored my request. Instead he threw back his long cloak. "Look, I have one like it." He slipped the duplicate off his upper arm. So fine was the gold, it could be bent to any form without breaking. On me, the heads came together and locked; on him, they remained separated.

While he held his bracelet in his hands, he said, "They were my manhood gift from my father. When I came of age, old enough to be a warrior and go Viking at his side."

"If they were a gift from your father, then I do not think I should accept it." Surely that was a plausible reason for returning it. I started trying to separate the dragon-headed clasp, but before I could get the bracelet off, he handed me his.

"Here, put mine back on for me, will you, while I pour the wine." As quickly as possible I slipped it around his upper arm, feeling the muscles tighten when I touched him. With the other hand he filled a single goblet. "I hope you won't mind sharing. With the jug, I could only manage one."

What with my ordeal in the sea and the emotional upheaval going on inside me, I was grateful for the warm and soothing effect of the wine. While we drank, however, passing the goblet back and forth, I began feeling strangely uncomfortable under his steady gaze. His eyes had a new, tender look that upset me more than his usually stern or mocking expressions. Again I tried to remove my bracelet, but I couldn't get the intricate clasp unfastened.

"Please take it off, Rorik. I really do not want it."

"I cannot, Tara. It means you are now my wife."

"Oh, no!" I closed my eyes against the pain and anguish that welled up and threatened to force the very breath of life out of me. "I've not agreed to it."

I know not whether I screamed or moaned, but immediately Rorik had me in his arms.

"It matters not," he whispered hoarsely. "We are married now. 'Tis an old Norse custom, the bracelets and the drinking from one cup. We will have a more formal ceremony when we reach Hordaland."

"You said I had time," I cried, trying to free myself from his grasp. "Until the end of the voyage."

"I could not wait," he said with a passion that sent tremors through me as I sensed its urgency.

With that, he lifted me off the deck and carried me, weeping and struggling to the prow.

Now I was engulfed by the one great fear that had tormented me since he'd first said I was to be his wife. Even as I kicked and clawed and beat him with my fists, I knew I was not fighting him but myself.

All physical strength to resist him was gone, but I was still determined not to give in without one last attempt at defying him.

"No!" I said in a surprisingly even tone. "I'm not going to let you touch me."

"Tara, look at me. I know you're frightened, but I'll not be cruel and brutal like those you saw at the abbey."

"Please, Rorik, not yet. I'm not ready. You don't understand."

There would be no way to make him understand the anguish I was suffering. I was being torn apart inside, struggling between my loathing of the situation I was in and the throbbing desire I felt for him when he touched me. It was not his making love to me that I feared. Once I submitted, once he made love to me, I would no longer be the person I was. A woman once possessed is no longer free. For her it must be the beginning of something, of a new life. For a man, the moment of love can be the end of the pursuit. I would no longer be able to conceal my need for Rorik and his strength, and if he let me down, I would be destroyed.

His voice came to me as through a fog. "I'm not dishonoring you, Tara. Ours was a real marriage, even if not to your liking."

"You don't know what you're doing to me," I cried.

I had become so hysterical, I was finding it hard to breathe, and Rorik began shaking me. "I know I intend to bed my wife before the night is over," he said sternly, "no matter how much she kicks and screams."

With that I gave in.

In less than a moment I was in his arms. When his body sought mine, I throbbed with a desire that transcended the hatred I'd once felt for him.

"Hold me close, Rorik, hold me very close," I whispered.

"You're no longer afraid?"

"No, not of this."

I clung to him as I clung to the rock when the surging waves pulled at me and I thought I was going to drown. When we reached a climax simultaneously, I bit his lip; and the taste of blood was bittersweet on my tongue.

Then, suddenly, it was all over, and I knew he had won. Whatever or whomever I gave myself to, I gave completely, relinquishing all, withholding nothing. My ties with the past were now severed. But, oh God, I prayed, let it be the beginning of something, not the end. Now that my life belonged to Rorik, don't let me be betrayed as I was before. Even greater now than my physical need for him was my emotional need, and I could not bear it if I were cast aside.

Chapter Four

THE MOST SENSUOUS, the most luxurious sensation in the world must be the feeling of soft, warm furs against a bare body. When I awoke once before dawn, I took a moment to stretch out full length and then snuggle down deeper between the skins. Still asleep, Rorik moved his arm down from across my shoulders to encircle my waist. When I tried to remove it, he tightened his hold and pulled me closer to him. Once more held possessively against his chest, I succumbed unashamedly to the desire that had surged through me, violently and unstilled, when I finally surrendered to him just hours before, a desire I had kept subdued far too long. If once I thought having this man make love to me would be loathsome, I now found myself caught up in the rapture of giving myself to him completely.

All night we were sheltered by darkness. When the morning sun lit up the prow, the first thing I saw was a strange little statue perched on one of the timbers near me. Carved from wood, it was the figure of a man, looking more like one of our elves than anything human, squatting on his heels. Some kind of long stick seemed to grow out of the ground between his feet. Looking more closely, I examined his bulging eyes and impish grin. I blushed with sudden shame when I realized that what I thought was perhaps a branch or cudgel of some kind was not a thick, knobby stick but a grotesquely enlarged part of the male body. I heard Rorik behind me chortling with half-suppressed glee.

"What—what is that obscene thing?" I asked.

Rorik threw his head back and laughed uproariously, his teeth showing white and strong beneath his full mustache. "That, my beloved Tara, is Frey, God of Fertility."

" 'Tis hideous and—and blasphemous! Get it out of here."

"No, no," he said, ceasing his laughter and becoming more serious. "Frey is always present on the wedding night, and he remains in the sleeping loft to assure there will be plenty of strong, healthy children."

For the moment I tried to ignore the words "sleeping loft." They conjured up visions of a barn or communal sleeping area rather than a private room in a house, and I shuddered. But there was time enough to learn the specifics of a Viking living quarters; I was not ready to face still more uncomfortable truths now.

"I will not have it near me," I said as positively as I could.

"Yes, you will," Rorik insisted, with that tone I was to learn meant I was to be an obedient wife. "You will be allowed to worship your way, but as my wife, you will also be expected to worship our gods."

"I cannot. Our God is the only God, and he allows the worship of no other gods."

"I think you will find you can, Tara." Now his voice frightened me. "You will do exactly as I say when it is time to join in our celebrations, or I will expel the other Christians from our land."

I knew then that Rorik could be cruel when denied, and I also realized that for my own peace, I had to acquiesce. "Yes, Rorik, I will do as you say." But I would find a way to get rid of that ugly little statue as soon as possible. I didn't need him to remind me of my duty as a wife.

When the crew came aboard, they cheered the news that I was now the wife of their chieftain. Having spent a day and a night in revelry on shore, they no longer resented a woman on the ship. Instead of mumbling complaints under their breath or leering at me whenever I came near them, they now treated me like a queen. Mine was the first plate served, and they waited for my approval of what they cooked. They had killed game while ashore and brought back an assortment of fresh vegetables, so there was variety in our diet.

When Rorik steered, I sat beside him at the tiller, and he showed me how to judge the distance from the shore, watch for signs of dangerous shoals, and use the dragon head as a direction guide against more distant landmarks.

If anyone had asked me, I could not explain why I took now such pleasure in being with him, when only a few days earlier I had dreaded seeing him come toward me. The battle within me was over. If the victory went to the basic emotional need of being loved, I did not think it one I would regret. Rorik seemed to sense immediately my change from an outwardly strong-willed, independent person to one who looked to him for strength and guidance. More important, his need for me was as great as mine for him. No, I did not think my trust would be betrayed this time.

As promised earlier, he taught me the secrets of steering by the stars, and soon I learned which ones could be relied upon to keep the same positions from night to night and which moved around the sky. Rorik said every Viking knew the stars as well as he knew the rivers and streams of his own land.

"We have to, Tara." I had expressed wonderment at such knowledge. "The sea is our life. You will better recognize why when you see our land. It is a land of water and mountains, great fjords and rivers, with many islands. Do you know what *Viking* means?"

In spite of having gradually changed in my attitude toward the crew because I now belonged to Rorik, the word still stirred bitter memories. "Yes, scourge of the sea. To go Viking means to raid and kill. I have not quite forgotten that yet."

"Oh, no, Tara. That is only a small part of it. *Vik* is the ancient Norse word for fjord. A Viking is a son of the fjord, and he is proud of that title. You will be proud, too, when you have sons who are Vikings. They will have your beauty, but they will be strong like me."

Yes, I would give him the sons he wanted, and daughters, too. Rorik was a virile man, and I might already be carrying his child. Many times each night I felt the force of his love rush through me, and I wondered each time if I quickened with new life. If not yet, it would not be long. They would be Vikings, but even if it had to be in secret and with a threat to my life, they would be baptized. My sin must not be their sin, too.

One evening we watched the sun set over the western horizon.

"You know what's out there, Tara?"

"Ireland." The land of my forefathers, the roots from whence I had sprung. My paternal grandmother had traveled from her home in Ireland to a strange land with her husband. Now I must emulate her, learn to accept and become a part of the land that was as yet mysterious and unknown to me. My children would be the blending of two quite dissimilar heritages, and I prayed they would draw the best from both.

"And beyond?" He pointed to where the cloud whisps trailed in the sea.

"I don't know. The end of the world perhaps."

"There are more islands, some inhabited, some only explored, and others just waiting to be discovered. The sea goes on and on, Tara, and I want to know what is out there. I watch the horizon disappear as I sail toward it, and someday I am going to reach it and cross over to whatever is on the other side."

This was a side of my husband I had not seen before: the dreamer, the adventurer on a quest. Of a certain ruthless courage he had plenty, that I knew; but this wish of his to explore and dare the unknown was a revelation to me, and I was stirred with a new admiration for him. I was beginning to think I would not be sorry I had been forced into marriage with him.

"And if there is nothing there?" I asked, half-challenging, half-serious.

He threw back his head and laughed. "I shall turn around and come home. But I will have been there. That is what counts."

"Might it not be very dangerous? What if you cannot turn around?"

"Then I'll sail on and on. Will you come with me?"

I looked into his eyes, and I knew what he was really asking. Yes, I was his now and I would go with him wherever he was bound, but like him I was not yet ready to put into words my deepest and innermost feelings. Perhaps my response to his specific question would suffice to answer the unasked one. "Yes, but I hope we'll not drop off the edge."

"No fear of that. We follow the birds."

"The birds?"

"When a Viking explores unknown waters, he takes along a crate of ravens. Once out of sight of land, he releases a raven from time to time. If still close to home, the bird will fly back there, and the ship will sail on. If there is no land near in any direction, the raven will return to

67

the ship. More birds will be released until one flies away from the ship. A Viking will then follow it, knowing the bird has somehow sensed the presence of land not far off. That is how we have explored and found new lands where people said there were no lands."

"And if they never fly ahead? If they keep returning to the ship?"

"We keep going on." He looked out to sea as if he wished he were doing that now.

"I should be frightened. They might be warning you not to go on. There might be a drop-off or horrible monsters."

"No, my little Freya, there are other lands beyond, and I mean to find them someday. My *Raven of the Wind* will lead me there."

Now I knew why his ship had been named thus.

Another day, while I sat on the stern deck, Rorik asked, "Can you really read the runes?"

"Yes, I was taught by the abbess."

"Will you read them for me now?"

I reached in the deep pocket of my robe. "Here, you can see what they say for yourself."

"I cannot. I don't understand them."

"No?" I could not conceal my surprise. " 'Tis your language carved on them."

Rorik hesitated. "I know, but I cannot read at all. A Viking has no need for such knowledge. We have wise men and seers for that."

"Oh." I hastened to cover his embarrassment. "Well, 'tis right you are. Knowing the paths of the stars and the ways of the sea is more important. Shall I read them now?"

I held the flat stones in my hand and chanted as I had been taught. Rorik evidently recognized the chant, for he looked startled as I intoned the words, strange to me but known to him. Carefully I tossed them on deck and then looked intently at the pattern they formed as they fell. When I hesitated too long in speaking, Rorik said, "Well, and what do you see?"

It had been a long time since I'd read them and then only in the nature of a game, but I recognized the signs of danger immediately. Should I tell him, or would it be better to let him think they indicated nothing out of the ordinary? I did not believe in them, and yet something told me not to mock their powers. Then I realized it would do no harm for Rorik to be prepared in case the *Raven* was heading into dangerous waters. "Some trouble ahead for the ship. The stones will not tell me what it is, but be careful how you sail her."

"Anything else?" He looked worried, as I knew he would.

"No, 'tis all the stones will say for now." I gathered them up and slipped them once more into the deep pocket.

"Trouble," he muttered. "I wish I knew what kind to prepare for. The sea is calm and the sky too clear for a storm. There have been tales of other raiders off the north coast of Ireland. I should have kept all four of our ships together instead of sending two of them on that mission to our settlements there. I could change course and meet up with them sooner than planned. Might be safer." He looked toward the western horizon. "But 'twould delay arrival home. No, we'll go on. Probably not more than one ship raiding this time of year. Most are out of water by now. We should be, too."

I was sorry I told him what I saw in the runes. Yet, it was better to be prepared than fall victim to a surprise attack. I had had enough of those already.

Surrounded by the soothing atmosphere of the sea, and having subdued my feelings of guilt at being married to a heathen, I found the voyage pleasant except for one thing. When Rorik and I retired for the night behind the woolen shelter, I was disturbed by the close presence of the men, some sleeping on their benches, some gambling, and others on watch. No more than the thickness of the shelter separated us from the nearest of them.

"Please, Rorik," I begged, "wait until at least most of them are asleep and those on watch move to the stern."

"Hush, Tara, no need to fret. Our being together is natural. They're not thinking about us. You'll soon learn there is no shyness between Viking men and women."

"I like it not. It makes me uncomfortable."

"You must learn to get over it then. You call some of their comments obscene. To us they are jokes. The women, too, are very frank about certain matters you think should be kept private, so you had better be prepared for questions you might think it embarrassing to answer."

Now I had a new dread to torment me. What questions

would they ask? What kinds of remarks must I listen to? Who were these people that I was going to live among? I cringed at the answers that came immediately to mind. If they were as open and unreserved as Rorik implied, I could never be like them, nor did I think I wanted to be. I visualized hordes of barbaric men and women swarming around me and causing me to blush with every word they uttered.

"I cannot possibly prepare myself for that," I shuddered. "Will we have no privacy?"

"For our moment alone together, yes. But do not be surprised at a certain amount of curiosity about those moments. You have seen my statue of Frey."

Indeed I had. It was the first object I saw on awaking every morning. If this was a common household idol, then I supposed they had no hesitation about asking very personal questions.

"Then," Rorik continued, "you know there are no secrets about parts of the body and their functions. Size and prowess of both men and women are the subjects of many of our jokes, so learn to take it all in good humor."

Held close in his arms, I continued to shudder at what I feared would be a most hideous reception by the Viking community. Rorik had said little about his family, and I could not help but wonder how they felt about accepting a stranger into their midst. This was before I learned it was traditional for Vikings to capture and bring home the most beautiful women they found on their raids. These wives and their daughters were very proud and lorded it over the native-born women.

We awoke one morning not to the brilliant sunshine we had enjoyed so far, but to overcast skies and heavy seas. Rorik dressed quickly and raced to take the tiller. Breasting the waves, the ship pitched and tossed until it was almost impossible for me to remain on my feet. Giving up, I retreated to the pallet. The men were too busy to think about food, but one of them brought me flat oaten cakes, always kept stored in a dry place against such emergencies. With a few sips of mead, it proved to be a satisfying meal. I lay back, thinking to fall asleep, when suddenly I had to rush for the rail. Now I knew how I would fare in rough seas: very badly. I thought that if I rid myself of the meager breakfast, I would feel better. But I did not. Again and again I headed for the rail, hoping that once my stomach was empty, the retching would cease.

To add to my torment, the high waves were accompanied by gale winds blowing rain and sleet into our faces. During a brief reprieve in my illness, I watched the men furl the sail. The wind was blowing it about so wildly, I thought it would soon be ripped apart. I was amazed at what followed. Heavily battered by the wind, several men made their precipitous way up the mast to the topmost spar and released the ropes used to hold the sail secure. Carefully they took the sail down and laid it, rolled lengthwise, along the deck.

My wonderment increased when I saw several of the huskiest heave and strain until they lifted the great pine mast out of its base in the hull. With a single, swift, sure move they lowered it until it lay the length of the ship, each end fitting easily into notches made just for that purpose in the prow and stern. Over the mast, now utilized as a ridge pole, they laid the sail. Once securely fixed along each side, the red and white sail became a protective shelter for all of us.

While the storm continued with no signs of abatement, I found I fared best if I ate a few morsels and took sips of wine from time to time. I was no longer ill, but I preferred remaining in one place to moving around.

I had finally dozed off into a catnap when a sudden lurch jolted me, and I was drenched by a tremendous wave sweeping over the bow.

All during the storm, the men fought to keep the ship headed into the waves. With no sail and the wind blowing from all directions, this proved an almost impossible task. At times when the prow slid up the crest of a wave, the ship rode almost vertical. Coming down the other side, the tiller rose out of the water and for a brief, crucial moment, the ship was at the mercy of the elements. The one thing that must not happen was letting the ship swing sideways into a trough between waves. As strong and seaworthy as the *Raven* was, she would be in danger of capsizing within minutes.

In spite of their best efforts, Rorik and his most able men pulling together could not steady the ship when the tiller was more out of the water than in it. The *Raven* fell into a trough and was soon awash and foundering out of control.

While I lay terrified at the thought of drowning, the men baled and strained at the oars to right the ship. Frantically I reached for the cross which lay beside me. I touched the rune stones as well, and clutching all of them, I sat shivering and praying. Waves continued to wash over the bow, and soon I was not only soaked to the skin, but half submerged in a prow filled with water. Dear God! I thought. We'll all drown even before the ship sinks. When I tried to stand up, I was tossed like a sheaf of wheat in the wind from one side to the other, and I clutched at anything within reach. I touched a crossbeam, the timber on which Rorik had placed the little statue of Frey. Looking down, I saw the wooden idol, still grinning, bobbing around in the water. A lot of good you are now, I thought. If you were the god of the seas, you might save us.

During one violent roll, I hit my head against the side of the prow, and I felt myself falling slowly—very slowly —into the water. I remember thinking, if this be death, 'tis like being embraced by someone you love.

"Tara." The voice came faintly as if from a long distance, from somewhere in memory. "Tara, drink this." Rorik was holding my head up and forcing strong drink between my lips. " 'Tis all right. The storm's over, and we're nearing the Orkney Isles."

"We did not drown?" I was still alive, and I offered a silent prayer to all the saints.

"No, and the ship did not capsize. I told you the *Raven* would bring us through."

"Where are we?"

"Just off the Orkneys, and soon heading straight for home."

Home. Not my home, but Rorik's. Would it ever seem like mine? I was curious but no longer frightened about its strange customs. I was alive and that was all that mattered. Rorik was holding me close in his arms, and I felt his strength encircling me like a sheltering cape. As long as I was with him I would never be frightened again. True, I might never return to my own land, so I must needs learn to tolerate and adapt. I had done it when I entered the abbey. There I had learned self-control along with the ability to mask my true feelings. It would not be hard to fashion another mask more appropriate to a different situation: the wife of a Viking.

Chapter Five

ONCE THE STORM WAS OVER, we recovered quickly from its rough treatment. Once again I could stand by the rail or walk the length of the ship and sit by Rorik at the tiller.

We put in briefly at one of the Orkney Isles, just long enough to repair damages to the ship and replenish the food supply. While I remained on board, the men set up an encampment on shore. When it was ready, Rorik wrapped me in furs and carried me to land. I never thought steady ground beneath my feet could feel so good.

The weather was bitter cold, and I huddled inside the warmth of the furs. Without them I would have frozen, and I knew now why the Vikings headed for their home ports before the fall equinox. On shore, however, I soon warmed up. Within a circle of fires, the crew erected a large woolen shelter hung from four poles. The top of each pole was carved in the likeness of a different grotesque animal. "To ward off evil land spirits," Rorik said.

While I rested within the shelter, the men shot game, collected fresh water in wineskins, and foraged for vegetables. After this, they turned to the ship and repaired the ravages of the storm. Night brought out the stars, and I joined the men and some women from a nearby settlement around the fire. Whether they had come willingly or been abducted, the women soon quaffed enough flagons of mead to respond unashamedly to the Vikings' advances. Sensing my embarrassment, Rorik suggested we return to the shelter. I needed neither mead nor a flaming fire to find pleasure in his nearness. In spite of my earlier resolve, I knew that, heathen or not, he was the man I was destined to belong to.

We sailed at dawn. After days of choppy but not dangerous seas, we were watching the horizon for the first sign of Hordaland. The purple and gold of the dragon gleamed in the sun, and the *Raven* rode before the wind in proud majesty. The two ships sent to Ireland met up with us as we crossed the great Northern Sea between the Orkneys and Norvegia. With our dragon-headed prows facing the morning sun, we were an impressive armada of serpent ships.

After what we had been through, I gave less thought to how I looked than to the fact I could soon be off the ship for more than a brief sojourn. I had combed my hair, but oh, how I longed to wash it in rainwater and brush it until it shone once more. There was nothing I could do about my attire except wrap one of the furs, now lank and musty from being water-soaked, around me in an awkward attempt at a cape. It was a dreadful way to meet my new family.

Carrying a large bundle, Rorik came to stand beside me. As he held it, he grinned like an impatient child, and I knew he was testing me to see how long I could keep my curiosity in check.

"All right," I asked, "what is it?"

"A surprise for you. Want to see what it is?"

"You know I do." I loved surprises, and now I was the one who was impatient.

He removed the wrappings and unrolled a magnificent white fox cape. The skins had been meticulously sewn together to bring out the full beauty of each pelt. It was shaped to fit the shoulders, not just be wrapped around the body; and when Rorik draped it over me, it hung to my feet. Two intricately wrought brooches held it together at throat and breastline. In addition, it had a hood that fit loosely but securely over my head. I could scarcely articulate my admiration for the soft beauty of it. I had never seen such luxury.

"Oh, Rorik, 'tis truly magnificent. But where? I mean, how did it survive the storm undamaged?"

"This is my secret for now. You do like it?"

Let him have his secret. I cared not how or where— now I had something to give me the self-confidence and pride I needed when meeting his family. "Like it! For certain no woman ever had anything more beautiful. 'Tis so warm. I shall never be cold again."

"Well, you had to have something to cover that hideous robe. Sorry I've nothing at hand to replace it."

"There is nothing wrong with my robe," I said huffily.

"Soiled, yes, but an honorable badge of my vocation—my previous vocation."

" 'Tis filthy, and you know it."

He was right. My vanity screamed at the idea of not being able to tear the filthy robe off and replace it with something clean and untorn. But I was not going to give him the satisfaction.

"This cape should keep you covered," he said. "You're going ashore beside me as my wife, not a slavey who walks behind. More important, you will be appearing to the people as a future queen."

A queen! I was too stunned to speak. I knew from the beginning that Rorik was more than an ordinary chieftain, but I'd no idea he was of royal blood. I could not help but wonder if it would have made any difference when he first said I was to be his wife. I was glad I had not known then, because now my feelings for him were too strong to be affected by considerations of station. As a Viking queen, my future would certainly be far different from what I'd anticipated. Suddenly I wished Ian and Deirdre could know, and then I was ashamed that I should let them enter my thoughts. They were part of the past life I had to forget.

"Did you say a queen, Rorik?"

"I did, Seabird. My father is a jarl, a powerful leader. At the next Supra-Thing—the meeting of all chieftains and jarls—he may well be elected king. As his eldest heir, I have a position to uphold. So wear the hood until we land, then push it back. In the sun, your hair is more like silver than gold, and silver is a very precious metal here, rarer now than it used to be. They may see in you the Goddess Freya just as my men did."

The thought of appearing as the reincarnation of a goddess frightened me less than how I would be accepted as a woman, a foreigner introduced into their midst as wife to one I surmised was a favorite. In addition, he was eldest son of a man admired enough to be a potential king. I must be all that he expected of me.

To lessen my anxiety, I tried thinking about the important conclave he'd mentioned, and I hoped women were invited. It would be interesting to see if these older leaders were as rowdy as their sons, and I was curious to witness the election process he spoke of, having always believed that kings were born, not chosen.

When a lookout atop the mast espied land, a shiver of anticipation ran through me. Very soon now, I would meet the people with whom I seem destined to spend the rest of my life. Would they be friendly or hostile? Would I find my place among them, or would I remain a stranger?

To my surprise, we continued to sail past many obvious landing sites. Then I learned we had still a good many leagues to travel.

"What you are seeing now, Tara, are islands. There are hundreds of them along the coast which protect the inner shoreline from heavy storms and form an advance lookout for anyone trying to attack. Our trading ships and warships remain inland in sheltered harbors. In case of attack, word can be sent to us quickly to prepare our defense and ready the ships."

For some time, we sailed on through the straits between the islands. We had reached Hordaland in Norvegia, but how much longer before we sighted Rorik's home?

"Do these islands go on forever?" I asked.

"We've passed the islands. We're now in a fjord leading inland. 'Twill not be long now."

Someday I, too, would learn to distinguish between a strait and a fjord, but for now, I was glad the voyage was nearly over.

Rounding a headland in the high-walled fjord, we sailed up to a grassy, gently sloping plain that seemed to have been hacked out of the sheer, towering cliffs surrounding it and extended from the hills in the distance to the water's edge. Several of the seamen had already furled the sail, and now in a proud salute to those on shore, the rowers raised their oars in unison on a signal from the helmsman. They then lowered them again and rowed in steady cadence. On the stern deck, Rorik hefted a long, curled horn to his lips and blew three mighty blasts. A Viking high atop one of the cliffs responded with an equally reverberating clarion welcome.

As we approached the settlement I had time to observe it closely. It was much larger and less crude than I had anticipated, and hope rose in me that at home Vikings were more civilized than I had been led to believe.

Avidly I took in everything I saw and committed it to memory. This was to be my home, and it behooved me to become familiar with it. There were well over a hundred structures, more than in many of our villages in Britain, and they were of various sizes and styles. There appeared to be at least two roads leading down to the shore, and through an open space I sighted another cutting across them in the distance. The most amazing sight of all, however, was a high, earthen rampart encircling a good three-quarters of the town, beginning and ending at the shoreline. With the wooden barricade atop, it must have risen a good twenty to thirty feet above the ground. The town was well protected. I later saw two openings in this earthwork: one for the stream that provided water and one for a road leading into the countryside.

Rorik now came to stand beside me, and I was grateful for his comforting presence. I did not feel quite so alone or overawed at the strangeness of it all. He pointed to part of the waterfront that was a flat strip of sandy beach.

"Those smaller boats you see," he said, "can moor there all the time. The larger ships have been beached for the winter months. We're late in returning. That's why there are so many already hauled up, awaiting the spring tides."

We sailed up to a long, quarter-circle arc constructed of sturdy tree trunks and planks that jutted out from shore, and to this mole or breakwater, the men tied up the ships. Once the strong ropes had been secured around the bollards, Rorik helped me to alight. The crew had gone running and leaping the length of the mole into the waiting arms of women on shore, and I could feel the tension in Rorik's arm as it circled my waist. Was he as anxious as I to see how I would be accepted? We walked toward the elderly man who came halfway along the narrow breakwater to meet us. This was his father, the one I knew it was most important to please. I tried desperately to control my shaking as he approached.

Thorne was a powerfully built, ruddy-complexioned man whose upright stance and strong features belied the quarter century difference in age between him and his son. Beneath his long cape, identical to Rorik's, chest muscles strained against his short leather coat. His heavy mane of hair, more red than blond, was lightly thatched with gray as were his long mustaches and full beard. Everything about him bespoke pride and overbearing assurance in his position as chieftain and jarl.

I awaited a formal greeting, but to my surprise and

relief, Thorne wrapped his arms around me and almost smothered me with his bear hug.

"You son of Thor!" he shouted. "Whose ship did you scuttle to capture this beauty? By Gunger, the spear of Odin, if she were not wife to my eldest son, I'd bed her myself."

It was well I'd been warned by Rorik what to expect, or I might have embarrassed everyone by blushing, but in truth his words were more loving than obscene.

"Tara is from Britain, sire, and I scuttled no ship for her. We did raid an abbey, though."

"An abbey, you say!" His eyes lit up. "And you captured more than this pleasing wench, I trust. Though no doubt you've found she delights as much as gold or silver. If she gives you strong sons and daughters, she'll prove as valuable, too. Has her belly quickened yet with your seed?" If a man would speak thus in front of me, what could I expect from the women?

"Come, Tara." Thorne threw a burly arm around my shoulders. "We've had feasts prepared for days, and the women are getting impatient. What kept you at sea so long, lad?"

"A storm, sire. Very bad one, too."

"Well, you're here now, you and the *Raven* both brought safely home by the gods. As you instructed, the thralls have prepared sleeping quarters for you and Tara."

Sleeping quarters? Instructions? Like the fur cape, these words titillated my curiosity, but Rorik only answered with a tantalizing smile when I questioned him. Well, let him keep his secrets. I might have one to nurture, too.

From the near end of the breakwater, Rorik led me toward and then lifted me into a high wheeled cart. Its shallow body rested on two curved supports constructed from sturdy limbs. The ends of each, like the poles supporting the shelters put up on shore, were tipped with carved animal heads. The cart itself was ornately carved all over in a serpentine design. The seats were more comfortable than they looked, and I watched with delight as Rorik waved to the people who came to the wharf and lined the streets to welcome him home. I had surmised rightly; he was much beloved by the people in the village.

As we were pulled slowly along by a single horse, I looked at the buildings we passed and the people who stood in front of them. An initial sinking feeling was fol-

lowed by a cold sweat and nauseating stomach pains. I
wanted to like the place and the people, but there was
little about the town that appealed. The buildings all
looked like hovels no better than what our serfs lived in.
There was nothing that looked like the home of a chieftain. Was I to spend the rest of my life in one of these
small, cheerless cottages, some rudely constructed of rough
logs, others of finished boards with wattle-and-daub siding?
To my relief, I finally saw, here and there, a sturdy edifice
of stone or clay, ranging from twelve feet square to eighteen by twenty feet in size. All were roofed with turf. Few
of the buildings had windows, and then only narrow,
shuttered slits. All the doors were too low for a man to
walk through upright. Not all the structures were houses.
As Rorik pointed out, some were craft shops, storehouses,
and forges. In open spaces between them, sheep grazed.
Strange that sheep should make me feel homesick.

While Rorik waved and spoke to the people, I felt no
qualms about staring at the men and women who were
also scrutinizing me and making no pretense of hiding
their curiosity. My heart tightened with a sharp pain. It
was all so unfamiliar, so strangely different from what I
was used to.

During the voyage, Rorik and the crew had spoken to me
in a dialect similar to our language. With all their travels
around Britain, they could communicate easily with me.
The same was true of Thorne. I had forgotten this would
not be the case with those who stayed at home. The guttural voices coming at me from all sides sounded like a
barnyard gone wild, and I caught myself wanting to
laugh for the first time since we landed. I managed to
stop at a smile, and this seemed to please them. They
waved and smiled back, helping me to feel better. Maybe
everything would be all right. These were people, real
people, not ogres or trolls. I tried a tentative wave, and a
young woman raised up the red-cheeked baby she was
holding so that I could see it better. They were ready to
accept me. I must have the same attitude toward them.

Rorik's home was not in the town, but on a farm some
distance away. Our horse trotted along the well laid
pebble road that ran from the shore to the earthwork. We
passed through this last by way of a narrow tunnel supported with timbers. Beyond this was a deep moat crossed

by a wooden bridge. More and more I saw that things were not so far different from home.

Now that there were no people to greet, I asked Rorik about the cape and the villagers' advance knowledge of my arrival.

"So your curiosity has you bursting, has it? You want to know my secret?"

"Yes, I do."

"I would have waited if my father hadn't spoiled my surprise. I sent one of the speedier ships on ahead and ordered ours to slow down. It met us again another night. And you, my little seabird, were not observant enough to notice. 'Tis glad I am you didn't see it, but as a Viking wife, you need to use your eyes more. It could have been an enemy raider sneaking up on us." His tone was humorous, but under it I sensed a more serious note.

"But the way they came and went all the time, how was I to know?" He had put me on the defensive, and I was half-apologetic and half-chagrined.

"From now on, you will." He said it kindly but still seriously. "It could save our lives."

"I promise," I said, in the same serious tone. As a Viking wife, I had much to learn.

The house to which Rorik led me was much larger than those in the town. Although dissimilar in design to the manor houses I was familiar with in Britain, it was obviously the home of an important and wealthy man. Rorik had used the term *jarl* several times, which I now assumed was comparable to earl or duke. Cruder than I hoped, the house was at least of a size to hold a family comfortably. Even though I was still apprehensive about ever feeling really at home here, the tension was beginning to ease somewhat.

Of an irregular rectangular shape, the house was some seventy feet wide by forty feet deep. Here and there small additions jutted out, and I wondered if these were storerooms or the separate sleeping quarters Thorne said were being prepared for us. That alone had relaxed me considerably and done much to ready me for what the next few hours would bring. A stone foundation supported wooden walls and turf-covered roof. There was a narrow doorway in the center of the front wall but no windows. I shuddered at the thought of its being like a cave or dungeon inside. Even the towers at home had windows, and those in many of the manors were glazed.

We stepped into the great hall, or *skaalen,* which extended the full width and length of the main building. I looked around the long room, and wanted to cry at its crudeness. I did not see how I could ever get used to living in it. I looked down at my feet. At least the rushes on the earthern floor were fresh and aromatic, but they could not mask the strong odors of boiled cabbage and stewed meat. At home and in the abbey, the cooking was done in a separate room or building, and we were not constantly surrounded by its smells. If I could have, I would have turned around and run out; but with Rorik's guiding hand on my arm, I knew I was now a part of his family and I needs must make the best of it. Not only outwardly, but within as well. Only I would suffer if I did not. To that end, I opened my eyes and really looked at my new home.

Mid-center of the rush-covered floor was a deep pit, lined and rimmed with stones, in which burned a fire to heat the long room and around which a number of women busied themselves with cooking. I soon learned that one thrall or slave had the single duty of keeping the fire going. Day and night he sat squat-legged or lay curled up beside it, leaving only to bring in more fuel.

Around two sides of the hall was a wide, raised ledge, divided by upright planks into compartments and covered with piles of furs. With a shock, it dawned on me that these were for sleeping. But for the family or the servants? I saw no curtains that could be drawn to permit privacy. I hoped when Thorne referred to sleeping quarters, he meant a room in another section of the house.

In spite of the first crude impression, I soon saw the room was richly furnished. A third wall was partially covered by a red and yellow tapestry depicting Viking warriors in various battle poses. There was one long table, several smaller ones, benches, and comfortable-looking chairs. To my surprise, the table was covered with a fine cloth and set with silver spoons, earthenware plates, and both silver and earthenware bowls. The house presented a strange contrast of roughness and gentility, an amalgam of barbarism and luxurious wealth.

Immediately we entered, we were surrounded by several women carrying bowls of warm water and towels heated over the fire. If there was warm water to greet guests and returning travelers, then there must be provisions for bathing, and once more hope rose in me that these people lived better than peasants.

After the women boisterously welcomed Rorik and more shyly smiled at me, they returned to the business of preparing food. Amid the confusion of coming home, Rorik tried to identify all of them for me, but I was lost in the welter of names. In speaking of them, he seemed to make no distinction between family, serfs, and thralls, and they were all equally busy getting a meal on the table.

Once inside for a few minutes, I realized why the single fire was sufficient even for so large a room. The thick walls kept all the heat in. A stifling, airless heat that clogged my mouth and lungs. I was a child again, smothering, gasping for breath under a goose-down quilt. The heavy, turgid smoke hung low in the room. The soot-darkened walls seemed to close in on me and raucous voices pelted my ears. Then all at once everything receded, and I stood alone by the fire, a stranger in the midst of convivial bustle. I heard Rorik laugh. He stood at one end of the room with his father and brothers, Ruskil and Adair. Adair was tall and blond, more slender than Rorik but with the strength of long, taut muscles. He had an ingenuously boyish countenance. Unlike his brothers, Ruskil had dark hair. He was strong and square like Thorne, and his thick, heavy muscles bulged like knotted ropes. He had a face that laughed but never smiled.

At the other end of the room, beyond the fire, a woman shouted an order to a slave. Through the smoky haze the tall, blond women looked like duplicate images of one another, and they moved in a ritualistic dance between the cooking pots and the table. From time to time they cast covert glances at me. With the heat, the tension, and weariness, I was sweating profusely beneath my cape. As soon as I removed it, the women stared openly at me. First one, then others came over and began fingering my soiled and tattered robe. I wanted to run, but I dared not insult them. I stood still, waiting. One more courageous than the others tugged at it, ripping a weakened seam apart.

"Oh, no!" I tried to pull it back together again.

Instead of stopping, they laughed at my feeble attempts to keep it from tearing further. Now they were all pointing and jeering at me. I had never imagined this kind of welcome, and it took all my self-control to keep from crying.

They were hateful! Never had I felt so alone and vulnerable. One of them patted my belly and looked at me inquisitively. I couldn't understand her words, but her meaning was clear enough. When she pointed to Rorik and then back to me, chattering all the while, the others laughed and nodded their heads. My face grew redder and hotter. If their gestures embarrassed me, it was probably well I did not understand their words.

I looked at Rorik and his brothers, toasting each other with large mead horns, sparring with words and gestures in mock familial battle. I was loath to disturb him, but the way the women were tugging at my robe, I feared they would soon have me stripped naked. Under their intense stares, I already felt naked, as if everything about me—my thoughts, my fears, my loneliness—were revealed in stark clarity.

Then through the undertone, I heard my name mentioned, and the men looked my way. Seeing the predicament I was in, Rorik came immediately to my side and shooed the women away.

"I am sorry, Tara. It was thoughtless of me not to get you a gown. We'll see about it right after we eat."

" 'Tis all right now. If only I could talk to them."

"You'll learn soon enough. 'Tis not that much different, and you will pick up new words every day. Just do not be frightened. No one here means you any harm. 'Tis just our way."

And a way I liked not. No, never would I feel a part of this family. They were crude, vulgar heathens.

The meal was the feast Thorne had said it would be. At least I could enjoy that. Twelve of us sat down to *nadver*, the evening meal: the four men in the family, a visiting chieftain who arrived just as the meal was served, and six women besides myself. Slowly I was beginning to distinguish between family and servants, but I had to learn the place each woman held in the family. Were they wives or daughters? And of whom? Time and Rorik would sort them out for me. Before we finished, five small children and a baby were brought in and fed at a separate table.

Servants passed platters heaped with fish prepared in various ways, chunks of boiled meat, tiny game birds, and sections of boiled cabbage. On separate plates were cheeses, butter, fruits, and long loaves of dark rye bread.

Beside each place was a goblet kept filled with wine. At least the meal was edible and not too different from what we had at home. In fact, it was really good, and I was amazed at how hungry I was.

"Rorik," his father said, putting aside the bones of a small bird he had finished stripping, "your grandmother is ill. I hope you will go to the cottage after we eat. 'Twill do her good to see you again. She has been awaiting your return."

Out of consideration for me, sitting between them, they spoke in words I could understand.

"I will, sire. I want her to meet Tara. Is her strength waning?"

"It is, son. We have begun work on her ship."

His words puzzled me, but his voice told me she was dying. I wanted to meet her. Rorik's mother had died some years earlier, but by one of life's ironic twists, his grandmother had lived to be eighty-two and was the most beloved member of the family.

Aside from that, the dinner was a gay one, with much laughter at jokes which Rorik tried to explain to me. Most of them centered around us. Some, concerning my husband's prowess, my fertility, and the size of my belly, had me blushing. Rorik squeezed my arm.

"Laugh with them, Seabird; they do not mean to hurt you. If they didn't like you, they would be deathly silent."

It helped some to think they were accepting me. So after he explained each joke, I laughed and felt more at ease among them. Soon they were teasing each other, and in turn, I laughed at them. When they began singing, Rorik and I slipped away.

"My grandmother has always been very strong," he said. "You think my father is, but it was she who held our family together when my mother died. There is nothing on the farm she cannot—or could not—do, though we've always had thralls for the hard and menial tasks. 'Tis sad to think of her lying helpless. I do not believe I ever saw her lying down."

We left the house and walked through a courtyard, scattering several chickens and a belligerent goose, to a small cottage. With no windows, the wattle-and-daub hut was dark inside. A small hearth glowed near one wall. Along another was a low, narrow ledge on which the old woman lay. Seeing her lying thus in such miserable and uncomfortable conditions, I was assailed at the idea that she had been cast out by her family and put in this dreadful place because she was dying. I felt a great sadness and pity— pity for her and for those who would do this to her. Had she been removed from the house because the dying were cursed or would place a curse on the house? I was completely ignorant of their religion and superstitions, and I knew I had much to learn.

Rorik knelt beside her and spoke to her in the language I did not yet understand. Her voice was low but still strong for a woman as feeble as she. Rorik took her hand and then motioned for me to come closer. He put my hand in hers and bent low to hear what she was saying.

"She says you are very beautiful. She welcomes you to the family. She is tired now but wants to see you again tomorrow."

"Tell her I thank her, and I am pleased to be here."

Rorik kissed her on both cheeks, and I did the same. Her wrinkled skin was hot and dry, like old parchment withered by the sun. Her thick hair was neatly braided so as to form a beautiful silvery crown around her head. Her clear eyes still sparkled, and the smile she gave me was filled with love. I knew I could have loved her in return, and I felt a strange emptiness at the thought that I would not have the opportunity to get to know her.

"Thank you, Tara." Rorik took my hand, and we walked back to the great hall.

"She is beautiful," I said sadly.

"We will feel the loss of her greatly," he answered.

I wanted to ask why she was in the small hut, separated from her family, but something—fear of what I might hear or of seeming out of place—held me back.

The men were still sitting around the table drinking and talking. Some of the women were preparing the children for bed, settling them in the compartments along the wall of the *skaalen* and putting up curtains they brought out from open chests nearby. The sight of the curtains offered some comfort, but I still hoped Rorik and I would have a separate room.

Before we reached the table, Rorik asked, "You're tired, aren't you, Tara?"

"Yes, a little. 'Tis been a long day with so much that is new." I was grateful for his concern.

"Let me tell my father goodnight, and we'll go to our room."

So there was a separate room. Once again I found myself relaxing a little.

Four of the rooms which jutted out at odd angles from the main building at the end were not large, but they had doors with bolts. In ours there was a bed, a real bed with pillows, eiderdown coverlets, and a fur spread. There were also two large chests, heavily carved and ornamented with inlaid silver. On one wall were pegs for hanging clothes. I knew then this would be more than separate sleeping quarters; it would be a room to retire to, where I could be alone amidst the large household. I had always felt a need to get away, to be by myself at times, and being able to do this here would make endurable things that otherwise I could not have borne.

"Will this always be our room, Rorik?" I asked apprehensively.

"I don't know about always, but for some time at least."

"What do you mean 'for some time'?" I had hoped I would never have to relinquish it to someone else.

"Until you have our first child. That is the tradition."

"And then?"

"If you don't like the idea of moving to the compartments, I think there are enough rooms for us to have one. And," he smiled, "the bed will be more comfortable." I sensed he had recognized my need for time to become accustomed to his way of doing things.

"Thank you, Rorik."

"Now," he whispered, "shall we see if the bed is as comfortable as it looks? And keep the tradition going?"

If anyone had asked me how I could have gone from hating Rorik to finding pleasure and security in his arms, I could not have answered. It was not love, not as I had loved Ian, but it was a sense of belonging to someone who gave me his strength and to whom I could respond with the passion I had long tried to deny. Far better that than a cold, passionless marriage with a man who might have been my father's choice, not mine.

Chapter Six

WHEN I AWOKE IN THE MORNING, Rorik had already left the bed. There was a small window in one of the walls which I had not noticed the night before and the inside shutters had been opened to let in the daylight. Thinking it would also let in cold air, I huddled under the eiderdown; but I was sheltered from the wind by an oblique wall angling out from the house. Brilliant sunlight bathed the room, infusing it with a feeling of cheery warmth.

I thought I was alone until I saw a young woman standing just inside the door. She was smiling shyly at me. Tall and buxom, she wore her straw-colored hair in two neat braids wrapped close to her ears on each side of her head. A long, full, unadorned garment of rough material hung loosely from her shoulders.

"Good morning, my lady. My name is Astrid. I am to be your maidservant." She spoke hesitantly, as if she had memorized the words.

"Good morning, Astrid."

She moved to one of the huge chests, and after opening the heavy lid, took out a number of garments. First she handed me a chemise of fine, very lightweight wool. It had a narrow yoke on which the body was gathered in narrow pleats. Modestly I slipped this on while still lying under the covers. Only then did I feel unembarrassed about standing in front of her.

Next I donned a long dress made from two pieces of heavier wool, which were fastened together with ornamental buckles on each breast. Over this Astrid draped a long, sleeveless cape, also of fine wool and decorated with silken braid trim. For my feet there were leather slippers. Although simple in design, everything was beautifully made. I admired the fine workmanship and exquisite stitching. These were not the crude garments I had envisioned wearing. Now I was dressed like the other women in the household—rather than in a tattered gown—I felt ready to join them again. Pride and self-respect would go a long way in conquering what fears I still had.

Astrid produced a brush and worked with my hair until it was once more smooth and shining. Then she twisted it into a thick knot over which she fastened, with bone hairpins, a gold mesh net.

"Thank you, Astrid." I hoped she understood what I was saying.

"I am happy to be your personal slave. I speak your language, but slowly. Please to be patient."

"Oh, Astrid, I will. I am glad you understand me." She was the first person other than Rorik and Thorne I felt close to. "But why are you a slave?"

"I was taken in a raid. My home in far north, on other side of mountains. I am strong, my lady, and I will serve you well."

"Thank you, Astrid. I am sure you will." Someday maybe I would understand the ways of the Vikings. Of one thing I was certain: she would know only kindness from me.

"Yes, very strong. My father had five daughters to live. No sons. I milk and plow and reap. But I want to serve you."

"And be my friend, too. I need a friend. A woman to talk to. You understand?" I hoped I had not confided too much too soon, that she would not think me weak. I thought not, since she too was a stranger.

"Yes, my lady. I will always do what you say. I be near when you need me. It is now time for you to go to *davre*."

"*Davre?*"

"The morning meal. Your husband is waiting for you."

It took a few days, but I soon accustomed myself to the traditional two meals a day in a Viking household. There were always fresh fruits in the summer and dried fruits during the other months to nibble on between meals. Among the dried fruits were two I had never seen before, dates and figs. Their taste was strange but delicious. Rorik told me they were among the many items brought back by traders from Constantinople in exchange for furs, seal ivory, and timber.

"Good morning, Tara," Rorik greeted me. "You look quite lovely this morning."

"Thank you. Astrid is a most capable servant, and I do feel much better gowned like the others."

"And the clothes fit. I'm pleased."

Before we finished eating, Thorne came in and spoke to his son in low whispers; then Rorik turned to me.

"My grandmother has not many more hours to live. She waited to die until I came home. Her sons and grandsons are finishing up her boat as speedily as possible. She asks to see you one more time."

I was again puzzled. This was the second reference to "her boat." I was equally disturbed at the idea she could determine when she would die.

Once more I followed Rorik along the short path to her hut, and we stood beside the ledge on which the elderly Signe lay. Weakly she lifted one arm, and Rorik indicated she wanted me to hold her hands. Her voice was much fainter than it had been the evening before, but her eyes looked steadily into mine.

"She says," Rorik translated, "to guard the runes carefully. To remember them when the raven flies through fire and ice. They are a precious gift you have brought to our family, a gift from the gods. She thinks you have come from the gods, too. She called you a Frost Maiden. A great honor because Odin's mother and wife were Frost Maidens."

"Tell her I will guard them with my life and will always use them wisely." I trusted I would know the meanings of "raven," "fire," and "ice" when the time came.

Signe closed her eyes and we left.

"She had no words for you, Rorik?"

"Yes, and I'll tell you someday. This is not the appropriate time." Was it always to be a land of secrets? Confused, I shook my head.

"I do not understand your saying she waited to die until you came home. Did she will her own death?" It was an eerie, unnatural thought that had me frightened.

"Not exactly. She knew the time had come for her to leave us. I told you she was a strong woman, also remarkable in many other ways. She had the gift of prophecy, thought to be given her by the gods. That is why your coming meant so much to her. She thinks you will carry on the tradition in the family."

"Oh, I do not know. Such things frighten me."

"Only when you feel the calling to read the stones, Tara. You will know."

I put those thoughts aside for the moment. "If she knew she was dying, why didn't the family insist on moving her into the main house where she could be properly cared for?"

"I didn't tell you last night because I thought it would disturb you. But she was moved out there when she became ill. It is called the House of Night, and all who know they are dying wish to slip away from there. She receives as much care from her personal slaves as she would in the main house, and also more peace and quiet."

I thought of the infirmary at the abbey. The House of Night was not really that different. At least Signe's death would be easier than those of Sisters Ilsa, Sarah, and Berthe. But I must force myself not to dwell on that, I must not think of them except in pleasant memory.

"Rorik, what is Signe's 'boat' you keep speaking of?"

"You will see tomorrow. Now, will you help the women prepare the burial feast while I work with my father and brothers?"

I was glad he'd suggested it. Not only did I have something to keep me busy, but I began to feel more a part of the family, and I slowly became acquainted with them and their traditions.

Rorik had introduced me to all the women of the household, but their names were a confused blur of strange sounds. And I still had not learned their places in the family. By the time we returned to the main house, many wives and daughters of other nearby chieftains and important men in the town had joined them, and I simply gave up on trying to figure out who was who.

The rest of the day was a hectic flurry of preparations. On one large spit erected over the central fire were two cauldrons in which chunks of mutton were stewing. In another small room I had not noticed before, called the fire room, more cauldrons filled with fowl and vegetables were bubbling. The Vikings preferred meat boiled rather than roasted, and from time to time some of the broth was ladled into the pots of vegetables. In the ashes, on the edge of the fires, loaves of bread had been set to bake.

Shyly, one of the younger women walked up to me, took my hand, and put it on her chest. "Thyri," she said.

90

I smiled back, put her hand on my chest, and said, "Tara."

She led me to two large casks and indicated I was to ladle great chunks of honeycomb into smaller bowls to be placed on the table. It would be used as a spread for the bread, I knew, but I was surprised to see Thyri dip dried figs and dates into it and then place them in dishes as one would sweetmeats. She smiled and offered me one. It was indeed a delicacy. Fermented honey was used to make mead, and we valued it as a sweetener, but I never thought of coating dried fruit with it. I smiled back a thank-you.

When I finished that, I helped with the other foods. There was no formal sitting down to *hadver;* everyone ate when they were hungry. Word came in the middle of the day that Signe was gone. The men were away from the house, so I didn't know how they reacted to the news. The women stopped their work and, crouching around the fire, began wailing in sounds much like Celtic keening, which they kept up the rest of the evening. I sat to one side, feeling very much the outsider during this moment of bereavement. If only Rorik would come back. Finally he did, but only to leave again immediately.

"I'll see you in the morning, Tara. Sleep well."

"You're not coming to bed?"

"The men will stay up all night to watch. 'Tis our last duty to Signe."

Because Thorne was a wealthy and important man in Hordaland, all who could travel the distance in one day came for the burial of his wife's mother. In addition to tables laden with food, there was wine as well as mead to drink.

Late the following afternoon, we followed the cart containing Signe's body to the family burial ground. She had been bathed and attired in her most exquisite finery by her favorite slave. Her gown of silk from a Far East empire was fastened at her breast with gold buckles. Over it was a many-colored brocade cape trimmed with bands of fur. In her hair, around her neck, and on her arms had been placed her finest jewelry of gold, silver, and pearls. Even in death she was accorded treatment worthy of a dowager queen. I was continually amazed at the violent contrasts between great wealth and barbaric customs in this strange land.

A second, less ornately carved cart followed hers. In this lay the body of her favorite slave. Because Signe was not to be cremated, the slave had mercifully been killed. In some cases, favorite slaves were buried alive when the dead were interred, or burned alive during the master's or mistress's cremation. Although it was an accepted custom, and the slave was ready to go with the deceased protector, I couldn't bear to look at the cart containing the body of the young woman whose faithfulness was rewarded with death. I trembled uncontrollably as I walked behind. One minute I was drawn to Rorik's people by their friendliness; the next, I was revolted by their heathen ways. Would I ever understand or really feel I belonged?

Everyone in the funeral procession was dressed for a celebration rather than in my idea of traditional mourning. The women had donned their finest silks, brocades, woolens, and furs; and they wore most of their jewelry: delicate filigree brooches, braided armbands, torques, pendants, hair ornaments, and breast chains. All were of gold or silver, many inlaid with enamel or set with pearls.

The men were equally festive in long-sleeved, thick woolen coats; long, tight-fitting trousers; and their ankle-length, twin-pointed, heavily embroidered capes. Each wore the traditional arm bracelets of wool covered with silk and embroidered with gold thread, and the *hlad,* long silk ribbons with gold embroidery fastened around the forehead.

We walked in stately procession, the women following the men, until we reached the burial ground. Then I saw it. Signe's boat. Although as beautiful in design as the *Raven,* it was not nearly so large; but it had obviously served its time at sea. There was evidence of its having been refurbished with the fresh paint and repairs that had kept the men busy the last few days. A shallow trench had been dug slightly longer and wider than the boat, and into this the vessel was being placed, balanced with rough wooden beams.

Rorik, his father, and his brothers lifted Signe from the cart and placed her on a narrow bed within an open pavilion erected in the center of the ship. A number of thralls laid the slave on a pallet beside her. I stood to one side, making myself as unobtrusive as possible. I really wanted no part of this pagan ritual that both sickened and horrified me. I was saddened at the thought of not having gotten to know Signe well, but otherwise I tried to remain as unemotional as possible. If I gave in to my true feelings, I could not have stayed for the entire ceremony.

Female friends and women of the family carried a variety of housekeeping items and personal belongings aboard the boat: Signe's cloth loom, her smaller ribbon loom, earthen tableware, iron kettles, dishes of foodstuffs, several gowns and capes, shoes, and more of her jewelry. I found it impossible to understand their belief that she would need all of these things in the afterlife, but when I had tried to explain the concept of the soul to Rorik, he only laughed and said no Viking would accept an idea that denied having a physical body after death. The men had already filled the ship with much of her furniture in addition to the bed—with four magnificently carved posts— on which they laid her. There were chests, mirrors, chairs, and barrels filled with more food. At the last, the women of the family put pillows under her head and covered her with fine eiderdown quilts.

When all this was finished, one man stepped forward, a neighboring chieftain who was acting as priest. Walking slowly around the ship, he intoned a repetitive chant and sprinkled dried herbs and small plants from a basket he carried. Following him were four men who carried bronze statuettes of Odin with his spear, Thor with his hammer, Frey, and Freya. Because she was a woman, Signe would not go to Valhalla, last resting place of warriors who fell in battle. The chant sung by the chieftain-priest was not to either Odin or Thor, the major gods, but invoked Freya to take Signe to her side and prevent her from being captured by Hel, the fearful goddess of the Netherworld, and carried to Nifleheim, the dark region of the earth. The prow of Signe's ship faced the fjord so she would be able to sail when called.

Once the long ceremony was concluded, the women returned to the house to set out food and drink for all the guests. The men stayed behind to begin mounding earth over the ship after spreading it with branches from evergreen trees. Members of the family would begin the mounding, but most of the laborious work was concluded by thralls.

By nightfall I was exhausted. The walk to the grave, although not far from the house, the standing throughout

93

the ceremony, and the long feast following had been tiring. More than that, I was emotionally drained from the realization I had taken active part in a pagan ceremony. As Rorik's wife I had been one of those entrusted with carrying aboard and covering Signe with the eiderdowns. When I looked into her face, I remembered her admonition to guard the runes and carry on in her position as seer. Involuntarily I shuddered at the thought I might someday be lying in a similar ship, being chanted on my way to a pagan afterlife. Had my actions completely robbed me of any right to call myself a Christian? By such actions, if not belief, had I recanted the vows taken for me at baptism and my later vows as a nun?

While most of the company continued throughout the night with the feasting and drinking, I retired to my room. When I finally dropped off to sleep, it was to fight my way through nightmares in which I was being buried alive while the statue of Frey danced around the grave and cackled incantations with a hideous laugh. I awoke in a cold sweat, shaking and sobbing. I fought my way out from under the covers as if wrestling with a demon determined to capture my soul, and in the dark made my way to the window. The fresh air revived me somewhat, but if I could have I would have fled the place even though it was the dead of night. I wanted nothing more to do with Viking rituals.

Too soon, however, I found myself involved in a second pagan rite—a formal marriage ceremony.

On the morning of the second day after the burial, while the numerous guests who had come for that event were still in a festive spirit, Astrid came to my room to array me in my wedding finery. Rorik had not come to my bed since the death of his grandmother, so I could not spill out my fears to him, nor would he, I realized, have understood them. I dreaded taking part in the ceremony, yet there was no way I could stop it. I seemed to be propelled by a force over which I had no control. I felt like one in a trance who was simply allowing anything and everything to take place.

First Astrid led me to the small fire room where she had brought a large brass tub and filled it with hot water. She helped me to bathe and to wash my long hair. Once it was dry, with the help of the fire and rough towels, we returned to my room.

This time my chemise was of soft, pleated silk. The two-piece gown she handed me was also of silk, embroidered with gold thread and beads. The intricately entwined breast buckles were of gold, and hanging from them were gold chains holding scissors, a knife, and keys. I would now be an accepted member of Rorik's family and a woman of the household. The long, sleeveless cape, traditionally worn back over the shoulders, was of gold brocade, also re-embroidered with beads and colored threads. While she garbed me thus, I made no move to help her, but let her do it all, as if I were a doll being dressed to go on display. From time to time, she voiced little reassuring sounds, but I dared not reply for fear of breaking into tears.

Instead of gathering my hair into a large knot encased in a mesh chignon, Astrid brushed and fashioned it into long braids. Into these she entwined gold chains and pearls, and the braids were wrapped like a crown atop my head. And like a queen, standing tall and proud, I would go to my wedding. I would not shame Rorik, and no one would know my inner feelings of despair. I could have lived with him after the brief ritual on the ship, but I did not like being forced to take part in these heathen rites.

All of the garments and jewels had come from the family treasure store, but when Rorik greeted me in the *skaalen*, he fastened a necklace of pearls around my throat, his own personal gift to me. In his eyes I saw a new tenderness, and I forced back my earlier revulsion.

Once again we walked away from the house in solemn procession. Rorik and I, carrying sheaves of rye, followed his father across a harvested field to a grove of trees. Those who walked with us held branches of evergreen. Within the grove was a tremendous evergreen with widespreading branches. From almost every one of them hung a golden chain. Nearby, a sparkling fresh-water spring cascaded over several layers of flat rock into a shallow pool. On either side of the pool stood two oblong stones, approximately shoulder high, heavily carved with runic inscriptions. Scattered among the trees, cairns held statues of numerous gods, many more than the four carried at

Signe's burial. A hush came over the company as we entered the sacred grove.

Rorik and I stood before his father as chieftain-priest. After we washed our hands in the sacred spring, we exchanged bracelets as we had on the ship. We then drank from a single goblet of wine. During all this, Thorne intoned a melodic chant. With both of us holding the goblet, Rorik and I walked to the statue of Frey and poured a libation on the ground at the foot of the cairn. The goblet was refilled, and this we poured over the statue until it was dyed a dark, bloody red. I winced each time I looked at the hideous, grinning god, now looking more like a symbol of death than a creator of life. It was my blood I was pouring over him, drop after drop draining away my life. Only Rorik's strong arm kept me from fainting.

To the wine on the ground was added the blood of sacrificial lambs and goats, and all the grove seemed drenched with the ghoulish red of wine, blood, and raw flesh. Sickened at the sight of it all—the slashed throats, the dripping meat hanging from branches of the trees—I buried my face in the sheaf of rye I still carried. The supple stalks with their heavy clusters of seed were symbols of life and fertility; and in the midst of all the death and sacrifice I needed to hold onto something alive. Portions of the meat not left for the gods were taken back to the house and cooked for the feast that night. I knew I would eat none of it.

In the long hall, Rorik and I sat in two large chairs to receive the congratulations and best wishes of the family and friends. The large gathering overflowed the house out into the yard. The women sang as they cooked. The men gambled, laying bets as to who could hurl a spear, an axe, a knife the farthest. Musicians filled the air with shrieking, head-throbbing rhythms, and many couples began a wild, exuberant dance around the fire. My hands clutched the arms of my chair, my fingers rubbing and rubbing the carved wood. Then I was clawing it with my nails, and I felt them break one by one. My head ached from the frenzy around me and my chest hurt from trying to subdue the emotions that threatened to explode and burst free.

"Enjoying your wedding, Tara?" Rorik leaned over and took my hand.

"I—I think so." How could I tell him about the tears I had silently wept, the shudder that went through me as

I poured the wine over Frey, the revulsion engulfing me now. I was truly his wife now. I wore the golden chains of a Viking housewife, and ironically I was chained to a way of life I once loathed.

" 'Tis all very strange to you now, Tara, but soon you'll feel a part of us. I'll be right here with you until spring when I go Viking again. By then, all this will be familiar to you."

I was already learning more of their dialect; and when I could chat with the women, I knew I would feel less ill at ease. As for their religious beliefs and customs, I would take part; but within myself, I would never foreswear my Christian beliefs and I would find time to be alone for my private prayers.

With an infectious laugh, Rorik took me in his arms and we joined the dancing, which for a woman, meant taking a few steps and then being flung around high in the air. Soon I was breathless, but Rorik only laughed and said I finally had some color in my pale cheeks. Then I was twirling in the arms of a tipsy Thorne and, finally, passed from one male guest to another.

Caught up in the gay, rollicking mood, I began feeling as heady as if I had drunk a dozen goblets of wine instead of the single one I'd sipped. Held in the strong arms of one dancer after another, I discarded all caution along with my heavy brocade cape, and was soon leaping as wildly around the fire as any of them. My hair had long since been loosed from the tightly braided coil Astrid had so carefully fashioned and was falling in disheveled tangles around my shoulders. As light and giddy as some bird just released from a cage, I laughed when one partner flung me, twirling like a top, high into the air. I was in an hysterical frenzy. Instead of crying, I was releasing my emotions in this wild abandon. When I saw Rorik standing to one side—legs apart, arms across his chest, one eyebrow raised—I winked at him. He grinned and winked back.

Flushed and exhausted, I finally collapsed into a chair, feeling as I had when, as a child, I flung myself with the same abandon into rolling down a hill or galloping across a meadow. My mother often said she thought I had gypsy blood in me. Maybe she was right. Perhaps if I tried the life-style of a heathen and learned to revel in pagan pleasures, I might be able to let the past slip into memory so that it would no longer torment me.

The drinking, story-telling, and singing lasted well into the night. Finally Rorik suggested we retire.

"You slip away, Tara, and I'll be along soon. No one will miss us now."

I fully expected Astrid to be there, waiting to help me disrobe. I was not prepared to find a strange woman who I assumed had come from town since I had not seen her with the family when we first arrived.

"Good evening, Tara. I am here to help you prepare for bed." Her voice was cold and forboding. I took an immediate dislike to her, and my apprehension was stronger than my curiosity at just what she was doing in my room.

"Where is Astrid?" I was more than a little afraid of this dark-haired stranger, and I didn't like being alone with her. "I thought to see her here."

"Not tonight. It is traditional I be the one to disrobe you and see you safely in bed."

"I see." I was feeling more and more uncomfortable at the thought of her undressing me. No one had explained such a tradition. Who was she and why was she, rather than a member of the family, doing this? Why had Rorik failed to warn me? Perhaps she was a priestess of some kind with one more religious rite to take me through. Tall and voluptuous, she was darker of hair and skin than any of the other women I had seen. There was something frightening about her eyes as she looked at me. Already she had removed my gown, and she was beginning to brush my tangled hair and pick out the jewels caught in it.

"Who are you?" I asked. "I have not seen you in the house before."

"My name is Raghild. It is traditional that I be the one to help you on your wedding night."

I knew it was foolish of me to be so disturbed, when all I needed to do was ask who she was. "Are you a priestess? Or the wife of a chieftain?"

"My husband is Rorik. I am his first wife."

The room swirled around me, and I reached for the tall bedpost. I would not faint in front of her. I would not! I felt sick to my stomach, and I had to swallow hard to control the nausea.

"Here, drink this." She handed me a goblet of wine,

98

poured from a carafe prepared for Rorik and me to share later. Still shaking, I took a few sips. My stomach continued to churn, and my heart was beating wildly. I could feel the blood rushing to my head, while my legs and arms were so weak I could scarcely stand or hold the goblet.

"You did not think you were his only wife, did you?" she asked. "Surely you have seen Thyri and their daughter."

Thyri. The woman I had worked beside while preparing the funeral feast. The one who had been first to make friendly overtures toward me. How could she have done it, being Rorik's wife, too? And I had played with her daughter, not knowing all the time that she was Rorik's child as well.

"Rorik is a wealthy man," Raghild continued. "He can afford many wives. You are not the first, and do not think you will be the last. I was the first, and the only one who really loves him. Thyri does not. She loves his younger brother, Adair, but she was given to Rorik by her father. And I know you were captured by him."

"But why—why if you love him, does he want other wives, Thyri and me?" I could not believe what I was hearing; I would not believe it, but I had to ask. I forced each question out, and the answers were like daggers piercing my heart.

"Because he does not love me," she said bitterly. "I have loved him since we were children; and he bedded me when we were very young, to prove he was a man. I encouraged him because then I knew he would marry me. He is an honorable man. It is important for him in his position to have several wives, so he did not refuse when Thyri was offered to him. Then he saw you, and anyone can see why he wanted you. He is like his father. His passions will never be sated."

"His father?" Rorik had said Thorne was inconsolable when Rorik's mother died. How could he have taken others?

"Thorne has three wives, all as young as his own sons."

I was shivering in my silk chemise, and I reached for a fur covering. My teeth were chattering; my skin felt as cold as ice, but the chill was not from lack of heat in the room. I knew I would never be really warm again.

99

"Do you live here?" I asked as dispassionately as possible.

"I did until I heard of your coming. I went to my father's house in the village. I could not bear to see who was replacing me in Rorik's bed. Thyri does not matter anymore. He slept with her only until she conceived. Now she and Adair have eyes only for each other, but of course they cannot marry. He would be killed and she sold into slavery if they were caught together. So I continued to satisfy Rorik, but I knew it would not last."

"And now?" Why did I persist with this questioning? What was I postponing? I was only punishing myself with each word either of us uttered.

"I must live here, of course. I am still his wife and must serve and obey him. Though I doubt he will call for me very often now. Only when you are unwell or he is displeased with you."

Or when I am displeased with him, I thought.

"Thank you, Raghild," I said. I could stand no more, and I hoped she was waiting to be dismissed. "You may go now."

She turned, still unsmiling, and walked out. I heard Rorik's footsteps outside and quickly I bolted the door. Wife to a heathen was one thing. One of several wives was something else.

First Rorik tried the door; then he rapped gently. When I didn't answer, he pounded more impatiently.

"In the name of the gods, Tara, this is no time to be coy. Let me in."

But I had already made my decision. Hard as it was to deny him, or regardless of the consequences to me, I would remain firm. "Never, Rorik! You will never enter this room as long as I am in it."

He knocked louder, but I refused to say anything more.

"Don't be a fool, Tara. If I have to tear the door down, the whole house will hear and come to see what is wrong. I'll not have them laughing at me."

I feared his anger, but for now mine was greater. He had deceived me, and I was determined he would suffer as I had when Raghild revealed the truth.

"Let them laugh."

Suddenly he lowered his voice to the cruel, menacing tone I knew allowed no argument. "Unbolt the door, Tara."

I realized then it would be better to have it out with him face to face, so that he should feel the full extent of my wrath. I opened the door and remained standing in the middle of the room, the fur wrapped tightly around me.

"What's the meaning of this behavior?" Rorik stormed.

"Raghild helped me to undress tonight."

"So? 'Tis the custom."

"So! As long as you have two wives, I will not be your third. I will stay here only until you can find a way to send me home." There was real danger in making such a daring statement, but I had to say it.

"By Odin! Getting independent again. No, indeed, you are staying here—and as my wife." There was no more gentleness or laughter in his eyes, only intense fury. "Since I bedded you on the ship you have been mine, and you're not getting away from me."

"That may be; I cannot prevent you from keeping me here. But I'll not sleep with you, so you may as well return to Raghild, or force your advances on Thyri. You lied to me. Don't ever touch me again." I was shaking at my audacity. I knew I might be beaten or sold as a slave, but I could not stop. Only by talking could I keep from crying.

"No, Tara, I did not lie to you. I never said you were my only wife. It is the custom for Vikings to have more than one wife."

"Speak not to me of custom!" I screamed. The dam had broken, and I could hold back my feelings no longer. "Just get out! You are vile! Evil! I was wrong to think you might be different."

"You know what happens when you start screaming." He pulled me suddenly into his arms and kissed me until I lost all breath. "By Frey," he whispered hoarsely, "this is our wedding night, and you'll not deny me what is rightfully mine."

With that he flung me on the bed and ripped my chemise from neck to hem. There were no gentle caresses or tender words. Like a man starved for the taste of flesh, he bit and clawed until my body was bruised all over and then forced himself on me so roughly I could not keep from crying out. There was no pleasure as I had known on the ship, only great pain.

"Never again tell me I am not welcome in your bed,"

he said. "I am leaving now, and I know not when I'll return, but I had better not find the door bolted."

With that he strode out, slamming the door behind him.

I'd come so close to loving him. Now I could do naught but try to hate him as I had when he'd first taken me captive. He had wooed me and taught me how beautiful it was to be loved by him. No! Not loved, but seduced. I'd been but a few hours of pleasure to him, nothing more.

"Oh, Rorik!" I cried into the pillow. "I do love you. How can I endure living in the same house with you and seeing you with Raghild and Thyri?" My heart and my beliefs would not allow me to think of myself as his wife anymore. I could not deny him entry into my room, but he would never know the suffering I endured when he touched me.

I could not stop my weeping, and I tortured myself by imagining Raghild enjoying the smug pleasure of having her husband seek her out once more. Pain greater than any physical pain I'd known engulfed me. Once again I had been betrayed.

Chapter Seven

EVEN BEFORE THE CEREMONY IN THE GROVE, I thought I was pregnant. Within a month I was certain of it. Once I would have been overjoyed to carry Rorik's child. Now it was one more bond tying me to him, making it impossible to sever completely the emotional ties. Nor would he relinquish his hold on the mother of his child when that child might be a son.

I waited fearfully for a second outburst of Rorik's wrath, but none came. Although the door to our room remained unbolted as he ordered, I slept alone. During the day he was busy around the farm, supervising tasks that needed to be finished before winter set in, so his presence was not always haunting me, constantly reminding me of our estrangement.

While the men gathered and stored fodder for the animals and harvested the last of the root vegetables, I was busy with the women, drying and storing fruits and vegetables, putting up great crocks of honeycomb, turning honey into mead, and hanging herbs to dry. These tasks helped me to endure the great loneliness I felt and also made me tired enough by the end of the day to fall asleep at night.

After the harvesting, the men turned to securing all of the buildings against winter storms. The clay barns, storehouses, and byres had to be made weather-tight with new layers of sod on both walls and roofs. When mornings found ice forming on the ponds, even the women were called upon to help with this task, and by the end of each day, my arms and legs were almost paralyzed with the strain of lugging great squares of turf. Only after Astrid rubbed me down with soothing oils was I able to sleep. Nor would the work be finished when the outbuildings were secured; the same must be done for the long house, but that would come last. Protection of animals and stor-

103

age of food took precedence in a land where one's life depended on both for survival during the long, cold months. The family could manage with leaking walls and roof by remaining close to the fire if necessary, but they would not last long without food.

I knew that if I revealed my pregnancy, I would be freed from such onerous labor, but I preferred the tiring hours and the painful muscles to having Rorik know of my condition.

Mealtimes were, as always, gay and noisy affairs. I listened, learning more of their words every day; and if I was more quiet than the others, it did not seem strange. Since the men sat at one end of the table and the women at the other, I was not forced to be near Rorik. I could not close my ears to his voice, but I could keep my eyes averted. It was enough that his features were so engraved in my memory that his laughing eyes and mischievous grin never left my mind's eye.

At night the women retired early with the children while the men sat around the fire drinking and settling on what needed to be done the next day. Rorik and I had no time to be alone during the day even if we wanted to; nevertheless, I was always uncomfortable when he was near—reaching for a slab of turf I handed up to him or passing close to me at the table. At such times he acted as if nothing were amiss between us. He simply did not come to my room at night. We were both playacting for the benefit of the rest of the family, and I wondered how long we could keep it up. I felt as if I were holding my breath, like one waiting for the rain to fall after hearing the early rumbles of thunder.

Once tucked under the eiderdown by Astrid, I lay alone in the big bed waiting, dreading to hear his footsteps outside my door, yet having to admit I longed for him to come in and demand that I play the part of an obedient wife. If I gave in too quickly, more quickly than one who had ordered him out of the room should, I could always pretend it was because I was too tired to protest or I was merely carrying out our agreement. It sometimes seemed that my condition had heightened my desire and increased my longing for him. Yet never would I humble myself to go to Rorik or leave my door ajar at night. If I were his slave instead of a third wife then I would have accepted my place instead of feeling demeaned by it. But I had made my position clear, and I would not swerve from it. Pride had to take precedence over desire. If I cried when I knew Rorik had gone to Raghild's bed, I at least was able to remain calm when we worked together or when he strode about the house or played with Asri, his daughter by Thyri. As I wept I tried to ease the ache in my loins and breast by thinking about the child I carried and the joy I would have in caring for it.

I had two brief interludes of peace when Rorik was away from home for extended periods of time. During the first he accompanied a group of serfs up to higher ground where the cattle had been grazing and breeding during the summer. It took several days to make the trip on horseback, gather up the animals, and drive them back to the farm. Soon after this, he joined some of his crew in the harbor where they set about beaching the *Raven* and securing her safely on land. During the winter they would completely re-caulk the hull, mend her sail, and make other needed repairs. For the present, it was enough to see she would be pulled safely above the high autumn tides and out of danger from the fierce gales that blew down the fjord during winter. With him gone, I could breathe more easily, and the tight feeling in my chest gradually relaxed.

During this time I became more friendly with Thyri. Knowing that she too had been taken against her will and was equally unhappy drew me to her. Our mutual feelings toward Rorik gave us a common bond and separated us from the others, although at the time she was not aware why I felt close to her. Raghild simply ignored me, and no one seemed surprised by it. Multiple wives might be the custom, but that didn't preclude jealously between them, as I saw by the bickering among Thorne's three spouses. At least there was no open bitterness among Thyri, Raghild, and me.

Thyri was small and delicate, so frail in fact that she seemed more like a child than the mother of one. Her skin was pale and delicate, reminding me of a translucent flower petal. Deep blue eyes gazed sadly from her wan, thin face, yet her lips were always gently curved in a sweet, girlish smile. I found a certain peace in helping her care for Asri, a beautiful little girl who was the image of her mother. Asri flitted around the long hall like a little honeybee, oblivious to the fact the other children—sons and daughters of Thorne and Ruskil—were given more attention and special treats. Asri was the innocent victim of her mother's status as Rorik's rejected wife. I wanted to scream at the unfairness of it. Although ignoring Thyri, Rorik often held his daughter on his lap. But only Adair, not married but obviously in love with Thyri, played with the child as if she were a special member of the family.

Once I had been shown the chests of materials belonging to all the family and told to choose whatever I wanted, Thyri and I sewed together through the long afternoons. I loved working with the fine woolens, sewing on silk braid in the traditional designs Thyri taught me, and trimming a heavier woolen cape with bands of fur. For a few hours I could forget where I was and the chasm of deceit separating Rorik and me. The white fox cape had been laid carefully away in a deep chest. I did not ever want to see it again.

When I completed what I thought would suffice for my needs, I helped Thyri with dresses for Asri. Tenderly I embroidered them and watched with delight when Asri squealed over the design of beaded birds I had put on her cape. Soon I would need to make smaller garments for the child I carried, but that could wait. In my long, full gown, my secret need not be revealed yet. I especially did not want Rorik to suspect, and since he no longer slept with me, he was not aware of the gradual swelling in my belly.

With Thyri's patient assistance I learned to spin the Viking way and work the wool looms. She had her own ribbon loom, a most prized possession, and she taught me to weave into intricate designs the delicate silk threads imported from Byzantium.

As was my duty, I made Rorik woolen trousers, and I wove new ribbons for his *hlad*. I would not be called remiss in my wifely responsibilities. He thanked me quietly with, "They fit well, Tara," but no other words passed between us except when he required me to do something. Since the men and women had different tasks, the two groups seldom came together except at mealtimes, making it easier for us to pretend all was well between us. Raghild surely knew the truth, but avoiding me as she did, I was spared seeing it in her eyes.

While we worked together, Thyri made the afternoons, now getting darker every day, pass quickly by relating her favorite Norse legends.

"I am proud to be the daughter of a chieftain and wife to a mighty warrior," she said. "We are children of Rig and Mor."

I'd never heard those names before, and I was puzzled. "You and Rorik are related then?"

"No, no. Rig is the father of all Norse peoples. He is a god. But chieftains and warriors are children of Mor, the mother."

"And others?" She had aroused my curiosity in these strange beliefs of theirs.

"You would like to know?" she asked eagerly. "About the beginnings?"

I nodded, expecting in my ignorance to hear the Norse version of Adam and Eve in the Garden of Eden.

"The God Rig wandered the earth. He came to a shabby cottage where lived Oldefar, great-grandfather, and Oldemor, great-grandmother. They could offer him nothing more than lumpy bread and a bowl of broth. Rig slept with Oldemor and nine months later she had a son called Trael. He was dark-haired and ugly, with rough skin, large knuckles, thick fingers, and crooked back. All children of Trael are serfs.

"Rig wandered again and came to a hall with a fire in the floor. Near it sat Bedstefar, grandfather, and Bedstemor, grandmother. They were dressed in neat, well-made clothes. He was busy making a loom, and she was spinning. Rig slept with Bedstemor, and nine months later she had a son, Bonde. He was ruddy and clear-eyed. The children of Bonde are free peasants.

"Once more Rig wandered the earth. He came to a great hall with rushes on the floor. While Far, father, worked busily making a bow, Mor, mother, set the table with a cloth. On this she placed silver bowls and mugs, pork and game birds, and jugs of wine. Rig slept with Mor, and nine months later she had a son, Jarl. He had blond hair, pale cheeks, and bright, piercing eyes. He learned to read the runes. The children of Jarl are the chieftains and warriors."

Thus slowly did I learn about the people among whom I was a captive. On other afternoons she told me the Norse version of the creation and of the prophesied end of the world. When the Giant Ymir was slain, his flesh became earth; his blood, the seas and lakes. His bones formed the mountains. From his skull came the sky, and his brains became clouds. Separated from earth by Bifrost, the trembling rainbow, was Asgaard, the home of the góds. Just as death is the destiny of every living thing, so would come Ragnarok, the doom of the gods and the end of the world. It would be sword-time and wolf-time, culminating in awesome natural catastrophes and the unleashing of the wicked giants and monsters. Viking beliefs were frightening and foreboding, born in the gloom of their lightless homes and the long, dark days of their long, bleak winters.

Thyri was a good story-teller and I an avid listener. It was an enjoyable diversion to wile away the time, and the tales helped me to understand the moods and attitudes of those around me. Viking life was harsh and the people had to be strong and rugged to survive, with little patience for weaklings. It was no wonder their gods were often cruel and ruthless, too.

Foolishly, I tried to think that no one was aware of the estrangement between Rorik and me; but in a house with many eyes, there are no secrets.

There were many mornings when Raghild greeted me with a smug, satisfied smile on her face, and I knew Rorik had spent the night with her. I tried to cover my hurt by telling myself that at least it kept him away from my unbolted door. The worst pain came when I saw the slaves laughing with her when they thought my back was turned. More difficult for everyone were the days when Raghild did not smile. She screamed at the slaves, beat them for their slovenly habits, and whipped those who did not instantly obey. As trying as those times were, however, I could tolerate them because she dared not take out her wrath on me.

The situation finally became intolerable when Thyri appeared one morning with one eye swollen and discolored and an ugly bruise on her neck. Her face was flushed from weeping. All laughter at the table ceased, and conversation became a low mumble. Rorik and Ruskil, the only men at the table, paid no attention to her. I knew it would be best for me to do the same. Inside I was seething. Rorik had abused her, and I loathed him for such brutality.

The oppressive stillness did not last long. Adair came in from tending to the animals; and when he saw Thyri, he grabbed Rorik and pulled him out of his chair. Taken by surprise, Rorik fell to the floor and Adair attacked. He had his older brother down, and he made the most of his advantage. Both were powerful men, broad of chest and with muscles made strong by hard work. But Adair could not keep Rorik pinned down for long. Over and over they rolled on the floor, grappling with each other and reaching for the most vulnerable spots. Again and again they pummeled chests and stomachs, gouged at eyes, and struck each other across the face with their fists. Before long, Rorik's nose was bleeding and Adair had a deep cut below one eye. I watched fearfully, dreading each moment to see one of them deal the other a lethal blow.

Suddenly Adair was on top again. Straddling Rorik with his powerful legs, he grabbed both shoulders and pounded his older brother's head against the hard earthen floor. I stuffed my fist in my mouth to keep from screaming, so certain was I that Rorik would be killed. In spite of my loathing for him, I felt a rush of pity and fear. I hated him, but I did not want him slain. I could not forget so easily that he had been my lover and was the father of my unborn child.

Thorne appeared in the door. I waited expectantly for him to stop the fight between his two sons. With a grim frown on his face, he merely stood and watched. All the while, Ruskil remained seated at the table, sopping up gravy with a chunk of bread and seeming to relish the mayhem between his brothers.

I did not see how Rorik could take much more and still live. His head was wobbling when Adair raised it up, and he was nearly unconscious. I started to plead with Thorne to intervene. Those were his sons fighting to the death, and I did not believe he remained unmoved. Then I saw the steely look in his eyes warning me off: remember, only the rugged survive and are worthy of becoming chieftains.

I should have known better than to worry about the man who could command a crew of Vikings and bring the *Raven* through the fiercest storms. With one swift, sure move he raised up and lunged for Adair's throat. Releasing his hold for a fatal, brief moment, Adair was caught off guard, and Rorik kneed him swiftly in the groin. Moaning in agony, Adair clutched himself and curled up on the floor. Thyri started from the table and then sat down again. She dared not go to his side. Rorik strode to the table and resumed eating, oblivious to the blood dripping into his mouth.

The danger was over for the moment, but nothing had been settled. This had not been a simple brotherly squabble, and it would be only a matter of time before something else stirred up the bad blood between them. Fortunately, Rorik left immediately afterward to bring down more cattle from the high ground, and there was once more peace in the house for a few days. Upon his return, he stayed out of Adair's way and Raghild was smiling again.

The snows began, and we frequently awoke to a crystalline white world. In the mornings I stayed under a double layer of eiderdown until Astrid came in with a bowl of hot broth to warm me up. With each day that passed, I was growing heavier and finding it harder and harder to get out of bed in the morning. The sun shone for only a brief time in the middle of the day, and it seemed as if no light ever entered the darkened long hall. No amount of fire or torchlight could dispel the ever-present gloom which matched my mood of despair and loneliness. I longed to get away, but I knew that such was hopeless.

"Tara!" I turned to see Rorik standing behind me. "Get your fur cape. We are going for a ride in the sledge."

"I put the cape away," I said quietly. His words stirred something in me I preferred to have left untouched.

"Get it out."

After seeing what he had done to Thyri, I knew better than to disobey.

The wheels of the cart we had ridden in from town had been removed and runners attached in their place. Pulled by a pair of horses, we rode across fields covered with several feet of snow and topped with a hard-packed crust of ice. The sun sent sparks of fire off the branches of the trees, and the whole world was silent save for the hard clop-clop of the horses' hooves and the hissing of the runners as they slipped across the ice.

"You are carrying my son, aren't you, Tara?" I should not have been startled at his words, but I was.

"I am carrying your child."

"It will be a son. Thyri has given me only a daughter. Raghild is barren. As mother of my son you will be honored and given first place among my wives. Will that satisfy you?"

My heart was stirred by his words, but they were not what I really wanted to hear; the offer was not enough.

110

"First or third, it makes no difference as long as there are others."

"Even if I say I will never take another wife or be husband to the others?"

I knew what it cost him to say this. He, too, had pride and would be defying tradition, but I could not give in, much as I wanted to.

"And did you tell them the same thing? Promise to be true only to them?" I had to sound hard and cold or I might weaken. If I were being unkind, I was no more cruel to him than he had been to me.

"There was no need. They knew the custom, and I am a wealthy man. They accept what cannot be changed."

"As Raghild accepted it by fleeing to her father when she learned of my coming?"

"She is a fool. She thinks to halter me by claiming to love me."

Too quickly I said what came first to my lips. I could then have bitten back the words. "So you admit that any woman who loves you is a fool."

He turned on me such a look of savage desire I shivered in spite of my cape. "I do not ask for love, Tara. I ask only for what we shared on the ship—a response equal to my needs."

I might once have said that was all I wanted in turn, but it was too late, too much had gone wrong between us.

"I want to go home, Rorik. I want to return to my people where I am loved and I am not forced to follow alien ways."

Suddenly the whole mood of the moment changed. There was no longer any hint of affection or concern behind our words. Instead we were lashing out at each other in anger and frustration.

"Never! You belong to me," he shouted.

"Is it me or the child you are thinking of?"

"It is you and you know it."

"Then let me go, I beg you."

"Your place is here with me."

"And you would force me to stay, knowing how unhappy I am."

"You think the abbey would take you in? As which— wife of a heathen or mother of a . . . bastard?" He was right, but I could have killed him for saying the words.

111

"If I am to be scorned, I will at least be among my own people."

"No, you will remain and be delivered of my son."

"If that is all you require of me, if my child is really all you want, then find another to fulfill your needs and give you a son. I am sure there are many eager to take my place."

"Be careful, Tara," he said harshly. "I've acceded to your desire to be left alone, but don't begin taunting me. Were you not carrying my child, I should be tempted to sell you into slavery."

It was not an idle threat, but I had one sure refuge. "Not as long as your father lives. He has the final word, and he is fond of me. I have faithfully carried out all the tasks assigned to me in Thorne's house. Nor have I bolted the door to our room. It is you who stays away."

"But it is you who keeps me away," he said bitterly, and I felt a certain satisfaction in knowing he wanted me to make the first move.

"I am surprised you consider my wishes—any more than Thyri's."

"Don't mention her name! She is a mewling weakling, not fit to be a Viking wife."

I feared then I had trod too far into dangerous waters, but I was determined to let him know how I felt. Maybe it would help him understand why I found his presence hateful.

"And that is why you mistreated her, beating her so brutally she was ashamed to be seen."

"She cried when I went to her sleeping ledge. As my wife, she should have welcomed me to her bed. She needs to be reminded from time to time who she belongs to. Remember that."

"I am not likely to forget. I need only look around to be reminded I am a captive in your house."

"And my wife." The lines were grim around his mouth.

"In your eyes, not mine. My door is unbolted. I will not resist you, but do not expect me to welcome you either."

"When I do come, you will receive me as you did on the ship. I do not want to beat up the mother of my son, but I will not be denied."

With that, Rorik laid whip to the horses and turned the sledge around. We had exchanged bitter words, and they were like gall on my tongue. What we had once shared now seemed irrevocably destroyed.

The days remained dark and cold; one winter storm after another kept us in the house, and everyone became more testy at the enforced close contact. Tempers flared again and again, and no one knew when the wrong word or an awkward action would start an argument. Only Thorne remained calm, as if all of his family were small children or animals who had to be tolerated during their temper tantrums.

I loved sitting beside Thorne in the evening, enthralled by the stories of his early days at sea, spent in both raiding and in establishing trading settlements. He had traveled to all the major ports in the Western world; and he told me about the different ways people lived in those faraway places. On learning I was pregnant, he was delighted and nothing was too good for me. From him I gathered the strength I should have been receiving from Rorik. I loved Thorne as I had never really loved my own father, and this made the situation between Rorik and me all the more sorrowful. Though Thorne never said anything, he was aware something was wrong; and he showed his deep concern by being especially kind to me.

"You are well, Tara?" He had an amazingly gentle voice for so large and rugged a man.

"I am well, sire," I smiled at him. "The child will be a healthy one."

"Rorik wants a son."

"I know."

"What do the runes say? Do they foretell a son?"

"No, only that the child is strong." I did not mention the other secret they held, one I would keep to myself until after the birth.

"Good. Eat well and do not work overhard. The birth will be in the spring?"

"Late spring, sire. Just before Midsummer Eve."

He slapped his knees and then laid a hand on my head as if in blessing. "A good omen. A new season, a new life."

One evening I was surprised to find Raghild waiting in my room. For some time she had been somber and glum, brooding over every seeming slight and retorting bitterly when anyone spoke to her. Once again the thralls were the victims of her sharp tongue and quick hand.

"Tara, 'tis time for you to return to Rorik."

I could not conceal my shock at her suggestion. "Oh, I should think you would be happy with the situation."

"You go to bed early. You do not see what happens. He chooses the youngest and prettiest of the slaves to share his bed. They are pleased to sleep with such a man. But they are laughing at me now."

"As you had them laughing at me, Raghild?" No revenge of my doing could have been sweeter to me. I felt no pity for her.

"That is over. 'Twould be better if you invited him to your bed again."

"Never! The custom of multiple wives is abhorrent to me." I would not have her know the door was unbolted, that the choice to stay apart was his, not mine.

"Tara, whatever you did or said, try to appease him." Pride and arrogance had been replaced with abject humility that did not become her.

"Appease? I simply forbade him to come near me. He is honoring my request." Then I wondered at the reasons for her request. "Why do you want him to return to me? He would no longer come to you."

"I told you, he is not satisfied with me. He takes the slave girls to the compartment next to mine. You are doing me no favor by your refusal to sleep with Rorik. And if—if he touches Thyri again, Adair will kill him."

"Who are you most concerned for—Thyri or Rorik?" I asked.

"I love Rorik," she pleaded. "Thyri is a little fool. She is married to the greatest warrior in all Norvegia, and she prefers his weakling brother. It may be Adair who is killed and Thyri sold into slavery if they are not more cautious. Or it may be Rorik who is killed."

I was grateful the subject had shifted away from me, and I pressed her for more information. "They find ways to be alone together?"

"Too often. There will be a real tragedy. I care not for them. I could not bear it if Rorik were killed."

"I'm sorry," I said, "but 'tis no concern of mine. I cannot see where my returning to Rorik would make any difference."

"He would pay less attention. Back with you, he would

care less about what Thyri did as long as she was discreet, and his own life would no longer be threatened by Adair's temper."

"Again, I am sorry. But I cannot go against my beliefs to save two foolish people. Or to make your life happier. I suggest you try luring Rorik back to your bed. Now, if you don't mind, I wish to retire."

But Raghild's words had given me an idea, and I waited for a time when Astrid and I were alone in my room.

"Astrid, do your men have more than one wife?"

"Many do. Many hands are needed on a big farm. My father did not. He said my mother was worth three weaker women."

"I worry about Thyri," I said.

" 'Tis better to worry about First Wife."

"Raghild? What do you mean?" Astrid was always so quiet and unassuming, one scarcely realized she was around, but nothing escaped her notice.

"She hates you. She will do you harm. I do not like her eyes." Astrid shook her head sternly.

"She cannot hurt me, Astrid. Rorik—nor Thorne—will ever let her."

"Just be wary." There was real concern in her voice. "Do not make her mad. She has ways the men do not know about. Do not let her near you when your time comes or get close to the child."

This was the most I had ever heard Astrid say at one time, so I knew she did not think her fears groundless; but I refused to see any danger for myself.

"I can take care of myself, Astrid, but what can I do for Thyri and Adair? Their unhappiness may cause real trouble."

"Do you think they would leave here?" she asked. "Go somewhere far away?"

"I think they might, so long as they were together."

"Wait here for me, my lady. I will return soon."

In a moment Astrid was back with an old piece of linen and a stick of charred wood. On the cloth she began to draw a rough map. She knew the route over which, as a captive, she had been brought from Norrland near the boundary of Finnmark. It was a treacherous route she diagrammed, traversing mountain passes where there could be snowslides at any time, across swift rivers with unex-

115

pected rapids, and through vast forests where a traveler could find himself moving in circles. She thought, however, the map would guide Adair and Thyri to her father's farm where they would be welcomed and given a home.

When we called Thyri into the room, she reacted like a frightened child. "Oh, Tara, I could not. 'Tis too far. It would be wonderful to go, but we would surely get lost."

"If you follow my map," Astrid said, "you will not. Here is the high meadow. From there you see the mountain pass."

"But how do we travel all that distance?"

In spite of myself I was getting impatient with her. I could not understand her reluctance to escape with the man she loved, no matter how rough the going.

"You walk," Astrid said. "You cannot worry with horses, not through the mountains."

"But my things. How can I leave all my precious things?"

"Thyri!" I spoke harshly, more harshly than I really intended, but we were putting ourselves in danger by trying to help her, and I expected a more positive response from her. "Listen to me. Do you want to be happy with Adair or do you want to stay here and be brutalized by Rorik? Do you really love Adair, or are you just making everyone miserable with your self-pity?"

"I love him. I truly do, Tara."

"Then look at the map and listen to Astrid. We could both be sold into slavery over doing this for you."

"I am sorry, Tara. I was not thinking. Please, Astrid, go on."

"The pass is a valley. You will follow the river to the other side. Then across several leagues of meadow. Adair can follow the stars. It is in the forests you must be wary. You can go in circles and get lost. They are very dark and thick, but there are paths if you look carefully for signs."

"Tara," Thyri said, clutching my hand. "I'm afraid again. We'll not get through alive."

"Have you no faith in Adair? He is a Viking." And I felt a strange pride at hearing myself say the word.

"Yes, but he knows only the seas. Not the mountains and forests."

"If he can sail with no land in sight, he can find his way through the forests. And then you will be free, free

116

forever from the threats of Rorik. If my child be not a son—" I did not need to finish the sentence; she knew what I meant. Rorik would once more demand she sleep with him until she conceived. I saw her wince at the thought.

"Will Asri be able to survive such a journey?" she asked.

"Asri will stay here," I said. I did not mean to be cruel, but she had to face this truth immediately. "Rorik may not follow you and Adair, but he will never let his daughter go."

"No, no. I cannot leave her."

"If you want to be with Adair, you must. I will love her and care for her as if she were my own. You will have other children. Rorik will let no harm come to her. If real tragedy is to be avoided, you cannot think of her but of the future you and Adair will have together."

Then I worried that I might be wrong, wrong to urge her to run away, wrong to defy a custom just because I did not approve of it. Was I doing it for her sake or mine? If she were gone, there would be only Raghild between me and Rorik. Did I hope to find a way to get rid of her too? I wanted Thyri to face a truth, but was I afraid to face one about myself? In urging Thyri to run away, I could be sending her and Adair to their deaths. She was not physically strong. As hesitant as she was, I feared she also lacked strength of will. No, if she did not want to go, I would never mention the subject again.

All through our conversation, Thyri's eyes had been heavy-lidded and downcast. Suddenly she looked up at me and her face glowed with a new anticipation. There was no more fear. Only elation.

"I will go anywhere, Tara, endure any danger, if Adair and I can be together."

I approached Adair more cautiously. Yearning for Thyri in his own home was one thing; leaving his family, his secure existence, and his future inheritance to set out on a journey to the unknown was another.

"Why are you doing this for us, Tara?"

"I think because I want someone in this family to be happy. Everyone—except perhaps your father—is torn apart by unhappiness, and I think he, too, suffers for his children. He knows about you and Thyri." I hesitated, then went on. It was right he should know. "He also knows there is something amiss between Rorik and me."

"What is wrong, Tara? You and Rorik were so happy when you first arrived."

Unexpectedly I found myself pouring out to this young man what I had been unable to tell anyone else.

"I was—well, not really happy but ready to learn to be. I had been captured, had seen the abbey burned and looted, and I hated Rorik for doing all that. Then, throughout the long days on the *Raven* I surprised myself by growing to like him. I adjusted to the fact I would be a slave, but I did not want to be his wife. However, he tricked me into marriage, and I wanted to hate him again. But I didn't. I—I found I wanted to be with him."

"My brother is known for his ways with women." There was bitterness in his voice.

"I am a Christian, Adair. By marrying a heathen, I condemned myself to eternal damnation."

"And you turned Rorik out of your room?"

"No. I was ready to live with him as his wife and to bear his children. I met your grandmother, and I vowed to perform the duty she charged me with. I was ready to be part of a Viking family. You don't know how ready, Adair, because I suspected I was carrying Rorik's child. Then I learned I was not his only wife. I could not live with him that way."

"Rorik is a good man, Tara."

"You can say that after what he did to Thyri? After he nearly killed you?"

"He is a Viking, and Thyri belongs to him. I had no right to attack him. She is his wife. He would not do the things he does if he had you back. Surely you must know he cares when he doesn't force himself on you. I have never known him to give in to the whims of a woman before."

"Whims!" I was furious that he should think my behavior whimsical. " 'Tis my deep religious beliefs. Do you call any of your beliefs a whim?"

"But you were willing to be his wife in spite of those beliefs. Are you sure it is your religion or the unwillingness to share him with other wives? Is that why you want to help Thyri and me? To get rid of one of the wives? What are your plans for Raghild?"

"I'm sorry, Adair. I thought I was helping you. If you

and Thyri are not interested in leaving, we shall say no more about it."

"I will think on it, Tara. The decision will be mine, not Thyri's, but I will consider her wishes."

I did not see him leave the room. He had opened a wound I thought was healed, and tears flooded my eyes. I refused to admit he was right, that it was pride not religion that kept me from returning to Rorik, pride and humiliation.

Chapter Eight

THE WINTER PASSED SLOWLY.

The men spent the long, dark hours mending farm equipment, making new plows, and stitching together a sail for their new ship from wide strips of red and white wool the women had woven and then embroidered with the traditional animal motifs.

I often watched Rorik's hands as he cut and joined leather harnesses or carved handles for farm implements. I could not take my eyes off his slim yet strong fingers and the lean, powerful muscles in his arms, bare now in his sleeveless leather jerkin. All moved together in a steady, ceaseless rhythm as he worked, and I longed to sit beside him as I had when he held the tiller of the *Raven*. I wanted to touch him, to be held in those strong arms, and to feel his fingers caressing me.

From time to time I caught him looking at me, his mouth set in a grim frown while he clenched and unclenched his fists or slid them along his thighs. I did not allow myself to get dowdy or awkward-looking. Instead I dressed with special care in my prettiest woolen gown and indoor cape. Astrid arranged my hair in its most becoming style. I needed to torment Rorik as he had made me suffer.

All this work the men did was not enough to dissipate the energy stored up now that they could no longer go Viking or labor on the farm. They drank too much and then gambled for high stakes until one lost heavily and started a fight. Rorik and Ruskil could wrestle to a draw and then get up and clink horns of mead. Not so when Rorik and Adair got into an argument. Twice they nearly killed each other, and Thorne finally intervened.

The atmosphere was getting more tense by the day, and I wished fervently for spring. Adair and Thyri had come to me saying they were ready to flee to Norrland. Together with Astrid, we met often in my room where they went over and over the map she had drawn for them. They would have to wait for the summer thaws in order to make it over the mountains. The rivers, swollen with melted snow in the warm months, would have been easier to traverse by sledge in the winter; but they dared not risk freezing to death in the forests or mountain passes. Aware of Thyri's frail physique, Adair agreed to use horses for riding but not to transport anything but the most vital necessities. I envied them planning for a new future. If not for the child I carried, I would have grown despondent in the face of their happiness.

In the midst of all this, Rorik's other brother, Ruskil, shocked everyone by bringing home a third wife, a girl from town, daughter of a free man. I had disliked Ruskil from the beginning. Unlike his tall, blond brothers, he was short and squat with red hair so dark it was almost black, like copper that has lost its sheen. His features were not unattractive, but he wore a perpetually surly scowl that made him look mean and ugly. He spoke little, except to issue orders, and then his voice was gruff and harsh.

No love had been involved in Ruskil's first two marriages, and he treated those wives more harshly than he did his slaves. His children he simply ignored. His latest action, however, was the worst insult of all. Ruddy and buxom, Helga was crude in habits and language. She was loud in her comments about Ruskil's sexual prowess, and bragged to all that he had bedded her within an hour after they met. To the disgust of everyone, it was her wont to climb on his lap and encourage him to fondle her. Even for Vikings, they went too far within sight of the family.

Rorik had calmed down considerably, and as far as I could tell, he retired alone to a bed on the ledge every night. I feared this new marriage of Ruskil's would stir him up again and send him on a rampage among the slaves or toward Thyri or me. Instead he became more quiet and reclusive, as if he saw in Ruskil's actions a reflection of his own.

I was the one who was stirred by my loss, and if I could, I would have forgotten my pride and opened my already unbolted door. Instead, I eased the ache in my loins by running my hand over my belly while I lay in bed and thrilled to the movement within me. And I wept.

I continued to read the runes for Thorne, who listened with interest even when the stones had little to tell.

"And the crops will be good, Tara?" he asked, leaning halfway out of his chair while I threw the stones.

"They will be good, sire, and the ewes will have many lambs."

"And you, Tara, you feel well?" he asked kindly.

"I am fine. I should have no trouble."

"That is good. We look forward to having another child."

"But there is already a houseful," I laughed.

"No man can have too many children or grandchildren. They are our immortality. What death holds, I do not know. With many grandchildren, I will be ready to go."

"Do not speak of death, sire. You are still young. You may yet have more children of your own."

"Oh, Tara, do not flatter an old man. But," he chuckled, "my wives do not complain of being neglected."

More and more I loved this powerful man, who treated me like a daughter. It made me all the sorrier I could not be the wife he wanted for Rorik.

With the coming of spring, the house was lively once more with preparations for a feast. It was the important festival celebrating the birth of new farm animals and the rebirth of the land. All must be made ready for the appearance of the gods who would come to bless the seed once it was sown. Pagan though the celebration was, I was as eager as the others to join the festivities, to feel alive again after the gloomy winter. Then, too, my own time was not far off.

The thralls were set to sweeping up the rushes which covered the earthen floor of the *skaalen*. Then the floor itself must be swept and reswept until all traces of the old rushes were gone. All these sweepings would be used for the bonfire on the day of the festival, the day of the spring equinox. The great fire in the *skaalen* was extinguished, with a few of the embers placed in a cauldron and kept alive to relight the fire. The pit itself was thoroughly cleaned out; it would then be relined with stones newly washed in the sacred spring in the grove.

Meanwhile, along with the other women, I had been busy spinning, weaving, sewing, and baking. For the festival everyone must wear all new clothes from skin out.

This meant chemises, gowns, and capes for ourselves and the children, as well as trousers, jackets, and capes for the men. Only the jewelry, the chains of housewifery, and the men's armbands and *hlads* could be retained. The men tanned leather to cobble new shoes and boots. They were also making certain all the farm implements were ready for us. Anything that had not been mended before the festival had to be destroyed.

We baked loaves of bread in the shapes of eggs and the sun-wheel and set them aside. I had always loved the smells of baking, and I joined in the singing while we kneaded and shaped the dough. Next we made cakes, mixing in whole grains from last year's harvest. The entire day before the equinox, thralls were busy lugging cauldrons of water to the small fire room. First the men took turns bathing in the large brass tub and rubbing each other down with rough husk towels. The hardier of them ran from the hot bath out into the yard and rolled in the fresh snow that had fallen during the night. New snow on the eve of the festival was a good omen, a sign from the gods that the crops would be plentiful that year. Only after rubbing themselves all over with the snow until their skin was glowing did the men dry themselves off and don the new clothes.

I joined the women, mistresses and servants alike, who stood just inside the door, laughing and cheering as the men rolled in the snow while pummeling and wrestling with each other to warm themselves. Rorik, like the other men, wore only a leather codpiece secured across the buttocks with thin leather thongs. His tanned skin glowed from cold and exertion. His muscles flexed as he pinned Ruskil in a snowbank. When he leapt up shouting, I ached to feel once more the firm tension of his stomach and run my hands over his slender hips and smooth loins. My breasts ached and my body began to throb, but I could not—I would not—recant the oath I made the night I sent him from the bedroom.

Next the women entered the bathing room, all frolicking and splashing until the floor, across which wood slats had been placed, was like a small pool. With my distended belly, I hesitated at first to disrobe in front of so many others, but they pulled me in with them. Even Raghild was laughing and carrying on like a child, and she joined the others in touching me—a pregnant woman—for good luck. Then we dried off and put on our new garments.

It was time to relight the great fire. Everyone in the family placed at least one of the new-washed stones in the pit and around the rim. As I laid mine down, I suddenly realized that once again I was joining in pagan ritual. The children had the honor of carrying in the dried branches of evergreen used at last year's festival and stored throughout the year. Then Thorne, as chieftain and head of the household, transferred the hot coals from the cauldron to the pit. When the twigs caught and the fire blazed up immediately, everyone cheered. It would be a good year.

Now came the spreading of the new rushes on the floors. First we women scattered sweet-smelling herbs to freshen them, crushing them under our feet until the aroma permeated the entire room. We carefully spread the rushes in an age-old, predetermined pattern: up and down and across in perfect north-south and east-west alignment until the floor looked as if it were covered by a huge woven straw carpet.

During all this I saw Rorik watching me, as he had so often throughout the past weeks, a little sadly but with the flicker of a smile. All I needed to do was smile back, but I averted my head to hide the tears and gritted my teeth.

The servants brought huge jugs of mead, and everyone watched through the night for the coming of the dawn. The women sang the old songs, and the men took turns reciting tales of the gods and the exploits of their ancestors. I had thought the night would be long; but well before I expected, the slave on watch announced the first rays of the sun had appeared over the distant mountains. We rushed out to welcome the dawn and the continued lengthening of the days.

With the children carrying newly cut boughs of evergreen, we went to the fields in solemn procession. Although the ground was still too frozen to sow the grain, one plowman cut three short furrows and scattered a few seeds. Next we moved to the cattle barns and stables where the loaves of bread were broken up and meted out among the animals and the celebrants. Just as all must work together to produce so all must share in the meal. The cakes with the grain from the previous harvest were crumbled into the seed bins to be plowed back into the earth.

Our final ceremony took us to the sacred grove. As we had shared bread with the animals, so now we shared wine with the gods. Libations were poured on the ground before the statues, invoking the blessings of all on the fields and animals. I looked at the image of Frey and remembered my feelings during my wedding. Although I had been bitter about having to go through with it, the unhappiness I suffered then was as nothing to my present misery. It had at least been a prelude to what I thought would be a joyous union with Rorik. Within hours all my hopes were destroyed, and I felt more bereft than when betrayed by Ian.

Next a pig, a goat, and a lamb were sacrificed and part of the meat laid on the ground before each statue. The remainder would be taken to the house for the feast. Here also Thorne announced that Haki, the oldest of the thralls, was now a free man. In days long past, such a thrall would have been sacrificed to the gods. With the passage of years, animals had been substituted, and the slave was set free or "reborn" into a new life. An excellent wood-carver, he was given a house in town and set up in his craft by Thorne. Haki would fare well as a free man, for good wood-carvers were always in demand. Each member of the family also gave him a gift to start him in his new life—food, clothing, furniture, and tools. In return, he presented miniature samples of his art in the form of strange animals or the gods to each of us. Mine was an exquisite replica of a seabird in flight. I was strangely moved. Rorik had to have told him it was his nickname for me. Did he yearn for me as I did for him?

When we returned to the house, the old rushes from the hall had been placed in the yard in a huge mound topped with more dried twigs and branches emitting a strong odor of pine resin. Soon a bonfire was blazing up, its flames shooting above the roof of the house and sending sparks into the sky. It was hoped the sparks would travel to the heavens to strengthen the light of the sun so it would increase in strength and duration until the mid-summer solstice.

The fire was kept going through the night, and the gala part of the festivities began in which everyone—family, serfs, and thralls—participated. The food was brought out, and we ate sitting around the fire. The flames were hot and the mood was gay, so no one minded that the weather still had traces of winter in it. We warmed ourselves with horns of mead and circle dances around the fire.

Through the flames I watched Rorik, who sat slumped opposite me, his drawn, tired face resting on his arms which were crossed above his knees. Thyri and Adair danced together, but he paid them no mind. When Raghild came to sit beside him and urge him to dance, he shrugged her off. In a fury, she invited a young stable boy to be her partner. Later I saw them hurrying toward the barns. I had no doubt she released her pent-up passions with a wild tumble in the hay. They didn't return until dawn, she wearing a smug, satisfied look and the boy grinning like a fool; it wasn't often a serf bedded the wife of his master. They were both fools. He could be banished or killed—either meant death, for no outlaw serf was ever accepted by another community—and she sold into slavery. If Rorik was aware of being cuckolded, however, he gave no evidence of it.

Thorne drank and romped with his young wives, all the while gasping and panting from the exertion until I feared he would have an attack. I loved him, and I did not want to lose the one protector I had in the family. I need not have worried. Soon he curled up beside the fire and snored like an old hound. Ruskil danced with wives and servants alike, occasionally flinging one so close to the fire she screamed in terror while he laughed with fiendish glee at her distress.

Neither Rorik nor I danced. We sat through the night, each staring into the flames, all the while avoiding the other's eye, until the sun rose again and we could return to our beds for several hours of sleep. I welcomed the exhaustion that kept me from lying awake and reliving the past hours when Rorik and I had been so close yet separated by something more impenetrable than a blazing fire.

Coming some three weeks before my time, the first pains surprised me, and I retired to my room with only Astrid and a slave-midwife in attendance. The labor was long and the pain severe, but in spite of my pleading, both insisted I stay out of bed and walk until the last possible moment.

"It will make it easier, my lady," Astrid encouraged me. "I know; I helped birth my younger sisters."

From time to time the midwife gave me sips of a herb tisane she said would relax the muscles needed to bring the child into the world and at the same time ease the pain. Finally Astrid said I could lie down, but labor continued for another full day and night. For the first time I began to fear I was not built to have children, and either the baby or I would die.

About the time I had given up hope and asked Astrid to hand me my cross, she smiled and said the head had appeared. All would be well. I think I fainted, for the next thing I remember was Astrid saying, "You have a son, my lady, a handsome little boy."

I watched as she wiped him off and then quickly laid him in the cradle old Haki had carved for me. But the pains had not ceased, and I already knew what her next words would be.

"There is another one, my lady! There is another baby." One final push and I heard her exclaim, "A little girl, as blond and beautiful as you." She joined her brother at my breasts, and with the two nursing eagerly, I felt a new sense of love pulsing through me. I had lost Rorik, but my life would no longer be empty.

For the time being, the twins slept in the same cradle while Haki was commissioned to make a second one as quickly as possible. All the family came in, exclaiming in awe and wonder at my producing twins.

"You have brought much good luck to our family, Tara," Thorne said, beaming broadly as he walked back and forth between the cradle and my bed.

"Thank you, sire. I hope they will continue to grow and make you proud."

"They look strong and healthy. Do you wish me to send for a wet nurse?"

"Not yet," I laughed. "I seem to have an abundance of milk." Nor did I want them taken away from my breasts. I did not want anything to break the special bond between us that had begun when I first felt life inside me. I needed to feel they were still a part of me, to assuage the loneliness I could not otherwise endure.

Only Rorik stayed away. Finally Astrid insisted on taking the babies into the long hall where he sat before the fire.

"It is not right, my lady," she said. "He should see them."

"Take them, Astrid. If he is too stubborn to come in here, we will at least not deny him that."

In a few minutes Rorik come through the door.

"I saw the children, Tara," he said almost shyly. "They are beautiful."

"You are pleased then?" I had done my duty. So far that was all I wanted him to acknowledge.

"I am pleased and very proud. They are to be called Signe and Eirik. You asked me once what words old Signe had for me. She said you would have twins and they were to be named thus."

"I know." This had been the secret I sheltered all these months. "I have already named them Signe and Eirik."

"But how—?"

"I understood when she spoke the names. When I felt the movement of two in my belly, I knew what she had told you."

"She—she also said I must care for and protect you."

"You have, Rorik." I could not deny he had treated me with respect at all times.

An eerie silence came between us, deathly still yet palpitating with emotion. Rorik paced the room, then suddenly he turned, and his words took me aback.

"She did not tell me to love you, but I do. I did not love Raghild or Thyri. I never thought to love any woman. When I saw you, I wanted you and took you. But now I love you. I have never said that to anyone else."

These were the words I had wanted to hear for so long, but I could not respond as I knew he wanted me to. I could not reveal my own love for him, and it pained me to have to answer him as I did. "It is not enough, Rorik."

"If I tell you that Adair and Thyri have fled, and I do not intend to follow them?"

They were gone. A great sigh escaped me. They had managed to escape, and I smiled for the happiness they must now be sharing. It was a good omen that Rorik did not choose to pursue them. They would be safe.

"And Raghild?" I asked. "Has she fled, too?"

"No, I've sent her to her father who has established a trading mart at Hedeby in Jutland. Once sent to her family and her bridal portion returned, she is no longer my wife. She was barren; I needed no other reason." He paused. Then he lifted my chin and forced me to look into his eyes. "You are my only wife, Tara."

128

For months I had ached to hear those words, yet I found myself unable to speak. There was still a barrier between us, a barrier of time and suffering. I could not be the first to break it down. But Rorik could. He pulled me into his arms; and my breasts, swollen with milk, pressed hard against his chest. All my longing, all my nights of aching loneliness were swept away with the touch of his body and the pressure of his lips. When at last he released me, I knew I wanted him to stay, to hold me close and reassure me, yet I murmured something about it being too hard on him to be near me and not be able to make love to me.

"Do you think that's all I want from you, my love?" he whispered. "It is enough now to feel you near, to have your warmth and loveliness belong to me again. You have never looked more beautiful, except perhaps when you were carrying Signe and Eirik. I desire you very much, but I can wait. I have something now to wait for."

"Oh, Rorik, please hold me close. I do love you."

He kissed me long and urgently and began caressing my breasts. Waiting would be as difficult for me emotionally as it would be for him to subdue his physical desires.

"It will not be too long," I said, all the while yearning to give myself to him completely. "I wish I could receive you, but I am still unclean."

With a special tenderness, he held me close; and we needed nothing more at the moment to renew our love.

Some three weeks after the birth of Signe and Eirik, I instructed Astrid to send for the wet nurse. She was a large-bosomed, comfortable-looking woman with a child of two she continued nursing in the belief this would prevent pregnancy. I was relieved her child was of an age to need her no longer. Many young mothers took wet nurse—slaves away from their own babies, and often these children died from being denied their mother's milk.

With the twins happily settled in their cradles in the long hall, I asked Astrid to prepare a bath for me. When Rorik came that night to bid me sleep well, he did not leave until the sun, shining through most of the night on the eve of midsummer, was high in the sky the following day. Lovers again, we renewed our love with the hunger born during long months of separation. We clung together passionately as if we could never get enough of each other. I was alive with a happiness I never thought to know again.

"How could you do it to me, Tara?" he whispered. "I felt imprisoned in a block of ice while a raging fire burned inside me."

I pulled his arms around me. "Did you think it was easy for me?"

"Then why? When we wanted each other so much."

"I do not know. I only know I was hurt, bitterly and deeply hurt, to learn I was not your only wife. For my faith, I was shocked, but I might have borne that. But when you took it for granted I would accept the situation, when you made no plans to divorce or send the others away—no, that I could not endure."

"So you admit, my love, it was pride that closed the door." His smothering kisses made it impossible for me to answer right away.

"If you admit," I finally said, "it was your pride that refused to open it."

"Enough! No more foolish separations."

"No more separations at all," and once more I melted in his arms, secure in the warmth of his love and aroused by the fire of his passion.

Chapter Nine

I RAISED UP ON ONE ELBOW and turned toward Rorik who lay asleep on his back. His blond, shaggy hair clung in damp patches to his forehead and cheeks. When I ran my fingers through the darker blond curls on his chest, he smiled in his sleep and put his hand over mine with the gentle pressure of need and possessiveness. I had not been wrong to return to him. That he still had two other wives no longer dissuaded me from wanting to belong to him. Since Thyri had fled and Raghild been returned to her father, I could pretend they did not exist.

"Rorik."

"Umm?"

"Did you mean it when you said you loved me?"

He opened one eye. "I love you, Tara, but don't ask me to show you how much. I have no strength left. If a scrawny, half-starved mouse crawled through that door, I'd be helpless to chase him out."

"Well, lie back and recover your strength. I have to feed the babies."

"Why?" He sat partway up. "They don't need you now. They have the wet nurse."

"Yes, but I need them. Look how swollen my breasts are."

"I am looking, and I like what I see."

"I thought you were too weak," I protested as he pressed me back against the pillows. Once more I looked up into the face of the man I had so often sworn to hate but could not keep from loving. The babies could wait.

With the passing of midsummer eve festivities, I knew the men would prepare to go Viking, and I dreaded the long summer days without Rorik. The ships had long since been made seaworthy and stocked with provisions. I often went down to the shore and watched as sails were once more unfurled amid great shouts and cheers and ships were towed from the beach and tied up at their breakwater moorings. Among those still on land was the *Raven of the Wind*.

"How soon do you leave, Rorik?" I asked, watching Ruskil leap boastfully from one long oar to another. Ruskil was a bully, and when I looked at him I involuntarily shuddered with a fear I no longer felt for the other Vikings around me.

"I'm not going this summer. There is important work to be done here."

He said no more at the time. Rorik had a knack of piquing my curiosity and then dropping the subject, but I was too happy at the thought of his not leaving to really care. When the time came for me to know, he would tell me.

Two days later he came into the *skaalen* where I was spinning, and told me to get ready for a journey.

"A voyage?" I asked. Were we, perchance, sailing to Britain? My heart leaped. Was he taking me home for a visit as he had at last promised he would?

"No, overland."

I should have known better. It was too soon. Even though my husband, he would be in danger as the leader of those who'd burned the abbey. I did my best to conceal my disappointment.

"A long journey?" I asked. "The important business you spoke of?"

"Three or four days' travel, then several at our destination. And, yes, it is very important."

Now I listened avidly as he explained the nature of our journey, partly because of my excitement at getting away after the long winter of being shut indoors but mostly because of where we were going.

"You remember, Tara, I told you about the Thing, the yearly gathering of all free men. This year the meeting is a more important one than usual. We are traveling to the Gulathing or Supra-thing, which serves the three shires of Sogn, Hordaland, and the Fjords. There will be hundreds of free men there. The purpose is to elect a chief jarl or king under whom all the shires will unite. Thorne is one of the jarls to be proposed as king. He should be chosen. He is older than the others, and his travels on many seas and as far south as Byzantium make him the most experienced."

So this was what Rorik had meant when he said I would be presented to the people as a potential queen. From nun to queen, a most unlikely transition for anyone to imagine. Never in my wildest dreams, when I first rebelled at the enforced seclusion of the abbey, did I consider going from the private, contemplative life of a nun to the public, convivial life of a Viking queen. The thought conjured up visions of everything from a huge castle where I would stand beside Rorik as he reigned over the newly established nation to continuing my role as a simple housewife on our farm. Then I shook myself back to reality. All of this was just dreaming. Since the Three Shires had never before been united under a king, it would be Thorne —if he were elected—who established the customs, and there would be time for Rorik and me to become familiar with the royal life. And then, too, Thorne was strong and would remain king many years; Rorik, when his time came, would also have to be elected. But the son was as popular with the people as the father, so I doubted not that someday I would be a queen.

Within a week we set out, part of a long caravan of warriors and serfs, who were free men not slaves. With Signe and Eirik I rode in a litter secured between two strong horses. All the warriors were mounted, and each carried spear, shield, knife, and battle-axe. Dressed in their finest woolen trousers, sleeveless leather jerkins, and heavily decorated capes that spread out over the horses' haunches, the riders formed an impressive phalanx fore and aft the long train. Their horses were caparisoned with reins and harnesses of the finest tooled leather, joined by ornately designed, highly polished brass buckles that glinted in the morning sun. Once again I was impressed with the sweeping grandeur of Viking life during great occasions.

More men joined us as we traveled along. They included all ranks of free men from impoverished peasants to small land-owners, tradesmen, shipbuilders, artisans, and wealthy Viking raiders. Some walked doggedly along or rode in broken-down carts; others rode fine horses. But all spoke with equal voices at the Thing.

The litter swayed gently, much like a ship on a calm sea. I would have preferred hitching up my skirts and riding astride, but Signe and Eirik required my constant attention. Rorik was so proud of our having produced twins, he insisted they come with us. Every unusual occurrence was to him and his family a good or evil omen, and twins ranked among the most felicitous. If truth be told, I did not want to leave them at home with the wet nurse either.

Although I envied Rorik and Thorne, who laughed and talked as they rode in tandem some distance ahead, I soon discovered I would not be bored. One or the other of the twins was always hungrily nudging my breast, and while Signe slept, I fed her brother. Then it was her turn. There were brief moments when they both slept, and I napped. Their birth and frequent feedings had drained my strength more than I realized at first. It was probably well I was not riding a horse.

We moved steadily along toward our destination, many leagues north of the farm in Hordaland. We traveled through dense forests, forded rivers on rafts we carried with us, and crossed meadows blooming with wild flowers. Each new vista was more startlingly magnificent than the last. I passed the time making posies to decorate the litter and a wreath for my hair. Feeling in high spirits, even Rorik and Thorne agreed to tuck flowers in their *hlads* and adorn the bridles of the horses. We were a gay group as we arrived at the meeting grounds just south of Sognfjord.

The men erected a woolen shelter, supported as always by poles topped with fearsome carvings to ward off evil spirits. Eiderdowns were laid atop piles of furs, and I soon had Signe and Eirik nestled on their own comfortable pallets. Rorik and Thorne stretched their legs and then settled in chairs to drink horns of mead. There was a chair for me too, as well as a goblet of wine. Both were most welcome after the long days in the litter.

The whole gathering—the laughing groups, the convivial chatter, the joyful reunions of friends long separated, the many small cooking fires—reminded me of the boar hunts and hawking parties my father had hosted back in Britain. I did not think of home often, at least not of my life before I entered the abbey. Those days had become mere shadows in my memory, far less real than the years after I left.

Once we were settled in and had eaten, we were well

134

into the long twilight. The sun would not set completely until nearly midnight. Before that it remained low in the sky, just barely touching the horizon, and the entire night was suffused with a rosy glow. Through it one could barely discern the feeble attempts of the stars and the moon to make themselves visible. Night had become day, and just as in the winter I wanted to sleep through all the dark hours, so now I wanted to stay awake almost round the clock.

"No, you don't," Rorik said, shaking his head at me the evening we arrived. "You'll not last long that way. You need your rest if you're to enjoy the excitement of the next few days."

Like a dutiful wife, I followed him to our pallet. There on our bed, well concealed from all those around us, we once more lay in each other's arms. The nights of separation on the way had whetted our desire for each other, and it was some time before we fell asleep. Thorne had gone off to drink and swap stories with some of his cronies, so we had the shelter all to ourselves. I felt joyfully uninhibited and free to give of myself completely with a warmth and passion that grew greater with each passing day. No longer need I hold back, fearful lest Rorik tire of me or I feel that my love was not returned.

Rorik woke me in the morning with a kiss. "I have to join my father, but you sleep awhile longer. Most of the morning will be taken up with regulations for opening the session. The excitement may start this afternoon."

Having slept little during the night, I was not averse to turning over and snuggling into the eiderdown once more. It was not long since the twins had nursed, one at each breast, so I would have at least two hours of uninterrupted rest. Rorik laughed at the way I sometimes fed them together holding one in each arm, their legs becoming entangled when they kicked. When they woke up simultaneously, it saved time and kept them happy. I loved to feel them pulling, sometimes in unison, sometimes in alternating rhythm, but always eager and ready to suck. My love for them gushed out with every drop I gave them.

By noon the day had become hot with a brilliant sun shining down on the assembled multitude. We were camped in a meadow carpeted with clover and wild flowers and situated at the end of a valley between small, rolling, fir-topped hills. On one hillside the chieftains and jarls

135

sat. Below them, the free men clustered, grouped according to territory and identified by the insignia of the jarl they owed allegience to. Some were as finely dressed as their leaders; others wore the most ragged of garments. But all were free, and each man's vote was equal to everyone else's. They were ready to acknowledge that their chieftains belonged to the ruling class, might even be descended from the gods, but they also knew the final power of authority lay in their hands.

The early afternoon was devoted to adjudicating minor crimes. The jarls sat in judgment, quoting the traditional laws from memory. Peasants were reminded that only the owners of the land had the prerogative to cut trees, and land owners were reprimanded for not allowing serfs and peasants to collect twigs beneath those trees.

Then came the more serious crimes. To these trials I listened avidly, eager to know how criminals were dealt with. Would the punishments be more lenient than those meted out in Britain, or would they be more barbaric? I was soon to learn that, although many seemed cruel, the verdict depended as much on the criminal as it did on the crime.

One man found guilty of stealing sheep was ordered to make payment in gold. Another, guilty of the same offense, had no wealth; and an executioner standing by with his battle-axe was commanded to cut off the thief's hand. The penalty was carried out immediately in the sight of all. The thief was ordered to lay his arm across a large tree stump, and the axe came down one time. I could not bear to look, yet I could not look away. My stomach tightened and I feared I would be sick. Was it always thus, I wondered. The wealthy feel no pain and the punishment lasts no longer than it takes to pay out the gold. The poor suffer unbearable agony, and the punishment continues for the rest of their lives. The poor man's screams were terrible to hear, and they continued while his bloody stump was immediately cauterized with glowing irons. In a near-faint he was led away by his weeping wife. It would be a long time before he learned to farm with one hand, and his punishment was meant to be a lesson to all who watched. Already too poor to pay for the sheep he had stolen, the man and his family would now face the threat of starvation. The Vikings were no less harsh than the land they lived in, yet only with such laws could all survive.

With one man being allowed to pay in gold and the other with his hand, I was reminded of an old adage, "The hangman's noose is the privilege of the poor."

A man accused of wooing away his neighbor's bees was ordered to return them as well as the honey they had produced and then was beaten until the skin on his back hung in shreds. Once again I cringed, as I thought he would surely bleed to death. A woman found guilty of souring by witchcraft the milk in the village cows was ordered sold into slavery. This was her third such offense.

The next two cases involved men accused of murder. As was the custom, both were supplied with jarls well versed in Think law to plead their cases for them. In spite of this, both were found guilty and sentence was passed immediately. Once again the executioner brought out his battle-axe, slowly and carefully honed it, and then tested it on the thigh bone of a sheep. The bone snapped cleanly in two.

The guilty men drew lots to see who would be executed first, and the loser of the macabre lottery stood by and watched. The first walked calmly to the stump and laid his head on it. When the axe came down, the head rolled off the block and onto the ground. It landed on a slight incline and continued to roll forward, the tongue lolling grotesquely from side to side in the bloody mouth. The second man become hysterical and lost control of his bladder. I shuddered and turned away. No criminal, no matter how heinous his crime, should have to endure such torture and humiliation. I looked at the faces around me for some sign of the pity I felt, but none showed any compassion. Screaming his innocence, the man had to be dragged to the tree stump and his head held down by the hair. In another second the axe ended his agony.

In addition to the executions, the murderers' families had to pay *wergeld,* the value of the men murdered, to the victims' families. In one case, the man had been elderly, living with his son's family, and no longer able to contribute substantially to its income. His *wergeld* was determined to be no more than two sheep and three lengths of woolen cloth. The second victim had been a wealthy farmer and Viking, the head of a large household, the husband of two wives. The panel of judges considered a long time before announcing that his *wergeld* was a large amount of silver, several sheep and cows, plus two thralls, a male and a female. It was just, and yet I wept for the family of the murderer. They were poor, and to meet the *wergeld,* two of its own members, a handsome brother and sister, had to serve as thralls. A second sister, also young and beautiful, would be sold into slavery to provide the silver. I could not argue with Thing law that said the victim's family had to be recompensed for their loss, but it did seem a pity that the murderers' families were also innocent victims of the crimes.

During these proceedings, I had seen a young man and woman standing to one side. They had not moved from their spot the entire time, and I suddenly realized they were tied to the tree under which they stood. I had seen fear often enough to recognize it when I looked at their eyes. Rorik had come to sit by me, and I turned to ask him if he knew about them. Before he could answer, they were directed to appear before the judges.

The two—each married to another—were accused of adultery. Having been caught together, they had no defense, and judgment was swift. They clung together during the short trial, making no attempt to hide their love for each other. Weeping and sobbing hysterically, the young woman was forcibly removed from the arms of her lover and led off to be sold into slavery. In her face I saw the face of Thyri, and I wept, too. With the help of fair weather and the gods, she and Adair should be well on their way to freedom. If it had not been for Rorik's generosity—yes, and his love for me—they might be standing in judgment before the Thing.

"Will he, too, be sold?" I whispered to Rorik.

"No, though the penalty for an adulterous woman never varies, the man has a choice—death by beheading or being whipped with the lashes."

The young man chose the whipping.

" 'Tis sorry he will be," Rorik said.

"Why?" I had felt a certain relief when he chose the lashes. "At least he'll not be dead."

"Yes, he will. Few men can endure the lashes and live. Worse, it will be a slow, painful death. The whip is made of five leather thongs, and on the end of each is a sharp, pointed stone. His body will be as torn to pieces as if he'd been set upon by wolves. Even if he lives, he'll be maimed for life, many of his muscles completely destroyed."

"You are a good man, Rorik." I hugged his arm.

"What makes you say that now?" he laughed.

"I was thinking of Thyri and Adair."

"Yes. I loved my brother, Tara, though I often fought him. I had to let him go. I knew it would someday come to this. More than that, it was what you wanted. I knew of the plans you and Thyri had made and of the map Astrid had drawn for Adair."

"And yet you said nothing." I was amazed at Rorik's calm selfless restraint. There were so many ways he could have used that knowledge to make our lives miserable or to destroy us. He could have prevented their going. He could have held it as a threat over my head to force me to do anything he wanted, or he could have won me back with a show of great compassion and sympathy for Thyri and Adair by agreeing to let them go. Yet he said nothing. He was willing to wait and let things work themselves out in their own good time.

"I would rather love than hate, Tara."

"Thank you, Rorik." Flushed with especially warm and tender feelings for him, I found myself becoming less and less sorry each day that I had been captured by him and brought to this strange land.

Discussion at the evening meal dwelt not on what had already occurred, but what would take place the next day —the election of the king. All the men being supported for the position were strong, powerful, and experienced. It would be a close election.

"Does Thorne want to be king?" I asked Rorik when his father had left us to join his comrades.

"I don't know. I think he appreciates the honor of being considered, but I have never known him to seek power for the sake of power itself."

"Will he have a strong following if he is elected, or will his enemies unite against him?"

"Whoever is elected will have the allegiance of all the shires. You ask if he wants to be? That is not important. What is, is that he is the right one."

"How soon will we know?"

"Before the day is over tomorrow. If you'll not mind, I'm going to wander among the other camps to see what the feeling is. Do not worry if I'm gone all night."

He kissed me long and ardently, reluctant to leave but

139

aware that the political business of the night was more important at that moment than his desire for me.

Soon after he left, Signe and Eirik awoke with lusty cries. While Eirik, always the more patient of the two, sucked on a sweet-tit, a rolled-up piece of linen dipped in honey, I nursed Signe. Once fed, she fell asleep, and then it was his turn. I looked at the two children, both mine and yet so different. Signe's hair was silvery blond like mine, yet it clung to her head in curls like her father's. Eirik's straight hair was reddish gold like Rorik's. Signe's demands had to be met immediately, whereas Eirik could be calmed by a little petting or rocking. My daughter could already get what she wanted by opening her big blue eyes, while her brother won everyone's heart with his dimples. Almost identical in size, they were healthy, plump babies. The miracle of having produced them still held me enthralled.

I had scarcely fallen asleep when I heard Rorik returning.

"I thought you were going around to all the camps," I said. "To see how the other men felt about Thorne."

"I did, and the outcome is all decided. They have agreed to name Thorne by acclamation." Even in the near-dark I could see the broad grin spreading over his face.

"By acclamation! Oh, Rorik, that truly is wonderful." His excitement became mine.

"King, Tara! You know what that means? He will be the first to rule over this whole united territory—over Hordaland, Sogn, and the Fjords."

"I can't believe it. There need be no election, no bitter feelings."

"He still has to be presented to the free men; and they, as you know, have the final decision. But unless they violently disagree with their jarls, they will approve."

We sat there with our arms around each other, savoring the victory of the moment.

"Rorik."

"Yes, love?"

"There is something I do not understand. Knowing your father might be elected king, why did Ruskil go Viking instead of coming to the Gulathing? I should think he would want to be present when Thorne was so honored."

"That's why he is not here," Rorik said bitterly. "Ruskil is ambitious. I think he stayed away on purpose, just so he wouldn't have to swear fealty to our father. Ruskil is his own man, and he doesn't want to owe allegiance to anyone."

"But his father!" I was shocked. As much as I disliked and distrusted Ruskil, I found it hard to believe this of him.

"No less his own father. I told you, he is ambitious. He wants to be king, and not over just three shires. I think he is doing two things that worry me—hoarding some of the wealth he brings back from Viking instead of depositing it all in the family coffers, and secretly acquiring a group of followers who will come out of hiding when he gives the word."

"He'd not lead an uprising against Thorne?"

"He would challenge Thor himself if he thought to succeed. Do not underestimate Ruskil. He will do anything to advance his position. Why do you think he married Helga?"

"I assumed because he loved her—or at least wanted her."

"He could have tumbled her in the hay anytime he desired. You've seen how she dotes on him and how easily he got her. No, it was not her body he was after. Nina and Andrea have given him only daughters. He wants a son. 'Tis certain I am that Helga feeds his insatiable appetite; more to the point, there is a chance she will give him an heir."

"But why, Rorik? What is it he wants that he has not already? He's a leader of men, a powerful Viking. He has wives who adore him. Someday he will inherit part of your father's estates and be a jarl in his own right."

"There is the problem. He doesn't want *part* of the land or be *a* jarl. He covets all of the land, and he yearns to be the ruler of the three shires and eventually all of Norvegia. I told you, he is an ambitious man. He craves power the way a starving wolf craves human flesh. And he would use it the same way, gouging and devouring those to whom he should stand for protection and sustenance."

"I cannot understand it. You're his brother, and you do not feel that way. Why is he so different?" Then I paused. A sudden deathly chill went through me as I became aware of something. "Thorne is not the only threat to Ruskil's ambitions. As the eldest son, you are, too. Thorne will not live forever, and Ruskil might be willing to wait if he could be assured of taking his place. You are the one who is really in danger."

"Don't worry. I know, too, and I can take care of myself."

Now I was beset by new fears. There was nothing I could do to protect Rorik. I would not have an easy moment anytime he was away from the house, and when he went Viking . . . I would have to watch him sail away while filled with dread that Ruskil and his men would choose to attack at sea.

"I cannot help but be frightened," I said. "It means never feeling secure as long as Ruskil or one of his henchmen is around."

"There, there, 'tis not something to worry about every minute. Remember, I have strong and faithful men around me at all times, too. Now go back to sleep. Tomorrow will be a long and exciting day."

In the morning a restless crowd of free men awaited the election for which most had come to the Gulathing.

Finally a senior jarl stood up. All fell silent almost instantly. Briefly he stated that the jarls had deliberated long and earnestly before concurring that Thorne should be proclaimed king of the united shires. The announcement was received with a confusion of noises such as I had never heard before. Every free man grasped his spear and banged it long and violently against his shield. At the same time they shouted with such fervor their voices reverberated throughout the surrounding hills.

"They approve! They approve!" Rorik was screaming along with all the rest.

The men continued to yell and applaud with their spears until Thorne stood up.

One at a time the jarls came forward to kneel and pledge fealty to Thorne. Rorik, as eldest son and newly acclaimed jarl, led those who accepted him as their liege lord. It was an impressive sight, all of the Vikings in their long pointed capes, heavily embroidered and fastened on one shoulder with large golden brooches. There was no crown or scepter, but Thorne needed none. His spear and *hlad* were enough. Tall in stature and strong of limb, he dominated the assemblage as if he had been born to be king. I could see the awe on the faces of all the free men

142

who witnessed the ceremony; to them he was already king.

As I observed the spectacle, I saw not Thorne standing there but Rorik. Someday he would be accepting their cheers. He would be a good king, and I would be proud to stand beside him as his queen. No, never would Ruskil usurp Rorik's position as heir to the crown if there were any power in me to prevent it. I thought of the elder Signe's last words before she died: "Remember the runes when the raven flies through fire and ice." Was Rorik the raven? And was Ruskil's burning passion for power and his cold, ruthless ambition the fire and ice? Up until now, I had read the runes for fun and to please Rorik or Thorne. Perhaps it was time to seek their wisdom with more serious intent.

When one of the elder jarls turned to the crowd and asked if they acknowledged Thorne as their new chief, they raised their spears three times and shouted his name each time. They quieted down only after Thorne held up his spear and indicated he wished to speak.

"I accept the charge you have laid on me today. With the help of Odin and Thor, we will become strong and mighty. Our power and wealth will increase each year."

I sat open-mouthed. I had never heard Thorne speak so eloquently. Laugh, yes, tell stories, scold his children, chat over the reading of the runes—all that I was familiar with. This was the first time I had seen him in his role as Jarl of Hordaland, now King of the Three Shires. He was an impressive figure of a man.

"More and more of our ships," he continued, "will sail forth across the seas, steering their dragon heads into the four winds. More lands will come under our control, lands not even discovered yet, but told us by the runes. Men of all nations will fear and respect us as they never have before. As your king, I now proclaim the unification of the Three Shires into a new nation!"

The thunderous din of rattling spears and shouting voices drowned out whatever else Thorne might have planned to say. One might have thought that Odin himself had ridden among them the way they greeted his words.

Now was the time for celebrating. First, however, there must be sacrifices to the gods and a visit by all to the local shrine, a magnificent fir tree laden with golden chains and precious pearls. Beneath its boughs were the usual cairns topped with statues of the gods. Thorne, now chief priest as well as king, offered the first sacrifice to Odin. I no longer cringed at participating in a pagan ceremony. Somehow it all seemed a part of me now.

The evening proceeded with feasting, dancing, singing, and drinking. As wife of a new jarl who was also son of the king, I found myself constantly circling from the arms of one man to another, both jarls and free men. Such gaiety made all equal and all wildly exuberant. Just when I thought I would collapse, I found myself looking up into the laughing face of Rorik.

"Hold me tight," I gasped. "I think I'm about to fall over."

"And 'tis the only reason you want me to hold you?"

"For the moment, yes. A little later, another one."

"Do you want some wine?" Rorik asked. "You look flushed."

"I don't know. I think I have had enough already. You look a little tipsy yourself."

"'Tis not surprising. I have toasted my father with everything from crude horns to silver goblets and plenty of large flagons in between."

"And been toasted yourself, according to all the cheers I heard. If you come closer, I shall toast you myself in my very own fashion." I kissed him long and ardently.

"Is that a toast or an invitation?" he grinned.

"A little of both. To let you know how proud I am of you and how much I love you. Oh, I am glad you didn't go Viking this summer. You might have raided another abbey or scuttled a ship with a lovely captive aboard who would charm you onto her pallet."

"Never, Tara," he answered quietly. "My love is yours alone. 'Twill never belong to anyone else. And now, little Seabird, shall we retire to our pallet. I'm not sure how much longer my legs are going to hold me up."

Laughing and tripping over nothing, we made our way toward the shelter and fell on the eiderdown. Whatever plans we might have had for continuing the celebration in our own private way, we both fell sound asleep without moving from where we lay.

Chapter Ten

ONCE WE WERE BACK ON THE FARM, life returned somewhat to normal except for the ever-increasing number of visitors who came to consult with Thorne about affairs in the Three Shires over which he now ruled. Rorik, as a new jarl, also had his share of those who wanted to plead a cause, petition for aid, or request him to intercede in personal disputes. Our great hall became more and more an audience chamber during the day and a convivial meeting place at night. I worked hard with the other women, feeding all the two gregarious men invited to share our hospitality and trying to keep the children out of the way. By the end of each day we were exhausted.

To accommodate the needs of his family, Thorne was finally forced to erect a second large *skaalen* at right angles to the long hall. Haki and other wood-carvers in town were put to work building tables and chairs for the new wing, and Thorne gave me the delightful task of purchasing more tableware and cookware.

Burdened with a small leather pouch of gold, I set out for the village. Laughing at my enthusiasm, Rorik had earlier cautioned me not to spend it all in one place, and then told me to pick out something special just for myself.

"Any little trinket you see, Tara, that you really want. As wife of a new jarl, you deserve a gift. So make it something pretty."

I rode in the small carved cart that had first carried me through the strange town and to my even stranger new home. Nels, a recently acquired thrall, held the reins. Like Astrid, he had come from lands far to the north and east. He seemed to bear no grudge against Thorne, who was a good master, and his work load with the horses was lighter than had been his tasks as a serf on a large farm. Placid at all times, Nels accepted his lot as one ordained by the gods, and with them he would not quarrel.

145

Never having had so much gold to spend at one time, I was apprehensive. I wanted very much to please Thorne by using the gold wisely, yet I feared he would think me extravagant if I purchased all the things I knew we really needed. I had spent two days making a very thorough inventory of the kitchen and eating utensils so as not to be spendthrift in my buying. While riding along, I again looked into the pouch of gold, and I assured myself that if Thorne had given all that to me, he meant for me to spend it.

I went first to the silversmiths to order platters, bowls, and spoons. Next, I walked to the dusky, smoky shop of the bronzemaker who stood humped over his blazing fire. Surrounded by artisans who shaped and decorated cauldrons of all sizes, he supervised their work with a keen eye and sharp tongue. I selected a few cauldrons and ordered more.

The walls of the new hall were still bare, and I wanted at least one large *tiald* or tapestry to decorate the wall opposite the sleeping ledges. The weaver usually worked only on special orders for pieces too large to be made by women on their own looms, but I hoped he might have one he had done with the idea of selling it. His hands were permanently dyed dark red and blue from the pigments he worked with every day. Sven greeted me and listened to my request. Yes, he had such a tapestry, but it was very large and very valuable. It was one his father had started before him, and on which he himself had worked for many years. It was a true labor of love, for he had no idea anyone would ever purchase it.

I gasped when Sven led me into a back room lighted only by sconces on the wall and the torch he carried in his hand. There it was, just what I was looking for. At least seven feet high and more than twice as long, the brilliantly colored *tiald* depicted the various acts and agonies of Odin in aiding, restraining, and chastizing mankind. He was at the well, removing his eye and giving it to Mimir in exchange for wisdom. Next he was riding Sleipner, his eightfooted steed, and brandishing Gungner, his great spear. In another scene he was hanging on the mysterious tree for nine days, suffering great pain in order to learn the secret of the runes so that he might pass it on to man. Then, in brilliant colors, he was depicted holding aloft the sacred runes, hunting the forests, sitting with his wolves at his feet and the ravens of Memory and Thought on his shoulders, and, finally, standing in the middle of a battle-field, his great blue cape billowing in the wind as he directed the Valkyries to carry away the slain warriors to Valhalla.

The cost of the tapestry was high, but I had to have it. It would hang in the old *skaalen,* dominating the entire room, a worthy backdrop for Thorne. The tapestry it replaced could be moved to the new room. Once I paid out the gold for it, instructing the weaver to deliver it as soon as possible, I had very little left. I began worrying again that Thorne had given me more than he really meant to spend. Most of the trading was done by barter, and both gold nuggets or the foreign coins captured in raids were used sparingly for outright purchases. But Rorik had said I was to get something for myself, and my feminine love for pretty things urged me on toward the goldsmith.

There were so many pieces of beautiful jewelry—torques, bracelets, neck chains, hair ornaments, buckles—I lingered over them until Nels slipped inside the shop to remind me it was getting late. Wistfully I looked again at a magnificent gold brooch set with amethysts. I knew I did not have enough in the pouch to buy it. Then I thought of the brooch on the cape I was wearing. Simple in design, it was nevertheless large and heavy. Unpinning it, I handed it to the goldsmith. He scrutinized it carefully and weighed it in his hand. Finally he nodded. Next to my pearls, the gold and amethyst brooch would be the most valuable piece of jewelry I possessed.

Fortunately Thorne and Rorik had gone on a tour of Hordaland to consult with the local jarls and would be away for several days. Plenty of time for the *tiald* to be delivered and hung in place. It took the combined efforts of several serfs and my careful instructions to get it positioned just right, but finally I was satisfied. Now the long *skaalen* looked like the reception room of a great king. Just wait, I thought, until the two new massive, heavily carved chairs arrived, along with the carpet imported from Byzantium I had found irresistible the moment I saw it at the rug merchant's. If Thorne were to be a real king, he had to have a throne room.

All was ready and in place by the day the two were expected back. I stood at the door eagerly awaiting them and yet dreading what they might say. I'd not slept the night before, and my stomach churned with apprehension.

Finally they rode up, and instead of rushing out to greet Rorik, I stood inside the room with the twins in my arms.

"By all the gods in Asgaard!" Rorik exclaimed before he even saw me. "Look what we have here. The mighty Odin himself to make us ponder well before we speak out."

"Oh, ho!" Thorne shouted, following him in. "I do believe our Tara would have us rival her kings of Britain in elegance and grandeur."

Quickly I handed the twins to Astrid and took from her hands the hot towels and bowl of warm water she had been holding. Meekly, like an obedient wife, I moved from my father-in-law to my husband.

"And a carpet at our feet. Do we dare trod on it, sire, or do we remove our boots?" Rorik pulled his off and then tiptoed around the edge.

"You do approve, do you not?" I asked hesitantly.

"How much gold did you part with?" Rorik asked.

"Gold, faugh!" Thorne grabbed me around the waist, almost spilling the water I still held. "There is always more of that. Indeed we do approve, my girl. This should impress the jarls from Sogn and the Fjords when they come for a meeting soon. You know, you almost persuade me to order myself a crown from the goldsmith's."

"Be careful, sire," Rorik cautioned. "Remember what the gods do to those who acquire too much pride in their power."

"A little luxury has nothing to do with power. We needed more beauty around here, and Tara has supplied it for us. I am pleased, so we shall say no more about it."

Still Rorik had not indicated he approved of my selections. Yet somehow I knew he was not displeased at the thought I had put into them. He walked over and put his arms around me.

"Miss me?" he asked.

"I did. I missed you very much." Then I smiled up at him. "But I'm glad you did not return any sooner. 'Twould have spoiled my surprise." Maybe now he would say something encouraging about what I had done.

"You had fun doing all this?"

"Oh, yes, Rorik. I saw the *tiald* and then I just could

148

not stop." If he were going to scold, even after what his father said, let him go ahead and do it now.

" 'Tis uncanny," he said thoughtfully, almost as if I were not there. "I have always wanted that tapestry. I have coveted it since I was a little boy and watched Sven weaving it. Every time we rode into town, I went into his shop and stood in awe for hours at the different figures of Odin."

I was puzzled. "But you seemed upset at my getting it."

"No, I just couldn't believe I was actually seeing it hanging on my own wall. Have you ever wanted anything so badly, over a long period of time, that you really began to think of it as your own?"

"No, but I think I know what you mean."

Rorik had thrown back his cape so he could draw me close into his arms. He began nibbling my ear, and then suddenly he let out a shout.

"What is it, love?" I backed away.

"Something scratched me, here on my chest. Look, 'tis bleeding."

"Oh, no! It must have been this." I showed him my new brooch.

"Where did you get that?" I could not tell from his tone whether he was angry or just merely surprised.

"You said to find some little thing I like for myself," I said hesitantly, fearful of an outburst like that when he first came in the door and saw the changes I had made.

"And you call that some little thing?" Now I knew he was really angry with me, and I wished I had not given in so easily to temptation. I couldn't bear it if he made me return it.

" 'Tis beautiful, is it not? I used some of the gold, but I also traded my old one for it," I said, trying to appease him. "Please say you like it."

Then he smiled and my heart beat faster, as it always did when he looked at me thus. " 'Tis magnificent, my little frost maiden, and you deserve it. Now, unpin it so I'll not be stabbed when I kiss you. Or shall we go to our room where there will be nothing to keep me from making love to you."

In addition to the new *skaalen*, stables and a lodge with sleeping facilities were constructed some distance from the main house to quarter the *hird*, the bodyguard or retinue now deemed necessary for Thorne—a perquisite of kingship. Rough, crude, and fiercely loyal, the hirdmen came from all three shires. Some were professional warriors, their outfitting and upkeep contributed by free men. According to Thing-law, every two or three families of free men had to send or support a fighter for the service of the chieftain, be he jarl or king. From poorer families came sons for a term of service; from more affluent free men came the wealth to pay a professional.

Surprisingly enough, there were also men of rank and wealth who found excitement in serving a strong leader. They were the nucleus of his army and they executed his official orders. All of them preferred fighting to more peaceful pursuits, such as collecting tribute and levies from foreign vessels, merchants, and proprietors, but these activities brought their rewards in a percentage of whatever was garnered.

As soon as all the buildings were completed, and the hird were settled in with their horses and thralls, Thorne bid us prepare a feast to celebrate his new title and honor his followers. The women of the family, dressed in their finest gowns and wearing all their jewels, were to serve the men.

A more festive evening I have never seen. The hirdmen, too, came garbed in all their finery—silk-ribbon *hlads*, gold armbands and buckles, and richly embroidered capes. Tables were set up along the four sides of the hall. Tall ewers filled with wine as well as pitchers of mead were lined up before the men, who drank from polished horns and silver goblets. The other wives and I carried in tray after tray of boiled beef, mutton, lamb, and fish; dishes heaped high with cooked cabbage, root vegetables, fresh fruits; and always the large, round loaves of rye bread. I thought I had seen trenchermen at my father's table, but never such as these.

While the men ate, the open area in the center of the *skaalen* became a stage for the entertainment Thorne provided—minstrels, skalds, acrobats, and jugglers. The festivities lasted all night, the men loudly applauding and toasting each new act, but the high point of the celebration was the distribution of gifts by Thorne. He gave each hirdman a sword with engraved hilt, a shield, a tooled leather battle harness, a pair of armbands, and a sable-trimmed cloak. To one man, who had endangered his own

150

life to save Thorne from an outlaw ambush on the last ride-about, was given an axe inlaid with silver. Then Rorik arose and presented the man with a pair of silver armbands.

Until that moment I had known nothing about the ambush, and now I was frightened, especially after what Rorik had said about Ruskil's ambitions. The ambush might have been one by simple outlaws, easily frightened away by a troop of hirdmen, or it might have been a well-armed group of Ruskil's hired assassins. Now each time Rorik set forth among his people, I would remain fearful until his return.

Sometime in the early morning, it was suggested that I and the other wives might like to retire. The drinking had continued unabated throughout the evening, and now the jokes and songs were cruder and more vulgar. Those, however, were not the main reasons for our being summarily excused. The men were becoming restless, and it was time for the slave girls to be brought in. Some belonged to the hirdmen themselves. Others were provided by Thorne, who knew the wisdom of keeping his retinue happy by meeting all needs.

As I left the hall, I gave Rorik a hard, meaningful glance. Morning had better find him bedded down next to me, not on the rushes on the floor or in one of the sleeping compartments. When he grinned and winked at me, I knew he understood. Sometime in the middle of the morning, he stumbled into our room, muttered, "She was tempting, but I resisted," fell across the bed, and immediately began snoring. Well, I thought, any man, drunk or sober, who is a real man will be tempted. I pulled off his boots and tunic, kissed his frowsy hair, and left him to sleep it off.

All had been going too smoothly, and I had that heavy feeling one gets just before a storm breaks. Thorne and Rorik were away for several days at a time, and Ruskil had not returned from Viking. It was nearly two months until the autumnal equinox, and the men would stay out as long as possible. With no men around the house most of the time, the wives of Thorne and Ruskil began bickering constantly at the slightest provocation, and I found myself waiting for one of them to do something crazy or for a physical skirmish to break out. Except for necessary tasks, I stayed out of the long hall.

One afternoon I went into the byre to see the lambs born in the spring. I never tired of letting their wet noses nuzzle my palms for an extra bit of feed or feeling their rough tongues as they licked up the last bit of grain. I heard a strange noise coming from the adjacent barn. I listened intently, and thought it sounded like giggling. If two of the serfs were tumbling in the hay, it was really no concern of mine, except they could be whipped if caught away from their assigned tasks. Perhaps if I just opened and shut the door, to let them know someone was nearby, they would leave and hurry back to work. The door opened farther than I'd intended, and as I leaned in to close it, I heard a familiar voice and saw two heads rise up out of the hayloft.

"Oh, no!" Helga shrieked and burrowed back down in the hay. " 'Tis Rorik's wife," I heard her mumble. "Let me go, you fool."

At first I was too stunned to move. Then I waited, curious to hear what Helga would say. I had also recognized her lover, the young serf Raghild who had cavorted with at the spring festival. Helga was right. He was a fool, and he would be a dead fool if he didn't watch his step.

Helga climbed down out of the loft, still fastening the buckles on her dress. Her face was ashen and her hands trembled. Her body was already heavy with the child Ruskil hoped would be a boy.

"What—what are you going to do, Tara?"

It was no business of mine, and I had no intention of getting involved with Ruskil and his temper.

"Why should I do anything?"

"You saw us together, and I am wife to Ruskil."

"A pity," I said. "I pity you for acting so stupidly. You might have been found by someone else. You know the penalty for adultery."

"Yes, death or slavery." She began to weep. "But, oh, Tara, Ruskil has been away too long, and I cannot live without a man. Even when he be at home, he—he comes not near me. Not since he learned I was to bear his child. 'Tis all he wanted me for, to give him a son. He used me for his own purpose and then tossed me aside."

I knew not whether to despise her or feel sorry for her.

"Please, Helga, you should not be telling me this."

"No," she stormed, the tears still running down her cheeks, "you are so high and mighty and so beautiful you were able to force Rorik to get rid of his other wives. What kind of woman are you that you could get along without him all those months? You must be made of ice. I bet you freeze his spear when he pierces you with it. 'Tis the only way he can keep it hard."

I had started with pity, now I was roused to fury by her remarks. She had no right to speak to me in that way.

"Be careful, Helga. I said I'd not reveal what I saw here. But I could change my mind."

"No, no! 'Tis sorry I am. But I get so wrought up. I can't go on without the touch of a man to calm me down."

Well, I thought, there's no sense in getting angry at her stupidity. She was speaking to me out of desperation.

"Be calm, your secret is safe with me. I could not be the one to condemn you to slavery. But you tread on thin ice, and someone else may come along and pull you under."

"I know, I know," she sobbed. "I shall be more careful."

She had not said she would stop meeting the serf, but I was not the keeper of her morals. I had enough disturbing thoughts of my own to keep me occupied. Rorik and Thorne had been gone longer than planned this time, and I could not rid my mind of the ambush they had barely escaped on their earlier trek.

Chapter Eleven

EARLY THE NEXT AFTERNOON, the men rode up, and I was relieved to learn my fears had been for naught. I was not to be consoled for long, however. As I lay in his arms that night, Rorik told me he was going Viking after all.

With that I broke down and wept. All the tension of the days without him had brought me to the breaking point. He was trying to calm me, but nothing he said could soothe the new fears his going to sea had created.

"But, 'tis only a short voyage, my love. A group of renegades are marauding along the coast to the north. Some of us are going after them, determined to scuttle their ships. To go Viking for your jarl is one thing; to roam the seas as a freebooter brings disgrace and is worse than being a thief or murderer. They are attacking the ships of the other shires that Thorne is now sworn to protect."

I was so upset I became sarcastic instead of listening to him like an understanding wife. "So there is honor among the ravagers of the seas."

"Indeed there is, Seabird. Vikings are not pirates."

Now I exploded with bitterness to cover my real feelings. "They only act that way at times!"

"You do delight in baiting me, don't you?" His soft voice made me feel ashamed of myself, and I could not stay angry long.

"Yes," I said more quietly, "because when I first met you, you were a very wicked man."

"And am I so different now?"

"No, I think I am the one who has changed. Toward you, at least."

Rorik smiled down at me. "I remember the vow you made when I captured you. To go back someday and avenge the destruction on the abbey."

"Nor have I forgotten, but 'tis not your men on whom I

seek vengeance. They did wrong, and I cannot forgive those who killed. No, it is the Britons who betrayed us I shall seek out. 'Twas their lust for gold that brought about the rapine destruction."

"So you still hope to return someday?"

"Not to stay, Rorik, but to carry out my vow and see the abbey and my family. Will you promise me that?"

If he agreed, I would have something to look forward to, something to help subdue my fears while he was gone.

"I promise. I cannot say how soon, but I do give you my word."

" 'Tis enough. How long will you be gone this time?"

"No more than a month, nor will we ever be far from this coast. I think the renegades work out from one of the fjords, sweeping down on single ships a lookout spots for them. They may also be raiding the north coast of Britain; but if so, we will lie in wait for their return."

In spite of my resolve the fears returned, and I wrapped his arms tighter around me. I could not bear the thought of losing him after these few weeks of newfound happiness. "I'm frightened. 'Twill be dangerous."

"Not with so many of us. Remember, the *Raven* always brings me home."

"Yes, but alive or dead this time?"

"Very much alive, I assure you. Do not forget: I have someone special to come home to."

"I shall be very lonely. More so even than when you and Thorne go counseling with the jarls. At least then I know you will be home in a few nights."

"The weeks will pass quickly, Seabird." He kissed the tip of my nose and held me close against his chest. "We shall be back before the first day of autumn, and then you and I will spend the long winter evenings doing nothing but what we want."

"Like now?"

"Like now." And once more I was swept up into the sublime ecstasy of making love with him.

Watching Rorik sail away on the *Raven*, I was overcome with a dreadful foreboding. The runes had not forecast danger to him on the ship, but I could not dispel the fear that took hold of me when I no longer made out his figure on the deck. Once home, I cast the runes again, to see if there was evil coming upon the house, but for some reason they did not speak to me. Upset, I threw them to one side and tried to convince myself it was all just foolish superstition anyway.

With Rorik gone, I had too much time on my hands. I began taking long walks through the surrounding meadows, sometimes as far as the nearby forest through which ran the small stream fed by the spring in the sacred grove. The water was clear and cool, with a tangy, refreshing taste from the mint and thyme growing along its banks. I frequently lay on the soft bed of pine needles and napped. More often, I took off my shoes and waded in the stream or lay on my stomach and watched the leaf boats floating lazily by on their way to the river and thence to the fjord.

Sometimes after wading in the water, roiling up the pebbles and sand from the bottom and causing little whirlpools where I walked, I watched it return to its normal, placid, clear flow. Nothing had been changed by my presence. Or had it? Maybe a pebble, lying for years in the same spot, had been dislodged and was now being carried down to the sea by the stream. Here and there underwater flora had been disturbed, bent down by my feet. Was a person the same way? On the surface appearing unaltered, moving along as always, with no apparent difference in character, but underneath changing from day to day because of encounters with people and events?

With the weather consistently warm and sunny, Astrid and I frequently took Asri and the twins into the meadows or the woods. While the twins lay on their pallet, and Asri picked flowers or played with the babies, she and I talked for hours about how completely different our lives had been before we both found ourselves brought to Hordaland as captives. She had become the friend I hoped she would when I first saw her, and I never thought of her as a slave. As with Nels, Astrid's life as a slave was far less onerous than it would have been on her father's—or a husband's—farm. But unlike him, she missed her family and dreamed of the day she could return home. I had often been tempted to tell her she was free, no longer a slave, and then try to find a way for her to get back to Norrland. But, though she was my servant, she belonged to Thorne, and I hesitated to request he free her. I had to confess, too, I knew not what I would do without her. When Signe and Eirik were older, I would think about it more seriously.

Ofttimes at night, after the children were fed and bedded down, I felt restless and found it impossible to sleep. It was then I wrapped a light cloak around my shoulders and left the house. Some distance from the barn was a stone wall, low enough for me to sit on and swing my feet while I breathed in the cool night air. After a spell at this, I felt somewhat eased. Already the days were becoming noticeably shorter, and the moon was more clearly visible in the dark blue sky.

I thought of Rorik on the dragon ship and wondered if he were at the tiller, steering by the same stars I was now trying to recognize from the lessons he had given me. Was he looking at the moon, too, and thinking of me? I hoped he would return soon. Not only was I lonely for him, but I worried lest the few renegade ships they were hoping to scuttle turned out to be a large flotilla, well manned and strongly armed. The renegades, secluded in the coves in the northern fjords, had the advantage of being able to remain hidden or attack suddenly, whichever would assure their not being captured. I was less concerned with Rorik's putting an end to the pirates' ravages than I was with his coming home safely to me.

Ruskil returned from Viking earlier than expected, and in a demonic mood. His voyage had been something less than successful, with nothing to show for his months at sea. I thought about Rorik's suspicions—that Ruskil was hoarding much of the loot he garnered. Was his hangdog look a mask to cover glee at having kept it all for himself this time? Yet, there was a kind of fear in his voice, as if he had barely escaped capture, possibly by the very renegades Rorik was seeking out. But he made no mention of this.

I waited expectantly for an outburst of some kind when he learned Thorne had been elected king, but he was ever the dutiful son, seemingly proud of his father's newly acquired honor.

I watched Helga's face for any sign she was once more content now that her husband was home, but her features told only of fear and longing. Ruskil's other wives were always in a surly mood and stayed off to themselves. Usually bickering, they were still intimate allies, choosing to remain apart from the rest of the family when their household chores were completed.

Knowing that autumn, with its chill winds and blustery

days, would soon be upon us, I enjoyed every opportunity to walk in the woods and delight in the late-blooming wild flowers. Soon Rorik would return, the cattle would be brought down from the upper meadows, and winter would close in, enveloping us with its hoary breath and deep snows. This winter Rorik and I would be spending the long hours together; I looked forward to sitting around the fire.

One afternoon I wandered deeper into the forest than usual. I was not afraid of losing my way, because I followed the stream away from the sacred spring, to where it widened and then branched into two rivulets. Here the air was particularly redolent of pine, mint, and horehaune. The breeze carried a multitude of sounds: birds singing, small animals skittering through the pine straw, foxes barking, and the crackling of dead branches. The last made me stop. Only a large animal would snap the twigs that way—a boar or a wolf. I walked on. The crackling continued, but when I stopped, so did it. I knew then that some person, not an animal, was following me.

As always I had my scissors and small knife hanging from the chains around my neck, but they would be of little value if someone intended to harm me. Strangers were few in our parts, and someone friendly to the family crossing our land would have called out and identified himself. It could be an outlaw serf making his way to the fjord, and I would be in real danger.

I knew I had to remain alert and at the same time find a hiding place of some kind. First I took refuge under a large tree with limbs hanging so close to the ground that I thought I could conceal myself behind them. Then I decided to climb it and hide among the leafy branches. From there I could see what approached from all directions while being screened from view.

In spite of the long skirts that impeded my progress, I made it to higher branches and settled myself comfortably with my back against the trunk. For a few minutes I thought I had been mistaken. Then the crackling sounds resumed, and I waited breathlessly as it came closer and closer.

I almost fell out of the tree when I saw Ruskil approaching, ambling along with casual, easy strides. He stopped, bent over to scoop up a handful of water, and then sat down among the roots of my tree. Although he was boorish, vulgar, and uncouth, I had never felt personally threatened by Ruskil; I just did not like him. Yet something about the way he had been following me without identifying himself cautioned me to beware. I held my breath, praying he had not seen me climb into the tree. If only he'd go away. I could hardly stay there all afternoon and night. It was not to be. A leaf brushed my face, and when I tried to stifle a sneeze, he looked up at me and stared.

"Tara, what are you doing up there?" His leering grin told me that all along he'd been deliberately stalking me like a marauding animal seeking out its prey.

"Hiding." I had to cover my fear, to be as casual as possible. I might only be imagining a danger in being alone with him, but I wanted to get back home as quickly as possible. "I heard you in the woods and was afraid it was a wild animal."

Ruskil laughed, and I didn't like the sound of it. He lifted his arms to help me down, and I let him. I did not dare make him angry or let him know I was afraid of him.

"Yes," he nodded, once I was on my feet, "the woods can be dangerous for a young woman alone, especially one as attractive as you."

"I believe wolves and bears are more interested in the scent than the sight of their prey." I wanted to keep the conversation light. I brushed off my skirt and moved as if to walk back to the farm. I had no desire to linger alone with him. "Now that I have some protection, I think I should be returning."

"No need to hurry, Tara. 'Tis much too pleasant here in the woods—just the two of us, no one else around."

"Yes, 'tis peaceful. And so I come here often." His reference to our being alone alerted me that I had not been wrong in wanting to get away. Once again I started walking back toward the farm without seeming to be alarmed.

"I know," he said "I have seen you come this way. 'Tis why I followed you today."

"You followed me. Why?" I had to keep him talking, and try to speak with a casual curiosity, so he would not be alerted to how really afraid I was.

"Are you always this naive, Tara? Blind to my desire for you?"

Quickly I decided on another tack, to appeal to what

159

few morals he might have. "Ruskil, I am your brother's wife, and you have three wives who are eager to obey your every whim. I will forget what you just said if you never refer to it again and return immediately to the farm."

He moved closer and put both hands on my arms. I was sweating with fear and disgust.

"Oh, no, Tara. I've waited for this moment since Rorik first brought you home. I had already begun to tire of Nina and Andrea. So I married Helga, thinking she would satisfy the urge I had for you. She is a lusty wench, to be sure, but hardly able to stir a man's blood now."

I managed to shrug out of his grasp. "And you know, of course, I shall tell Rorik if you put your hands on me again." Only after I spoke, did I realize how dangerous was my statement. Seeing the fire in his eyes, I knew I should not have threatened him.

"I think not." Ruskil moved closer, backing me toward a tree and pinning me helplessly against it with one arm on each side. He was leering at me maliciously and licking his lips. "Not after you enjoy a roll on the grass with me. I can pleasure you in special ways my brother never thought about."

"Get away from me! Now!" I strained to keep the terror out of my voice. Although my legs felt so weak I could scarce stand and I was shaking all over, I tried to remain cool and firm.

He began caressing one breast, and unwittingly it swelled and responded to his touch.

"You like it, Tara," he said breathlessly. "You know you do. Rorik's been gone a while, and you must be hungry for the taste of a lively spear."

Fury at what he was suggesting gave me a new, stronger voice. "You disgust me, Ruskil. Put your arms down. I'm going now."

In two swift movements, Ruskil had a knife at my throat and his trousers loosened. He was ready to attack, and if I tried to resist, I would be dead instantly or, worse yet, left to bleed to death. When I was finally found, blame would be laid on an outlaw roaming the forests. Even if I submitted, I was still not out of danger. To avoid incurring the wrath of Rorik and the penalty for rape, Ruskil would still have to slay me. I was dead either way unless I could find some way to free myself from the clutches of this maddened animal. The knowledge I had little to lose gave me the courage to wait for the most propitious moment, and fear was replaced by determination.

Ruskil had already lifted my skirts, and his hot body was pressing against mine. He was panting, and the hand holding the knife was beginning to shake. I moved my hips restlessly, as if suddenly eager to consummate the seduction. I could knee him in the groin or fall to the ground; but I still felt the cold steel of the knife blade against my skin, and I knew he would slash my throat before I succeeded in doing either one. Somehow I had to get him away from me, far enough away that I could run before he knew what had happened.

The very second that Ruskil was most vulnerable, I would have to move quickly or miss my opportunity. Moaning hungrily and begging him to hurry, I bent to one side so that a hank of my hair fell between the knife blade and my skin. I then lurched forward. Too wrought up to realize what I was doing, Ruskil was caught off balance and fell to the ground, hitting his head on a gnarled root of the tree.

Having him unconscious was more than I hoped for, but I wasted no time in taking off for the farm. Not until I reached my room did I realize how shaken I was by the experience. When Astrid greeted me, my legs gave way and I began to sob hysterically.

"Are you all right, my lady?"

Still choking with fear, I could hardly speak. "Yes—no. I've had a most terrifying encounter."

"I help you to the bed. Lie down. I remove your gown. 'Tis all covered with dirt."

Between sobs, I told her of Ruskil's attack. Her horror at what he had dared was as great as mine had been, and she wanted to go right to Thorne.

"Please, Astrid," I said, "say naught to anyone about this. I do not want them to know."

"I think the jarl should know, but if it is your wish, I will say nothing." She covered me with a light eiderdown and gradually I became calmer.

"Remember," I cautioned again, "this must remain between the two of us." I did not want her blurting it out to Rorik when he returned.

"He is an evil man. You must take care."

"I will, Astrid. Oh, believe me, I will. No more walking in the woods or straying from sight of the house. Not until Rorik returns."

"You rest now. I get food. You eat in here."

"I do not intend to argue with you, Astrid. I've not the strength."

I ate a light supper of stew broth, crusty bread, and mild wine. Astrid explained my absence from the communal meal to the rest of the household by saying simply I was not feeling well.

For a few days Ruskil avoided me as much as he could in a household whose members all congregated at mealtimes. In spite of being surrounded by the family, I was not yet free from fear. I had eluded him once, but I might not be able to again. His own fear that I would reveal to Rorik what had happened made him doubly dangerous.

The earthen walls of the house and outbuildings deadened most sounds. However, there was no disguising the muffled screams I heard from inside the storehouse as I walked through the inner yard.

Concerned lest someone had been seriously hurt from a fall or some other mishap, I gave no thought to the idea my interference might not be wanted or that I was involving myself in something which was none of my affair.

In the middle of the storehouse, Ruskil stood over Helga, who was cowering on the grain-covered floor. From the blood on her face and shoulders, I knew he had more than once used the whip he held. The stable boy was huddled in a corner, one arm cradling the other, which hung at a bizarre angle from his shoulder. He was moaning, and his face was green with fright.

"You whore!" Ruskil shouted. "I knew you put the horns on me while I was at sea, but I could never prove it. I did not think you'd be fool enough to let me catch you. Get up!"

He grabbed her by one arm and hauled her, sobbing hysterically, to her feet.

"No, no, Ruskil. Not that. I swear!"

"No?" he asked with a sneer. "Playing chess, I suppose, on the floor behind the sacks? Or making the beast with two backs!"

"We—we were just talking." Helga was weeping so

162

hard she could scarcely get the words out. She was too frightened to think of what she was saying, and she had good reason to be.

"By Thor, don't lie to me! My eyes are not blind or clouded with love. I am going to see that whimpering fool over there dead. And sell you into slavery; just as soon as the child is born. If it be my child!" He twisted her arm behind her back so that she was forced to kneel at his feet.

"You know it is," she pleaded. "You know you were the first. You saw the signs."

"Oh, no. You women are clever. It could have been chicken blood."

"No, I swear, Ruskil. I lost my maidenhead to you."

"On the chance you speak the truth and the child is mine, I will be easy with you until after it is born. Then you become a slave."

All this time I stood there, an unwilling spectator, not daring to say a word. I should have left, but I could not. As much as I feared Ruskil—and as stupid as I thought Helga was—I had to stay around to be with her when he left. She was still a woman about to bear a child, and I did not know what his beatings might have done to her. I made myself as inconspicuous as possible, though I doubted anyone was aware of my presence.

"And my child?" she asked.

"You swear 'tis mine, so I keep it."

"No, please, Ruskil," she pleaded. "I'll not mind slavery. No one could be unkinder or—or less attentive than you. I may get a master who appreciates my favors and does not ignore me." She was sobbing harder now. "But my child! You cannot keep my baby."

"Stop whimpering. You make me sick. If it be a girl, you may take her with you. Your master will get two slaves for his gold. But—if it be a son, he stays here."

With that Ruskil strode out, giving orders to the head serf to tie up the stable boy until the time of his execution.

Helga collapsed on the floor, biting her fists and moaning.

"Get up, Helga," I said gently. "Come with me to my room. Astrid will bring you something to ease the pain of the lash."

She moaned again and then let out a low scream.

"What is it, Helga? If you can walk, I'll help you."

" 'Tis the baby," she moaned again.

"So soon?" It was not quite her time; the beatings had brought it dangerously early.

Helga nodded and stuffed her fist in her mouth to keep from screaming again. I hurriedly found two serfs who carried her to my room. Once there, I let Astrid take over, and I followed her instructions without question. Helga was built to have many children easily, and within two hours we delivered her of a fine, healthy son.

"A boy," she sighed, and I knew what she was thinking. Once she recovered, she would be sold, and she had to leave her baby with Ruskil.

"He is beautiful, Helga." I looked down at the boy nursing hungrily at her breast, and I remembered my own feelings just after Signe and Eirik were born.

She smiled down at her son, running her fingers across his cheeks and examining his sturdy body. "Maybe 'tis better this way. If I took him with me, he would never be anything but a slave. Here, he will someday be a jarl. And —and if I am not too far away, I can know what he is doing."

"Do not think of that, Helga," I tried to comfort her.

"I do not mind. And I really think I will be happier away from here."

"If you spoke to Thorne?"

"Only to be with my son, Tara. I would do anything to keep my son."

When Helga fell asleep, I went in search of Ruskil. As much as I feared him, I was too moved by Helga's plight to worry about any danger to me. I also thought my plan just might remove that danger.

I found Ruskil training a new horse, and from the fury with which he went about it, he was going to break either his neck or the mount's.

"Ruskil, you have a son."

I thought he would be elated, but he stared at me as sullenly as ever.

"How soon can Helga be sold?" he asked coldly.

"She is not leaving, Ruskil. She is staying here as your wife and mother to your son." I had finally gotten up the courage to hold a threat over his head.

"You are daring to tell me what to do?" His surprise at my words was evident, and there was shock more than fury behind his question.

"Yes, and you will never lay hands on her again. Do this for me, and Rorik will never hear about what happened in the forest."

"And if I do not agree?"

"You will be the one to feel the lash or the axe." Now that I had dared to take this step, I no longer felt afraid of him.

"You would do that, wouldn't you?"

I nodded.

"For a slut like Helga?" His lips curled in a sneer.

"She is a mother, Ruskil, and your wife. I shall expect you to remember that."

"How can I be sure you will keep your word?" His voice took on a menacing tone.

"Because I am an honorable person, and I expect you to be the same." I turned on my heel and walked away. I had no desire to stay and talk further with him.

Ruskil would never know I had done it for myself, not Helga. By removing from Ruskil the fear I would tell Rorik, I also removed any threat to me that Ruskil would have to get rid of me to prevent Rorik from finding out what had happened.

Helga wept and clung to me when I told her she was to stay. Life with Ruskil would be something less than tolerable, but she would not be separated from her son. The stable boy was to be sold, for disobeying orders and endangering the horses, so no one would ever know the truth.

"I—I know not what you said to Ruskil," she sobbed, "but I will never forget what you have done for me."

Neither of us knew at that point that soon there would be a way for her to repay my kindness.

Chapter Twelve

RORIK RETURNED IN A DESPONDENT MOOD, embittered over the inability of his ships to locate any of the renegades. Instead of gathering in the fjords, as anticipated, the pirates had evidently chosen to scatter and either head for a fastness in Britain or return to secondary home bases.

"No way to follow them," Rorik mumbled, "with all of the Northern Sea to get lost in."

"As you say, my love," I tried to console him, "the sea is huge, and you couldn't explore every fjord along the coast."

"Not a sign of them. 'Twas as if they had been forewarned by paid lookouts."

I thought of Ruskil's hasty return, his lack of booty, and his obvious relief that Rorik was at sea. I wondered whether to voice the nagging suspicion that he was one of them. Not just yet, I thought. Time enough for that when spring came and the men returned to sea.

"What do you plan to do now?"

"Nothing. With winter setting in, there will be no Viking for many months. We will bide our time until summer. Meanwhile, we will have lookouts of our own."

After the eventful summer—the exhilarating days of the Gulathing, Thorne's election, the problems with Ruskil, and Rorik's long absence—the placid winter routine was a welcome relief. Only a few of the hirdmen remained as an abbreviated retinue, the rest returning to their homes until spring. The cattle and sheep were brought down from the high meadows, and all buildings were again made ready for the onslaught of cold weather. As the nights grew longer, they also became quite festive, with the remaining hirdmen joining us around the fire for singing, dancing, story-telling, games of chess, and the inevitable gambling. Yes, it was placid, but not dull.

Before one of the trips to bring back cattle, Rorik asked if I would like to go along. This time he would merely make certain all was going well, and the ride should take no more than two days. The babies would be fine under the care of Astrid and the wet nurse.

We started out while it was yet dark, traveling eastward toward the rising sun. I wore trousers and boots under my gown so I could hoist up my skirts and sit astride. It would take many hours of hard riding if we were to reach the high meadows before dusk. We watched the sky ahead of us lighting up in long streaks of gray, pale lavender, and pink. Then suddenly we both stopped at once, to gaze in awe and wonder as the sun burst forth in a ball of flaming red above the jagged horizon. Its rays trapped the peaks of the mountains and set them on fire. It was magnificent and it was frightening.

"Oh, Rorik, is it always as beautiful as this?" These were the mountains he had talked of so often, and I could see why they inspired such love in him.

"No, nor as dangerous," he said quietly.

"What do you mean?" What was there about a sunrise to inspire the thought of danger?

"A sun rising red like that can mean trouble."

"Superstition or natural lore?" I thought perhaps the first, and yet I knew how much he depended on natural phenomena to guide him.

"Sailors' lore. It usually presages a storm, at least at sea. But the sky is clear. I see no storm clouds gathering. To be safe, though, we will make camp at the first of the upper meadows, and I will ride out from there. That way we will have a shorter road to travel home tomorrow."

Since he did not seem concerned enough to turn around right then, I cast all worries aside. He would not put me in danger.

We continued on as speedily as possible, crossing cold, narrow streams rushing and tumbling through the glens to the fjord. The horses were often forced to pick their way carefully among loose boulders dislodged from the mountainsides eons ago, when the giant Loki shook the earth. Finally, after stopping only briefly for a meal of cold meat, crusty bread, and water from a stream, we reached a spot Rorik thought would be an ideal campsite.

"I'll set up the shelter," he said while I stretched my cramped legs, "and get a fire started. I should be gone no

167

more than two hours. I just want to make certain the cattle and sheep are rounded up and ready to be moved down."

"And leave me here alone?" I shuddered at the thought of his being away even a few minutes after what he had said about the sunrise. Then I wished I had not complained. I was being foolishly, unnecessarily alarmed.

"You're too tired to ride farther, and you'll be perfectly safe," he assured me. "The herders are ranging all over this area, so have no fear. With all these animals to protect, the men keep all predators well away from the grazing lands. If you should hear or see anything to frighten you, just call out. The sound will echo for leagues, much farther, in fact, than I will be."

"If you say so." I laughed to show him I had gotten over my momentary fear. "But don't stay away too long."

"Keep busy arranging our pallets and cooking up something hot and tasty. I'll be back before 'tis ready."

Rorik kissed me teasingly on the tip of my nose and rode off. Of course it was foolish of me to be frightened, and I knew it. I only wished he'd not left quite so quickly; but the sooner gone, the sooner he'd be back. So I set to work as he suggested.

The shelter he put up was just sufficient to cover the two of us and had barely enough headroom for us to sit up. But it would certainly do for one night, and it was strongly secured between two large trees. I took the pallets from my horse, and struggling on hands and knees managed to smooth them out over the soft layer of moss. I arranged them so we would have fur both outside and against us for added warmth.

Once I had the shelter set to my satisfaction, I rigged a tripod of long branches over the fire as Rorik had taught me to do. After filling a small brass cauldron with water from the nearby stream, I hung it from the tripod with leather thongs. The fire was going well, but before beginning to prepare the meal, I gathered several armloads of faggots and set them beside the shelter. I felt better knowing I had plenty of fuel. From a leather poke I took strips of dried meat, cut them into chunks, and dropped them into the now boiling water. To this I added pieces of cabbage and onion. The stew would be no great delicacy, but it would fill our stomachs after the long, hard ride. With coarse oat flour and more water, I stirred up a thick batter which I spread on flat stones to bake near the fire.

I knew not how much time had elapsed, but I thought it would be at least half an hour before Rorik returned, and while the stew simmered and the bread baked, I would have time for a short nap. More tired than I realized from the long ride, I fell asleep as soon as I settled down on the pallet.

A chill, fiercely howling wind awoke me. Through the shelter's flap door which I'd left open for air, I saw it was as dark as midnight outside. How many hours had I slept? And where was Rorik? Then I saw something else: the foot of my pallet was piled high with snow. I reached for my cape and, sitting up, awkwardly threw it around me. When I finally crawled out, to my dismay I saw the ground covered with snow and a fierce blizzard adding to it every minute. The violent wind was piling the snow against trees and boulders in drifts more than three feet high, and my shelter was already almost buried on one side, the direction from which the wind was blowing.

My first reaction was panic. Then I remembered what Rorik said about men being close by all around me. I called as he said I should. There was no answer but the roaring of the wind. Again and again I called, louder and louder until my throat was raw from shouting and from sheer fright. But as I had feared all along, there was still no answer.

Again I gave in to panic and began crying. But when the tears froze on my cheeks, I knew I had to pull myself together and do something positive or I would die in the storm. I took a deep breath, wiped the tears from my face with the back of my mittened hand, and surveyed the situation.

My eyes went immediately to the fire. Partially protected by the two huge boulders between which Rorik had dug the pit, a few damp twigs were still sputtering, but the coals were wet. Unless I tended to it immediately, I would soon be without a fire. Snow covered the piles of faggots I had gathered, but when I dug into one, I found dry twigs underneath. Cautiously I arranged them in a criss-cross pattern over the tiny flames, and then cupping my hands, blew gently but steadily until some of them caught. When I finally exhaled, I realized I had scarcely breathed from the time I laid the sticks until I saw a real fire going once again. I piled more faggots on the stones around the fire so they would be dried by the time I needed to refuel the flames.

The snow was coming down faster and, melting near the fire, was forming a puddle that would soon drown it out. Usually a fire pit is a good idea, but not under conditions such as I faced this night. Pulling away the flat stones, now covered with soggy, burned oatcakes, I began desperately digging a downhill trench with my hands. Again I sighed with relief when I saw the water draining away. Even so, the snow and wind would soon extinguish the fire if I did not find some way to protect it. I was trying to think of what I could use when I heard a mournful sound coming from the trees. The horse! I had completely forgotten about my mount, tethered to a tree near the stream and within reach of plenty of long grass. In my panic over the fire, I had forgotten a cardinal rule of the Viking: see to your mount before you see to your own needs. Of course, when I'd lain down, Fenris was well situated and comfortably tied. If left unprotected in the blizzard, however, he could soon freeze to death.

Somehow I knew that Rorik would not be returning soon. I was alone and I must put my wits to work. If I were to survive, I had to have the fire, but neither could I let my horse perish. I had the shelter, the double-layered fur pallets, a thick saddle blanket, and my cape. How could I utilize them best to get us through the blizzard?

Taking out my knife, I quickly ripped apart the layers of furs. Fenris was partially sheltered under the broad branches of the tree to which he was tethered, and with two layers of fur covering his neck, back, and haunches, he should remain warm as long as he wasn't buried by the snow. It looked as if the storm might be lessening. Only the wind kept blowing, swirling around us like an invisible maelstrom.

Once I had Fenris settled as comfortably as possible, I tended to the fire. Wind and snow kept threatening to extinguish it, but I piled on more twigs until I had a good blaze going. Around the tripod I wrapped the cape in a cone, with a small hole at the top and a narrow slit at the front for ventilation. The cape was long enough to spread out like the train of a skirt and hold to the ground with the heavy, flat stones. There was a considerable lessening of heat, but at least the fire would not die out altogether.

When I became too cold, I could open the flap and get warm again for a few minutes.

To prevent becoming dangerously chilled, I crawled back into the shelter, lying on one fur and covering myself with the other and the saddle blanket. After what seemed like some two hours, I saw that as long as I checked the fire about every half-hour, it would not go out, and I could get some rest. Only then did I realize I had not yet eaten. Opening the cape, I looked into the cauldron. The stew was still bubbling away, thick and juicy and smelling like the ambrosia of the gods. Sowewhere under the snow were buried all our eating utensils; but I still had my knife. Now I knew why Viking wives always hung it from one of their breast chains. With it I speared pieces of meat and vegetables. Never had anything tasted so good.

Looking to the east, the direction from which the wind came, I knew the blizzard was much worse in the upper meadows where Rorik had gone to check on the cattle. I knew, too, that he was probably stranded up there, and many hours would pass before he could get back to me. Strangely, I was no longer afraid, but I well knew that a dangerous complacency was typical of the snowbound and could lead to freezing to death. That meant watching the fire carefully, using only as many twigs as needed to keep it going, and adding more meat and vegetables to the stew from time to time. With the snow there was no lack of water, and I had hung the poke of food on a branch as Rorik had cautioned me to do.

The rest of the night and the next day passed in a blur of tending the fire, eating a few bites from the cauldron, and resting when I could. By evening the snow had stopped completely; but the wind continued to howl down from the mountains and through the trees. With the fire in less danger of going out, I thought I dared get some sleep. I pulled the fur and the blanket over me, but it was some time before I could relax enough to sleep. All sorts of horrors went through my mind: the fire would go out; I would freeze to death; Rorik had frozen to death trying to get to me; I would never get back to the farm and the twins. And Asri would suffer the loss of a second mother. Not daring to cry, I checked the fire one more time and forced my mind to become a blank.

Some hours later I awoke to a new sound. Not the blowing of the wind in the trees or the chomping of the horse, but something disturbing the branches around me. I listened more closely. There was definite movement outside the shelter; something or someone was stalking round and round. Worse, it was getting closer. Then like an unexpected clap of thunder, I heard a growl, a single, long-drawn-out growl that turned my already cold blood to ice. It was followed by a series of short huffs and the sound of something first scraping against one of the trees to which the shelter was secured and then scrambling up the trunk. The movements seemed too ponderous to be those of a man. Just then I heard the crack of a branch, followed immediately by a heavy weight thudding on the ground.

Now my curiosity was greater than my fear; although when I saw what had been haunting the camp, I suddenly became terrified at what might have happened to me. In the now bright moonlight was the silhouette of a huge bear running as fast as he could through the deep snow. I looked up at the broken branch from which hung the shredded scraps of the thongs which had once held my poke of food. It was unusual for a bear not to be in hibernation before the first snow, but a blizzard this early in the year was even more rare.

I sat back on the fur. I now must be more frugal with the remainder of the stew. By adding more snow, I could increase the amount of broth and subsist on it, if necessary, once the meat and vegetables were gone. Surely someone would find me by then, and I prayed it would be Rorik.

The fire was burning steadily, so once more I allowed myself to fall asleep. With no more nightmares or unwanted intruders, I slept until after sunrise. The wind had eased off to a slight breeze; and while snow was still piled in drifts, the air was less frigid than the day before. The sun shone at last and, wrapping a fur around me, I sat before the open fire. In its way, the day was beautiful, and for the first time, I thought there was real hope Rorik would return soon.

I saw the shadowy forms in the distance and leapt up. The sheep! If they were being brought safely down, surely Rorik was with them. They moved steadily toward me, and I started to run to meet them. I only wondered why there was not at least one man on horseback leading them.

Then I heard the howls and realized with a start that the shapes were all dark, not white. Now they were running, and I was shocked into an awareness of the new danger—a marauding pack of wolves. Desperately I tried to remember what Rorik had told me to do if ever trapped like this. The tree? No, even if I could climb it, the wolves would circle below until I froze or starved to death. The shelter was no protection. They would have it ripped apart in seconds. The thought of their fangs slashing and tearing through my flesh sickened and terrified me. My hands were shaking, and I instinctively put them closer to the fire, as if by warming them I could stop the tremors.

The fire! That was it. Moving as quickly as possible in my benumbed state, I clawed aside the stones holding the cape down and pulled it off the framework. There was still a good pile of faggots, and frantically I threw piece after piece on the fire until the flames blazed up as high as the top of the tripod.

I wrapped the cape around me and huddled as close to the fire as possible. The wolves approached and began circling the camp, their open mouths emitting steamy breath and low howls. Their sharp fangs glistened bone white in the sun. With each snarl they came nearer, and I piled on more wood. The animals were closing in, and unless the flames halted their advance, I would soon know the pain of an agonizing, bone-crushing death.

Suddenly they raised their muzzles in the air, their nostrils sniffing some new scent. In another minute I tried to close my ears to the piteous cries of Fenris screaming in pain as the wolves attacked, stripping off pieces of horseflesh. None too soon the cries stopped, and I heard only the sounds of low growling and the crunching of bones.

I had prayed I would faint before the wolves attacked me. Once that danger was past, and they fled into the woods, I must have passed out from relief or exhaustion. The next thing I knew, strong hands lifted me up and held me against a broad, comforting chest. Still only semi-conscious, I felt someone wrapping me in furs and rubbing my hands and feet to restore warmth. In another minute I was snuggled in Rorik's arms and sobbing against his shoulder.

" 'Tis all right, my love," he whispered. "You're safe now."

"The bear—the wolves," I sobbed. "And the snow. I kept the fire going, just like you said."

"You did fine, just fine. I'm proud of you."

He gave me more broth and then tucked me between the furs where I fell asleep once again.

Several hours later, men sent to the farm returned with a sledge. The trip back took longer, requiring a more circuitous route than on horseback, but Rorik insisted I was in no condition to ride. When I fainted, I fell back into the snow, and only the heat of the fire kept me from freezing to death. How long I had lain there, Rorik did not know, but the fire was almost out when he arrived.

Surrounded by furs and held close in Rorik's arms, I enjoyed the trip home in the sledge far more than I had the ride up the slopes. I was not only more comfortable, but more important, both of us were still alive and together.

Many of the cattle and sheep had foundered in the deep drifts and frozen to death. Rorik had left the care of the animals to his men and tried to get back to me when the first snow began to fall, but the onset of the blizzard was so sudden, he was bogged down and trapped by drifts before he traveled less than halfway. Frantic with fear for my safety, he could only hope I was able to remain warm in the meager shelter. Only his sure belief I would keep the fire going kept him from doing something desperate, like trying to make it to me through the deep snow in which he certainly would have died himself.

"I nearly went crazy," Rorik said, "when I saw you lying on the ground and the fire almost out. Never—never again will I leave you alone like that. The red sun was a warning, and I was a fool not to heed it."

" 'Tis all right, Rorik. I'm safe now. Just hold me close and keep me warm."

The terrifying experience was over, but I wondered how long my dreams would be shattered by the hungry howling of wolves and the death-throe cries of Fenris.

After the great blizzard, we had several weeks of almost mild weather. The snow stayed on the ground, and the streams and ponds were frozen over, but the sun shone every day and the wind had stilled. We went for short, exhilarating rides in the sledge, I in my fur cape and the three children bundled in fur-lined bags.

Then one afternoon Rorik suggested I dress warmly,

with trousers and boots under my gown. He had a surprise for me.

"Not another long ride," I protested.

"No, my love. Something I think you will enjoy much more."

We climbed in the sledge, and the horses trotted off along the ice-ridged road and then across fields of hard-packed snow. In his hands Rorik held what looked like four pairs of runners for doll-sized sledges. They were made of carved bone, with one side honed to a sharp edge.

"What, pray tell, are those?" I asked.

"You will soon see." He grinned but left me as curious as before. He was involved in fitting leather thongs through slits in each runner and securing them in twos to what looked like a heavy boot sole.

"Now," he said, "I shall explain. These are for gliding over the ice."

"We send them sliding across the ice?" I tried to visualize it. "The way we sent little leaf boats down a stream?"

"No, my little frost maiden," he answered and then began laughing so hard he could scarce speak. "We fasten them to the bottom of our boots—tie them on with these straps —and then *we* skim across the ice."

I must have looked stunned, trying to picture what he had just told me.

"You'll see when we reach the lake," he nodded. "I think men first made these for travel on the rivers when the snow on the ground was too deep to walk. Then people must have seen they could be used for fun as well. The frozen surface of the rivers is usually rough, so we do most of our gliding on the lake."

We had reached the small lake by now, and I saw what he meant. Its frozen surface gleamed in the brilliant sunlight like a smooth, solid sheet of pure silver. On it several people moved as if they were flying, or sailing like boats before the wind, and I gasped in amazement. To be able to move like that, with such speed and no apparent effort, must be wonderful.

There were rough, crude benches near the edge of the lake, and one tremendous bonfire around which a group of laughing people were warming themselves. It did indeed look like fun.

"Now," Rorik said, leading me to one of the benches. "We will try these out. They should work smoothly. Some runners are made of wood, but wood absorbs water, and then the runners begin to stick to the ice. When that happens, look out! It's a painful fall."

He fastened one double set of runners to each of my boots, securing the leather straps across my feet and around the ankles. "There, those should hold." Then he put on his own. "Now," he said, "stand up."

I did, took one step, and immediately fell down—hard.

"I thought this was supposed to be fun," I said, chagrined at my ignominious failure and furious with him as he stood laughing over me.

"It will be, when you learn how. Here, give me your hand. We'll glide together."

Even with his arm around my waist, I found it hard to navigate. My feet kept wobbling and sliding out from under me, and I could not keep my ankles from turning in and out.

"No, no," Rorik said, "don't take such short steps. Don't step at all. Just glide. Here, watch me."

He sat me back down on the bench and went sailing off across the ice, in long, even strides, like a seagull skimming the surface of the water. I watched closely and began to figure out what he was doing.

"Ready to try again?"

"Yes, if you hold me real tight so I can feel each time you move your legs."

Again he led me out onto the ice. This time I followed his movements as one does in a dance. Yet only his arm around my waist kept me from falling several times. I finally learned to glide without raising a foot off the ice, and discovered it was really fun.

We spent all afternoon at the lake. When we tired of gliding, we joined those around the bonfire. There was plenty of mead to warm us inside while the fire thawed frozen fingers and icy cheeks. Rorik had also brought chunks of bread and a basket of honey cakes. Famished after expending so much energy just on trying to stay upright on the ice, I dug into them ravenously.

In the long twilight, we started for home.

"Want to come back again?" Rorik put his arm around me as he headed the horses toward the farm. Gloriously tired, I could only nod my head and then fall asleep on his shoulder.

Chapter Thirteen

THE MILD WEATHER CONTINUED well past the New Year. Then, without warning, the Frost Giants blew their frigid breath over all the land, and the Time of the Wolves began. There were great blizzards, pelting us not with soft snow but with sharp needles of ice. Inside the house, the water in basins and crocks froze, and the thrall in charge of the fire in the long hall was hard put to find enough fuel to keep it hot enough to ward off the chill that settled in everyone's bones. To move even a few feet from the fire was to be pierced to the bone with a chill that no number of fur wraps could ease. Day and night the room was fogged with our steamy breath.

I had never felt such cold. I put on layer after layer of gowns under my heaviest cape, and I was still shivering all the time. My lips stayed blue, and my fingers and feet finally grew so numb I no longer felt the cold. That was a danger signal. To ward off frostbite, and the threat of losing fingers and toes, we massaged each other's feet and hands to restore circulation.

" 'Tis the worst winter in my lifetime," Thorne muttered, "and many a cold one I've lived through."

There were no more rides in the sledge or trips to the lake to glide. One went outside only when absolutely necessary. Fortunately we had an enclosed well, and by breaking the surface ice, we could always get water. With the barnyard wells frozen, it was necessary to lug water to the barns for the animals. The serfs and thralls took turns keeping cauldron fires going near the stalls to prevent the animals from freezing.

Around the fire in the long hall, the men entertained themselves with chess and gambling. A second fire pit was dug in the room near one end for cooking; and between preparing meals and seeing that the children stayed warm, the women were kept busy.

Signe and Eirik had been crawling for some weeks, and they seemed to delight in scooting off, like ferrets loosed from a trap, in opposite directions as soon as I thought I had them settled by the fire.

In one way, being closed in the way we were gave me more time to devote to Asri and the twins. Each day's new trick or expression increased my delight in the twins. Sometimes they played happily together with small wooden toys Rorik made for them; in another minute they would be fighting over a favorite carved horse. Signe was adept at pulling Eirik's hair when he wasn't looking and that brought squeals of pain, until he learned he could punch her in the stomach to get what he wanted. Only Asri, in her quiet way, could calm them down and get them playing peaceably. I had come to love her as much as I did my own babies, and she in turn was a little mother to them.

They had a kind of hide-and-seek game where one crawled under a chair and remained there until the other found him. Or I hid behind a chair, and oh, such gales of laughter when they found me! Then I picked them up and hugged them until I thought my heart would burst from the love I had for them.

As much as I loved them, no one adored them more than Thorne. Their favorite place was on his lap, pulling his beard or being tickled by him. He told them stories about animals, and even at their age they listened intently while he mimicked the chirping of birds, the chattering of squirrels, the growling of bears, and the lowing of cattle. Then they pulled and tugged until he was down on the floor on all fours and they were riding around on his back, their hands clinging to his shaggy hair while he jounced up and down like a trotting horse.

I sat back and thought how fortunate I was to have been captured by a man I had come to love and to belong to a family with a father like Thorne.

One morning I awoke burning from fever and shaking with chills. For a time the whole household had slept in the long hall, not wanting to stray too far from the fire. Soon the lack of privacy made everyone peevish, and I, most of all, wanted to return to my room. With a brazier of hot coals kept burning day and night to alleviate the cold, the room was not much less comfortable than the *skaalen* and far more quiet.

Convinced I was suffering only a simple attack of ague, I cautioned Astrid against letting the children in and stayed in bed, determined to sleep it off. Instead, I awoke to find my throat painfully sore and my chest so congested I could hardly breathe. I vaguely remember Astrid telling me Rorik and Asri would take care of the twins while she tended me. When I tried to answer, there was only more pain.

The next few days were a blur of hot, aromatic poultices on my chest; pungent, acrid-smelling steam for me to inhale; a warm concoction of honey and wine forced down my burning throat; and dozens of eiderdowns piled on to make me sweat. I burned and I froze. My eyelids stuck together, and I tasted blood on my cracked lips. For days I thought I was going to die, but Astrid would not let me.

Finally the fever subsided, and there was no more pain, but I was still too weak to turn over in the bed. In spite of not eating anything solid during that time, I had no appetite. Astrid helped me to sit up against a mound of pillows, and insisted I eat every morsel of the meat and vegetables she brought in several times a day. I gagged at first, convinced my stomach wouldn't accept the food, but she persisted and I was able to keep it down. When I wasn't eating, she entertained me with tales of what had gone on while I was sick.

"Asri played like a little angel with the twins, but the jarl Rorik took complete charge of feeding them," she said. "And, oh, it was something to see him chasing them both down when it was time to eat."

I laughed for the first time in days as she described his preparing gruel for them and trying to feed them both at the same time. Each had four teeth, and she said pandemonium reigned when he attempted to show them how to dip chunks of bread in their porridge and bite off soggy pieces.

"Oh, my lady, 'twas a sight. The master had gruel and wet bread all over him. And so did the little lambs. But never did he fuss at them."

I knew Rorik adored our children and he loved playing with them, but the idea of his taking complete charge of them and demonstrating such infinite patience was totally unexpected. I flushed with pleasure at the thought of him as the doting father, and if possible, it made me love him more than I already did. To think that when first we met I knew him only as a ruthless Viking!

"And they ate it all?" I asked.

"Some, I daresay. But most on the floor and on them. 'Twas a wonder to hear them laugh and carry on and a joy to see how he loves them."

"He is proud of them, Astrid. He feels having twins is a good omen for the years ahead." But I knew it was more than that. Many men equally proud would not devote so much time and care to their children.

"Indeed it is. They double your luck for the future. The gods will look with favor on your family."

"I hope so. I truly hope so."

I knew I was beginning to get well when the food began to taste good and I asked for more.

"Time for me to get up, Astrid. Does Rorik know the fever is past?"

"Indeed he does, and he is champing at the bit to come in here. Only the fear he would endanger the children has kept him away all this time."

"Then help me dress, and—oh, dear—to stand as well." I had no idea I'd be so weak. My body felt light enough to float away, all air and no substance, but my legs were so heavy I could not move them. I fell back on the bed. "Oh, my, I am really woozy."

Astrid helped me to my feet again. Still feeling unsteady, I stood with her arms around me and then tried a few steps. My feet tingled with tiny pin pricks, and I thought it best to stand still and hold on to the bedpost. Astrid removed my gown, and before she put on the chemise, I looked down at my body. I was shocked.

"Look at me, Astrid. All my bones show."

Indeed, I could count my ribs just by looking at them, and I thought surely my hip bones would pierce the skin, so sharply did they protrude. Worst of all, my breasts had begun to sag. My female vanity shrieked at the hag I'd become. Rorik wouldn't love me anymore. He'd married me because he thought me beautiful, and look at me now. My once smooth and fully rounded breasts looked like empty goat udders. One look at me, and he'd want another wife, one that's young and pretty. Now that I loved him, I didn't want to lose him, but what could I do?

"Oh, Astrid, Rorik will take one look at me, and that

will be the end of any desire for me. My skin hangs like parchment, and I've no color at all."

"Be easy, my lady. The fullness will return, and your skin is dry because of the fever. I'll rub it with sweet oils and soon 'twill be soft and glowing again."

"Do you really think so? But that may take days, and you said Rorik wants to come in now. Oh, dear, is there any way to make him wait, much as I want to see him? Tell him I've taken ill again."

"I cannot, my lady. He knows you are awake and well. He has been pacing the long hall since before sunup, as he has all these many days. I do not think he is a patient man. He has stayed away this long only because of the children. If it were not for his fear they would become ill, he would have stayed by your side this whole time."

"And my hair!" I moaned, looking into the small hand mirror. " 'Tis limp and gray like an old crone's instead of the bright silver he loves so well. At least take time to brush it, and maybe give it some life."

While she brushed, I cried inside. If I lost Rorik, I might as well die. Now we were together again, I could not bear the thought of losing him. But how could he love this ugly body of mine? He'd no longer find any pleasure in it, and I would not blame him if he sought out girls in the village.

An impatient knock on the door interrupted my thoughts.

"Quickly, Astrid, hand me that pink robe. Maybe the fullness will hide my ugliness."

"Please, my lady, you have been ill. No one will think you ugly."

The soft fleece billowing around me made me feel a little less gaunt, and the color seemed to add a rosy hue to my pale, sallow skin.

Astrid opened the door for Rorik, and then leaving quickly, closed it behind her.

Two great strides had brought Rorik into the room, and I was immediately enveloped in his arms. Never had they felt so comforting or his body so strong. A new warmth went through me, the warmth of being loved and wanted and needed. Yet a tiny fear still prickled inside. He'd not yet seen how really changed I was.

"Oh, Seabird, I thought we had lost you." He was kissing my hair, my throat, and finally my lips. My mouth opened eagerly under the pressure of his, and it was as if we were discovering the delights of being in love for the first time.

"You cannot get rid of me so easily," I whispered, when he released me for a moment. "I intend you should know you cannot live without me."

"You think I do not know that already."

"Then hold me tight and tell me how much you love me."

Once more I was crushed against his chest, feeling the hard, urgent pressure of his body against mine as an almost painful desire flooded through me. There was a hollowness inside me that needed to be filled by his body, and I wanted to feel his love pulsing and surging through me.

As if reluctant to let me go for even a second, with his arms still around me, Rorik bolted the door and then carried me to the bed. When he removed my robe and chemise, I dreaded seeing the look in his eyes that would tell me he could not bear to look on what I had become. I waited expectantly for the slightest shudder or cringe when he touched me and no longer found me desirable.

Instead he lay down beside me and began caressing my breasts just as if they were still plump and firm. I was so wrought up with fear and now relief, I began to cry.

"What is it, my love?" He took my face between his hands.

"I—I'm so ugly," I said between sobs. "I thought you'd no longer love me."

"Oh, my darling, did you think my love so shallow? You are alive, and that makes you more beautiful than ever. Did you think all I loved was your body?"

"Then you do find it changed. You don't find it desirable anymore." I began crying again.

"You've been ill and you're painfully thin, but I want to make love to you more than I ever have."

Under his touch my nipples hardened, and I could feel my breasts swelling. He still loved and desired me! 'Twas all I needed to feel well and whole again. When his body sought mine, all weakness left me, and I clung to him, moving in rhythm with him in a frantic passion that finally left both of us exhausted.

Sometime later Astrid brought in food and wine and replenished the coals in the brazier. No words passed between us, but she left with a very knowing, I-told-you-so smile on her face. Rorik and I remained closeted alone for another twenty-four hours, eating, making love, and resting in each other's arms. No longer did I fear losing his love; and by the time those hours passed, my skin had become soft and rosy under his caresses, and I believed I would be truly beautiful again.

The spring equinox approached with no abatement of the ice and cold. As a rule the festival took place amid snow and chill weather, but this year the layers of ice and snow resembled a deathly white wasteland and made travel any distance from the house impossible. The sacred spring and cairns holding the statues of the gods were hidden under snowdrifts layered with ice. In lieu of the traditional festivities—the symbolic plowing, the huge bonfires, the ritual libations to the gods—we had a simple ceremony in the *skaalen*.

" 'Tis an evil omen," Thorne said. "The gods will not look favorably on us this year."

I wanted to scoff at his superstitious mind that would base fear for the future on the fact spring was late in coming. My own beliefs did not allow one to foretell the future by such things. Then I remembered the red sunrise and the blizzard that followed. Thorne called the late spring an omen. Maybe it was just another way of saying that one could tell by natural phenomena what a season would be like. I knew of farmers who could forecast a cold winter by the fur on their animals and the time when squirrels gathered nuts. But that was knowledge garnered over years of experience, not superstition. That had to do with crops, not with events. Then I shuddered. Thorne's words moved me more than I wanted to admit. I did not believe in omens, but I was not ready to disbelieve completely what Thorne prophesied.

Truly it seemed that Thorne was right. There were several stillbirths in the cattle barns and sheep byres. The first planting of the seed was delayed several weeks, and even then the ground yielded reluctantly to the plow. When it came time to lead the animals to the upper meadows for summer grazing, many were too weak to walk the distance and had to be transported in carts and wagons to the lower meadows. There they could graze until strong enough to be led the rest of the way. In spite of the animals lost in the blizzard, the winter supply of fodder threatened close to depletion before the survivors could be turned out to feed on their own, and rations had to be cut in half during the last several weeks.

Finally spring burst forth in a dazzling display of color, and it really seemed that the world had been reborn again. In a festive mood we trooped gaily to the sacred wood for a belated ceremony of thanksgiving for the end of winter, and Thorne offered extra sacrifices in hopes of appeasing the gods. In spite of not believing in such pagan ideas, I found myself hoping that the gods would accept the sacrifices and look favorably upon all of us. Then I hastily crossed myself, and prayed that God would understand and forgive me. And keep us all from harm.

Just prior to midsummer eve, two exciting events occurred—one anticipated, the other most unexpected. Much to our delight, the twins finally decided to assert their independence and walk. In her own impatient way, Signe was, naturally, the first.

"Look at her, Tara," Rorik exclaimed. "By Thor, she's not going to let her brother get ahead of her."

"Watch her, Rorik! She's about to fall."

Signe had very simply let go of the chair she was standing by and taken off across the room.

"No harm done," he said, picking her up. Instead of crying, she laughed excitedly and took off again. From that moment on, she never relied on anything for support. It was awhile before she could take more than three steps without falling down, but undaunted, her childish laughter rippling through her whole body, she got up, walked, fell, got up again.

Our more cautious Eirik watched her for a few minutes, and I could almost see the wheels of his mind turning. Should he or shouldn't he? Finally he set his face as if to say, "If she can do it, so can I." Unlike her, though, he seldom let himself wander far from something he might quickly grab hold of; chair seat, table leg, or Thorne's sturdy knee.

"That's it, my boy," Thorne chuckled. "Always depend on your grandfather when the going gets rough. I'll not let you down. But if you're going to grow up to be a Viking like your father, you'd best be a little more adventuresome." And he'd give the wavering little boy a pat on the rump and start him off again. Eirik's progress around the room was slower than his sister's, but accomplished with fewer mishaps.

I laughed at all of their antics and their new inquisitiveness that had them trying to climb up alone into the sleeping lofts or seeing if they could pull the wool off the lambs when we walked through the farmyard. They chased the chickens and ducks, threatened more than once to fall into the well, and loved to tease me by scrambling up onto Thorne's lap when I tried to dress them. At the same time I was enjoying them, I felt a new sadness. They were no longer babies, and my body ached with a new hunger, the desire to feel new life within it. I wanted to give Rorik many children, and I feared I was now barren. After having become pregnant so quickly with the twins, I could not understand how a year had gone by without my conceiving again. Rorik said nothing, but I was certain he was wondering too.

Soon, however, Thorne made an announcement that set my head spinning and put all of us to work with needle and thread.

"Rorik," the elder jarl said, " 'tis time to send the tax money to Torvald."

"I know, sire. Who do you plan to trust it with, this year?"

"How would you and Tara like to go? 'Tis time we made a ceremonial visit to Zealand. Torvald is married to Esrig, my sister's daughter, you know, and I think such a visit would be most diplomatic and beneficial."

"I'd not thought about it, sire, but you are right. It would be wise for one of the family to take the tax money and make a formal, state visit."

"And let them know that the Three Shires are united and I am now king."

During all of this conversation, curiosity and excitement rose higher and higher until I thought I would burst if they didn't tell me what they were talking about. Tax money to some other king? A formal visit? What did it all mean? Yet they were so deep in serious discussion, I dared not interrupt.

"It would be a pleasant voyage, too, for Tara," Rorik said, "and very good for them to meet her."

I could not hold back any longer. "If I am to be part of

this pleasant but diplomatic journey, pray tell me what it is all about."

Thorne slapped his knee and set down his flagon. "By the gods, child, I forgot you were sitting there. While I ride to the fjord and see about getting the ship ready, Rorik, you tell her. Torvald will be expecting to see our ship in about a fortnight, so we needs must get preparations underway."

While I listened eagerly, Rorik filled me in on where we were going and why the trip was so important.

"Torvald, married to my cousin, is king of the Dani. They have more than one king, but he is the most powerful. He rules over lands on both sides of the Noric Channel."

"But he doesn't rule the Three Shires," I said. "Thorne does. Why should we have to pay him taxes?"

"Because he also controls the channel, and he demands annual tribute from all who use the waterway between the Vik and Svealand to trade with merchants from all other parts of Europe, especially from Constantinople."

"And Thorne is an important trader?"

"He is. Trade, not Viking, is the strong foundation of our wealth. To the big trading centers like Helgo, and Birka, we take amber, furs, honey, hides, walrus ivory, whalebone, and fish." He hesitated a moment. "And slaves."

I thought of the two young women I'd seen sold as slaves at the Gulathing the year before. What had been their fate? Slavery was a terrible thing, but I knew it was practiced almost everywhere and brought in too much revenue for it ever to cease.

"And from them what do we get?" I wanted to shut out the thought of the suffering that so many endured.

"Goods come to us from as far south as Constantinople and as far east as Samarkand. The silks and jewelry you wear, the silver for our tables, the spices we cook with, and wine and rare fruits."

"Like the dates and figs."

"Right, so that is why we must be able to sail through the channel. It is a very important lifeline for us."

"So you must pay taxes to Torvald. Cannot the other Norsemen join together and put an end to it?"

"Someday perhaps. The uniting of the Three Shires is a beginning. For now, we must continue to pay taxes every year. But that is why Thorne wants us to go this time. To show Torvald we are gaining strength. To that end, I want you to look through the chests and select the most beautiful of the materials in them and sew gowns that will make you the envy of the gods."

"Oh, Rorik, you do know how to reach a woman's heart."

"Or her vanity?"

Never had I taken such pleasure in carrying out an order. Like a beggar led into a room full of precious treasure and told he may take all he can carry away, I searched greedily through each chest, appraising every piece of silk, every length of brocade. Then Astrid and I began to sew.

The whole time I worked, my mind dwelt on Thyri and Adair. Little more than a year had passed since they started out on their long trek northeast to Norrland and Astrid's home near the border of Finnmark. I prayed often they had made it, or at least found some village along the coast where they were accepted. As well as being a good sailor, Adair was clever with his hands and should be able to find work as a wood-carver or leather tooler. We would probably never hear from them again, so I allowed myself to imagine them comfortably settled in a small cottage, perhaps with a baby of their own.

One day, between sewing sessions, I was out riding in the cart with Rorik when he told me we were not going in the *Raven,* and I shivered as a cloud passed in front of the sun. It was foolish of me to see it as an omen, and I crossed myself quickly.

"Why aren't we sailing in the *Raven?* 'Tis your own ship."

"The *Albatross* was built for ceremonial voyages. It will be more comfortable than the *Raven.*"

Once we arrived at the shore, I saw what he meant, and I shook off the incipient fear that was threatening to ruin the journey before we even set out.

Unlike most serpent ships, the *Albatross* had a complete deck from prow to stern. There were other unusual accoutrements such as a canopied and curtained bed near the prow, chairs with low-slung leather seats bolted to the raised stern deck for easy riding on the seas, a table which could be brought out for dining, and less primitive cooking facilities. Thorne had issued orders to put it in perfect condition and had selected the best men among all his crews to man it for us.

Two days before we sailed, I helped Astrid pack my trunk. Into it went finely pleated chemises of sheer linen, gowns of sea green, azure blue, honey yellow, and autumn russet silk. Carefully laid across the top were the two garments I was proudest of—a silver brocade cape edged in ermine and one of gold brocade trimmed with bands of sable. Both were embroidered with multicolored silk thread and jewels.

"They're all so beautiful, Astrid. I cannot believe I will be wearing them soon. Everything about the trip would be perfect if only Asri, Signe, and Eirik were going with us. I shall miss them most dreadfully."

"I know, my lady, but for only a fortnight. I shall take very good care of them."

"I have no doubt of that. I trust them with you as I do with myself. And I know they will be happier here than on the ship."

"And our lord Thorne will be here. He scarcely lets them out of his sight, so fond is he of them."

" 'Twill be a long fortnight," I sighed, "but maybe 'twill pass swiftly with all we have to do. I'll not deny I look forward to the sea voyage, more so than the days at the court. I learned to love the sea on the voyage over here, in spite of the violent storm we sailed through."

We shut the chest, and for some inexplicable reason the sound of its closing sent another shudder through me. A demon dancing on my grave? No, only the excitement of facing a new venture.

In spite of the preparations for the voyage, Rorik stomped around the great hall with a perpetual frown on his face. I feared he was disappointed at having to make the official visit to Zealand rather than go Viking. His restless nature demanded the kind of action and danger lacking at home or on a diplomatic mission of this kind.

That night, finally unable to stand the silence between us, I faced him with it in our room.

"Rorik, if something is troubling you, tell me. 'Tis not right to keep it from me."

"I've not wanted to mention it, but I am disturbed by strange words I keep hearing." He hesitated. "That Ruskil is the leader of the renegades. I know that he is ambitious, and I suspected he was hoarding some of his booty, but I never thought he might prey on our own ships and those of the Three Shires. I don't want to believe it, yet those who speak so are honest men."

Intuitively I felt I had been right in my suspicions the year before when Ruskil returned from Viking much shaken and with no treasure to show for his weeks at sea. Yet I had stopped short of telling Rorik of my feeling that his brother was one of the renegades. I fought back the revulsion Ruskil's name always evoked. Since the attack in the woods, and my threat when his son was born, he had avoided me with a studied condescension that implied I'd been the pursuer, he the pursued. I'd escaped inviolate from his evil grasp. Why had I suffered the pangs of guilt? Only Rorik's love had absolved me from feeling besmirched and unclean after the encounter. Now I felt clammy all over, simultaneously shivering and sweating. I should have told Rorik right away about my assessment of Ruskil. Not his attempted rape. Never that.

"Strange," I said, "I had the same feeling last fall." And I told him how Ruskil had acted on his return, how he had come home, badly frightened, with an empty ship.

"And you kept it from me! Why?" I shrank from his fury. How could I tell him that I would have revealed everything if I had spoken of his brother then?

"He is your brother. I thought 'twould cause trouble. 'Twas only a feeling I had, a suspicion, nothing more."

"We've more than a suspicion now." Rorik spoke more calmly to me, but I knew he was wrought up inside. "By Thor, I should string his guts on my spear! And dash them to the ground for the ravens to eat."

I knew my husband too well to think this was an idle threat. God knows, I had no love for Ruskil, and his death would not find me weeping, but I wanted no bloodshed between the brothers. Yet I knew, as surely as if I saw it in the runes, that someday it would come to that.

"No, Rorik, for your father's sake. Thorne has lost one son with the flight of Adair. If others capture Ruskil, so be it, but not you. Warn him, but do not kill him."

"I'll stay my hand for now and let others seek him out. I just hope the gods will not frown on me for seeming a coward."

"It is not cowardly to spare a life." I wanted to calm him, to assure him he was doing the right thing.

"I'll do as you wish, Tara, but do not preach Christian morals to me. I am a Viking, and you'd best remember that. To turn the other cheek is reckless wisdom; it is more apt to court disaster."

The next day I rode to the fjord to take the chests of clothes and check on the final provisioning of the ship. Rorik and Ruskil faced each other menacingly on the deck of the *Albatross*.

"Surely you jest, brother," Ruskil said in mock horror. "A renegade? And what, pray tell, should I gain by that?"

"Only you know that, Ruskil. But I say it again—you are a traitor to the family and to the shires."

Ruskil blanched, then resumed his self-assurance, as if resettling a cape he had let slip. He tried to pass Rorik's words off lightly. "Nay, 'tis not so. You are deceived by idle words. Jealous men mouth falsehoods as wishes as easily as they speak the truth."

"You lie, brother!" I could see Rorik's rising temper in his flared nostrils and frigid blue eyes. I feared he would attack Ruskil right there. As equal as they were in strength, I knew not which would be the winner, but I dared not move to come between them. The tension was like a taut spiderweb, almost invisible, unyielding to the power of their hate, fragile enough to be rent asunder. Rorik finally shattered it with his next words. "So this is a warning. One misstep, one wrong move, and you will be dead."

Ruskil said nothing, but turned and strode off the ship. He looked back one time, and the hatred in his eyes was more frightening than any words he could have spoken.

"That was most unwise," I told Rorik that night.

"It was your suggestion I warn him."

"Instead of killing him. I was wrong. Now Ruskil knows he has to kill you first."

"Not because of this. I became his enemy the day he was born. He emerged from our mother's womb fighting the world, and nurturing a special hatred for me, as one nurtures a viper in his bosom. Do not fret, Tara; if there is to be a final confrontation, I will win. He is cunning, but his hatred weakens his blood and erodes his energy."

With that I had to be content, but while Vikings talked

190

of the Twilight of the Gods and the Time of the Wolf, I foresaw a final cataclysmic battle in the House of Thorne.

We sailed with the tide on a perfect summer's day. No longer did the potential for violence seem to hang like a morbid miasma over us. Thoughts of anything but the voyage ahead were dispelled by the grandeur of the sea and the brilliant blue, sunshiny sky.

The voyage to Zealand was much more luxurious than the sail from Britain had been. As impressed as I was with the *Raven*, there was no denying the splendor of the *Albatross*, with its special facilities. Sitting in the leather-slung seats, we were able to keep our balance except during the roughest seas, which was vastly different from having to hang on to the thwarts to keep from sliding across the stern deck on the *Raven*.

We entered the bay at Zealand during the long twilight, accompanied by hundreds of fishing boats, all proudly displaying the mammoth hauls for which the area was famous. Zealand, the heart of the Dani, contained all that bountiful nature can provide—a seacoast with vast quantities of fish and multiple deep-water harbors, grassy meadows and plains for fodder and grain, magnificent forests for timber. It was no wonder then that whoever ruled Zealand controlled much of the Norseland.

"We of the shires to the west and of Svealand and Uppland to the northeast," Rorik said as we were convoyed to our mooring, "are looked upon as poor, barbaric relations by the Dani. That's why we came in the *Albatross* and why I wanted you to dress like a queen. We need to show Torvald and the Dani nobility that Hordaland can no longer be considered a primitive outpost. They must know that Thorne and the Three Shires will soon be a power to be reckoned with."

Thus when I stepped off the ship in my sable-trimmed gold brocade cloak, I saw looks of astonishment on the faces of those who came to greet us—jarls and nobles in the court of Torvald—and an amazed expression in the king's eyes.

A fine mount awaited Rorik and I was assisted into a cart—more comfortable but no more ornately decorated than ours in Hordaland—for our ride to the castle. Situated on a rugged headland above the bay, the castle consisted of four lofty, round, stone towers built around a central courtyard and joined by covered walkways. On the lowest level of one, Torvald held court, while the round floors of the others were used for dining hall, assembly hall, and gathering place for his retainers.

The rooms we occupied were two flights up, above the dining hall, and we reached them by way of rough-hewn stone steps circling the inside wall. The view across the harbor from our slit windows was magnificent and well worth the awkward ascent. I felt as the men must feel who climb to the top of *Raven's* mast when I saw seabirds soar by me at eye level, and I fully expected one to fly into our aerie. At night I listened, enraptured, to the breakers pounding against the rocks so many feet below us.

Our visit was brief—only three days—but it was sufficient to accomplish our diplomatic mission. There was no overt acknowledgment of Thorne's increased strength, but there was an undertone of agreement that Torvald recognized the need for changes in their relationship, particularly in the area of trade agreements that would be of mutual benefit. Torvald needed goods from the Three Shires as much as our merchants needed access to the trading marts.

Rorik was satisfied, and I was proud I had carried out my task of impressing the Dani.

This time we embarked and sailed with the tide late in the evening. Too tired to change, I lay down behind the curtains of our bed while still wearing the silver brocade edged in ermine over a pale blue silk gown I had chosen for our final leave-taking. I have often wondered since what would have been my fate had I instead taken the time to remove them, place them in the chest, and put on a sleeping gown.

Chapter Fourteen

SLIPPING OFF LEATHER JERKIN, long cloak, and boots, Rorik lay down beside me. Earlier he had asked if I would like to sail farther east, to visit the famous marts at Helgo and Birka.

"They are a sight not to miss, Tara. Such wonders to see and things to purchase as you have never dreamed of."

"Another time, Rorik. I miss the children."

"As you wish, Seabird."

So we sailed out of the harbor, heading north by northwest toward the Vik.

I was rudely awakened from my slumbers by something slamming hard against the ship from the port side, rocking us roughly back and forth. A moment later, we were rammed from starboard. I feared the worst: in the dark we had hit hidden, underwater shoals and were capsizing! My mouth went dry and fear gripped my heart.

Rorik was off the bed and trying to reassure me. "It's all right, Tara; we're all right."

"But we'll drown!" I wanted to scream, but I could scarce get the words out.

"Stay calm. We're not far offshore. There should be fishing boats around." But his voice sounded anything but calm. "If we foundered on rocks, they will hold the ship out of water enough to keep us afloat." Was he trying to convince me or himself?

After he left the bed, closing the curtains behind him, I clung to the covers, trying not to be afraid, to concentrate on what Rorik had said about fishing boats and rocks holding us afloat. How much of the ship had to remain above water for us to cling to it safely? I heard the sound of feet scurrying and scuffling on deck. Maybe they had righted the ship. Maybe there was no real damage. It certainly didn't feel as if we were sinking.

I was about to lie back down, comforted by the thought that Rorik had been right and he would soon return. Suddenly I was jarred again by another violent thud. The ship shuddered from prow to stern. It continued to rock back and forth, and I hoped it was settling among the rocks, slowly and not dangerously. Why didn't Rorik at least come and tell me what was happening?

In the dull silence a scream pierced the air. Then another, followed by a guttural, liquid moan that rent every nerve in my body. Something was desperately wrong. Rorik had told me not to move, but if he were the one hurt, I had to know. I could no longer remain passive on the bed.

Before I could pull the curtain aside, I heard the unmistakable clash of steel, the sound of many footsteps pounding the deck, and a series of wild yells to Odin and Thor. For a moment I was dazed. Then the truth dawned on me. We were being attacked by renegades!

There was now such a barrage of sound—painful shrieks and victorious shouts—I was torn between trying to remain safely hidden and rushing out to find Rorik. I had to know if he were safe, but I was halted by the dread of what I might see. Memories of the attack on the abbey claimed all my thoughts, and fear manifested itself in cramps that clutched my legs like hot pincers and rendered me helpless to move. It was the agony of not knowing that finally forced me to action.

I pulled aside the curtains. I felt the scream start somewhere deep inside and sear its way through my heart and lungs and throat long before it exploded from my mouth.

Rorik stood bound to the mast between two huge guards, a knife at his throat and a spear pressed against his chest between his ribs. His head hung down at a grotesque angle. Blood matted his hair and poured from his nose and multiple slashes on his face. There were more wounds on his chest and arms. Only the blood spurting from a cut in his side assured me he was still alive. But barely.

Blood on the deck and the bodies lying in it told me our men had fought gallantly. Those still standing had been subdued and forced to stand together in one spot, aware that one untoward move by any of them would mean death for Rorik.

My scream turned everyone's attention on me.

"Look here, we had not counted on this prize."

"No, and she will only be more trouble. Bring her out and tie her up with the crew."

Although I could understand every word, it did not mean the men were from Norvegia. The Norse dialects were all so similar, they could have been from any one of several Northlands. If I were to be tied up, what did that mean? Were we to be held captive only long enough for them to loot the ship? It was a futile wish, for I knew it was more likely the *Albatross* would be scuttled or set afire. Inwardly I collapsed at the thought of either sinking slowly beneath the waves or being engulfed by flames, struggling to free myself from the bonds and gasping hopelessly for air. I fought to keep from fainting.

"You don't intend—"

"Aye, that I do."

Or would we be enslaved? I looked at Rorik. It did not matter what they intended to do with us. He would not live long enough to suffer any of those threats if he were not tended to. Now that I had been seen, it made no difference what I did, and I started to run toward him.

Rough hands grabbed me brutally from both sides. Although I offered no resistance, I was not permitted to walk between my captors, but was struck across the face, knocked to the deck, and dragged over it. If their intention was to hurt me, they succeeded. My cheekbone cracked when I hit the deck, and my arms were scraped raw. But if they meant to humiliate me, they failed in their purpose.

With ropes that sliced through my ankles and wrists, I was tied up to the thwarts alongside the crew. I tried to smile at the sympathetic look on the face of one, but the pain brought tears to my eyes. I knew what he was thinking. He had signed on fully aware of the dangers of life at sea, but I was a helpless woman, unprepared to cope with them. And at the moment I was ready to agree with him.

Once the searing pain had subsided into a dull, throbbing ache, I was able to raise my head again and look over to where Rorik remained tied securely to the mast. He was beginning to regain consciousness, and his moans were pitiful to hear.

"Please," I begged, "untie him and let me tend to him. You can see how he suffers. At least let him lie down."

The answer was another slap across the face and the butt of a spear in my ribs. A single thought flashed through my mind. These were not just renegades looting a ship. There was a much more dastardly purpose behind the attack. We were victims of an evil engendered by a demented or vengeful mind. Tears washed over my cheeks, but the crying I did inside was more terrible. It tore me apart. I wept for Rorik and I wept for myself.

"Heathens! Tyrants!" I screamed, amazed I had voice left to call out. "Turn us loose or you'll feel the wrath of both Thorne and Torvald. They'll not let these acts go unpunished."

"Shut up! Shut her up, Gunner."

This time it was a boot on my shins and a spear across my belly. The pain from both took all my breath.

"Best to remain quiet, my lady." The voice coming through the haze was one of our crew. " 'Twill not take much for them to kill the jarl."

I had not more strength to fight. Sagging against my bonds, I wove in and out of consciousness. I was hollow inside. There was void where my heart and lungs and stomach had been. The ropes no longer hurt, and I floated above the deck. It was a nightmare, and I would wake up from it. I would open my eyes and be on the bed reaching for Rorik's strong arm.

Then something roused me, and I did open my eyes, not to awake from a nightmare but to face the horror of reality. I watched them untie Rorik from the mast and drag him toward the rail. Oh, God! He's dead. He's dead. The words repeated themselves over and over in my brain like a demonic chant that would not cease. A single movement and I knew he was still alive. But where were they taking him? I saw it then, the ship jammed close beside ours.

"Rorik! Oh, dear God. Rorik, don't let them take you!"

Helpless to struggle against the men who held him, he turned a piteous look on me that would haunt my sleeping and waking for the rest of my life. I watched, unable to avert my eyes, as they hauled him from one ship to the other and again tied him up. Once more his eyes were closed. Mercifully he had passed out.

I no longer thought of what lay ahead for me, only that Rorik was gone from me. I would never see him again. Now there was new pain, so intense I had to fight back the nausea that engulfed my whole body. I would not let them know how I was suffering.

"We send her down with the rest?"

" 'Tis what he said."

The words were muffled, as if coming to me through a fog. At the time they had no meaning. In a few moments the meaning would be tragically clear.

"A pity. She's so young and beautiful."

"Everything ready to go?" This from the man called Gunner.

"Yes, sire. She, too?" A hint of pity in his voice.

"Why not?" A surly growl that grated on my already raw nerves.

"I just thought—take a look at those jewels and that cloak. We're sailing south, and I just thought—"

"Untie her and put her in my ship."

For a minute my heart sang and my hopes rose. I would go with Rorik. I could bear any pain, endure any suffering if I were with him.

All too soon I realized I was being carried to yet another ship. I fought with all the strength left to me. It did no good. I soon found myself leaning against the side of a ship sailing in one direction while watching Rorik's move steadily away toward the opposite horizon. Tears streamed down my face. All reason told me I would never see him again; yet every beat of my heart assured me I would— someday.

Looking toward the stern, I saw flames devouring the planks and rigging of the *Albatross*. That was the meaning behind those ominous words. It was to have been my fate, too. My skin crawled with the thought of it, and my stomach churned with apprehension over what was to be my fate now. The skeleton of the ship remained motionless for a moment atop the waves, and then it sank. With all hands aboard, those already dead and those who suffered all the agonies of hell in the flames. It was a horror not to be borne. And a dreadful loss of good men and a stalwart ship.

Rorik was sailing farther and farther away from me. When someone spoke to me and I did not answer immediately, a fist sent pain searing through my head only long enough for me to turn around and be pushed heavily across an oar.

Days and nights flowed together in such a merciless fog of agony and grief, I had no awareness of the passage of

197

time. Awake I knew only stabbing, throbbing pain in my head, my back, my ribs, my legs. And I longed for sleep. Asleep I suffered the torment of the recurring nightmare: Rorik being dragged away and the ship burning with all our crew aboard. The pain was easier to bear. At least it was real and of the present.

Somehow—and for some reason—I was being kept alive. I knew also I was still on a ship. At times, between waking and sleeping, I imagined I was being rocked in my mother's arms. Stern she had been when she meant for me to be ladylike, but in other memories of my childhood she was gentle, loving. I think I called out "Mother!" more than once, and I felt myself soothed by the pressure of a comforting hand. I do not remember being fed, but I felt no hunger pangs.

Once, before falling back to sleep, I imagined a large figure standing over me, a giant of a man with a kindly face. When next I awoke, he was gone.

The seas became rougher, but I was not ill. I know I was kept drugged the whole time. When the wind whipped the waves into a turbulence that pounded against the hull and blew roughly across my bed, I felt someone lay more coverlets over me. But it was night, and my glazed eyes saw no one, nothing but darkness.

Of a sudden the waters stilled, and I had the feeling we were in a calm harbor. Our ship tied up to something, and I vaguely sensed I was being carried to a smaller boat and placed within a shelter of some kind. The water remained calm, as if we were now on a river.

After more days and nights, I was transferred to a litter, and we traveled across land. I still floated in and out of a haze. There were men all around me, and I could see their lips moving, but I heard nothing. The pain had eased considerably, and I was tormented less and less by nightmares. It was in my waking hours now that I could not rid my mind of the last sight of Rorik lashed to the mast of the strange ship. Was he still alive? The agony of that question was worse than any physical pain.

I was awake when we arrived on the shore of a second river, but I preferred to let my captors think I was asleep. I looked more closely at the men around me, but I recognized none as the figure of my half-sleep. They ignored me as if I did not exist, but I was still haunted by a fear

198

of being hurt again. One of them brought me broth and hard bread from time to time, and I ate. I was not hungry, but I knew I had to regain my strength. There was always strong wine, and after drinking it, I fell asleep immediately. I was never completely awake, but always in that state that comes between rousing from a short sleep and dozing off again.

Once more I was transferred from the litter back onto a boat. I was becoming more alert; and when one of the men brought me the wine, I wondered if it were drugged, if that was why I had been existing in a hazy limbo. I would not drink any more of it, but I would continue to feign sleep. In that way I could keep my wits about me, listen to all that was said, and try to learn where I was and what was to become of me.

In the enclosed shelter, it was impossible for me to see any of the men whose voices and footsteps now became a familiar part of my waking hours. Soon I became aware someone was talking about me.

"Are you still taking good care of her, Olav?"

"I am, sire."

"I have very special plans for her. With her fair hair and pale skin, she is just the beauty he has been wanting me to find for him."

I shuddered at the implication. I was to be sold as a slave. The promised price must be high if I had been kept inviolate among all these men on the ship and given good care. The thoughts this conjured made me wish I had continued to drink the wine and kept myself ignorant of the plans for me. But I had to become strong, strong enough to escape at the first opportunity.

Then I forced myself to face the truth of the situation. I had no idea where I was, how far we had traveled from Zealand, or in what direction. I could be in Central Europe, near the western coast, or on my way to the Far East. If I were on a well-traveled trade route, I might have a chance to find refuge with a caravan or on another ship. I dared not become impatient. I must bide my time and wait for the most propitious moment. And what if I put myself into the hands of others who saw me as a valuable piece of property? Slavers roamed Europe in a variety of guises, everything from merchants to mendicants to wearers of the holy cloth, supposedly on an errand for the Pope.

My situation seemed hopeless, and for the moment I wished I had died with the crew.

Footsteps approached the shelter, and I pretended to be asleep. Someone opened the curtain and remained standing by my pallet. Finally curiosity overcame fear, and I opened my eyes. I looked up at one of the largest men I had ever seen: tall of stature with broad shoulders, husky chest, and a massive head covered with shaggy hair. He was clean-shaven with skin as smooth as a girl's. I studied his face. With his kindly eyes and gentle smile, I knew he was the one I had seen before through a drugged fog. He must also have been the one taking care of me since my capture.

"Good morning," he said, in the familiar dialect of Norvegia. "I thought you were asleep. I did not mean to disturb you."

"No—no, I have been awake for some time." His voice did not belie my first impression of him, but I had to be careful. His gentle manner could be a trick to ingratiate himself with me and weaken any resistance I might put up. "Do you come in here only when I am asleep?"

"Yes, I did not wish to frighten you." He spoke kindly, and I would let him think I trusted him. If I did not show fear, I might learn something useful from him.

"I have been more frightened lying here alone. Wondering where I am and where we are going. And why."

"My name is Olav. If you listen carefully, I will try to answer all your questions. But I must speak low. Above all, do not be frightened. I am your friend."

Careful, I said to myself. Do not let down your guard. Move warily. Listen, but do not say anything.

"How—how can I be sure?"

"You are right to be cautious, Tara." His use of my name startled me. I could not believe I had heard correctly. My disbelief must have shown on my face. "Yes, I know your name. You are wife to Rorik, eldest son of Thorne, a jarl in Hordaland."

No, I thought, that means nothing. He could have learned all that from my captors. I must not be misled by his seeming concern.

"You want to be reassured," he said. "I come from a village in Hordaland where I was a shipbuilder. I helped to build the *Albatross* and the *Raven*. I sailed on the *Albatross* as a member of Thorne's crew. He was a good friend of mine. He was a jarl and I was a free man, but

200

we were comrades. We voyaged together on many raids and trading ventures. You will learn soon enough why that is important."

All his words could still be building a trap for me. I said nothing, but Olav seemed unconcerned at my silence.

"Let me show you something." He folded back his cape and held out his arm. On it was an embroidered wool armband. "Do you recognize this?"

" 'Tis an armband." That was no assurance. All Vikings wore them.

"Look closely at the design," he said. "It should look familiar."

I studied the interwoven serpentine design of red and dark blue with a border of gold. I had seen it before, but where? On an arm, a large arm. Thorne! A new alarm shattered my inward calm.

" 'Tis Thorne's. Have your people captured him, too? Where is he?"

"No, Tara, he is still wearing his. He gave this to me. I told you—he is my friend."

I thought of the great feast and the night Thorne distributed gifts to his *hird*. He would have been generous in the same way to favorite members of his crew. I was ready to believe. In trusting Olav lay my only hope. But I had to keep on testing him.

"Then why are you here?"

"On another voyage, under a chieftain other than Thorne, I was captured. I have been a slave for many years; sold to the man Gunner who led the raid against the *Albatross*. I was helpless to prevent it or to aid Rorik and the crew. When I was made your guardian, I knew my duty to the family lay in keeping you alive and then helping you."

More than anything I wanted to trust him, but why help me? What did he want of me?

"You wish to aid me because I am wed to Rorik—or is there some other reason?"

He must have sensed my unasked question. "Do not fear me, Tara. I cannot harm you. That is why I was chosen to guard and care for you."

I was more puzzled than reassured by his remarks. "What do you mean?"

"I am a eunuch."

"Oh, no! I am sorry." I had heard of the horrible practice, but I had never seen a victim of it before.

"I was castrated very soon after I was captured. The pain was great, and I thought I would die. I wanted to die, but I survived. So now I guard the women captives who are to be sold as slaves."

Once again I cringed at the thought of being sold. I had known all along that was to be my fate, but I had tried to ignore it, to push it to the back of my mind.

"And I am to be sold as a slave?"

"It was the plan, but do not be afraid. My master—Gunner—thinks to sell you in Constantinople to an Eastern trader who has been looking for one as blond as you for his—his collection. But I will not let you be sold. Just wait and trust me. When we get to Constantinople we will escape. I know the city well. I have explored it on previous trips. Just watch me and trust me and do exactly what I say during the rest of the voyage. No harm will come to you before then. Gunner will not approach you. He has plenty of slave women, and he is eager for the money he knows you will bring. Now—I have to go. We have talked long enough, and I do not want to arouse suspicion."

We sailed on, and Olav came to talk to me whenever he could. I came to trust him completely. If I were wrong in my judgment, he was a master at dissembling. I only knew I had to trust him if I were ever to be free and not locked within the walls of a seraglio.

Every day I found myself growing stronger, and I longed to stand by the rail as I had done on the *Raven* and the *Albatross*, but I also had no desire to come into contact with the man who had captured me. I had seen him, and his features were as ugly as his trading practices. One small glimmer of hope burned steadfastly inside my heart: Rorik was alive and also in slavers' hands. If Olav was right, if he did have plans for us to escape from Gunner, he would also devise a way to help me find Rorik. It was that thought alone which kept me going through the following days of unmitigated abominable horror.

Olav knew nothing about why the *Albatross* had been raided, why Rorik was captured, or where he had been taken. A slave, he could do no more than carry out orders. He knew only that the ship Rorik was on had sailed off in the opposite direction from ours. We had sailed across the Baltic to the mouth of the Dvina River. Once we had gone as far as we could on it, we portaged across land. The crew had actually carried the second, smaller boat all these leagues to the Dnieper River on which we were now sailing southward to Constantinople.

I did not know there were plans for stopping, but we came to a port where the boat tied up at a landing. Olav told me we would stay in Kiev for more than a fortnight.

"Kiev is a large trading center," he said. "You will see many ships tied up at berths established for the hundreds of merchants who come each year: serpent ships from the Baltic, biremes from the Black Sea and Mediterranean, galleys from Rome, smaller dhows from Arabia, and many others."

Olav led me ashore and into a tremendous pavilion whose several sections were demarcated by silken curtains. The ground was covered with rugs from the Orient, and more silken curtains hung in front of the ox-hide outer walls. It was well furnished with tables, chairs, and couches of exquisite design. Soft cushions were scattered about on both divans and rugs; unusually shaped oil lamps decorated the tables. The lavish decor bespoke wealth, but its beauty was imbued with an aura of sordid lust and lecherous greed. All this had been bought with the proceeds from the sale of slaves captured in raids. As pleasant and comfortable as it looked, I would have preferred the fresh, clean roughness of life at sea.

I had my own alcove with curtains I could draw for privacy. Olav assured me he would be right outside at all times. "Make yourself comfortable, Tara, and ask for anything you need. We will be in Kiev for some time."

A pretty, young slave brought me a selection of lightweight, loosely hung garments; and after I selected one, she led me to a second room where a large brass tub filled with hot, fragrant water awaited me. She assisted me out of the once beautiful but now soiled gown and brocade cloak. Gently, with comb and fingers she loosed the tangles from my hair, carefully removing and setting aside what pearls still clung there. Once I settled down in the hot, soapy water, I let her wash and rinse my hair while I scrubbed my body all over. I felt like the Paschal lamb being prepared for sacrifice. Olav had said we were destined for Constantinople, but I would not rest easy until we left Kiev. Who was to say that Gunner would not change his mind? If Kiev was a large trading center, that meant trafficking in slaves as well as other goods. All this bathing and dressing might well be in preparation for exhibiting me to prospective buyers. Olav had promised to protect me, but in Kiev, surrounded by hundreds of merchants eager to buy, we were two mice in the midst of a swarm of hungry cats.

When I was dry, I let Kiri massage soothing, fragrant oils into my skin and brush my hair. No use denying myself these pleasures, and I forced myself to remember that Olav had said to trust him. I put on blousy blue silk trousers, wrapped at the ankle, and over them a long, full skirt. The soft silk blouse had full sleeves gathered into bracelets at the wrist. Kiri brought a tray of food and a goblet of wine. I hesitated to eat or drink until I saw Olav nod his head, assuring me it was all right. At night she prepared one of the couches for me to sleep on. Once certain I was not going to be disturbed, I relaxed and fell asleep.

So my days went, in easy, indolent luxury. I had permission to walk some distance in front of the tent, but I was not to go near the waterfront. Kiri carried out her duties without speaking and only shaking her head when I spoke to her. With her long, straight black hair and slanted, sparkling eyes, I knew she had come from far to the east. She did not remain in the tent at night, nor did I see where she went when she left.

From as far as I was permitted to walk I looked out over the river and watched the ships and studied the cargo they offloaded or took on. Black and dark brown slaves did most of the menial tasks, while men in a fantastic variety of dress supervised them. There were Norsemen—called Rus by the others—Bulgars, Greeks, Orientals, Moslems, Egyptians, and many more. I became used to the sight of the great variety casks and crates piled on the wharves, but I never ceased to be horrified at the large numbers of slaves being transported in all directions. With every group I looked hopefully for a beloved, familiar face, but Rorik was never among them. Sad and downcast, I returned to the tent. What I would do if I saw him, I did not know, but at least I would know for certain that he was still alive. Deep inside I knew that as long as both of us lived, we would someday be together again. It was the only thing that kept me going.

For a few moments at a time I could ease my aching loneliness by observing all the activity around Kiev. The city was located on a series of bluffs on the west bank of the Dnieper River, which during summer months was more than a league wide. Although traders came from all directions, Kiev and the surrounding area had long been dominated by the Norse, or Rus, who had set up a permanent town. Around the perimeter and across the river were a variety of temporary shelters: circular frameworks covered with gaudily woven materials of many colors, cone-shaped tents of dun-colored hides, and the simplest structures consisting of a roof slung over four poles.

On the days the slaves were being traded, Olav suggested I stay in the pavilion with the curtains drawn. But I could not. There was always the chance Rorik would be among them. We might at least be able to discover who bought him. So I insisted on watching every time. I thought I was shockproof, but with the first sale, I learned I was not.

The slave mart was no more than sixty or seventy feet from me. The unfortunate captives were lined up, on a large platform and I watched—horrified—as all of them, men and women alike, were stripped nude so they could be inspected by prospective buyers. One thought possessed me like some evil spirit that will not let go: I might yet be put on the block in Constantinople. Olav was certain we could escape once we got to that city, but his self-confidence had yet to be put to the test.

It sickened me to see the slaves being pinched, prodded, and examined thoroughly. Teeth, breath, hands, nails— nothing was overlooked; my stomach churned and I felt my gorge rise, hot and burning, when even their private parts were massaged or explored to make certain they were not diseased or carrying jewels or contraband drugs. I clung to a pole of the pavilion, certain I was going to faint, and I tried to look away. But I could not. I stood immobile, unable even to close my eyes. All that was happening to the slaves was being done to me; and like them, I felt humiliated and dehumanized, ready to obey any order. As a child I had seen puppets dancing on the end of a string held by a puppeteer, able to move only when and as he wished. Some will stronger than mine seemed

205

to take over now, and I felt I would be powerless to resist even the most degrading manipulations.

Through all this the women were able to see what was being done to them and to look at the faces of those about to bid for them, but the male slaves were blindfolded so that the sight of so many alluring female bodies would not arouse them.

By now my flesh was crawling from the filthy hands and rough fingers that had vicariously ravaged me with brutal force. Venomous hate so filled my lungs I was scarce able to breathe, but I was determined to wait for the bidding. It was horrible and yet it was fascinating. I was watching evil incarnate, and I was its captive as surely as were the slaves. Olav had come to stand beside me, and I was grateful for his presence. I might yet need his strong arms.

As each slave was put up for sale he was led to a higher platform so all could see. From time to time Olav identified a buyer—a merchant from far to the east, another from Constantinople, a Bulgar prince, and the emissary of a khan. The women were bid for first; and as each was sold, she was led off to an open-sided wooden structure on one side. And each time, Olav directed my attention back to the slave block.

One young girl, no more than a child, caught my attention. She was no more than eleven or twelve, and I could not take my eyes off her sweet, sad face and the tears running down her cheeks.

With her manacled hands, she was trying hopelessly to hide her shame. I wept for her humiliation when the auctioneer roughly raised her arms so that she stood completely vulnerable to all the leering faces. Like the others, she was led by her former owner to the open shelter. The prospective buyer followed a few steps behind. She was ordered to lie on a couch, and the man who was about to sell her coupled with her in the sight of everyone. Her screams were most terrible to hear as he ravished her, and I felt her searing pain in my own loins. The horror of it obsessed me. I could hold back no longer. I became violently ill and rushed for the tent.

" 'Tis the custom, Tara," Olav said, following me inside. There were no more words between us then, but he brought me a carafe of wine, and I drank it all before collapsing on the couch. This was what lay ahead for me if Olav was wrong and we were not able to flee from Gunner in Constantinople. But I must not dwell on that. I must remain hopeful that all would be well.

A few days after we arrived in Kiev, one of the Rus merchants, a man who had lived in the city a long while and become a prominent figure there, died from a sudden pain in his chest. With others like him, he had become wealthy not only from trade but also from collecting revenues from the vast lands surrounding the city by demanding tribute from all who traded and lived there.

"You are familiar with Norse funerals," Olav said, and I thought of Rorik's grandmother and the heathen rituals I'd been forced to participate in. "There are some customs here, however, far different from anything at home. I think it best if you stayed inside."

"Worse than the slave market?"

"In many ways, yes. I do not think they are for your eyes."

"Am I forbidden to leave, or may I be the judge of what I can and cannot tolerate?"

"You can go if you wish. I merely advise against it."

I thought for a long moment. Only by seeing everything, every horror, every despicable act conceived of by man, could I strengthen my own will to survive whatever I might yet have to endure. "Will you go with me?"

"I would not let you go alone. Cover your head with a veil. I'll put on a burnoose and no one will recognize us."

The dead man's ship had been tied securely, sidewise, to the wharf, and a long ramp led from it to the shore. We watched men erecting a canopied shelter in the center of the ship while many women undertook the task of sewing new woolen trousers and cloak for the deceased and silken curtains for the shelter.

"They are his friends," Olav said, "and they do this as a last duty to the dead man as well as out of love for him."

During all this, those who worked and those who watched drank flagon after flagon of intoxicating beverages. After two or three hours the air was filled with loud singing, and many began a riotous orgy of dancing and gambling.

"This does not seem too much different," I said, wondering why Olav had cautioned me about seeing it.

"There is more to come. At the moment the man's slaves were notified of his death, one of them came forward and offered to go with her master into the halls of death."

I thought about the elder Signe's faithful servant, and once again I was filled with abhorrence for the obscene and barbaric practice.

"Will—will she be killed mercifully?"

"I will let you be the judge," Olav said sternly.

Now what did he mean by that? Either she would or she couldn't be saved from a torturous death.

"At the time she offered herself," Olav continued, "she was dressed in the richest of garments, with jewels in her hair, silver bracelets around her wrists, and small bells on her feet. For the past twenty-four hours she has been the center of all attention and plied with one goblet of liquor after another. All her senses will be numb by the time she is carried aboard ship."

The last sentence alerted me to the ordeal the girl faced. Since the ship was still in the river, it would be set afire and floated toward the sea. That meant only one thing: the girl would be burned alive as our crew had been. How could Olav think I might consider this merciful?

"It is terribly, terribly wrong," I said. "No animal treats its own kind so cruelly. Did she know what was ahead for her when she chose to go with her master?"

"She did. To her it is an honor, as well as what—" He stopped in mid-sentence.

"There is something more, isn't there? Something so shocking you don't want to tell me. What is happening to her now?"

"She has been going from one tent to another of the dead man's comrades, and there in sight of all, the men have coupled with her. After each time, the man says loudly, 'Tell your master I have done this out of friendship for him.'"

All my senses revolted at what the girl was enduring. But she knew—or did she?—what was required of her when she offered to be her master's companion in death. That she would be used this way for other men's lusts. Did the honor negate the brutality and shame?

Now it was time for the dead man, dressed in his new garments, to be carried aboard ship and laid on a couch in the shelter. While he was being transported, other Vikings stood by and banged their spears against their shields. The man's spears, shield, axe, and knife were laid beside him. All this I was familiar with, but I waited in a state of acute apprehension to see the girl carried aboard. Was there yet more torture for her to endure, or had she quietly been slain by one of the men while they lay in close, orgiastic embrace?

Then I saw her. She was still alive. Her once magnificent dress was torn and besmirched, and her hair fell loosely around her face. She was so sodden with drink now, she could not walk unaided, and four men helped her up the ramp.

"She has to walk aboard," Olav said quietly, and then lapsed into silence.

Gratefully, I realized she was long past knowing what was being done with her. I, too, was numb, but not from drink. I was intoxicated with a more potent elixir: fear, anxiety, and horror at the bestiality that lies dormant in the heart of every man until aroused by raw, naked passion. Conception, birth, women's moon periods, and death —especially death—awaken such passions, for they are the great mysteries of life, the great enigmas in the progression of life which bedevil man. The gods jealously guard these secrets from man, and man must not play god or he will be destroyed.

Once aboard the ship, the girl was laid on a couch next to her master, and three of his relatives coupled with her in his honor. I should have felt something at this, but I did not, because this was merely the penultimate act, and I was waiting—waiting—waiting like the others for the ultimate. They knew what it would be. I did not. I could only wait.

The sheer curtains were pulled around the sides of the shelter, but I could still discern the shadowy forms within. An old woman, a giantess, followed the girl aboard. Six men held the young slave while the woman removed a veil and wrapped it around the girl's neck. My hand went involuntarily to my own throat and I clutched at it until I felt the nails draw blood. While Vikings beat upon their shields to drown out her screams, three men took each end of the scarf and pulled until her neck was broken.

I swayed and brushed against Olav. The sleeve of his burnoose was rough and scratchy, a reality I could cling to. What I was seeing was real, not an illusion or a mirage conjured up by an Eastern fakir. The sheer veil floated mistily before my face, and the people around me wavered like shadows on the water.

Torches ignited from a bonfire set the ship ablaze. It was towed to the center of the river and sent floating downstream, amid wild yells to Odin and Thor to send their former comrade on his way to Valhalla. Still clinging to Olav's strong arm, I watched the flames cascade into the water as bits of timber charred and fell off. Sparks from pitch leapt skyward, carrying prayers to Odin and Thor. I wondered how many leagues it would move downriver, a ghost ship without tiller or sail, floating inexorably toward its own destruction. How long would it burn before it sank, hissing like a live serpent, beneath the waves?

"Olav," I asked, "I thought he had to die in battle to earn the right to go to Valhalla."

"As long as he died with a sword in his hand. It was placed there before he took his last breath."

Strangely, those words eased the tension in my breast, and I felt an odd kind of relief.

Chapter Fifteen

AFTER A FORTNIGHT, the trading for which Gunner had come to Kiev was completed, and we were told to prepare to set sail. I had seen the man a few times—squat, dark-visaged, and cruel-looking—when he came to check on me. He merely nodded sullenly and walked away. I thought of Thyri's stories, the Norse legends of the beginning of man and those who had been born to be serfs. Somehow, Gunner had risen above his origins, but he had not lost the crude, vulgar ways of his ancestors.

After having seen the slave market in Kiev, one thing puzzled me. "Why, Olav, was I not sold here? Why is he taking me all the way to Constantinople?"

"Because the price he thinks to get from a merchant there is many times what you would bring here. Nor does the Byzantine buyer ever send emissaries to purchase for him. He trusts neither their taste nor their abilities to keep their hands off his property. He prefers to deal directly with the seller. Be glad Gunner did not intend to sell you here. We could not have escaped from Kiev. Do not worry. You will not see the merchant."

"How can you be so certain?"

"Because I have been making plans. I know the gates by which the ships enter Constantinople. The city is a maze of broad avenues and twisting streets. There are bazaars, squalid vermin-filled tenements, and sprawling palaces. Once inside, one can disappear for weeks or forever. Have no fear. You will never be found by Gunner once we have left the boat."

I had to believe him, have faith in him. There was no reason not to. If I did not, there was no reason to live and go on. Yet why had Olav waited until now to end his own slavery?

"If you have been to Constantinople before, why have

you not sought refuge for yourself? Why have you remained a captive?"

"My captivity is within my own despoiled, lacerated body. It would do no good to escape from Gunner. I could never escape from myself."

I said no more. It was enough that he had revealed his misery to me. I would not humiliate him with further questions.

The swiftly flowing Dnieper carried us first to a small, stockaded trading post where Gunner waited to join up with two more ships for the hazardous journey ahead. As wide and deep as the river was, I thought our downstream voyage would be an easy sail. Olav's words quickly dispelled that notion.

"Oh, no, Tara, the river would not flow so rapidly were it not constantly descending as we travel south. And in descent there is always danger. Not far ahead of us and spanning a distance of some thirteen leagues is a succession of treacherous cataracts. It is not safe to navigate them. We must stop, unload the goods, and portage around each one. Some men dare the smaller rapids rather than face ambush by brigands who wait to kill off the unwary and steal their goods. Either way, we will be in real peril until we pass the Courser."

"The Courser?" Was this another river, or a new town? Always nourishing the hope that we would be free once we reached Constantinople, I wanted nothing to delay our arrival.

"The worst of the cataracts have been named, and well do they describe them. Let me see how many I can remember." He braced his elbow on the rail of the ship and began rubbing his forehead as if pulling each name out. "The Yeller, the Sleep Not, the Gulper, the Ever-Fierce, Wave Force, Portage Force, the Laugher, and finally the Courser."

If their names bespoke their peril, we did indeed have a rough journey ahead. Was it the tumbling currents that yelled or the people on the ships? And who did the laughing?

"Can any of them be traversed safely?"

"Two or three, with the right men in the water and on board to guide the ships. All in all, portage is still the

212

surest way to get safely past and on one's way to the Black Sea."

"What will Gunner do?" I looked at the man, scowling as he sat at the tiller while shouting orders to his crew.

"He is a cautious man. We have always portaged. But not a man lays down his spear when we do."

So, I thought, Constantinople is still many leagues and many dangers away from me. I may not even reach it. The great city had assumed all the attributes of a shrine to which I was making a pilgrimage. Each delay, each hazard, was like a station of the cross where I must do penance before continuing on my way. I had no idea what Olav planned for us once we arrived. He was being irritatingly secretive. But he had become both friend and faithful servant—the only friend I had now—and I knew he had some particular destination in mind.

As we neared the treacherous stretch on the Dnieper, the river narrowed between high, rocky cliffs, its mighty force compressed into a channel of churning waters. Olav was called to the stern by Gunner. He returned, mumbling under his breath.

"We are going to run the cataracts." This was the first time Olav had outwardly shown he was upset about something, so I knew he was genuinely worried.

"All of them?"

"All of them. He is in a hurry, and this will save time. But I like it not. I think he will kill us." Now I sensed a deep, sane fear in his voice, fear engendered by reason not emotion.

"Has it ever been done?" I, too, was shaken by the news and I craved reassurance of some kind.

"I don't know. There are tales, but who can believe them. Stay here and do not move. No matter what happens, do not move. The prow rides high, and the going will be easier for you. Also safer."

Truly, as swiftly as the channel ran now, we should traverse the thirteen leagues very rapidly unless halted by some natural force. I thought Olav to be an alarmist, for surely Gunner would not put his life in jeopardy to save a few hours', or even days', time.

At the first sound of the rapids, for they were heard well before they were seen, several of the crew stripped themselves naked. Others picked up stout poles and stood poised at the stern, near the prow, and amidship. Once

213

we reached the churning waters, the naked men went overboard. They felt their way among the hidden rocks with their feet and guided the ship between them. All the while they shouted orders to those on board who used their poles to assist in the maneuvering and keep us from foundering against large boulders that showed above the surface or from being ripped apart by those beneath.

I was afraid to look, and yet I was fascinated by the expertise of the men. The ship rocked and its timbers shuddered and crunched as she was guided through the cataract. The men in the water were in constant danger of being sucked down into furious whirlpools or becoming trapped among the rocks. Those on board were equally in peril of catching their poles beneath a boulder and being flung off the ship and into the water themselves. Through it all, I did as Olav instructed and stayed close inside the prow.

Miraculously we traversed two rapids without mishap, but they would become successively more treacherous as the river's flow increased with each league of descent. I was heaved from side to side until I discovered that if I slid as far up into the prow as I could and held on to the crossbeams, I swayed back and forth but was not so painfully jolted about.

At the third cataract, more a series of short waterfalls than swift-running rapids, we lost two of the men in the water, who were sucked under the ship as it threatened to capsize. Those with the staffs righted it before it took on much water, but I was certain the ship was going to break up. Olav had said hang on, but I was so rigid with fear, I could not have let go if I'd wanted to.

Olav put down the pole he was handling and came forward to see how I was faring.

"No matter what happens, Tara, keep holding on to something."

He was like a mentor preparing me for a trial I must undergo, forcing me to be ready for the danger but calming my nerves at the same time. It was not enough. I had to know exactly what we were facing, what it was I must be prepared for.

"What are you trying to tell me, Olav?"

"I don't think the boat will make it through the next one. Gunner is getting careless. 'Tis not like him, but he's gone crazy."

"We're going to be killed." I was amazed at how coolly and calmly I spoke the words. I was facing the end of my life, a brutal, mutilating death, but I was drained of all fear.

"No!" He shouted it like a challenge. "Just remember, hold on!"

In another moment we reached the cataract. The ship crashed against the rocks and was swirled around like dry leaves in a violent gust. I heard the timbers creaking and watched like a disembodied spirit as the boat, with one long, agonizing moan of despair, split crosswise at midships. Most of the men in the water were pulled under and dragged along by the current, zigzagging over and around the rocks. Many of those on board foolishly jumped over, only to meet the same fate.

Still mysteriously held together by the force of the water, the boat spun and was breasting the waves sideways rather than head on. A large boulder directly in front of us severed the stern, and the last I saw of Gunner he was spinning through the air like a flat pebble. I wondered obscenely if he would skip once or twice across the surface of the river. More rocks completed the rupture at midships; and still in a dreamlike trance, I felt the prow capsize and fill with water.

Olav's words kept repeating themselves over and over in my brain: "Hold on. No matter what happens, hold on." I had not seen him since the first sickening crunch of timber, but like an obedient child I did as he told me. Even when the prow began to break up, pounded unmercifully against the rocks, I found one sturdy timber and clung to it.

Then I was falling toward the churning water, breaking the surface, and finally being sucked under the roiling force to the calmer waters beneath. My hands still clung to something, some piece of the prow. I had to breathe, but I dreaded surfacing through the turbulent rapids. Soon the choice was not mine. The timber rose up and I with it. Together we traveled, that bit of wood and I, along a route charted willy-nilly by the current. Around large boulders, over skin-scraping stones. But always moving steadily forward.

After being carried some distance downriver, battered by every obstruction along the way, I found myself lodged securely between two boulders. Or rather the timber was stuck, with me still clinging to it. I could breathe deeply again. Never knowing when I would be suddenly sucked under or tossed into a wave, I had been afraid to take more than a quick breath each time I surfaced. I was dizzy and sick. Every part of me was sore. My clothes had long since been ripped off, and the rushing waters laved my bare, bruised skin. I was churning as violently inside as the waters swirling around me, and I clutched more tightly at my fragile support while I threw up all the water I had swallowed.

Fortunately, one of the boulders rose high enough out of the river for its flattened top to remain dry. It took me several minutes to get up the courage to let go of the timber that had carried me so far. But I was shivering, and I knew I had to get out of the water. I looked cautiously for likely handholds and footholds and then slowly clambered to the top. The rock was hot from the sun; and when I lay down, the sun quickly dried me off and warmed up my body.

I know not how long I lay there, but it was well into the afternoon before I felt strong enough to sit up and look around. There was not another human being in sight. The sheer cliffs on either side of the river rose straight up from a narrow strip of grassy shoreland. The rapids extended behind me as far as I could see, to the series of cataracts over which we had tumbled, and downriver to where, in the distance, I espied calmer water.

Weary and desperate, I pounded on the boulder with both hands. Holy Mother of God! What was I doing on a rock in the middle of a foreign river? Somehow I had survived certain death in the water. Was I now to die here on this boulder, alone and stranded with no hope of rescue? Two huge birds circled in the air above, the only signs of life visible. No, not life. They were vultures, looking for carrion to feast on. Oh, God, could they already sense I would soon provide a feast for them, or were there other bodies nearby for them to gorge on. Now I prayed I would at least be dead before they attacked me, picking out my eyes and pulling the flesh off my limbs. Was that to be my end? A pile of whitened bones lying atop a flat boulder in this alien land?

"I don't want to die!" I screamed, and "die—die—die—" taunted me from the surrounding cliffs. I want to live, I sobbed to myself. I want Rorik to hold me in his arms, warm and secure. Oh, God, Rorik, where are you? Are you alive or dead? There must be a way, there had to be a way to get off the rock and through water to land.

I looked downriver again to the calmer water, but a series of rapids separated me from it. Then I looked toward the shore. If I could manage to maneuver through the rocks, I might be able to make it, especially if I moved at an angle that would put me close to land. I had managed to remain alive while tumbling through the cataract, so daring the water again seemed no more futile than remaining on the boulder.

I looked at the water around me. I needed something to aid me in getting to shore, a stout pole or a short piece of wood. Scattered remains of the boat floated in the water, were trapped between rocks: broken timbers, shattered planks, crates, leather sacks, many still intact but all beyond my reach. Like Tantalus in Hades, I was surrounded by everything I needed to remain alive but none of it within my grasp.

I lay back on my small island refuge. I was not yet strong enough, after my ordeal in the water, to attempt leaving it. The top of the boulder was well above the surface, and I determined my wisest move would be to get some sleep.

Lying very still I was more aware of the sounds around me. The water rushing and swirling, wind rustling the grasses on the shore, night birds screaming, and more wreckage from the boat crashing through the nearby rocks. Then a new sound. Something thudding and bumping against my boulder. I sat up. Night had come quickly, but it was not too dark for me to make out the shape of a large leather sack lodged precariously against the side of the rock. Any minute the water would swirl it away again. If I could just pull it up first. I tugged. Not too heavy, just bulky. One more heave and I had it beside me. The water-soaked thongs were intent on defying my attempts to pull them apart, and my fingernails were too badly broken to do much prying. Finally the thongs loosened, and I pulled the neck of the sack open.

Oh, Holy Mary, thank you! Inside were several lengths of cloth, enough to wrap around me and protect me through the night. Smoothing out the sack, I lay down on it and curled up under the heavy cloths.

The moon came out full, and I began counting the stars.

I could not sleep. The night breeze was cool, but I was no longer uncomfortable as long as I shifted position from time to time. The stars were amazingly bright, and I tried to remember which ones Rorik had identified for me.

"Oh, Rorik! Why aren't you with me now? I need you to tell me what to do. I have the will to survive, but I know not if I have the strength. I don't like having to be strong. I want to be sheltered and protected and loved. I want you, my love. No, I must not think like that. I must think about staying alive and knowing I'll find him someday.

As the moon rose higher, its light became more brilliant, lighting up the river and making a silver path to the shore. Its beams flicked across short grasses, were reflected off bits of metal in the rocks, and came to rest on a flattened patch of weeds. Something had lain there recently. I looked intently into the shadows but could see nothing. I closed my eyes to accustom them to darkeness, avoided looking at the moon, and stared intently at the darker areas on either side of the flattened place. But still nothing. Whatever had been there was gone.

I finally fell asleep, awaking only when the morning sun touched my face. Now I was hungry as well as thirsty. The last I took care of by scooping a handful of water from the river, but it did not stop the gnawing in my stomach. I had my choice. I could stay on the boulder and die from starvation and exposure, or I could take the chance of getting to shore. The calm waters ahead would mean the end of a portage, and if I could keep myself alive until more traders came downriver, there was a good chance I would be rescued. At this point I cared not who they were or where they were going.

Surveying the river and shoreline to see if I could possibly make it across, something disturbed me. I no longer saw the flattened area the moon had shone on the night before. That was not surprising. The grass would have straightened back up during the night. What was confusing was a new flattened place no more than two body lengths downriver. I knew I was right about the original site, right below a sharp outcropping of rock. Something had been there, and whatever it was had moved and only recently left the second spot.

While concentrating on the shore, I had ignored the river itself, but that changed when I saw a figure hauling a crate from out between rocks where it had lodged. I was not alone! I had no idea who else was still alive, or even if the man was from the ship. I remembered the brigands Olav had spoken of. They waited for boats to capsize so they could gather up the spoils as well as ambush the traders who chose to portage. If this were one of the vandals, it would not be long before he saw me. But capture by him could not be much worse than what Gunner had planned for me and certainly better than my present predicament. I had learned how beautiful life was.

I watched the man lug the crate to shore, leave it, and return to the river for more. He was facing away from me. Then suddenly, in spite of the strange clothes, I recognized the broad back and hefty arms. I tried to call, but my voice caught as sobs in my throat. I could not believe my good fortune, but I had to get his attention. Still shaking and sobbing, I called out again.

"Halloo! Olav! Halloo!"

When he turned around, I began to weep uncontrollably, loosing all the pent-up fears I had forced myself to keep inside.

"Tara!"

Whatever else he said I could not hear, but I watched anxiously as he opened and ransacked two crates. Could he possibly rescue me? Oh, God, let him find a way. He pulled out a long rope. Still fearing to breathe, I saw him secure one end around a boulder near the shore almost directly opposite mine.

"Don't worry, Tara," he called. "I'll have you off there before long. Just be patient."

I could wait now. He would not let me die, and I refused to think we could both die in the attempt to rescue me.

Working his way carefully between rocks and through the rapids, he played out the rope as he came toward me. He slipped and fell, but I held back the scream that burned in my throat. By pulling on the taut rope, he regained his footing. At last he was on the boulder and sitting beside me.

"Let me get my breath, Tara, and we'll start back."

I could not yet believe he was with me, that I was no longer alone.

With Olav behind me holding the rope and offering encouragement every step of the way, we made it to shore.

From one of the crates he found a blanket to wrap around me, and only then did we talk.

"You held on, Tara, just like I told you. 'Tis what saved your life. Now we have to plan carefully how to get away from here."

"To where?" I was exhausted and less optimistic about traveling downriver than when I'd been stranded on the rock.

"To Constantinople. Once there, we can still follow my original plan."

I sighed. He was a dreamer, a lovable old dreamer. "We'll not make it. 'Tis too far."

"We will make it." He shook his hands as if he'd like to be shaking me. "But only if we move cautiously and take everything we need for the long journey."

"And where do we get what we need?"

"From the crates still caught among the rocks."

Leaving me sitting still despondent, he once more strode into the river. I thought Rorik was strong, but I had never seen anyone as singleminded as Olav in his determination that we would have a goodly supply of provisions. Once he had salvaged several unbroken crates and a large waterproof leather bag, he dried himself off and searched until he found food.

Insisting we needed another two days of rest before starting out, Olav had me empty the crates while he sorted and made preparations. I did not argue. Keeping busy left me no time to dwell on the hopelessness of our situation: two people struggling the leagues to the mouth of the river and then trying to get across the Black Sea. It seemed an impossible venture, but I would not let Olav know I thought all our plans were in vain. For me he found woolen trousers and blouse, a leather jerkin, and soft boots.

"They're not pretty, but they will be more comfortable and offer more protection than a gown. Tuck your hair under this knitted cap. Anyone seeing us will think us two men. You will be safer that way."

"Is there danger of ambush?" I had not forgotten his earlier warnings.

"I think not. The brigands will have seen the boat capsize and will return to the portage route. I do not think they will bother two poor travelers."

Olav laid two blankets on the ground. We had found

dried meat and dried fruit. He put a generous supply on each blanket.

"We can use the blankets for shelter at night," he explained. "As soon as we have put everything we need on them, I'll fold them into packs for us to carry."

Perhaps we would make it. Olav seemed to know what he was doing. Trust him, I said to myself, trust him and do not give up hope. You are alive and you are not alone.

To the foodstuffs we added spare clothing, lengths of rope, and extra knives. I already had both a knife and dagger attached to my belt. Olav folded the blankets into neat squares, tied with strips of cloth. He attached one pack to my back by running my belt through two of the lengthwise straps. More strips of cloth ran from the straps to my belt in front, and the pack rested securely and comfortably across my shoulders.

The leather bag he had found contained a most unexpected treasure. Inside were four smaller pouches, and I gasped when he poured their contents on the ground. Each contained a king's ransom in jewels: uncut rubies, emeralds, and sapphires as well as fistsful of pearls.

Olav sat back on his heels. "Now I know why Gunner was in such a hurry to get to Constantinople. He was trying to stay ahead of someone who knew he had these and either wanted to steal them or recover them. He would indeed have been a wealthy man."

I looked at the riches spread out before me on the rough blanket. They were ours, every one of the precious gems. I had never seen such wealth, but I cringed as I looked at the stones. They had been purchased with lust and avarice; they were stained with the blood of the men who died when the boat capsized because of Gunner's voracious greed. Reason told me not to be squeamish; we could put them to good use. And they were certainly of no value to the dead.

"I had thought to plead for aid in Constantinople," Olav said. "Now we can more than pay our way while in the city and for passage home."

Home! I wanted to go directly back to Hordaland. With all I'd been through Constantinople no longer offered the allure it once did. It had been a gateway to freedom, but I was now free.

"Do we even need to go south?" I asked. "Can we not just start back upriver?"

"No, Tara, that route is far more dangerous, and the rest of the way south is much shorter now. There we can find a ship. It will be a comfortable and safe voyage home."

Again I had to trust him. At least twice he had saved my life. He had traveled this way before and would know the best route. He divided the jewels into two piles and put half into each pouch.

"Here, Tara, put one of these in your pack. That way if we get separated, or one pack gets lost, we'll not lose everything."

The boat had capsized about a third of the way through the dangerous stretch of cataracts, so I judged we had about nine leagues to travel before we reached safe water again. Depending on the terrain, Olav thought we could make at least four leagues a day. By early morning of the third day we passed the last of the falls. There seemed to be no reason to hurry, so we traveled at an easy pace during the day and slept under a shelter of limbs and blankets at night. On the second day, we saw the bloated body of Gunner, one foot caught between two rocks. His obscenely swollen face was a mottled mass of green and purple. One eyelid had been ripped off, and the orb stared at us, no longer menacing but still terrible in death. We never saw any of the other crew members.

Once we reached calmer waters, Olav began looking for a boat or raft to carry us the rest of the way. Luck seemed against us, and we continued making our way on foot. My muscles were so sore they cramped with pain when I stopped to rest. Even a long night's sleep did nothing to assuage the bone-weariness that had invaded my whole body. But Olav insisted we go as far as possible each day. Instead of thinking about the leagues still to travel, I concentrated on each step, using all my energy to put one foot in front of the other. We seldom talked, husbanding our breath against exhaustion.

At last we came to a village just before nightfall and made camp on the near side. But we did not sleep. As soon as it was dark, and there were no sounds from the village, we packed up and returned to the shore. Lined up in the water were a dozen or more small, single-sailed boats. Olav had no idea whether we could sail one across the Black Sea, but it would suffice to get us the rest of the way downriver. For a long while I found myself looking back over

222

my shoulder for someone following us, but once it was evident we were not being pursued, I relaxed and enjoyed the journey. What a relief it was not walking! The rudder and sail were in good condition, and there were two oars if the wind failed. Olav took the rudder, and I followed his instructions for handling the sail. With the boat moving swiftly across the water, I felt good. We would make it now. Many of the fears of the past days faded into memory, and I was buoyed up with very positive hopes for the future.

By the time we reached the entrance to the Black Sea, the weather was stormy and the sea rough. Olav knew our small boat would never make it across open water. Although it was the longer route and would delay our arrival in Constantinople, we followed the shoreline, keeping land always in sight. Sailing on the river had eased my tired, aching muscles, and I was able to enjoy the excitement engendered by seeing boats of all sizes around us, from crude fishing dugouts to well-manned ships.

At the first sizable town, Olav put ashore. He traded two pearls for a handful of coins. The merchant scrutinized our faces and clothing with his narrowed eyes, but he made no comment. With the coins we purchased fresh fruit and two skins of sweet water. We were now in no danger of starving, for the sea yielded up great quantities of fish and there were enough market towns along the shore to replenish our supplies.

Weary with many days of traveling, our skin burned from sun, wind, and salt air, Olav and I at last sailed into that narrow strait between the Black Sea and the Sea of Marmara known as the Bosporus. Many times the wind had failed us completely, and we had to row, every muscle in arms, legs, and back straining to pull the heavy oars. Ahead lay our goal: the Golden Horn, a huge, crescent-shaped, landlocked harbor that allowed Constantinople to control the great north-south and east-west trade routes.

Through the long journey, Olav had sought to lighten the days and ease bodily soreness by entertaining me with descriptions of Constantinople. His words were so descriptive, I could see it in my mind's eye long before we arrived. A city of magnificent palaces and three- and four-story pestholes of poverty, of broad avenues lined with trees and narrow alleys heaped with refuse, of open-air bazaars and blocks of arcades filled with craftsmen, of

223

many churches, forums, the Hippodrome, and the heart of Byzantine Christendom—the Hagia Sophia. The city's first impression on me, however, was of one tremendous, unending stone wall, bisected at irregular intervals with gates.

We had arrived. It mattered not what the city looked like. All it meant to me was the end of our long travail and a place to rest our weary bodies.

We sailed through an arch of the bridge spanning the harbor and by two of the fortified gates. I had long since passed the first stages of exhaustion, and I thought I could not pull another stroke.

"How much farther, Olav?" Would he never stop?

"To the next gate. 'Tis the one nearest our destination. I know you are tired, but once in the city we will have quite a distance to walk, and I want to spare you as much as possible."

The harbor was massed with ships, a vast armada of merchant vessels and fishing fleets. In our tiny boat I felt like a water bug skittering among a huge gathering of hungry seagulls. When we reached the Plateia Gate, we had to hand over more of our precious coins, to assure the authorities we had money to support ourselves.

Once moored inside the gate, we walked along broad avenues, past the church of St. Savior Pantocrater, and beneath the great viaduct of Valens. I was far less interested in being given a guided tour than in knowing where we were headed. We made our way between massive stone buildings, small craft shops, and through a colorful, open-air bazaar. I gazed in awe at the milling, crowded procession of donkey-pulled carts, aristocratic-looking men on horseback, fancy equipages that Olav told me were cars, two-horse chariots, palanquins carried on the shoulders of slaves, and many, many other people who were walking. As one gilded palanquin passed, I saw a hand laden with jewels draw aside a curtain. Within sat an elegantly gowned woman, more jewels in her dark hair, and a haughty, disdainful expression on her face.

I glanced down at myself. My trousers and blouse, now torn and heavily soiled, had seen good service on the long trek; but they were most unsuitable for making an appearance in this cosmopolitan city. I still had no idea where we were going, and Olav merely urged me on, saying we would soon rest.

"We have no way of knowing," he said, "whether any of Gunner's men also survived the wreck. If so they would recognize us."

"Then we are still in some danger because of the jewels we found?"

"We are, but not for long."

Somehow I also sensed that there was someone other than Gunner who would be interested in knowing we were still alive and that I had not been sold as a slave.

Olav began to take longer strides as if he had found the place we sought. Stopping before a broad wooden gate within high stone walls, he knocked with no hesitation.

"But, Olav, this looks like a home of great wealth."

"It is." Nothing more, no explanation.

"Should we be here?"

"We should," he said tersely, as if chiding an impatient child.

When a slave opened a small door in the gate, Olav announced grandly, "Tell your master that Olav, friend to Thorne the Jarl, wishes to see him."

Without questioning us further, the man opened the gate, and we were invited to wait in a large hall. My eyes gazed in wonder at the marble floors, the gloriously colored mosaic walls, and the soaring archways supported by carved and enameled pillars. I scarcely had time to look and wonder at it all before the slave returned and asked us to follow him. We walked down corridors floored with both intricate mosaic and brilliant blue tiles, around an open courtyard filled with a variety of colorful flowering shrubs and a plashing fountain, and were finally led into a small, intimate chamber. The floors were covered with Arabian carpets and the walls hung with silken curtains. It was well Olav would be doing all the talking. I was too tongue-tied to have uttered a word.

The man who rose from a divan and came forward to greet us was gaunt and stooped, but I could see he had once been of a commanding height. His eyes still flashed with power, and he walked with a majestic, almost arrogant step; but he spoke with a kindly voice in words we could understand.

"Welcome Olav, friend to Thorne the Jarl."

Olav bowed slightly—in honor but not servility. "We are most pleased, sire, you remembered me and have agreed to receive us."

"And I am most pleased to see you again. It has been many years."

How? When? Questions chased one another around in my brain. I was stupefied by curiosity and elated with relief that our pilgrimage had ended here and not in one of the vermin-filled tenements.

"Ali Habib, I would like you to meet Tara, wife to Rorik the Jarl, son of Thorne, now King of the Three Shires."

I had walked a few steps to the rear of Olav, trying to remain in the shadow of his broad back. Only after he spoke my name did I step forward. Ali Habib held out both hands in greeting, and I imitated Olav's gesture of bowing slightly.

"Welcome, my child. It is an honor to have you here. But come—come and sit down. I think you have much to tell me."

He had made no comment about our sudden appearance or the condition of our clothes and skin, but I knew only courtesy prevented his asking a direct question.

"Yes, sire," Olav said, once we had been seated on divans across from Ali Habib, "we do have a long and sad story to tell, and we have come to you for refuge."

A servant brought in carafes, goblets, and a platter of small cakes.

"Something to eat and drink first," Ali Habib said. "My faith forbids me to drink wine, but I think you are in need of something stronger than fruit juice. Then you must tell me what brings you here, and why you must seek refuge."

With the first sip of wine, I felt my head reeling and the room begin to spin around me. As from a distance, I heard the calm voice of our host.

"Help her, Olav, she is fainting."

I did not pass out completely, but I was glad to be lying down on the couch rather than trying to sit up. Olav was rubbing my wrists while Ali Habib directed a slave to bring cold water.

"I have been thoughtless," our host said. "I should have seen at once how exhausted you both are. You must bathe and rest before you try to talk."

He rang a small silver bell on the table, and a young female slave appeared.

"Tara, this is Cyri. She will take you to rooms I have had readied for you in the women's quarters. I will go with Olav to his. We will meet again at supper. Do you think you are strong enough now to walk?"

"Oh, yes, sire. I don't know why I became giddy. It was the wine, I think."

I followed Cyri along more halls, to a room off a small walled garden with flowering shrubs and a sweetly singing fountain. Silk hangings covered the walls and surrounded a double-width bed. Through archways I looked into a larger garden in which tiled pathways wound between garden plots, and colorful birds flew among the trees. A peacock strutted before two peahens, flaring and shaking his magnificent tail. Such beauty did much to restore strength to my weightless body and to help me forget the rigors of the arduous days I had just endured.

In a small alcove off the main room was a sunken tub of blue and green tiles into which water flowed from gold pipes. At the end of each was a handle of gold and jade which Cyri turned to regulate the water. It was more magic to amaze me in this house that seemed created out of fantasy. Near the top of the tub and in the floor around it, blue and green tiles alternated with mosaic designs of birds and flowers in unusual and brilliant colors. I had heard of the Roman baths, fed by running water from large cisterns, but I never thought to see one. Flower petals floated on the surface of the warm water, which was perfumed with attar of roses. If I had just concluded weeks of a nightmare existence, I thought I was now dreaming. Cyri helped me bathe and wash my hair. As she brushed my hair with lightly scented oils, I looked at my face, hands, and arms in the silver mirror she handed me. Would they ever be pale and smooth again?

Having put on the long silk tunic Cyri handed me, I slid between the silk sheets in the large bed and immediately fell asleep, without taking time to wonder who Ali Habib was or why he had made us so welcome.

Some hours later I awoke to see Cyri standing by my bed. I changed into a second long tunic, this one of green silk, with long, tight sleeves. Over this Cyri draped a somewhat shorter and fuller brocade tunic with wide sleeves cuffed just below the elbow. There were soft velvet slippers for my feet. Once more I followed her through the wide halls to a dining area overlooking the first inner court. Like the garden, it was filled with carefully tended flower beds, shrubs, and trees, all in full bloom. Olav and our host were already seated in latticework chairs drawn up to a low table, and they rose when I came in. Both wore long, beltless tunics similar to mine, but with sleeves that were fuller and wider at the wrist. Around Ali Habib's neck, and covering much of his chest, was a heavy silver chain, from which hung several large silver pendants, each centered with a precious gem.

"I hope you were able to rest, Tara," he greeted me.

"Indeed I did, and very comfortably, too."

"Olav has been telling me much of your story, and his own tragic tale as well. I am quite bereaved over all of it. But again, I am forgetting my manners. Sit down, and while we eat we shall discuss your future plans and tell you why Olav brought you here."

Never remiss in matters of courtesy, whatever Ali Habib did, he did with a purpose, including having me stand long enough for him to pass an appraising eye over me.

The table was covered with a cloth of fine damask, its intricate cutwork design re-embroidered with silver threads. There were smaller cloths of the same material at each place beside crystal finger bowls. The dishes and platters were of fragile, almost translucent porcelain decorated with delicate tracings of blue and gold and green. All of the eating utensils were heavily embossed silver. We used silver spoons in Hordaland, but we brought our personal, short, bone-handled knives to the table. I was curious to see how silver blades cut through meat until I tried it and realized that Ali Habib's cooks had some special way of making it very tender.

There was also a strange, new implement I had never seen before. It had a handle like the spoon, but it ended in two long, pointed prongs. Unsure what it was used for, I watched our host, and was amazed to see him spear and pick up pieces of meat with it rather than with his knife. Later I learned it was called a fork and had been designed by the Empress Theodosia herself. It took me awhile to learn how to handle it without feeling awkward, but soon I was holding meat with the fork while cutting it with the knife. Since one's fingers never had to touch the food, it was a much more fastidious way of eating.

Having eaten only a little fruit in the morning and then fainting before I tasted even a mouthful of the dainties set out when we first arrived, I was famished. We dined on small, whole birds stuffed with a spicy orange and raisin dressing, slices of cold lamb with a hot mustard sauce, a fruit compote baked in a tangy sauce, several varieties of fresh fruit, cheese, and small cakes. This time I waited until I had eaten something before tasting the wine. The meal concluded with dishes of sweet fruit sherbet—fruit juice blended with snow brought down from the mountains—and small cups of a hot, dark brown beverage with a strong, pungent odor.

"It is made from the coffee bean," Ali Habib said, suggesting I dilute it with hot milk until I became accustomed to the taste. It was delicious and soothing after the rich meal.

The curtains leading to the court had been pulled apart, and while we ate, we could smell the heavy aroma of exotic flowers, hear the songs of tiny red, yellow, and green birds, and watch the spray from the fountain sparkle in the soft light of many tapers.

I waited anxiously for Olav and Ali Habib to answer my unasked questions. Finally our host spoke.

"Tara, I am a wealthy merchant, although it has not always been so. I am a Moslem, and I inherited from my father a small trading shop in one of the bazaars. Some twenty years ago, I was set upon by an angry mob of over-zealous Christians who wished to rid the city of all non-believers."

"They were fanatics, to be sure," Olav said, leaning forward in his chair and shaking his head to emphasize his words.

"I knew the situation was dangerous and I was in dire threat of having my head cut off when Thorne came to my rescue with Olav at his side. More of their crew arrived within minutes, but the two of them were already busy breaking heads and brandishing their axes with very effective results. I owe my life to them. More than that, it is because of Thorne I am now a man of great wealth. He used his influence to persuade other Viking traders to seek me out. Soon I expanded to larger shops and gradually accumulated a fleet of my own. My ships sail to many ports.

"So you see, Tara," he continued, reaching over to touch my hands, "it is my real pleasure to have you here and give you whatever help you need."

"Thank you, sire. I cannot tell you how grateful I am to be here after all we have been through."

"You are to stay as long as you wish, and we will try to find transportation home for you. Olav told me of the jewels you found among the wreckage of the boat, and he has offered to repay my hospitality, but I will not hear of that. You must keep them for your journey back to Hordaland. Meanwhile, my home and everything in it are at your disposal."

"You are most generous, sire."

"Nothing I can do for Olav and one of Thorne's family will ever repay my debt to them. Your rooms are in the seraglio, near the women of the harem. I think you will enjoy living among them and getting to know them."

Harem? I had known of course that Moslems, like the Norsemen, often had more than one wife. I was not shocked at hearing the word, but was startled at the prospect of living amidst one.

"As a guest, of course," he continued, "rather than one of the harem, you will be free to come and go from your quarters as you wish. You will be informed of which rooms you are not to enter and which will be closed when I am entertaining guests. There will be a palanquin and slaves at your disposal so that you may travel throughout the city whenever you wish. I encourage you to visit the many bazaars, and I know you will want to see the numerous churches. I urge you to have Olav go with you. He knows the city well, and you should not go without protection."

Already life in Constantinople was taking on the aspects of an enigma. I was free and yet bound by restrictions; I should explore the city, but not without protection. This was the mysterious, exotic Orient. A tangled web of beauty and intrigue, of great godliness and despotic evil. The center of a great Christian empire, its wealth generated by heathen trading practices. It fascinated me, and I wanted to see all of it, to drink in all of its beauty and richness and mystery.

Ali Habib lit up a pipe of aromatic tobacco and offered one to Olav. After puffing a few minutes, the merchant leaned back and turned to another subject.

"Olav, have you any idea what might have happened to Rorik?"

"I have some thoughts, sire, but nothing definite. The most obvious is that he was taken to be sold as a slave."

"I do not think so." Ali Habib shook his head. "There is an active, fast-moving line of communication among the traders. If a man as important as a jarl were sold as a slave, that information would have been received here by now. I have spies as well as ships' crews sending back news all the time, and I think I would have known immediately. The fact his capture has remained quiet makes me suspicious. I think he was not carried very far from where he was taken, and he was kept a prisoner by those who captured his ship."

"For what reason?" Olav asked.

I wanted to know, I wanted to hear every one of Ali Habib's ideas about where Rorik might be, but each word was a painful thrust. Why was he taken if not to be sold? Why kept a prisoner? Or had he been killed in some way more torturous than going down with his burning ship? It was a rebus with no clues, yet one thought plagued me. The raid on our ship was not a random one; it had been carefully planned.

"You heard nothing, Olav," Ali Habib asked, "before your master reached the *Albatross*?"

"Nothing. I heard nothing about a raid. I thought we were going to Frisia to pick up slaves. That would be the reason for my being aboard. I did not know it was to greet Rorik and make him think it was a friendly meeting. He was first told we had come to escort the *Albatross* home."

So that was how we were taken by surprise, lulled into complacency by men Rorik knew.

"I suspect then," Ali Habib said, pulling on his sparse white beard, "that he was held for ransom. I can think of no other reason for taking him prisoner."

"You think he is alive then?" My voice rose along with my hopes. If Rorik were alive, then there was a chance we would be together again soon.

"I do. If they meant to kill him, they would have done so on the ship, or they would have tied him to the ship when they set it afire. No, he was kept alive. If my thinking is correct, he has been ransomed by now and returned home."

"Oh, no," I wailed, disturbed by a new worry. "He does not know where I am. He must be sure I am dead. He might even be thinking I went down with the ship."

"Not for long. I have two ships ready to sail for Kiev,

231

and they will carry word that you are with me. From there the news will be sent on quickly."

Ships going north! That could be our means of getting home.

"Could I not return on those ships?"

"I think not. My ships go no farther up the Dnieper than Kiev, and I do not know who would take you the rest of the way. We will wait for a ship captain I can trust who is taking the Mediterranean route. It will be longer, but more pleasant. Meanwhile I will do all I can to make your stay comfortable."

I was disappointed. Somehow I knew I was going to be in Constantinople for several months. At least I was comforted by the thought that Rorik was probably alive and at home. Soon he would know I was alive, too, and we would eventually be reunited.

When I lay again between the silk sheets with my head on a soft silk pillow, I could not sleep. The bed was much too large for one person, and my whole body ached to feel Rorik's arms around me and his chest pressed against my breasts. How long—oh, how long—before I could respond again to his caresses!

Chapter Sixteen

TRUE TO HIS PROMISE, Ali Habib sent word the next morning that a palanquin and slaves were at my service whenever I wished to go out. I was forced, however, to defer the pleasure of discovering the wonders of the city. On awakening I was suddenly struck with such a weariness I felt completely debilitated. It hurt even to place my feet on the floor. I was much, much more tired than I first realized. Cyri helped me out of bed, but it was physically impossible for me to stand unaided. It was not so much that my body ached, but that my muscles simply went limp when I tried to use them.

With hand motions, Cyri indicated I should spend the day in the garden, and I agreed with a wan smile. Once I was settled on a comfortable divan she had ordered other slaves to carry out there, she plumped soft pillows behind my head and some under my feet. Next to the couch she placed a small table with fruit juice and delicacies, so I need do no more than move my hand to reach them. First, though, she brought me a cup of strong, sweetened coffee, with no hot milk in it, and I immediately felt somewhat less lightheaded.

I napped off and on during the day. In between I watched a pair of green and blue songbirds teach their brood of fledglings to fly. I wondered at their patience and their method, incomprehensible to me, of communicating with their offspring. So intently did I follow their first faltering attempts, I felt like the proud mother when each one finally made it safely from a lower branch to a higher.

In another tree, a yellow bird and his tawny mate took turns guarding their nestlings and collecting bugs for them to eat. I caught only a glimpse of the downy-feathered babes, but I heard their demanding chirps and saw their wide-open, almost transparent beaks when one of the parents returned with food.

A young male slave in sandals and short tunic came in to tend the shrubs and flower beds. He nodded and smiled and then went silently about his work. He was slim and bearded so I knew he was not a eunuch, and I wondered at his being allowed so near the women's quarters. I learned later that the harem were not allowed in the garden, and they could come to my rooms only at my personal invitation and then if I drew the thick draperies usually kept open. As well, there was a heavy, iron-bound wooden door separating the seraglio from my quarters.

I also learned the young man, Paul, was a deaf mute, and while our communication was limited to smiles, nods, and hand motions, we still managed during the next few days to carry on lively dialogues about the beauty of the flowers and birds, the right way to cultivate each variety of flower, and the fact that both of us came from lands far from Constantinople. When he rubbed his eyes as if he were weeping, I knew he was as homesick as I, and another bond was forged between us.

I rested thus for three or four days before I felt my strength gradually returning. Although the weather was warm, there was always a good breeze in the garden, perfumed by the many flowers and refreshed by the spraying water of the fountain. Day or night I could walk out there and feel a new awareness of life surging through me. It was pleasant to lie on the couch during the day, but I enjoyed it even more at night when all around me was quiet with the stillness of sleep, and I had the feeling I was all alone in that strangely beautiful world. It was my world and none could trespass but visions of Rorik and memories of our hours together. Separated as we were by vast amounts of time and space, strangely I felt closer to him than I ever had before. It was as if his presence walked beside me the whole time, and I had the eerie feeling that if I but looked around I would see him. It was a premonition that both comforted and haunted me.

While Cyri tended me, I began to learn the language of the harem, a unique multilingual dialect comprised of equal amounts of Greek and Arabic and embellished with words and expressions from a variety of tongues. We started with parts of the head and face, then moved to the rest of the body. From there we turned to various toiletries and items of clothing. Soon I could ask for anything I needed or wanted done. Having picked up the Norse dialect quickly, I knew it was best to learn first the names of specific objects and only later worry about expressing myself in full sentences.

Finally the day came when I was ready to be up and doing, but not quite prepared to venture into the city. By pointing to me and herself and then counting on her fingers, I learned there were some twenty women in the harem as well as a number of small children and babies. Cyri rocked her arms four times, so I knew there were that many under a year old. Ali Habib might appear aged and gaunt, but the evidence proved he was still a virile man. I hesitated when Cyri suggested I enter the seraglio and meet the women. Remembering my experiences when I first entered Rorik's house, I was wary of facing so many strange women. Cyri must have caught the confusion on my face because she grabbed my hands and laughingly pulled me along.

"I—you—to Thalia. Thalia—you—to—" and she pointed to me, all the while counting again on her fingers. She would introduce me to one who would help me meet the others. She repeated the name Thalia over and over, each time holding up a solitary forefinger. Finally I nodded. Thalia was first or number-one wife. She probably ruled the harem like a martinet. Cyri was shrewd. She knew Thalia had to be appeased and would be affronted if I had been introduced to someone else first.

Ali Habib's palatial home consisted of three attached buildings, each successively smaller as one proceeded from the avenue to the high rear wall. The first two were three stories high and built around inner courtyards. The third was a single, one-story rectangle facing a walled garden. The lowest level of the first building contained the merchant's offices, reception rooms, a large dining hall, the small dining room where we had eaten, and other rooms for entertaining guests. The floors above contained his personal living quarters as well as those for his sons, his younger half-brother Ben Hassem, male guests, and male slaves.

I was living in the third or smallest section, built originally for Ali Habib's mother and aunt. Both had been wives of the merchant's father and were therefore widowed at the same time. Being dowager widows, they had been relieved of many harem restrictions and allowed the freedom to go escorted into the city, shop the bazaars, and attend certain outdoor events. Since their deaths, the rooms had been unused.

The second building was the seraglio or the accommodations for his harem. I followed Cyri through the inlaid, heavily carved doors, usually locked, into this middle building. Previously I had been led along a long hall that extended the length of an outer wall of the women's quarters. Although there were windows on the second and third floors overlooking narrow side streets, there were only solid walls on the first floor. All entrances were carefully guarded by gigantic, knife-wielding eunuchs who could kill without changing expression.

I found myself in a large pavilion opening onto a center garden court. There were doors that could be closed when the weather grew chill. Much of the tiled floor was covered with soft, thick carpets of delicate design in pastel colors, and there were numerous divans and finely wrought tables inlaid with patterned mosaic tile or wood. Later I learned the second and third floors contained the sleeping quarters of the women, some of their children, and the female slaves. Daughters stayed with their mothers until they were married, but sons remained in the seraglio only until their sixth birthday when they were removed to their father's quarters.

To walk into a seraglio and to hear the heavy doors shut behind one is to enter a strange, unreal world peopled only by beautiful women and delightful children. It is a world of long, somnambulent days and luxurious tedium. The atmosphere had a light, ethereal, pastel quality that reminded me of the fragile mimosa blossoms in the garden adjacent to my room. Soft, lilting, dulcet voices were interspersed with squeals and laughter from the children with an occasional baby cry. It was a totally feminine world which no deep voices or heavy footsteps ever disturbed. When Ali Habib visited, he went to the private rooms or suites on the upper floors; more frequently, he had the children and women brought to his own quarters.

Most of the women wore long, loose tunics of white or pastel silk similar to mine. Some were barefoot, others were shod in light sandals. Two or three were garbed in bloused trousers and jackets much like the ones I wore in Kiev, and their heads were swathed in veils. On others were garments completely unfamiliar to me. All were adorned with gold or silver necklaces, bracelets, and earrings, many inlaid with precious stones, which provided a constantly tinkling undertone to their voices.

I walked slowly into the room, unsure how I, a stranger, would be received. I need not have worried. They approached with a shy temerity which dispelled any fear I felt. Once Cyri told them I was a guest, not a new member of the harem who would challenge their positions or compete for Ali Habib's favor, they immediately surged forward, surrounding me and chattering like a bevy of cooing doves. Memories of my first greetings in Hordaland overwhelmed me with longing and I was close to tears. It had been frightening at the time, but at least I had Rorik beside me. Now I must make my way alone.

Having learned enough of their language to cover the amenities, I was able to greet each woman by name and exclaim over the beauty of the children clustered near their mothers. Five older women had no children, but they were quick to indicate they had married daughters as well as sons now living in the men's quarters. Four younger women stood to one side with downcast eyes. With no children hugging their knees and no babes in arms, they were pariahs amid all the fecundity in the seraglio. Before long I would become friends with one of the youngest and prettiest and learn the cause of the tears that frequently came unbidden for no apparent reason. A cause that very nearly led to irreversible tragedy.

All that, however, was still in the as yet beclouded future.

Through the following gentle-morninged days, I learned to know and love many of the women who, in the midst of a large, busy, Christian, metropolitan center, lived out their lives within a few hundred secluded square feet of one building. Like generations before them, once they entered the seraglio, as wife or concubine, they never saw any man other than husband or master. From that moment on, his will was their will; his commands were their pleasure. They watched the change of seasons in their small garden court as the apricot trees budded in the spring, flowered in the summer, and bore fruit in the early autumn. Their only sight of the bustling city of Constantinople was through latticed windows with a limited view of passersby on the narrow side street. There were no visits to the noisy, colorful, aromatic, treasure-filled bazaars to bargain with merchants. Nor could they walk freely along the streets, attend exciting contests in the Hippodrome, or simply ride in an enclosed palanquin along the wide, tree-shaded avenues. They lived out their lives entombed in a luxurious monument to one man's pride in his wealth and virility, embalmed by a tradition rooted in religious dogma.

In spite of this, all seemed serene on the surface as one placid day followed another, and I spent many enchanted hours with them. Only gradually did I become aware of an insidious element in the harem: tedium begets inertia and inertia breeds petty irritations and jealousies. I learned early that Ali Habib's eldest wife, Thalia, was the acknowledged matriarch in the seraglio and all acquiesced to her wishes. A stern yet gentle mother figure to the younger women, she set an example of immediate compliance with her husband's desires that she quietly expected all the women to follow.

Although nearly as old as Ali Habib, Thalia was still a strikingly beautiful woman. Though of less than medium height, she seemed to tower over all the other women, and her silver-streaked hair framed her face like an aura. From the very first she took me under her wing, having been apprised by her husband of all I had been through. It was from her I learned much about life in the harem not immediately evident to my eyes. I was surprised to learn that not all were wives to Ali Habib.

"Oh, no," she said, the furrows between her eyes deepening. "As an orthodox Moslem and follower of the Koran, he is allowed only four wives at any one time. We are the most honored among the women."

"And the others?"

"Some are ex-wives. In order to comply with the Koran, he is allowed to divorce a wife when he wishes to take a new one. Sometimes it is for business or political reasons. Sometimes," and here she hesitated, "personal ones. He is, however, expected to continue supporting all ex-wives or allow them to marry again."

"You are the eldest and yet you are still his wife." I had thought to say it to myself. Such curiosity was rude, and I had unwittingly voiced it aloud.

"I will never be put aside. Ali Habib married me for love, in spite of his family's objections. They had chosen one they thought more suitable."

"For love? You met Ali Habib before you married him?" This was unheard of in the Moslem tradition.

238

"I was reared in the Moslem faith, but I was privileged to enjoy the greater freedom accorded Christian girls in Constantinople. I met my husband when I shopped at his booth in the bazaar. After we married, I worked very hard behind the heavy curtains of the booth while he met the customers in the front." She laughed. "He will be the first to tell you I am as shrewd a merchant as he. Since becoming wealthy, he has taken many wives and concubines, but he still loves me and relies on me for advice." She smiled a secret smile. "And I still visit him at night. I have given him three sons and two daughters. No, I will never be put aside."

"How," I dared ask, "having been brought up with the freedom to come and go almost as you please, could you settle so easily into harem life?"

"There you are wrong. It was not easy. I struggled for years, but finally I accepted it. The reason is simple: I love Ali Habib."

Her acceptance of her husband's way of life amazed me. It was the very thing I could not do when I married Rorik. She loved her husband enough to follow tradition. I loved Rorik too much to be dominated by custom.

Below the wives in this stratified world were the concubines who had given Ali Habib children, especially sons. Although he was permitted only four wives, there was no limit on the number of concubines he could acquire. Next to the lowest level, and the ones who suffered the abuse and mockery of the others, were the concubines who remained childless. At the bottom were the female slaves who took orders from everyone else.

Although I enjoyed my hours with the women, I began to feel the need of an occasional foray out of the smothering atmosphere of the seraglio. Nor could I remain long among the children without my heart beginning to ache with loneliness for Signe, Eirik, and Asri. The twins had not been walking long when we left. Were they now running around the long hall? Signe had delighted in trying to imitate the clucks and honks of the chickens and geese. Maybe she was now chasing them across the farmyard. I hoped Astrid was taking them to our favorite cluster of fir trees beside the stream. Eirik was the water baby, always had been. I could see him now, running and splashing where the shallow part of the stream gurgled over the small rocks.

239

Maybe he was sailing leaf boats down the narrow current, watching them twist and spin around in the crystal-clear eddies. They were seldom out of my mind, but my heart really ached for them when I was with the children in the harem.

To help ease that longing, I began exploring the city, riding in a palanquin carried by slaves. Always Olav went with me, insisting no woman should venture into the streets unescorted. Cyri showed me how to form a headdress by winding a scarf around my head, letting one end fall to the shoulder. Over my long, beltless tunic I wore a cloak with a hood I could pull up to conceal my head completely.

The palanquin had curtains which could be closed for privacy, but they also obstructed the view. The first time I went out, I kept them open, not wanting to miss any of the strange, new sights around me—the masses of people, the impressive buildings, the vibrant colors, and the variety of conveyances. Within minutes I learned for myself why most people kept the curtains drawn.

We turned off the broad avenue into a narrow street leading to one of the bazaars. Suddenly I was surrounded by beggars, jostling the palanquin and thrusting their bony arms and skinny fingers through the openings, all the while wailing in high, shrieking cries. Olav and the slaves tried to push them back, but that only seemed to make them more violent in their demands, and they clawed my tunic or stretched their hands right up into my face. I was convulsed with both terror and pity for the gaunt men and women whose bodies were barely covered with shreds of material. Some were crippled and maimed. Mothers were trying to suckle babes against their dried-up breasts. The diseased, covered with sores, sickened and revolted me. Yet I could not ignore them. I threw out a few small coins on each side. Too late I learned that was the wrong thing to do. Now more and more swarmed around, threatening to overturn the palanquin.

"Olav!" I called frantically. "Tell the porters to turn around. I want to go back."

"No need to do that, Tara." He was standing close beside the palanquin, keeping the beggars away from that side. Our slaves had been stopped by the crowd, now jostling one another so violently I feared we were in real danger. "Pull the curtains and hand me a few coins. I'll walk head and toss them out. That will make a path for you."

In a minute we were in the bazaar and the beggars were gone, but from then on I kept the curtains drawn. It was an effort, but I soon learned to ignore the pleas of the pitiful creatures when I rode or walked through the streets of the city.

Ali Habib had advised us to put most of the jewels we had found in his locked chest for safekeeping, to be held against paying our passage home and for our needs on the journey. For the rest he recommended a particular dealer in fine gems who paid us their full value. He assured me all our needs woud be met while we stayed with him, and I should sell only enough for what trinkets I might wish to purchase in the bazaars. He steadfastly refused to accept anything for his hospitality.

I loved walking through the open-air bazaars or along the streets of open arcades specifically designated for certain crafts. I delighted in the sensuous pleasure of inhaling the exotic odors of spices, rare woods, perfumes, fruits, and new leather or of listening to the chantlike bargaining between merchants and customers. The colors and sounds and smells surrounded me, enveloped me like one of the oriental carpets come to life, and I reveled in the lush extravagance of it all.

I often bought fruit to eat as I rode along, sucking out all the flavor of the juicy pulp in the same way I was sucking out all the riches the city had to offer, licking the drops from my fingers so as not to miss any of it. As I explored the bazaars, I was looking for something. I wasn't certain just what, but I wanted to buy something typical of the Byzantine craftsmen. There was so much to choose from: thick, softly piled rugs, embroidered hangings, exquisite jewelry, delicate, paper-thin glassware. I went from one to another of the booths. Then I saw it. A small wooden icon, oblong in shape but coming to a cathedral point at the top. The Madonna and Child were finely detailed in brilliant shades of blue and red and gold, stylized in the Byzantine fashion yet amazingly lifelike.

True to my feminine vanity, however, I also had to have a few pieces of jewelry, and I selected a number of gold and silver bracelets. I stood a long time looking at earrings. I had never seen earrings before coming to Constantinople, but all of the women in the harem wore them, and I was fascinated by the way they swayed gently whenever they moved their heads. I went from one pair to another, trying to make up my mind, they were all so beautiful. Olav never complained about these shopping forays of mine, but always waited patiently by the palanquin for me to select what I wanted and make my purchase. I could never learn to bargain, always paying the first price mentioned because I was too easily intimidated by the merchants to do otherwise. I know they thought me a gullible fool, and I'm certain I paid twice what I should for everything, but the thought of haggling over coins turned my stomach. While I was looking at the earrings, I could see Olav out of the corner of my eye. He was shifting from one foot to the other. The day had become hot and oppressively muggy with no breeze stirring in the crowded streets. I knew he wanted to get back to the cool courtyard, so I quickly chose several pairs of filigreed birds and half-moons.

If I had known the pain these were going to cause, I might never have given in to temptation so easily. Not having known about earrings before, I did not realize I would have to have my lobes pierced in order to wear them. I was sitting on a cushion in front of my mirror when Cyri walked in. She immediately began laughing in her high, musical giggle. I was trying to stick one end of the gold wire inside my ear and then wrap the rest of it around the bottom of the lobe.

"No, no!" she said, then began laughing again.

"What do you mean, 'No, no'?" I was hot and flustered. "Come show me how then. They keep falling off."

"You must use holes. In your ears. See." She pulled her hair away from her face.

I was stunned. I'd never noticed that all the women had holes in their ears for the wires.

"But, Cyri, I don't have any holes." Frustrated, I threw the earrings down. All those coins I'd spent, all those beautiful silver birds and half-moons lying on my table and I could never wear them.

"We make them for you," she said matter-of-factly. "We punch them out."

"Oh, no!" My hands shot up to cover and protect my ears. No one was going to poke holes in them.

"You wear earrings," she nodded, "you have holes."

I looked again at the exquisite pieces and thought of the money I paid. While I was trying to decide, Cyri took my hand and pulled me through the door into the seraglio.

"I do it," Thalia said. "I do many ears, all my daughters. It'll be over in a minute."

The sight of her heating a long needle in a candle flame did nothing to ease my qualms. I felt like one of the lambs being led to slaughter. The first quick, searing jab raised me up off the cushion. With all the women staring at me to see how I would react, I had to grit my teeth to keep from screaming while Thalia pulled the bit of silk thread back and forth through the opening. I almost fainted when I touched the spot and then saw blood on my fingers. And we were only half finished. There was still the second ear. The agony finally ended when Thalia slipped the gold wires into each hole. I was not sure, however, as for several days, I kept moving the gold wires back and forth to keep the skin from closing around them, that my vanity was worth all the hours of soreness. Thalia gently rubbed numbing salves on the lobes several times a day, which helped some, and soon I found I could change from one pair to another with little discomfort.

With Olav always by my side, I explored most of Constantinople: visiting the forums of Constantine, Theodosius, and Arcadius; riding through the old Golden Gate in the original wall of Constantine; viewing the Imperial Palace and many of the harbors. I never tired of watching the vast numbers and sizes of ships arriving every day from foreign ports. Ali Habib had promised to find us a ship, and as I looked at each, I wondered if it would be the one to take us home. I was enjoying the pleasures the city had to offer, but underneath all the gaiety, like a faint moan beneath laughter, was an intense longing for Hordaland.

My greatest pleasure came when I entered one of the splendid churches and I gazed in awe at the magnificent mosaics around and above me. From a distance, the scenes from the Bible, the life of Christ, and the lives of saints and martyrs seemed painted on the walls with some sort of glistening substance that captured and reflected back the light from the many candle flames. A closer look, however, revealed that every picture was created from thousands of tiny pieces of stone, all almost identical in size, meticulously fitted into place. Sometimes bits of glass and even jewels were used to add to the brilliance. Shadows and contours were created through the use of delicate differences in the shades and colors used. The glittering backgrounds were created by setting the stones at different angles to the light. Marble, with its great variety of white and gray and pink and green hues, was a favorite stone. The vast amount of gold found in halos and robe decorations was made by annealing gold leaf to the bottom of clear glass. I don't know which impressed me more, the mosaics themselves or the artistry and craftsmanship that went into designing them, all done to glorify God. These were unlike any churches in Britain; and yet sitting in them, I found time and distance evaporating. I could have been in the abbey again.

The queen of all the churches was the Hagia Sophia —Holy Wisdom—built first by the Emperor Constantine and later rebuilt by the Emperor Justinian. I did not enter it until I had visited many of the others, but I often looked at it from afar. Its tremendous center dome sheltered the heart of Eastern Christianity, and its patriarchs wielded great power over both secular and sacred affairs of the Byzantine empire.

I had heard so much about the impression the first sight of it made on a visitor, I postponed going, knowing I could have that experience only once. I did not know then that each subsequent visit would reveal new and more glorious sights which human eyes could not absorb all at once.

As imposing as the Hagia Sophia was in size, its bare exterior walls of brick were really quite unprepossessing. I wondered if its grandeur was in the imagination of the viewer. I walked through the atrium, surrounded by porticoes, and then into the narthex, which opened into the church through nine doors.

I stopped. It was as if I were almost blinded by a great light. For a few moments I was too overawed to move, and I felt like one who had been allowed a vision of Heaven.

Slowly I walked through the wide nave, flanked on either side by aisles with galleries above them. Overhead loomed the enormous dome, supported by four arches resting on a quartet of tremendous piers. Above and around me was a splendor so dazzling it was hard to believe it had been designed and created by man.

Tall columns of porphyry, white marble, and verd antique had marble capitals sculpted with goldsmithlike delicacy, highlighted by accents of blue and gold. Walking on the pavement of marble and mosaic was like walking through a garden frozen in stone. The walls were covered with sheets of marble in a variety of tones and hues which blended one into another in one continuous sweep. On the curves of the vaults, within the domes, and in the arches were brilliant mosaics against dark blue and silver backgrounds.

But all that faded from memory when I approached the farther end and my eyes moved from the silver pulpit to the iconostasis enclosing the sanctuary in chased silver. A silver canopy, with silk and gold embroideries between the columns, was raised over an altar of solid gold, decorated with enamel and embellished with precious stones.

I left the Hagia Sophia after my first visit with only a swirling impression of gold, silver, sparkling gems, ornate marblework, and detailed mosaics. I returned many times before I could get over the feeling of awe and really look at all the separate creations that together made up the Great Church. I went there to admire, not for moments of meditation and prayer. For those I sought out smaller churches.

I often spent an entire afternoon in one or another of them, finding in their quiet, peaceful beauty a surcease from the almost constant agony of worry about Rorik and the children. As widespread as Ali Habib's network of spies was, no word had reached him about Rorik's fate. With the coming of fall, there were no longer any ships arriving from the North; so we must wait for late spring or summer for news. That meant months of delay unless we located a ship bound for Britain or the North Sea by way of the Mediterranean and the great World Sea. In spite of what he said about feeling that Rorik had not been sold as a slave, I still felt that Ali Habib really thought that he had been and might yet be brought to Constantinople, the greatest trading center of them all. There seemed no other reason for his insistence that I stay with him. It would not be that hard to find a ship for Olav and me. So I stayed, ignoring the feeling in my heart that Rorik was moving farther and farther away from me. I refused to think of him dead.

Although I respected Olav's wish to accompany me whenever I ventured beyond the walls of the house, there were times I longed to wander to nearby streets alone.

"Really, Olav," I said crossly when he saw me in the garden with my cloak around my shoulders, "there is no reason I cannot walk a few blocks unescorted."

"There are many reasons," he insisted. "No woman of your station ever goes out alone. Only the poor and the prostitutes. In your fine clothes you are obviously not poor. You would be accosted as one plying her trade."

I was getting more and more impatient for him to leave me on my own. I was not a child to be led by the hand everywhere I went.

"Not if I put the hood over my head and walk with eyes down. I am not ignorant of the ways of prostitutes to lure their customers. Nor do I wear the eye paint that is the badge of their trade."

"There are other reasons I prefer not to mention. You would not be safe."

He's always so mysterious, I thought. Always circling around a subject, never coming to the point. Well, I'll be the judge of whether I'm safe or not. I had no intention of wandering as far as the bazaars or entering an unknown shop. I merely wanted to stroll a few blocks and revisit a small church I had entered some days earlier after managing to escape Olav's vigilance.

"All right, I'll stay here," I assured him.

"I'm ready to go with you."

"No, I prefer to stay in the garden." I was being petulant and responding rudely to his kindness, but I was also angry. He left right away without saying anything more.

I waited until I knew he had returned to the men's quarters before slipping out the side gate into the narrow street. It was only a few steps along the one street and down another to the church. Smaller than most I had seen, it had an air of intimacy about it I liked, enhanced by age-darkened mosaics. The colors had mellowed to subdued, almost somber tones, although the pictures were as exquisitely detailed as those in the larger churches. Mary's eyes, in her mosaic over the main altar, had a soft, liquid look about them, as if filled with the tears she longed to shed. She was the sorrowing mother of a lost child, not the exultant mother of a risen Christ. In that was her appeal for me.

I thought I was alone until I heard the swish of heavy robes on the marble floor. A priest, all in black, came toward me. His spare figure and gaunt face bespoke the ascetic life, and his eyes shone with an almost unnatural, penetrating brilliance. They were accentuated by long black hair that hung to his shoulders and a beard that covered most of his face.

At first he only nodded and went about some business near the altar; but when I started to leave, he approached me.

"You are a stranger here?" he asked.

I nodded. I felt his gaze taking in every feature of my face, every aspect of my tunic and cloak. His eyes seemed to pierce through what was outwardly visible.

"You have come to see the relics?" he asked.

"No—no, I did not know of any here." I wanted to leave. Something about him sent cold chills up my spine, and there was a nauseating odor emanating from his robe, sweet like incense but overpowering like a drug.

Many of the churches displayed relics claimed to be associated with Christ or the martyrdom of a favorite saint, and I had viewed them with a combination of curiosity and disbelief. Withered hands and yellowed bits of bone held little fascination for me.

"Then come," he said in an insistent tone. "I will show you." He began leading me toward a door in the narthex. "We have one of the rarest which we keep protected in a darkened room. I will not tell you what it is. You will see and you will know."

I did not want to go. I was suddenly more afraid of what I might see than of the man himself. I shuddered at the thought of coming face to face with a complete skeleton or the mummified head of a saint. By now the priest had grasped my arm so tightly, I was helpless to do anything but move along with him.

He was asking more questions. Where was I from? How did I get here? Where was I staying? Something cautioned me not to answer, and I pretended not to understand.

Once inside the small room, with the door shut behind us, we were in almost total darkness. When the priest lit a

247

candle, I saw the walls and ceiling were covered with glass which reflected back more than a dozen images of the two of us, emphasizing the fact I was alone with him. Other than a couch and low table on which he placed the candle, the room was bare. I thought about the strange religious cults which demanded human sacrifices, and I was terrified. I was in the grip of a madman, and I dared not show my fear. I had to get out of the room, get away as quickly as possible.

"The relic," I stammered. "I'll see the relic and then I must go."

"It was not a dead relic you sought when you came in here alone; it was living flesh." Now his eyes gleamed with the fierceness of one transformed. "I have seen you before. I have watched you. Always you come here alone. You seek out Father Petros and what I can do for you."

With no warning he pulled off my cape and ran his hands along my shoulders and down my arms. I was feeling sick and dizzy from the cloying odors and the mirrors all around me. His hands were all over me. I was trying to struggle out of his grasp, but something about the smells was weakening me.

"Let me go! Let me go or I'll scream." The walls were thick and the threat a weak one, but I had to do something before I succumbed to whatever was putting me to sleep.

"Oh, no, my fair one. You will not leave now. Father Petros has been waiting for you."

Somehow I eluded his grasp. My legs threatened to collapse under me, but I managed to make it to the door. If I could just get it open. He grabbed me from behind, clutching me around the waist and dragging me toward the couch. Praying someone had come into the church, I screamed as loud as I could.

In a state of shock, I saw the door fly open as if my voice had activated it. Olav strode in, grabbed the astonished priest by the scruff of his neck, and threw him to the floor. I stood by, breathing hard and gasping in disbelief. In less than a minute we were standing in the street, and I was gulping in huge breaths of fresh air to clear my head.

"Now you know, Tara, the danger I spoke of," Olav said in a chastizing tone.

"But how—where did you come from?"

"Did you think I believed you when you agreed so quickly not to go out alone?"

"You followed me." I was disturbed and relieved.

"I did," Olav answered, hurrying me along.

"Surely you'd not anticipate I'd come to harm in a church."

"In that church? Yes."

"But why? Who would think someone looking like a priest would turn out to be a lecherous old man instead?"

"That man is the very one Gunner was planning to sell you to."

"Him!" I was stunned. "But you said he was a merchant."

"I said he was a buyer and seller of goods. And so he is. Such things as stolen valuables, illegal drugs, fake relics—there are some genuine ones—and beautiful young women. Those he often buys for himself, enjoys for a few weeks, and then sells to one of the more expensive houses of prostitution."

"But how dare he wear the robes of a priest? And in the church?"

"He is a priest. All the rest is done without the knowledge of the church. His official rooms are simple and bare to the point of poverty. He has other dwellings as opulent as the rooms in the Imperial Palace. He wears two faces and garbs himself accordingly."

"How do you know about him?" I was constantly being amazed at the vast store of knowledge Olav had about the city.

"I have made it my business on previous trips to learn such things. My fear now is that he has recognized me. I have delivered other choice wares to him. And he may well guess now that you are the woman he was promised by Gunner. Do you believe me when I say you must never again go out alone?"

Completely frightened and chagrined, I agreed with no hesitation. For several days I preferred the garden to the bazaars.

When Ali Habib had no guests, he frequently invited me to dine with him. We were often joined by his younger half-brother, Ben Hassem, an elegant man with a wit sharp as a scimitar's edge. He was handsome in a way that is difficult to describe because no single feature was particularly attractive. His lips were too full for his high-boned, saturnine face, and they moved into a sensuous curve whenever he smiled or spoke. Intense black eyes peered out of sockets deeply set in sallow skin. Yet taken all together, it was an arresting face. It was his habit to concentrate on whoever was speaking while saying little himself. When he did speak, it was to make a single, pointed remark. Invariably I felt uncomfortable in his presence, loath to say anything that would draw the attention of his sardonic, disapproving gaze.

It was, therefore, most unexpected when Ben Hassem sent word by way of Olav that he would be honored to have me accompany him to the chariot races at the Hippodrome. My reaction was strangely ambivalent. I was curious to attend some of the entertainments in the city, knowing there was more to Constantinople than shops, harbors, and churches, as fascinating as they were. Yet I hesitated. Constantinople was a city of bizarre customs, particularly among the Moslems. I was puzzled and more than a bit apprehensive about what my acceptance might imply. I did not know Ben Hassem very well; and although he had been apprised of my position as guest in the house, I wondered if he assumed that carried any special obligations toward him. What would he want in return if I went with him?

Deep inside I knew that all of these questions were really covering the turmoil I felt at his invitation. Why did I want to go? Was it the fascination of the chariot race or the thought of being in the company of an attractive man again? Something about Ben Hassem, so very different from Rorik, appealed in a way that was both disturbing and tantalizing. I couldn't put my finger on it. A sensuality not of hard strength and sweat but of languid ease and personal fastidiousness. He was never anything but immaculately clean, yet there was always the suggestion of a savagely masculine scent.

I was tempted to go with Ben Hassem. To test my own feelings and to see what he expected of me. Yet I knew it would be unwise. I trusted Ben Hassem to take the refusal of this first invitation with good grace. I did not trust how he would react to the refusal of a more serious proposal. After my experience with Ruskil in the woods, I was well aware that male conceit thought every woman ready to succumb at the merest of overtures, and masculine vanity thought every smile was an invitation. Nor should I try to bury my own emotions beneath a cool, complacent façade. Ben Hassem's presence stirred a deep need for male companionship, and I had been separated too long from Rorik not to feel a warm response when I was around him. I did not want to have to fight either him or myself. Nor, as Ali Habib's guest, did I want to insult any member of his family.

But I had never been one to resist temptation or to turn my back on a dare. I had fallen out of too many trees and jumped my horse over too many fences to deny that. I wanted to test myself, and I was curious to see just what Ben Hassem did want from me. As long as I knew I might be walking into a dangerous situation, I was sure I could keep things under control.

For the gala event, Cyri arranged my hair in the Greek style, forming several tresses into large curls which she piled high on the back of my head. Over my simple, long-sleeved silk tunic I wore a pellium, a long, wide strip of embroidered fabric with a hole at the center for my head. The back was long enough to form a train; and Cyri showed me how to bring this to the front and drape it over my left arm. I thought of the last time I had dressed carefully to make an impression. It was the last night at King Torvald's. We had left there feeling exuberant at the success of our mission, our proving to the Dani that the Three Shires were as civilized and cultured and, more important, strong as they. I had dressed with the same care, little dreaming that twenty-four hours later our ship would be sunk, our crew drowned, Rorik almost beaten to death, and I on the way to Constantinople.

I looked in the mirror. Was I dressing this way today just to feel good or to make another impression? Did I want to please myself or Ben Hassem. Impatiently I turned from the mirror and sat down to let Cyri put on my soft leather slippers, but I could not stop the blood from rushing to my face or the trembling in my hands.

Ben Hassem and I rode in an open, well-upholstered cart—or car, as he called it—along wide, tree-bordered avenues to the Mese which led through several forums to the Hippodrome next to the Imperial Palace. Cushioned seats had been prepared for us in Ben Hassem's pillared box near the emperor's loge. Being on the upper level, it commanded and excellent view of the entire arena.

251

Two young male slaves attended us, serving chilled juices, small cakes, and slices of fruit.

"Are you comfortable, Tara?" Ben Hassem asked, arranging a pillow behind my back. From the time we left Ali Habib's, his brother had spoken no more than a dozen words, and now I felt even more intimidated by his haughty and imperious attitude. Then I shook myself mentally. I was his invited guest, and I would take my cues from him. If he wanted to be cold and silent, I could be just as frosty and remote.

"Quite, thank you." I turned my face away to look at other spectators coming in. I loved watching people, their clothes, their expression when they thought no one was looking at them. It would suit me fine to spend the afternoon doing just that.

"All this must seem very splendid to you. You have nothing like Constantinople in the North. I understand it is a barbaric land."

I raised my eyebrows. I did not intend to be baited into appearing a naive, wide-eyed innocent. I had judged him rightly the first time I saw him. He was despicable, but I could not deny a certain diabolical charm. He had thrown down the gauntlet, and I would meet his challenge on his own ground.

"No, but it all seems very flat in comparison to our mountains. And of course you have nothing so magnificent as the sunsets on our snow-covered peaks. Or the gigantic fir trees sparkling with ice crystals."

Now his forehead furrowed in a row of exclamation marks. I had reached him. The first point was mine.

"Really?" He had not expected that answer. "You are not impressed with our city? With its seven hills it was built on this site to be a second Rome."

"There is much that is beautiful." I would grant him that. " 'Tis just a different kind of beauty from what I am familiar with."

"For real beauty you will have to see the mosaics inside the Hagia Sophia. Although I am a Moslem, I will be glad to take you there."

How generous of him to put himself out like that! "Oh, but I have been there, and I do not think its Christos can compare with the one in the church of the Holy Apostles."

Ben Hassem looked startled but made no comment. Point

252

two on my side in this verbal combat. He signaled to a slave.

"Would you care for something to drink?" Courtesy became him far more than pettiness.

"Please. I'm finding this heat rather oppressive." Actually the weather was extremely pleasant, but I dabbed at my forehead with a square of white linen as if I were feeling faint.

"Shall we call it a stalemate?" he asked, offering me a slice of apple from the silver platter the slave held.

"What?"

"In chess, when neither opponent can win—"

"I am quite familiar with chess," I interrupted, more rudely than I intended.

He laughed. It was the first time I had heard him laugh, and it was a very pleasant, sociable laugh. "I am now convinced there is little you are not knowledgeable about. So—shall we call it a draw and start all over again?"

"Agreed." I could not repress a smile. Maybe if I had been the seer the elderly Signe thought she saw in me, I would have maintained my cool, aloof exterior rather than tried to dazzle Ben Hassem with my wit. "Constantinople has been a revelation. I've enjoyed exploring it."

"Will you let me show you more of it?"

"I would like that." Time enough to worry about any feelings of guilt. I brushed aside the few twinges I felt now. I could handle seeing Ben Hassem if I thought of him as a friend and remained on the alert for any signs he wanted to be otherwise.

Now I concentrated on the action in front of us. The Hippodrome was an elongated oval some two thousand feet long and six hundred feet wide. Down the center ran the *spina*, or low stone barrier, around which the races were run. Along the top of the *spina* were many fine sculptures in stone and bronze. The finest was a tall obelisk of porphyry which Hassem told me had been brought from the Temple of Karnak in Egypt and placed in the arena some six hundred years earlier.

There were to be nine chariot races that day, each one more important and exciting than the last. Hassem explained what was happening as each race began. The first two in each set of three were called "heats." From four doors beneath the emperor's box, four chariots hurtled into the arena. To the cheers and urging of the spectators, and amidst great clouds of dust from sand and cedar shavings, the drivers raced their chariots four times around the course. The two winners from each of the heats met in a final third race to determine the ultimate winner. The first set of chariots was small and lightweight, pulled by a single horse. Before each race the air was filled with the raucous sounds of heavy betting. Once the horses appeared that changed to cheers and applause, urging the favorite on. During the first heat I sat and watched quietly, moving to the edge of my seat only when the race neared its end. Then I was swept up in the fervor of those around me, heated by the gambling fever I had caught among the Vikings. When the next group of chariots came out, I let intuition pick one for me, and I silently cheered the man on. He won, and with others around me I leapt up from my chair and applauded.

"You want to place a small wager on the next race, Tara?"

I suddenly became embarrassed at having shown my enthusiasm. I turned to Hassem. He looked amused at my outburst.

"I—I have no coins with me."

"You have your bracelets. I'll put up three bezants against a silver bracelet. Which is your man?"

"The chariot with the black horse."

"Stephanos. You have a good eye for racing. He is a champion."

"No," I laughed, "pure luck." I put my bracelet with Hassem's coins on the edge of the box.

Stephanos won, and I started to pick up my bracelet.

"Stopping so soon, Tara? At least give me a chance to get my coins back."

We bet on the next five races. I won three and lost two, so I was ahead by a few coins. The second set of races had been run by larger, two-horse chariots. We were now watching the third set, heavy, cumbersome battle chariots pulled by four horses. At times the four contestants ran side by side, and it was an awesome sight: sixteen horses panting and snorting as their hooves pounded the sand, and appearing to run headlong toward the wall at the end of the arena. Always, at the last moment, the drivers turned the horses' heads, and they swerved around the tip of the *spina*.

It was the final race. I had bet on Igor, a tall, lithe

driver from somewhere to the north of Constantinople. He had been brought to the city as a slave. When he showed his abilities at handling horses, his master trained him as a chariot racer, and he was usually a winner. He won the second heat easily, and I left my bracelet and coins on the rail. My money was still on him.

"You may be sorry, Tara," Hassem said. "He's good, but not as good as the new driver I've picked. My man hasn't raced long, but I've never seen anyone handle the reins as well as he."

"We'll see," I said and turned my attention to the race.

For three times around the horses ran side by side, not an inch separating them. They were gauging, testing one another, waiting to see who would pull ahead first. Igor moved forward. Immediately Hassem's man moved up beside him and slightly ahead. Now I was screaming and yelling with the rest of the crowd, ignoring the dust that encircled us and the hot sun that had my silk tunic clinging to my sweaty body. Igor laid on the whip, and sped a good two feet in front of the others. They were coming to the fourth and last turn around the *spina*. Hassem's man was next to and just outside Igor, and when it came time for him to swing the curve, he cut in short, ramming his chariot into Igor's. The horses went down, the chariots crashed into the *spina*, the men were thrown backward. The other two chariots swerved, trying to get to the outside of the ring and around the fallen horses. In doing so they crushed the two fallen drivers between them.

In less than a minute it was all over. In the sand beneath us lay two dead drivers and eight horses so badly hurt they would have to be destroyed. Around me the cheering grew louder. This was what many had come to see. The racing and gambling were not enough. They wanted blood. And now they had it. I picked up my bracelet and put it back on my wrist. There were fortunes won and lost that afternoon. I had won a few coins, but I had lost any desire to see another race.

Acrobats and jugglers, who had entertained us between each set of races, now came out and tried to keep the crowd's attention while the dead and mutilated were carried away.

"I'm sorry you're upset," Hassem said. "I should have warned you. There is usually at least one pileup every time. Today was really rather mild."

"I'm all right now. And I did enjoy it up to that point."

I returned to my room in a highly disturbed state, unable to decide whether I wanted to see Hassem again. Fearfully anxious, impatiently apprehensive, I waited for a second invitation. When it came, it was for an evening at the theater and I accepted. Then there was a third and a fourth, for a musical performance and a ride along the shores of the Bosporus. I had wrestled with my feelings of guilt and subdued them. Always Hassem was the courtly companion, friendly but keeping his distance. He was an intelligent, witty escort, and if for brief moments at a time he could relieve the tedium and help me forget my sorrows, I saw no harm in it.

It was true his attitude puzzled me, and I wondered why he wanted to see me. For most men, companionship was not enough, and always I was prepared to fend off any advances. If he were leading up to a seduction or the suggestion I enter into an affair with him, he was being most cunning. Nor did his presence leave me unmoved. Often I returned and lay awake a long time, imagining what it would be like having him make love to me. Then I forced myself to realize it was loneliness and not a real feeling for him that had me tossing and turning hour after hour. I ached to have Rorik beside me in the bed, and I would not let my emotions lead me to seek a substitute for him.

Chapter Seventeen

WHEN I FIRST SAW THE BEAUTIFUL women of the harem walking two together, arms linked or around each other's waist, it seemed only natural. They had been brought to this place as strangers and were now forced to find what happiness they could among companions not of their own choosing. Their backgrounds were as diverse as the countries whence they came. Some had been brought up prepared to spend their lives in seclusion; others had known the freedom of running through open fields and the joy of family gatherings. My heart ached for them each time I walked away through the door to my rooms—and freedom, knowing they could not.

Within one end of the four-sided pavilion, built around the garden court, was a sunken pool of glazed tile and mosaics. Similar to the one in my rooms, it was much longer and deeper. Two extremely lifelike, large bronze fish spewed water into three alabaster shells from which it spilled into the pool.

During much of the day, the pool was the center of activity; and while the women sat or lay on cushions around it, they chatted in their soft, lilting voices. From a laugh now and then, I knew they were gossiping, as women are wont to do, even before I understood what they were saying. Some laughter evoked a blush or a frown on the face of one of them, the victim of a joke or the subject of the gossip. When I learned more of the language, I knew the stinging remarks were aimed at those who were no longer summoned by Ali Habib.

One of the favorite ways the harem found to wile away the time was sitting before gilded mirrors, held by slaves, and artfully applying colored pastes to their skin—azure and turquoise on their eyelids, carmine on the lips, and paler pink on their cheeks. I was aware women in some countries painted their faces, but this was the first time I had watched makeup being applied. So I stood, fascinated, as their fingers moved from one jar of color to another and then to the face. Or, as with a long, slim stick of black kohl, they outlined their eyes and darkened their lashes. While one sat on a cushion, working steadily in front of a mirror, another brushed her hair and skillfully twisted it into curls or fashioned long braids. The women seemed able to spend long hours trying to accentuate their natural beauty.

From time to time one might begin singing a high, melodic tune but always with a melancholy undertone. When others joined in, two or three brought out ornately designed, stringed instruments to accompany them. Soon, the pavilion looked and sounded like an enormous gilded bird cage, the colorful gowns and lilting voices mirroring the feathers and songs of the exotic birds in the garden who did not fly away because their wings had been clipped.

As the day grew warmer, the women removed their long tunics and bathed in the fragrant pool. Like children—and with their children—they played under the plashing spray of the fountains, tossed handfuls of water at one another, or merely floated in the cool depths. With floral-scented bars of soap, they took turns lathering each other and rinsing off under the spray from the shells. Over and over I was reminded of the tales I had heard of beautiful water nymphs and sea sprites.

They often bathed for more than an hour before walking out of the pool by way of the sunken marble steps. Putting the children in the care of slaves, they dried each other off with large, soft towels and then rubbed their bodies with fragrant oils. While some immediately donned fresh tunics, others lay naked on the divans or near the edge of the water, letting the cooling breezes from the garden blow across them.

A few of the women had been well educated, and they often read aloud from books of poetry. Some listened with rapt attention; some returned to making up their faces; while others napped away the long, lazy afternoon.

As soon as the harem learned I was merely a guest in their quarters, they greeted me each time by gathering around and chattering like a bevy of hummingbirds. It seemed to delight them that I could not speak their language well, and they eagerly began to teach me. So good were they as teachers, 'twas not long before I learned enough to make myself understood and to know what they were saying.

From the very beginning they urged me to bathe with them, allow them to teach me the art of making up my face with paint, and to rearrange my hair. Since most of them were dark-complexioned with rich brown or black hair, they exclaimed over my fair skin and pale blond hair.

I hesitated at first to join in, still feeling very unsure of my place among them. When I realized I might remain with Ali Habib many months, I began to value their companionship more and more. I could not go shopping every day, and even in my garden the hours were long between waking and retiring. The pavilion soon became as familiar to me as my own rooms.

Although everything about the seraglio was very beautiful, it was a beauty that disturbed me with its seductively sensuous, exotic atmosphere. It seemed imbued with an evil I could not see or hear. More than just the obvious evil of slavery and the purpose of the harem itself, it threatened at times to suffocate me like a cloying, too-sweet fragrance. The cool waters of the pool offered an invitation I found hard to resist, and yet I did. 'Twas not from modesty I refused to remove my tunic. I had disrobed in the small fire room on the farm in Hordaland. Nor was I averse to having someone brush my hair and arrange it in various styles. Cyri did that for me every morning and evening. No, there was an elusive something that disturbed me.

So the women, thinking me shy I suppose, welcomed but did not pressure me. I listened to their chatter, learning many new words every day until I could laugh and talk with them. As the songs and poems gradually came to have meaning for me, I realized they all dealt with love on a highly erotic level. I observed the women more closely, and soon I became aware of what evil haunted the place.

While one brushed the hair of another, she frequently leaned over and kissed her throat and shoulders. When they bathed or rubbed on the sweet-smelling oils, they caressed each other. And those who fell asleep, still naked, lay close together on the divans or beside the pool. They were not paired merely in friendship. They were love partners.

I was shocked at the revelation, repulsed and sickened.

I did not think I could ever go near the pavilion again. I accepted the fact that all these women shared the beds of either Ali Habib or Ben Hassem. I enjoyed watching them play with their younger children. Now I tried to shut them out of my mind, locking them out of my memory by closing the heavy doors between us. It was not that easy.

During the next few days I remained in my garden or took excursions in the palanquin. And I did a lot of thinking. I was free to move around as I wished. I saw the Christian women of Constantinople in the bazaars and the shops of craftsmen or visiting friends. Slowly, painfully, I came to a new understanding of the situation in the seraglio. The harem women were slaves to loneliness and in thrall to a passionate need for love. Who was I, bereft of Rorik's love, not to understand? The ex-wives had long since been cast aside. Also, many of the older wives and concubines were, probably, no longer called to Ali Habib's room. Nor were they allowed a mother's natural prerogative of loving and teaching her children when and how she wished. The younger wives and concubines had known perhaps a month or a few weeks of love, and were now called for only occasionally. It depended on who was the favorite of the moment. Even then it might be less pleasure than merely serving a man's needs. No matter, their senses had been aroused, and now their own hungers cried out to be assuaged. Perhaps 'twas natural they should turn to one another to fulfill those needs.

While still hesitant to get close to any of them for fear of encouraging an intimacy I did not desire, I returned to the pavilion. I had earlier begun making friends with Irenia, the youngest wife. She smiled her delight at my return, and urged me again to join her in the pool. The day was warm and the water too inviting to resist.

I undressed and walked into the pool. The water came just to my breasts, and it was my first experience in not being able to sit down in a pool when I bathed. With my first move, I slipped on the tiles and went under, landing awkwardly on the bottom marble step. Someone grabbed me by the shoulders; and once I was able to stand, I saw them all laughing and clapping their hands. As frightened as I was—the memory of the day in the rapids suddenly overwhelming me—I was able to laugh too. Before long I was splashing under the fountain and playing with the children.

Next Irenia showed me how to lie on my back and float. Try as I might, I could not keep my feet from going straight to the bottom. Since I failed hopelessly at that, she told me to watch her and copy what she did. By lying on her stomach and moving her arms slowly out and back, she glided the length of the pool. I laughed and shook my head. I had seen others do it, and it looked easy; but I was certain I would sink right to the bottom.

"I insist," she said, nodding her head so fast her long, black hair sprayed water all around; and her amber eyes crinkled at the corners.

When at first she put her hand under me to hold me up, I tensed. Her nude body was too close to mine for comfort. Immediately I felt ashamed, realizing she was only trying to help me. Her constant companion, Tanyama, a swarthy woman some years older, stood nearby, and I made haste to learn how to swim. I was an alien in their midst, and I had seen the small jeweled scissors many of them kept among their powders and perfumes. A swift stab with one or a long, slicing cut with those curved blades could be as fatal as a knife wound. Once I was able to manage on my own, Irenia and Tanyama left the water together and stretched out beside the pool.

Usually I left the pavilion during the afternoon to rest and get ready for the supper Olav brought each evening I was not dining with our host. One afternoon, however, I was entranced by the readings from a new poet. I had learned enough of the language by this time to appreciate the evocative words of love and the sensuous, haunting rhythms. Gina, one of the younger concubines, accompanied the reader on a slim, long-handled lute. Like the others, I was caught up in the ecstasy of the moment, and my thoughts had been lingering on memories of Rorik. I yearned to feel his touch once more, the taste of his lips on mine, the pressure of his hands that set my blood racing and my flesh throbbing. I ached for the weight of his body and the final, exalting surge of warmth that left us both weak and yet strengthened by our love. It had been more than a dozen weeks since our ship had been captured, and in my longing I wondered if I would ever see him again.

Listening to the poetry and music, I let the hour slip past when I usually left for my rooms. I was still there when Ali Habib's personal eunuch came to summon the wife who was to spend the night with her husband. There was no pause in the reading, no moment of eager anticipation, no signs of disappointment. Just a calm acceptance of a normal daily routine. The one chosen merely left quietly to prepare herself for the evening.

The one called for this night was Thalia, the first wife. Though Thalia herself had told me she often spent nights with her husband, I was astonished that he hadn't called for one of the younger wives or concubines. Irenia must have noticed the surprised look on my face, for she flicked a finger at me and motioned for me to move over and sit beside her.

"Thalia is first wife," she said.

"I know," I nodded.

"She is very wise and still very beautiful. She sees Ali Habib every day and many nights. I think he loves her very much, and he depends on her for counsel."

I saw tears come to Irenia's eyes. Was it because she had not been called for this night, or was there another reason? I wanted to ask her how she felt about sharing the affections of her husband with so many others, but I dared not. Did she love him or did she feel nothing more than awe and respect for him?

Now that my curiosity had been aroused, I remained late many afternoons. Not every evening did Ali Habib summon one of the harem to attend him, but such days were rare. I was amazed that a man of his age was so virile. Maybe that was one of the advantages of a harem. Variety provided a titillation of its own.

I never ascended to the sleeping quarters on the second and third floors. I would not let my imagination dwell on whether the women not chosen by Ali Habib slept alone or shared their beds with another lonely partner. Their desires were not mine; and while I did not condemn them, I preferred not to think about them either.

Through the weeks, the many slaves became as familiar to me as the wives and concubines. Each had her own place in the female hierarchy: nursemaid, teacher, personal servant, general servant, and so on. A few had unique abilities of their own. One recently arrived from Persia often entertained us with her particular talent, an exotic style of dancing much admired in the Near East. Aimee hesitated when I asked if she could perform Salomé's famous dance of veils. I thought at first she'd not understood me. At last she nodded but frowned. I thought maybe the dance carried a curse of some kind. Then I learned she considered it shameful, preferring the traditional dances of Persia. Eventually she did the veil dance; but once I had seen the traditional ones, I understood why she demurred at my request.

Aimee wore long, tightly fitting trousers, a blouse with full sleeves caught at the wrist, and a long skirt gathered at the waist. The material was a heavy silk, bordered at hem and cuffs with wide bands of gold embroidery. She had tiny bells on her soft leather slippers, and fastened to the middle finger of each hand was a pair of small cymbals which she clicked against her palms. The impression she made, as demure and modest as a nun, was quite different from what I had imagined of an oriental dancer. There were no sheer veils and no exposed flesh.

Three slaves with small drums, a lute, and a reed flute provided the music. The first notes were soft and low, played in a smooth, easy rhythm. Aimee moved slowly across the floor, undulating her hips slightly, gliding more than stepping. Very gradually the tempo increased, and her steps became shorter and more rapid. She twirled as she moved in the wide circle formed by those of us watching. The music grew louder and faster, and Aimee's feet and cymbals kept perfect time. The little bells on her shoes tinkled continuously, providing a high descant to the lower tones of the drum and lute. She moved to the center of the circle, bent gracefully into a deep backbend, her hips still undulating, until her hands touched the floor. Just as gracefully she rose up again, and then went into a rapid spin, gradually raising her arms from her sides until they met high over her head. She continued to whirl until I thought surely she would grow dizzy and fall.

As I followed her movements, they became more than the movements of a beautiful, sensuous dance. Her body spoke a silent language as rhythmic as poetry, as intimate as a whisper. It spoke of tender love and passionate desire, of longing to touch, to arouse, and to console, of heartbreak and despair. Each gesture, every sinuous motion uttered a sentiment too often silenced by modesty or estrangement. With such a language, love needed no words spoken aloud.

Although I sat absolutely still throughout the performance, I felt my inner body moving in time with hers. By revealing my own needs and hopes, the dance seemed to

reach in and bring to life memories that needed to remain
buried until I was with Rorik once again. I forced myself
to concentrate on Aimee and the others around us. It was
the wrong place for weeping.

Suddenly she came to a complete stop in front of Thalia
and fell in prostrate obeisance before the first wife.

There was a stunned silence at first, and then we began
applauding. Many of the harem danced, but none had seen
a performance as beautiful as this. The women clamored
for her to teach them. Thus it was I learned oriental
dancing. I tried to imagine the look on Rorik's face when
I danced for him. He would be a little amused, somewhat
perplexed, but underneath, enjoying every minute of it.
Then I laughed to myself. 'Twas Thorne who would really
appreciate the performance. I could already see the smile
spread into a grin across his bearded face and hear the
chuckles begin deep in his stomach and finally burst forth
in loud guffaws.

On impulse one day, after we had been dancing and
were resting by the pool, I reached for the lute laid aside
by the slave and began strumming it. It was many years
since I had played, and I thought about the evenings at
home, sitting before the fire in the manor, and singing my
father's favorite songs. Gradually my fingers found the
notes again, and I began singing one of the old ballads. I
scarce realized that the other women had ceased their chattering and were listening to me. When I stopped, they
begged me to go on, and I found I remembered more and
more tunes, both ballads and love songs. As it had been
their pleasure to entertain me with their gifts, so now I
could do the same in return; and I taught them the words
and music. It helped me, too, to bring a touch of my home
into theirs.

Ali Habib had told me I could invite members of the
harem to my rooms as long as there was no one in the
garden outside, the heavy draperies were drawn, and I requested a eunuch to stand guard outside the door leading
to the main hall.

Thalia came several times, and we talked about our
lives before we met. She asked many questions about
Thorne and the family and about our life in the North.

"I remember well," she said, "the attack against Ali
Habib and the rescue by Thorne and Olav. I rushed out

from the back, from behind the heavy curtain. I knew my husband was going to be killed. I tried to get help from nearby merchants. They were afraid. It was not wise for them to side with a Moslem against Christians. I wept and pleaded. It did no good. I would have been forced to watch Ali Habib die if your Vikings had not intervened. It is a very deep gratitude we feel. It is a debt we can never repay."

"You are more than repaying it now." I told her about the attack on the ship, and she murmured her sympathy over my fears for Rorik. Always the talk eventually turned to our children, and I told her all about Signe, Eirik and Asri while I held back the tears.

"Cry, my dear," she said. "It will help you."

"I'm sorry. I didn't mean to weep. But I have no idea how they are or if my babies remember me."

"I know. I have not seen two of my sons for several years. And I—I will never see my daughters again now they are married and in harem."

" 'Tis not fair, Thalia. Not the way you were brought up."

"It is the custom, Tara. I was the exception. I must abide by my husband's wishes and those of their husbands."

Thalia looked around my rooms and pulled the curtains back to gaze into the garden. I wondered if she loved her husband enough to wish him a long life, or if she thought about the time when she might move to this suite when her eldest son became master of the house.

Irenia refused shyly when I first asked her to visit, but finally she accepted an invitation to have supper with me. I was sorry I had to keep the heavy draperies pulled. The garden was beautiful in the evening and the breezes cool, but I would do nothing to displease my generous host. From then on, Irenia came frequently, often eating with me and asking many questions about my life and family.

One night as I was preparing for bed, I heard a frantic knocking on the door leading to the pavilion. Cyri ran to answer.

"It is Irenia, my lady."

"This late? What can she want." Something had to be seriously wrong for her to come to me without an invitation. In the past she had always waited for me to ask her.

"She is crying."

"Go quickly and find a eunuch to stand at the outside door. Then tell Irenia to come in."

I hastened to pull the draperies to the garden. There was probably no need to do this. No one could see in from the street, and I was alone, but by this time the action had become automatic.

By the time Irenia joined me, she was too hysterical to speak. I made her sit down while I bathed her face. Finally I was able to ask some questions, but only one word came from her lips: Tanyama. Her constant companion and, I assumed, her love partner. Something had happened to Tanyama.

After many minutes Irenia calmed down enough to tell me what was troubling her. Tanyama was an ex-wife. She had chosen at first to remain in the harem, because of her two children, and had seemed satisfied once she'd taken Irenia under her wing. Gradually, however, she became restless and requested Ali Habib to find her a husband as she was permitted to do. Irenia knew nothing of this until earlier in the day. Amid many tears she bid her intimate good-bye.

"I am so unhappy, Tara. You are my friend, but now I—I have no one—"

I knew what she was trying to say. As distressed as I was by their relationship, I understood her loneliness.

"Irenia, you have been very close to Tanyama, but you must now keep your thoughts on your husband. Your—your relationship with him is a natural one. You must have known yours with Tanyama was not really normal."

"You don't understand, Tara. I love her."

"I know." I had to be careful if I hoped to retain her confidence and help her. If I said too much, if I tried to moralize, she would turn away from me completely. "And you will not forget her. But you will be happy again. Certainly when you have a child, you will have a wonderful new interest."

"No—no!" She began crying again. "There will never be a child."

"You are young, Irenia. Give yourself time."

"You do not understand. I am still a—" She groped for the word. "I am still untouched."

"You have not slept with Ali Habib?" I was stunned. With her petite figure, glossy black hair, and sparkling

266

amber eyes, she was one of the most beautiful in the harem.

She sobbed a few times and then told me her story. When still very young, only fourteen, she had been given by her father to Ali Habib. She had brought a large wife-portion with her; and her father, also a merchant, had gained many advantages.

She was still at her mother's side when her father announced the betrothal and said she was leaving for Constantinople immediately. Her mother protested, saying there was much she still had to teach her daughter, but the father was adamant. Thus Irenia arrived ignorant of many of the nuances of lovemaking. She was startled when she first saw her husband. She had not been told he was older than her father. Ali Habib welcomed her with a gentle kindness, and she thought maybe she would get used to being his wife. After an intimate dinner, slaves prepared her for bed and left her alone.

"I could not please him. I did not know what to do—what he needed to—"

I said nothing but merely nodded. Ali Habib was no longer young, and he required certain stimuli to become aroused. Irenia had not been prepared for that.

"He has never summoned me again. I may soon become an ex-wife before I am ever a wife. I have learned what love is, and I do not know how I can live without it."

There seemed to be no way I could tell her that what she had experienced with Tanyama was not really love but merely physical stimulation. I had to find some way to help her.

"Go back to bed, Irenia. You are tired and should sleep now. Do not do anything you will be sorry for. And come here whenever you wish." I feared that in her despondency she would try to end her life.

The solution came sooner than I expected, but unfortunately it placed me in a very tenuous position with Ali Habib.

Irenia accepted my invitation and came almost every evening. I told her more about my own life and forced her to talk as much as possible. Always I had the guard at the door, and I closed the draperies. Late one afternoon she walked to an arch leading to the garden, and before I could stop her, she thoughtlessly pulled the curtains aside. At that time of day there was usually no one there, but

267

this time I saw her start back. Then I saw why. She had come face to face with Paul, the young deaf-mute slave, who was working among the plants on the loggia.

The glances that passed between them were like a single bolt of lightning flashing from one cloud to another. I should not have been surprised. I have said how beautiful she was. Paul was fair-skinned, slender, of medium height with blond hair and fine but strong aquiline features. His long, slim fingers moved tenderly among the plants. He had been captured in Macedonia, and I often thought he came from much higher than peasant stock.

I immediately rushed over and pulled the draperies together again.

"You must leave immediately, Irenia. Ali Habib must never know that Paul has seen you."

She did as I bid her, scurrying away like a little mouse that has barely escaped the trap, but not before I saw the smile she gave Paul and the tears that glistened in her eyes as she left. I felt sorry for them, but it would be death for them and banishment from the house for me if I let them see each other again. When Irenia went to her rooms in the seraglio, I thought that was the end of it.

The days had become cooler, and it was more pleasant than ever to ride through the bazaars. Twice more I went to the theater with Hassem and again to the Hippodrome, where this time there were no accidents to mar the excitement and thrills of the race.

Late one afternoon I returned from browsing among the craft shops. I had seen a pair of exquisite blue blown-glass vases ornamented with gold chasing. The price was high, but they would be a real treasure to take back North. I walked rapidly down the hall, thinking I would sit in the garden for an hour before supper and ponder whether to make the purchase. I knew I would end up going back for them. I had always been able to rationalize why I needed whatever it was I wanted. I turned the handle of the door, but nothing happened. It was bolted from the inside. I paused. That was most unusual. Cyri never locked the door when I was not there. I knocked and waited. I knocked again. When she finally opened it, she was flustered and out of breath.

"I'm sorry, my lady. I—I was busy getting your bath ready. I don't know how it got locked. The bolt must have slipped."

The bolt was far too heavy to slip. It was difficult for me even to work it into place. But I let the matter drop. I trusted Cyri with all my things. If she had been trying on my gowns and jewels or bathing in the tub, I could easily forgive her. She was too fine a servant to chastise.

Irenia came to visit less and less frequently, and I assumed she was either adjusting to the loss of Tanyama or found it painful to be in my rooms when Paul might be in the garden just on the other side of the curtains. Near enough to touch yet forbidden to look at each other. I should have been more alert. Forbidden trysts are the most delectable.

Two, maybe three weeks later, she again sought me out, weeping, unable to speak. With shaking hands she pointed to her belly and encircled her arms in front of it. She was pregnant! But I couldn't understand why she was so distraught. She should be happy that Ali Habib had at last taken her to wife and she would have a child. I didn't like mysteries, and this one in particular was disturbing me.

"Irenia! Stop crying at once. You should be laughing and smiling. You said you wanted to be a real wife, and now you're going to have a child."

With that she collapsed in my arms, and I had to call for Cyri to help me. She finally calmed down enough to say one word: Paul.

Oh, dear God, no! That was why Cyri was so upset the day I came home earlier than expected. She had been a party to the affair. I should have beaten her right then and there for the trouble all of us were in. Instead I sat her down and talked as calmly as I could under the circumstances.

"Cyri, tell me everything. It is obvious that Irenia can't tell me."

"She and Paul. They love each other." Deathly pale with fear, she spoke in short, jerky sentences, knowing she herself was in great danger. "She come back. You not here. They go into garden. Then—then in here."

"And you let them? You didn't send Paul away? How did you dare disobey Ali Habib's commands!"

Now Cyri began crying, and I had two hysterical children on my hands, for neither one was any more mature emotionally than a twelve-year-old.

"Answer me, Cyri! I have to know. Maybe there is something we can do."

"They so happy," she sobbed out. "I enjoy seeing them happy."

She was right. There was so little joy in either one's life. I might have been tempted to do the same thing. But those few moments of happiness could end in great tragedy for all of us.

"How often, Cyri?"

"Three, maybe four times. That is all."

I had almost forgotten about Irenia, lying on the bed, her head buried in the pillows, the cause of all this misery. Now she tugged at my sleeve.

"Ali—Ali Habib. I must see him."

No, I thought, he would never understand.

"I must sleep with him, Tara. Soon. Please see him and tell him of my desire."

That would do it, but who was I to interfere between husband and wife? I was already involved, however, and certainly I had nothing to lose.

I usually dined with Ali Habib, Ben Hassem, and Olav at least once a week. I could only pray he did not have a full schedule of important guests. Two days later I received the invitation I waited for impatiently. Would I please join my host for a simple supper.

The problem was how to broach the subject. Conversation during the meal was light and informal. Hassem kept us laughing with witty stories, and Olav entertained with wild tales of the sea.

"You have been very quiet, Tara," Ali Habib said. "Are the men monopolizing the conversation?"

"No, I enjoy listening to them." It was time to speak, but I did not know how to lead into the touchy subject. I was sorry I had agreed to speak to him on Irenia's behalf. Then I decided it was best to get right to the point. "I—I do have a message for you."

"Well? Tell me."

"I am not sure how to say it. As you suggested, I have become friends with many in the harem."

"I know." Why did his voice sound foreboding to my nervous ears?

"Yes," I smiled, trying to work up my confidence. "And many confide in me." I searched for the words to make him understand. "Irenia tells me she is unhappy. She feels rejected."

Ali Habib frowned. "She should not have spoken to you. What is between her and me should remain private."

"I know, sire." I had begun and I could not stop now. "She is very fond of you and is disappointed you do not summon her more often." I prayed my dissembling would aid the cause, yet convince him I did not know the truth.

Ali Habib raised his eyebrows. Had I convinced him? "So she misses me, does she?"

"Yes, sire." I breathed more easily. He was accepting my story.

"Well, as I said, you should not have been the one to tell me this, but I will see—perhaps in a few weeks."

A few weeks! That would be too late, but I dared not say more.

"Oh, come, Habib," Hassem said, "send for the pretty little thing, if she is that impatient to share your bed." I had to catch myself from sighing too loud with relief. Never would he know how his few words had saved the situation.

"All right," my host laughed, "if it will please her. Since you are acting as messenger, Tara, you may tell her it is my wish to see her tomorrow night."

I had counted on one thing, and it had not failed me. Ali Habib would not want me to know he was not a real husband to her.

As I expected, Irenia was waiting for me when I returned to my rooms. She had nearly passed out with the agony of waiting, and now she shook with relief when I relayed his words.

"You will know what to do," I asked, "so he will not suspect?"

She nodded. "I have learned much since I came here."

"But you must promise never to see Paul again."

We had managed to find our way out of a labyrinth of deceit, but I vowed I would never again get myself involved in harem affairs.

Chapter Eighteen

I KNEW THAT ALI HABIB, in spite of his seeming good humor when I relayed Irenia's message to him, was highly displeased at my interfering in his affairs. Three weeks went by and then a fourth with no further invitation to dine. I became despondent. Shopping no longer entertained me; and the garden, once an idyllic spot, seemed to get smaller and smaller, the walls closing in on me like a prison. I wanted to go home.

Olav spent a part of every day at one or another of the harbors, always on the lookout for a ship going to Britain or Norseland. With winter setting in, it looked as if our only hope would be to sail to Rome and then travel over-land to Frisia or Jutland. I trusted Olav and would leave the final decision to him. At one point he hinted that he was in no hurry to leave until spring. Perhaps he, too, had a premonition that it was in Constantinople we would get word of Rorik. My ambivalence—wanting to go home and yet feeling we should stay—kept me taut to the point of screaming.

If it had not been for the happy smiles on Irenia's face, I don't think I could have lived through the next months. She had been summoned not just once but several times by her husband, so I was certain he would not look with suspicion on a child born a few weeks early. If only the child did not have blond hair.

In spite of my many concerns, the days were not all gloomy. I forced myself to look around and see how much better off I was than if I had been sold by Gunner. I was being well cared for, I was in pleasant surroundings, and I was neither a prisoner nor a slave. We would leave someday.

To relieve the tedium, I continued to make occasional outings with Ben Hassem. In many ways my host's younger brother remained a man of mystery. His dark, passionate eyes seemed to hold secrets that I longed yet dreaded to fathom. He had a powerful intensity about him that he kept in check like one holding a tight leash on a ferocious animal that wants to burst free. When we rode in a car or palanquin I could feel the tremendous effort he made to keep from touching me. He only relaxed when we were talking intently about something or he was pointing out various sights around the city.

He was not the only one disturbed by the enforced closeness when we drove out. He was becoming more and more attractive to me, too attractive for the emotional state I was in after the affair between Paul and Irenia and months of longing for Rorik. I decided I had best refuse any further invitations before something happened that I could not handle. Something had been holding Hassem back, keeping a respectable distance between us, but I felt it weakening each time we were together. When our hands inadvertently touched, or he looked down at me and paused while talking, I felt myself go limp. He would have to be the one to break down the barrier, but I knew that when he did, I would no longer have the will to resist.

I had already agreed to go sailing with him. But that would be the last time we went out alone. From then on I would find some excuse to refuse.

In his own twelve-oared galley we sailed across the Bosporus to Galata where we visited the famous Tower of Galata, tallest point in Constantinople. The boat was resplendent with magnificent appointments. We sat on cushioned seats in a small pavilion whose silk curtains were drawn back so that we could see everything. Descending the tower, we sailed to the brothers' villa overlooking a harbor on the Sea of Marmara. From a sculptured, colonnaded wharf on the sea, we ascended by marble steps to the lawn and gardens. Within the villa was every luxury available: mosaics, statuary, silken curtains on silver rods, tapestries, exquisitely carved furniture, and more marble. I gasped. I thought the house in the city was magnificent, but now I was surrounded by more beauty than I had ever seen before. Through all the arches blew soft breezes from the sea, carrying with them exotic aromas from the gardens.

A light repast was awaiting us before we returned to board the galley, and while we ate, Hassem began questioning me as he never had before. Even as I answered him I was worried. He had never before probed so deeply into my feelings. Always the conversations had been light, and it was for that reason I had enjoyed being with him. It kept me from thinking about my situation.

"Do you think your husband is still alive?" He speared a small shrimp on the tines of his fork.

"I guess I really have no reason to believe he is. I can only hope."

"If he were, would he not have found you by now?"

"Not if he were enslaved, or being kept prisoner." He is alive, I told myself. He is alive and you are his wife. "It may take years, but I think we shall someday be together again."

"Perhaps he thinks you are dead and will give up looking." Is that what he wanted? To make me think of myself as a widow? It had never before occurred to me that Hassem might want me to enter his harem. Now the idea came as a shocking revelation. This was what he had been leading up to all the time.

"I'll not believe that," I said defiantly. "Your brother has spread the word I am here. That word will get to him somehow."

"Do you think of your children often?"

"Constantly. Scarcely an hour passes they are not on my mind."

With that the conversation ended. Had I perhaps told him, without saying it in so many words, that nothing could keep me in Constantinople once I found a way to leave?

When we returned to the galley, it had begun to rain, just a light drizzle but enough so that the curtains of the small pavilion had to be closed to keep us from getting wet. I sat back against the cushioned seat, listening to the steady pull of the oars against the choppy waves. It was dark in the enclosure, and I looked up through the sheer curtains to watch the stars. Oh, Rorik, why aren't you here when I want you so much? Why are you always gone when I need you? In the woods with Ruskil, on the flat boulder in the Dnieper, and now.

I could feel the warmth of Hassem's body close beside me. We were not touching, yet for all the tension within me he might have been holding me in his arms. I concentrated on the stars, trying to stop the rapid beating of my heart, the erratic pulsing of the blood through my veins, and the aching, throbbing desire ripping me apart. It was Rorik I wanted, not Hassem, but Rorik was gone. He might be dead. Hassem was next to me and very much alive.

With no words spoken I was suddenly in his arms, crushed against his chest. He was exploring my mouth, caressing my breasts. I felt his legs touching the length of mine. For a moment there were two thin layers of silk between us. Then there was nothing. My nails clawed into his back, and I felt blood on the tips of my fingers. There was no love in the act. No words of endearment. It was pure animal lust, a physical response to a deep, primeval need.

When it was over, I turned away from Hassem and opened the curtains. The rain had stopped, but the breeze was cool on my flushed cheeks. We were approaching the landing. In a few minutes I would be back in my rooms. I would never see Hassem again. I felt neither shame nor misery, bereavement nor guilt. What had happened had been inevitable. I had known that from the first time I accepted his invitation to the Hippodrome. We had both played a waiting game, and now it was over. Like the fatal race or a stalemate in chess, neither of us had won or lost. Hassem said nothing about extending the seduction into an affair. For him, it seemed, the goal had been reached.

Thus, I was surprised a few days later when Cyri announced that Ben Hassem was waiting for me in the garden. He had entered through the side gate. I was shocked to realize I did not fear seeing him. Whatever feelings I'd had for him had been burned away in those few violent moments.

"Good morning, Tara."

"Good morning, Hassem."

"I had forgotten how beautiful this garden is. I used to come here when my mother was alive." I remembered then. His mother had lived in my rooms after his and Ali Habib's father died. I waited for his next words. I felt nothing for him, but I would prefer not to talk about the night on the galley.

"Yes, I enjoy many hours out here," I said.

Paul was working in one of the flower beds. He tended the plants as carefully as ever, but he no longer smiled much. I knew he missed Irenia, but he had to have been aware of the danger they would be in had their affair continued. I never told him about the child.

"Ali Habib says you are looking for a ship to take you home." Hassem's words broke into my thoughts.

"He has promised to find us one, and Olav goes every day to the harbors. But I am afraid it is for naught. There will be none sailing until the spring."

"That is what I came to tell you. I have a friend, a merchant who trades with the northern countries. By profession he is a physician, but he augments his income by trading. He has a ship sailing for Frisia within a week."

Frisia! On the northern coast of Europe, almost within sight of Hordaland. I could not believe our good fortune. With luck I would be home within a few weeks.

"He takes passengers?" I was almost afraid to ask.

"It could be arranged. Would you like to meet him?"

"You know I would. We have waited months for word like this."

"I am dining with him tomorrow night. He would be delighted if I brought you along."

Ben Hassem was again the friend I had first known. A dinner in someone else's home could not possibly put me in the vulnerable position that the cruise on the galley had. Riding in the car, we would be on busy streets. This might be my only chance for months to find a way home.

I dressed carefully for the dinner, this time to please Hassem's friend rather than him. I knew how important my appearance might be. Over a long, slim, pale blue silk tunic I wore a deeper blue wool dalmatic, or short full tunic with wide sleeves coming just to my elbows. Both the hem and the sleeves were edged with a wide border of colorful embroidery and gold braid. The long white pellium, which fell in a train carried over my left arm, was embroidered with gold thread and encrusted with semi-precious stones. On my feet were soft, blue velvet slippers. With all this I wore my finest filigree earrings set with blue stones. Ben Hassem would not be ashamed to introduce me to his friend.

Cyri worked for an hour fashioning my hair in the Greek style once again. Our host was originally from Epidaurus and had settled in Constantinople some years earlier.

The night was pleasant and we rode in an open car, which relieved somewhat the slight tension I was feeling.

"Polybus made his fortune in Epidaurus," Hassem explained as we rode along, "but on a voyage to the Golden Horn for his health, he decided the climate here was better for him."

"He suffered from some ailment?"

"Yes, you might say that. Something was endangering his health. At least he feared he would not live long if he stayed in Epidaurus."

We were met at the door by slaves, one taking charge of the car, another leading us to a reception room. I never ceased to be astounded that in a city so dominated by the Christian church, the Roman laws regarding slavery were still in force. It was a strange anomaly I never quite got accustomed to. We were ushered down a long hall whose walls were emblazoned with intricate mosaic designs and pictures. I paid scant attention to them, thinking they were the usual ones depicting lives and martyrdom of the saints, until one suddenly caught my eye. I was first shocked and then horrified. Each very graphically illustrated a form of lovemaking, some of them unnatural and grotesque to the point of being obscene. I wanted to run, to hide my head, anything to erase them from my mind. Then I pulled myself together. I was here because the man had a ship to take me home. If I kept that foremost in my thoughts, I could ignore his voluptuous, hedonic taste in art.

Even before I was introduced to Polybus, slaves offered us crystal goblets of wine and thin slices of bread covered with a paste of finely chopped goose liver. I did not hesitate to take the wine. Ali Habib always served it, but I was surprised to see Hassem take a goblet, drink it right down, and reach for another. He never touched it at his own house, and I began to feel uneasy.

It did not subdue my growing discomfort to meet our host. Grossly obese, with a bulbous red nose and puffy, inflamed cheeks, Polybus was already tottering on his feet from too much wine. I had the feeling, as he loudly admired my hair and pale skin, that he was slowly undressing me with his eyes. I found it more and more difficult to remain poised, but I forced myself to remember we were there for a very important reason, and for that I could manage to endure anything for a few hours.

I was grateful when slaves began bringing food to two tables set at right angles to each other. Hassem had already emptied three goblets of wine and was well into a fourth. I had no idea how often he drank intoxicants or how well he could tolerate them. As I looked at our host, I prayed desperately that Hassem would not pass out. His mood, however, seemed to get gayer and gayer, and I could only hope the food would keep him sober. I was disturbed when the slaves brought in divans for us to sit on rather than chairs. I did not want a repetition of the night on the galley, but I knew lounging on couches was one of the favorite Roman customs brought to the Mideast. I had to remain calm and not let Hassem see how nervous I'd become. If he had not thought of a second seduction, I did not want to put one into his mind.

I do not remember what we ate. My mind began to spin when Hassem informed me, drunkenly, why Polybus was really in Constantinople. He had made his fortune by selling illegal drugs and performing very expensive abortions on courtesans and prostitutes, who would fall out of favor if they became pregnant, and on wealthy wives who had to rid themselves of the fruit of an illicit affair. The voyage Hassem had earlier said was for the physician's health had been to prevent an early death by hemlock or decapitation. He hinted that our host had expanded his business affairs in Constantinople to include other lucrative interests. I did not inquire into the details, but remembering the priest Olav had saved me from, I became terrified. Were we here for a ship or for some other reason?

"The ship, Hassem," I whispered. "Have you asked him about the ship?"

"Later." His voice was suddenly amazingly clear. "It is not wise to mix business with pleasure. We will talk about it after dinner."

"Then there is a ship." I had to be reassured. "That is the reason we are here?"

"Certainly. Just relax and enjoy yourself. These things cannot be rushed, especially when we are seeking a favor."

Relax? How could I while Polybus stared at me with his deep-set, all-seeing eyes. And how could it be a favor when I was ready to pay my way as a passenger?

A young slave who had been serving Polybus joined him on the divan, and he began fondling her breasts and thighs, all the while looking at me and running his tongue over his thick lips. I was physically repulsed by the man, and I thought I would scream if we did not get away soon. Next to me, Hassem stuffed food into his mouth and emptied his goblet as soon as it was refilled. At least he made no move to touch me. Yet I knew he had brought me here for something more than finding a ship. Was he again playing a waiting game? Was he the cunning hunter waiting for me to fall prey to a different kind of bait? If so, he would be disappointed this time. By now, I had learned the rules of the chase. The evening would not last forever. He might have lured me here with the story about a ship, but that ruse was as far as he would get in tricking me.

Knowing that entertainment was a part of every dinner, I was not surprised to see three musicians enter and take their places on the floor near us. Good, I thought, once this is over I can urge Hassem to take me home. I was not prepared, however, for the dancing that followed.

The young woman might have been naked for all that the sheer gauze skirt and veiling hid her body. Her sensuous movements were less graceful than provocative and titillating. Her nipples, painted a bright carmine, protruded through openings in her short, tight jacket. Her breasts and hips undulated with every movement of her body, and her arms moved sinuously in a constant invitation. When she finished the traditional backbend, she rose up slightly on her knees and, legs apart, began a series of jerking, frantic motions in imitation of the act of love. Breathing heavily, her stomach rising and falling faster and faster, she left no doubt when she reached the moment of climax.

The revulsion I felt had my stomach churning. Gagging, I forced back the small amount of food I'd managed to eat. Polybus was sweating profusely. He turned his eyes from the dancer to me, and I saw the saliva running down his chin. Strangely, Hassem continued to ignore me, as if I were not even there. He had said nothing throughout the entire evening, except the few words about the ship. Nor did he seem stirred by the dancing he had just seen.

I was startled when, after his long silence, I heard him mumble something under his breath. "Wait for the next one. There is no one to compare."

My God, I thought, closing my eyes and forcing myself to breathe deeply, what will I be forced to witness next. All sorts of obscene visions passed through my mind, but none of them materialized. Not right away.

A young male slave, as lithe and graceful as the woman

279

dancer, glided in, his whole body moving as sinuously as a serpent. His only garment was a loincloth, so brief it left nothing to the imagination. On both arms were wide bands of gold; and in his ears hung jeweled rings with tiny bells. His face and body were heavily painted: cheeks rouged, eyelids shaded green and outlined with kohl. His nipples were carmined. He was young, no more than sixteen, and he was completely clean-shaven.

He was hideous and beautiful at the same time. I was horrified but fascinated. I assumed he was an acrobat, but I had never seen one painted like a courtesan before or one who worked alone. I waited for the leaps and twirls, the cartwheels and handstands. There were none. Instead he moved through the same sensual, voluptuous dance the woman had performed. His hips and thighs and arms constantly issued an erotic invitation. But not to me. I looked at Hassem. He was breathing heavily and licking his lips hungrily.

"He is beautiful, isn't he?" Ben Hassem's question required no answer from me. "I have waited a long time for him to belong to me, but tonight he will be mine. Polybus has refused every price I offered. Now, at last, I can give him what he wants."

At the conclusion of the dance, the boy came to our table, sat beside Hassem, and kissed him full on the mouth. Hassem could scarce keep his hands off his new treasure.

My mind whirled with questions. Why had he brought me here as his guest? Why had he escorted me around the city? Above all, why the seduction on the galley? Then I remembered one of the hideous mosaics on the wall as we came in: a scene with two men and a woman. If I had thought I was going to be sick before, I was now feeling violently ill. The room was getting hotter. I reached for the wine and drank it too fast, thinking that if something were going down, nothing could come up. The walls, the lights, the people were all spinning around me now. The last thing I remember was collapsing, face down, on the table.

I awoke to complete darkness and no idea where I was. My head ached so I could not lift it up and my stomach was still churning. I reached out my arms. I was lying on a wide bed, not the divan in the dining hall. I did not even know whether I was in Polybus' house or if Hassem had taken me home. Gradually, as my eyes grew accustomed to the darkness, I knew I was in a strange room. I was terrified, and I lay there shaking, unable to move. Like scenes in a nightmare, events of the evening flashed through my mind. The mosaics on the wall. The dancers. Hassem's description of Polybus' professional activities. The hungry look on Polybus' face when he stared at me. My mind gradually cleared. Now I knew. I was the purchase price for the male dancer. Hassem's cool, well-calculated seduction had not been for his own pleasure. He had been trying me out as one does a piece of merchandise to make sure I was worth the price. He could not offer Polybus a passionless, unyielding article. Unfortunately I had passed the test. Oh, how well I had passed it! Shame, revulsion, humiliation battled inside me, not because I had been unfaithful to Rorik, but because I felt unclean and sordid.

For a few minutes I cried, letting myself wallow in self-pity. Once that mood passed, I became calmer. I had to think rationally. No matter whether Polybus wanted me for himself or as a sporting partner for others whose unnatural tastes desired something obscenely unique, I was not going to let myself be victimized if I could possibly help it. That meant trying to escape. At first glance it seemed a hopeless impossibility. Then I took stock of my situation. I was still completely clothed; I knew Polybus had not yet used me in any way. I did not know how long I had been unconscious. The wine, of course, had been drugged to keep me from struggling when I was brought to this room.

On first trying to stand, I fell back dizzily on the bed. Then I forced myself to get up and walk around. The room was not large, and it was sparsely furnished. I found a door, but it was locked as I knew it would be. I felt the walls closing in, and I rushed to the window. I pulled aside the draperies, and looked out onto a moonlit inner courtyard one story below. I thought of jumping until I saw there was ornate grillwork reaching from sill to ceiling. There was no point in screaming. No one would come to help me. I fought back desperation. I had to remain rational and try to work out a plan.

More than an hour passed before I heard someone at the door, and during that time I was constantly tormented by the thoughts of what Polybus might want of me. At the

...ame time, the interval gave me time to regain some composure and clear my head.

The door opened and Polybus entered. In one hand he carried a small brass lamp; in the other what looked like a small bamboo cage.

"You are awake, my beautiful one. Good. I am sorry to have kept you waiting. I hope it has increased your desire as much as it has mine."

He moved slowly toward me all the while he spoke. He was now garbed in only a long tunic which clung to his sweaty body like a second skin, the shiny silk emphasizing every obese bulge. I averted my eyes from his grossly engorged member, more revealed than hidden beneath the tunic, as he stood spraddle-legged before me. I tried to brush the sight from my mind as well, but it seemed to grow larger and more hideous.

I had been standing at the window. He had not locked the door behind him, and I foolishly tried to make a dash for it. A pudgy hand grabbed me by the shoulder and swung me around to face him. There was amazing strength beneath the fat.

"No, no," he said, as if chiding a mischievous child, "you must not do that. I have very special plans for the night." He put one hand under my short tunic and ran it across my breasts. I could do nothing but try to control my breathing and keep from hitting out at him. I must not, I reminded myself, make him angry. "Did you like that? All I want to do is pleasure you, my dear. Hassem says you are well worth the boy I gave up. I shall expect you to prove that."

I glared at him and tried to pull away, but it did no good. He merely pulled me tighter against him.

"I am having a garden room prepared for us," he went on, exhaling his wine-soaked breath into my face. "Also a light repast. I think you will find it refreshing."

He kept rubbing his hands over my body; my skin shriveled under his touch. He made no attempt to get me onto the bed. Each minute I was spared from the violence of his body gave me added strength to fight when the final, demanding moment came.

"In a few minutes," he continued, "a slave will come and help you don the garments I prefer. If you wish, she will prepare a bath for you. She will let me know when you are ready and will lead you to me. Do not worry, she is an excellent slave, the most faithful one I have. But then, I expect all of my treasures to submit to my will."

With that he opened the bamboo cage, reached in, and pulled out a tiny, colorful songbird. "Beautiful, isn't it? So eager to please. But it does not sing as much as I like." With that he crushed the bird—very slowly—in one huge first and threw the dead body to the floor in front of me.

I rushed to the window. No longer could I keep back the sickness inside of me. I heard Polybus' grotesque laughter as he left, locking the door behind him.

I could not get away before the slave came nor while she was bathing and dressing me, but get away I must. I would either die or be destroyed like the bird if I remained, for I could never submit. My one chance might come when she left me to prepare the bath or bring it to the room. The question was whether she would leave me alone—and the door unlocked—while she did it. If I pretended to be very tired or eager to join her master or just bored by the whole thing, I might put her off guard. I would wait and see what her attitude was.

Within a few minutes she entered, carrying a sheer silk garment over her arm. She did not seem too pleased at having to perform these duties. If Polybus had not said what he did about her being such a faithful slave, I might have made my first mistake by trying to bribe her with some of the jewels off my pellium. Enthusiasm would not do either. She would be displeased or suspicious. I pretended both exhaustion and boredom when I suggested I would like to bathe. I hoped she thought I was too tired to move and that a night's activities such as those planned were no novelty for me.

My subterfuge worked. She tossed her head in disgust and left the room. The bath, she said, was down the hall. She would return when it was ready. Meanwhile I could disrobe.

The moment I perceived she had turned a corner, I left the room and sped down the hall in the opposite direction. I had no idea where I was going or how to get out of the building. There was always the danger of running into slaves or guards.

Quite unexpectedly I arrived at a broad marble staircase leading to the first floor. So far my luck had held, and my velvet slippers made no sound. In the middle of my descent I heard footsteps below, and I froze against the balustrade. As soon as I realized they were going away from me, I started down again. The stairs led into a small anteroom, and through arches I saw a reception room and the entrance hall beyond. The large room contained only several large, marble urns, placed at regular intervals and planted with flowering shrubs. I did not take time to wonder whether the outer doors were locked. As in most homes, they were probably bolted from the inside.

I reached the reception hall and was preparing to cross it when a long shadow spread across the floor. In the semidarkness, I could see only a huge figure looming up in the archway leading to the hall. The features were obscured, the entire body being one tremendous silhouette. Without waiting to see any more, I hid behind one of the tall, rounded urns. I knew as long as I stayed there, I could not be seen, and I breathed as quietly as possible. If only the man would leave! It was not Polybus, of that I was sure. He was too tall. But it could be a guard. I could hear him moving around the room, as if searching for something, and I feared my flight had already been discovered. I dared not look out to see which way he moved. I could only listen.

About the time I thought I could no longer keep from screaming in anxiety, he moved past me and headed for the stairs. Cautiously I crept from urn to urn, and finally gained the entrance hall. I sped toward the door. In the dim light, the obscene figures in the mosaics seemed to leer at me, and blindly I raced straight ahead.

Just as I reached the door and grasped the bolt, some slight disturbance made me turn, and I saw the huge shadowy form step into the hall. In a panic I thought I heard it whisper my name. Or was I so terrified I was hearing things? The bolt slid easily. I pulled open the heavy door and dashed out.

I had no memory of what streets we had taken to get from Ali Habib's to the home of Polybus nor how far it had been. No moonlight shone between the tall stone buildings, so the street was in almost total darkness. I moved swiftly from one narrow street to another and through muddy alleys, always hoping the next one would lead to a broad, familiar avenue. I looked in vain for some landmark, a church or other building I recognized. I dared not pause. I had done so twice, only to hear heavy footsteps following me, still some distance away but constantly gaining. I could try to outrun him, but I knew that was not possible. My only hope lay in turning one corner before he rounded the last and saw which direction I was headed.

I continued stumbling through cavernous alleys between three- and four-story buildings with balconies meeting overhead. The pavement reeked of rotten fruit and stale urine. I was in the most dangerous part of town, the tenements where footpads and assassins lurked. Fear had overtaken me completely, and I ran without thinking where I was going. Around another corner, and I heard the cry of babies. No, it was two squalling tomcats, their golden eyes glaring in the dark. A drunk lurched toward me, then halted in a doorway to relieve himself. I was breathing heavily now, and sharp pains gripped my chest. I had to take deeper breaths or I could not go on.

I found myself on a street of bazaars, but ones unfamiliar to me. I could still hear the footsteps of my pursuer pounding behind me, getting closer and closer. Each time I tried to lose him by turning a corner I heard him stop, walk slowly forward, and then finally pick up my trail. Only sheer terror and the loathsome memory of Polybus as I'd last seen him kept me from dropping from exhaustion. I had to find my way out of this forbidding confusion of streets. I remembered Olav calling the city a tangled maze of alleys where one could get lost forever. While I wished I could hide from my pursuer, I had no thought of remaining in this squalid section of rotting buildings and stinking garbage. My life would be worth nothing.

Always keeping in mind what would happen to me if caught, I forced myself to speed along. My skin crawled at the idea of Polybus touching me. I thought of the bird. So I must not be caught. His lust would have been aroused to the point that only the most vile atrocities would sate it. Which of the obscene acts in the mosaics would he force me to endure? I forced my tired legs to keep moving.

Finally I saw the dome of the Hagia Sophia haloed by moonlight, and I almost collapsed with the realization I had been traveling in the wrong direction the whole time. I would have to turn around and traverse more than half the city to get home. At least I knew where I was, not far from the Mese, the broad avenue leading away from the

Imperial Palace. I thought I would be safer there. It was well traveled even in the dead of night.

I turned into an alley, there being no letup in the ominous sounds behind me. Eyes fixed on the wide avenue just ahead rather than on my feet, I stumbled over something on the pavement and fell forward. When I reached out my hand to steady myself, I touched what felt like a body in ragged clothes. There was just enough light to see a woman lying there. I thought she was dead until I heard a moan and saw her start to turn over.

In spite of myself I screamed. She had no hair or eyebrows, and where there should have been a nose there was only a gaping hole. More pits marred her face, and she held out stumps in place of arms when she muttered something through toothless gums. Her bare feet and legs were covered with raw, suppurating lesions and scabrous sores. I had seen other lepers before among the beggars. I scrambled away as quickly as possible after tossing her three jewels I tore from my pellium. The chances were they would be stolen from her before she could sell them, but it was all I could do for her.

I had lost time, and in trying to make haste, I stumbled again when I reached the Mese. Before I could get up, powerful hands were lifting me from the pavement and forcing me against a huge chest.

"By the gods, Tara, you do give a man a mighty chase!"

"Olav! Oh, Holy Mother!" Through all my travail I had not fainted or given up. Now I was in such a state of relief and exhaustion, my whole body went limp. I could not believe I was safely with him instead of in the arms of one of Polybus' guards. I opened my eyes to make certain it was really Olav, and then closed them again. I was too tired to keep them open. "How—how did you get here?"

"By following the twisting path of a terrified young woman who would not slow down long enough for me to call to her."

"You mean—'twas you—all that time." I had begun crying, and I could barely get the words out between my sobs.

"Every step of the way."

By now Olav had led me to a bench outside a craft shop. I was shaking so hard from fear and shock, he had to wrap me in his long cloak. His strong arms held me upright while we talked.

"But why? I merely went out to dine with Ben Hassem. Why would you come into the house? That was you sneaking around in the dark?"

"It was. And I was there because of him. I know him too well. I dared not tell you, or let you insult Ali Habib by refusing his brother's invitations. But I could follow you."

"Did you follow us other times? When I went out on the galley to the villa?"

"No, I did not think you were in any real danger then. But I am well acquainted with Polybus' reputation. Only when I knew he was taking you there did I become afraid for you. When I saw him leave with the boy and without you, I suspected what had happened."

"Surely Hassem knew someone would miss me—you, Ali Habib."

"He must have been too infatuated with the boy to think straight. Or he might have had some plausible story ready. Even if one of us demanded an explanation of him and went after you, by then you would have had to endure suffering you cannot imagine. I was not thinking of all that—I never dreamed Hassem would dare such a trick—but somehow I knew I had to follow and see you safely home."

"And mighty grateful I am that you did." I had stopped shaking, but I still needed the strength of Olav's arms around me. Never—never—would I forget all that he had done for me, the many times he had saved my life. "How long were you in the house?"

"I dared not break in until after Hassem left and I saw the downstairs lights extinguished. I could only pray you were as yet unharmed. I was headed upstairs when I saw you dash for the door. I breathed my first sigh of relief when I saw you were still in your formal dress."

I started to speak and then didn't. I would never let Olav know the ways Polybus had abused me. Even though he had not succeeded in raping me, Olav would have returned and found a way to kill him if he knew the man had touched me.

"I could only whisper within the house," he continued, "but I thought surely you recognized me."

"I was too frightened to know any more than that someone was chasing and calling to me. I wasn't even sure I had heard my name. I thought fear had me hearing things. After all, you were the last person I expected to have chasing me. I dared not let you catch up to me."

"Do you feel strong enough to walk a few steps?"

"I think so. But it's more than a few steps to Ali Habib's."

"We're not going there. I have a friend, a silversmith, who will take us in and give us a place to sleep for the rest of the night."

I could barely manage the short distance, even with Olav's help. At last we came to the shop, Olav knocked on the door, and his friend showed us rooms where we could stay until morning.

But there was no sleep for me. All the horrors of the night, all the abominations I had witnessed and experienced tormented me while I tossed and turned like one demented. I was safe for the moment, but what about in the days to come. I knew Hassem too well not to think he would seek revenge from me. Polybus would demand payment of some kind; and Hassem, in turn, would find a way to make me suffer for it. More than ever, we had to get out of Constantinople as quickly as possible. As watchful as Olav was, he could not protect me forever. Daylight brought no peaceful calming of my fears. Instead I was burning with fever then shaking in a cold sweat. Olav ordered a palanquin to take me home, but for more than a week I lay ill and delirious from all I'd been through.

Chapter Nineteen

CYRI WAS KINDNESS ITSELF. I don't know how much Olav told her, but she never left my side the whole time I was ill. Whenever I opened my eyes, she was there. When I was finally strong enough to get up, she prepared a bath and laid out clean clothes as if nothing strange had happened. Neither she nor Olav would ever know all I had been forced to endure. The nightmare was mine alone, and sharing would only swell it to gigantic proportions rather than diminish it.

Olav was waiting for me in the garden when I walked out.

"You are to say nothing to Ali Habib about the other night."

I could not believe what I was hearing. Surely he would want to know the peril his brother had put me in. Yet I knew there was probably wisdom behind Olav's words. "Are you thinking of me or Ali Habib when you say that?"

"Both of you. He would act horrified and he would apologize, but he'd not like to be reminded of his brother's peculiarities or be made aware that someone else knew about them. Remember, Tara, this is a world quite different from the one you are familiar with. What displeases you does not necessarily disturb others. And—you are a guest in his home."

"You are right. I am a guest, and he has treated me most kindly. With luck, it may not be for much longer."

"I go to the harbors every day. I think we will find a ship by the beginning of summer."

However, it was a long time before I could be persuaded to leave the seclusion of my quarters and go into the city again.

Spring brought tiny new buds in the garden, and my favorite colorful birds began nesting in the trees. I sat in the pergola remembering the days almost a year earlier when we began planning our voyage to Zealand and watched the *Albatross* being refitted for the journey. I thought about Signe and Eirik taking their first steps. So much had happened to me in between, but what had they been doing all those months? Did they still climb on Thorne's back and demand he gallop with them up the long hall, or had they tired of that? Signe's hair must now be long enough to tie back. I wept. It should be I, not Astrid who was doing it for her. I never allowed myself to dwell on whether either of them took ill or were hurt. It was enough to be separated from them. I could not have borne to worry about them as well.

I was fortunate in that I seldom saw Ben Hassem. With spring came increased activity in trade, and Ali Habib had more guests in to dine. The few times I went, Hassem asked to be excused: he had another engagement for the evening. When I was forced to see him, I amazed myself by remaining cool and distant. Time had deadened my feelings.

On a pleasant morning in April, I called for the palanquin to shop the bazaars, and I sent word to Olav I was going out. I was finally going to buy a pair of the beautiful blue glass vases decorated under the surface with golden foliage and birds. They would match two cloisonné bowls I had purchased earlier. I was shepherding my money carefully, but I did want to take some Byzantine treasures back North with me.

Olav and the porters arrived together, and we headed for the street where the glass craftsmen had their alcoves. I opened the curtains to enjoy the beautiful day. At irregular intervals, the authorities doled out bread, oil, and wine to the poor; so on this day, the streets were relatively free from the beggars' pitiful whines.

The sky was a brilliant blue; the air smelled of spices from the bazaars. A holy-day pageant along a main avenue held us up for a few minutes; and I watched the Patriarch, head of the city's Christian churches, lead the parade of priests and important men in the secular world. All were garbed in heavily embroidered robes encrusted with gems. Wearing a high, jeweled crown, the Patriarch carried a mammoth gold cross studded with huge sapphires, rubies, and emeralds. Other priests swung braziers filled with smoky incense, and all were chanting as they walked along blessing those who stood by the roadside. I pulled the curtains wider apart, hoping to receive the special benison I craved.

Once the pageant passed, we went on. Our route took us by one part of the bazaar we usually avoided, but today I decided against taking the longer way around it. Much of the time this area was empty, but today it bustled with feverish activity. There were more than two dozen slaves being readied for the auction block.

As was customary, the women stood on one side, the men on the other. The slave traders and auctioneer were removing the few scraps of clothing the poor unfortunates wore. The thorough examinations I remembered from Kiev began, and the cries of the very young and innocent wrung my heart. I longed to climb out of the palanquin and comfort them. So abhorrent was the scene to me, I wanted to move right along, yet something had me bid the porters wait.

"Do not stop, Tara," Olav said, peering through the curtains. 'Twill only spoil your day. You know what agonies you suffer every time we come by here, even when there's no sale."

"I know. In a minute. For some reason I feel I should not leave yet."

"Not too long. You'll not take any pleasure in spending all your coins at the bazaar."

The women were to be auctioned first, and after they had all their orifices and private parts probed, they looked as if they would collapse from fright and pain. Only the fact they were chained together, each supported by the ones on either side, kept them from falling. I could see their feet were blistered and their skin was burned. They had recently been walked over a great distance. Complexions and hair were of all colors. I assumed they had been brought from various countries, herded together at another mart, and bought by the present seller.

While the women were being examined again by prospective buyers, the trader and auctioneer turned their attention to the men on the other side of the block. As usual their eyes were covered so they would not be aroused by the sight of nude female bodies. My eyes searched among them for a familiar, beloved face. Each time the disappointment was greater, and another part of me died.

Yet I had to keep searching. Rorik was alive. I would have known if he were dead.

Olav again urged that we move on, but I put my hand to stay his command to the porters. When the first woman stepped on the block, I noticed for the first time a little girl trying to hide behind the others. She was no more than ten years old. My heart turned over. In spite of the dirt and tangles, I could see her long hair was blond, and her blue eyes were filled with tears. Tiny rivulets streaked through the dry dust on her cheeks. I thought of Asri and of Signe a few years hence, and the vision of either on a slave block determined my decision. The blue glass vases could wait. If only I had enough coins to purchase her.

Olav had seen the look on my face and recognized what it meant. He patted the leather pouch at his belt. He would lend me what I needed.

The first woman, voluptuous and swarthy, had many bidders and was sold quickly. She would be able to take care of herself, I thought. The little girl was next, and Olav bid for me. It would not do for me to expose myself among the crude, uncouth buyers. Three others were also bidding, and I grew more and more frantic as the price continued to go up. Twice Olav looked at me, but I nodded for him to go on. Finally one after another of the buyers gave up, and the little girl was mine. She had no idea who her real purchaser was; and looking at Olav when he walked over to get her, she became hysterical with fear. He did present a formidable figure, and I could understand why she was terrified. Her previous owner started to slap her across the face; but he had no sooner raised his hand than Olav had him flat on his back. Then my good eunuch picked her up in his arms and carried her over to me.

Once in the palanquin, she snuggled next to me like a baby. It had taken most of our coins to buy her, but I knew I would never regret it. She had stopped her loud crying and was now sobbing against my shoulder. In another minute she was asleep.

I was ready to start off when a violent commotion broke out among the male slaves. One of them was grappling with his chains and lunging at the auctioneer. He was tall, and sinewy muscles bulged like knotted ropes from his gaunt frame. His skin was a deep bronze, paler where usually covered by clothing. Dark, heavily matted hair fell

292

over his shoulders, and his face beneath the blinder was covered by a full growth of beard.

My heart palpitated and swelled in my chest until I could no longer breathe. Waves of searing fire flashed through me, and yet I was shaking as with a chill. A certain movement of the man's arm, the tilt of his head, and I knew. It was Rorik!

Or was it? Did I want to find him so desperately that I would see him in every tall slave? Joy and doubt, elation and disbelief roiled inside me like a frenetic whirlpool. It had to be Rorik. It had to be! No, his hair was too dark, and there was nothing of Rorik's massive build about him. I turned my head away. I was only torturing myself more by continuing to look and try to turn him into Rorik.

Then a sound, a single word, and I looked again. He had thrown his head back, and I saw the blond hair beneath the filth. Starvation and heavy labor had taken its toll from the once magnificent physique.

I could scarce believe that, after all this time, I was at last seeing Rorik alive, and so close that a few steps would put me beside him. I wanted to leap from the palanquin and rush over to him. To fling my arms around him and assure him that everything was all right now. I was alive, too, and nothing would ever separate us again.

"Olav!" I dared not scream, but my voice was filled with urgency. "Olav, 'tis Rorik! I've found him."

"Are you sure?" Olav asked. "Are you certain 'tis not just because you want to find him?"

All my doubts had cleared away, and Olav's words only stirred up my impatience to the boiling point.

"Yes, I'm certain. And he's going to be sold. We've got to do something. Quickly. Talk to the trader. Oh, God, Olav, hurry. Tell them he is not a slave, then he'll release him to us."

"No, Tara, he will sell him to you. He'll not give away a slave he has already paid for and expects a good price in return."

"But we've no coins left," I wailed. Why this bantering? I just wanted Olav to go up and get him. I wanted Rorik in the palanquin beside me. My thoughts were incoherent. I didn't want to accept what Olav was saying.

"We'll get them from Ali Habib," Olav said. "He'll not let Rorik be sold."

"Go. Go! As fast as you can. I can't stay hidden from

293

him. I've got to speak to Rorik, let him know I am here and he'll soon be free." I was already laying the little girl on the seat beside me and pulling the curtains farther apart.

" 'Twould not be wise, Tara."

"What are you saying? Of course I'm going to him."

"No. You know not what Rorik might try to do. We will go back to the house and ask Ali Habib for the money. He will give it without question."

"You go. I'm staying here. I'll not let Rorik out of my sight now that I've found him. Nothing will move me until I see him rid of his chains."

He saw I was adamant. "Stay then, but in the palanquin. I'll be no longer than it takes to sell the women first."

In my heart I was running every step of the way with Olav, and emotionally I was just as exhausted as he must be. I could no longer see Rorik among the slaves. At his attempt to free himself, the slaver struck him across the head and knocked him to the ground. Was it imagination that heard him moaning? Or had he been badly injured. It took all my will to remain in the palanquin as Olav had ordered. It would do no good for me to alight among the rowdy crowd of buyers, but I did not see how I could stand it until Olav came back.

Ten minutes at the most had passed, but I was almost frantic. Hurry, Olav, hurry! I forced myself to keep from shouting aloud. He should be at the house by now. Ali Habib must be at home. He had to be. Was there enough in his treasure chest? Would he know how much a slave like Rorik cost? My head spun with these questions. He could use our jewels. I knew they were there. I had seen them.

I watched the women going up for sale. There were five remaining. No—six. How many minutes for each? The bidding was going too fast. Not enough men bidding on each one. Slow down! I screamed inside. Please slow down. Take time to count the coins. Argue over them. Anything to use up the time.

Where are you, Olav? There was a scuffle on the other side of the platform. Another fight. Good! It would make the minutes pass and delay the bidding. The fight was stopped amid wild yells and heavy moaning.

Two more women were sold. Now there were only two left. Olav had to return soon. What was keeping him?

Now the bidding was halted. There was no one on the platform. Why had they stopped? A buyer stepped from among the crowd and spoke to the auctioneer, who shook his head violently at first and then nodded in agreement with what the man said.

The two remaining women were led off to one side. My heart stopped. Rorik was being prodded up the steps. His hands and feet were manacled, and his face was bloody from the smashing blow to his head. They couldn't be selling him now! They couldn't. The women had to go first. They had to wait until Olav returned.

Several men pushed toward the platform behind the man who had spoken to the auctioneer. Rorik was still blindfolded, and he was trying his best to elude their hands as they grasped and poked him. I couldn't sit still. Nor could I remain in the palanquin. I alighted and stood beside it, covering my head with the hood of my cloak. The bidding had begun. It was fast and furious. Rorik was a prime prospect. Even though gaunt from starvation, it was evident he was still strong and would make a good worker. One bidder dropped out, then another, and I moved forward a few steps. The price was going higher. I turned and peered down the street. There was no sign of Olav. Another bidder backed down. There were only three left. The first man must have named an exorbitant price, for the other two shook their heads and wandered away.

By then I had moved ahead several paces. Now I began running the ten or twelve yards, pulling off bracelets and rings. I almost ripped my earlobes when I tore out the gold wires of my jeweled earrings. I would offer anything—the palanquin, the porters, anything—to prevent the man from taking Rorik away.

"Rorik!" The scream, coming from deep within, seared my throat.

"Tara!" With his iron-bound hands he tore off the blindfold.

In another minute I was within the circle of his manacled arms, kissing his heavy beard, his blistered lips. No words needed to be said. We were crying and moaning with relief and agony. The heavy iron bracelets bore into my back, but I felt no pain. The voices around us shouting imprecations and threats had no meaning for us. We were in a world apart.

I felt someone unlocking Rorik's chains. He would be free! Free to come back with me until we could sail North. Then a heavy hand clutched my shoulder and spun me around. Others held Rorik's arms to his sides. A heavy, surly man stepped between us, his face contorted with anger. It was the auctioneer. I could not understand his words, but I knew their meaning. I held out my jewels, but he shook his head. I turned to Rorik's buyer and pointed to the palanquin. He only laughed and ordered the two men holding Rorik to bring him along.

I wrenched myself free and once more flung myself into Rorik's arms. I was not going to lose him again. No one was going to drag him away from me. Men were all around and between us now, forcing us apart. Hampered by the chains on his feet, Rorik was fighting with all his strength.

"Don't let them take you," I cried. "Olav is coming with the money. Please, please," I begged. "I have the money. I'll pay you. Don't you understand? He's my husband."

I could have been shouting to the wind. It finally took four men to subdue Rorik. He was unconscious, and they had to drag him to a wagon. I lay on the ground sobbing, unmindful of the dust in my mouth as I choked out his name over and over. I watched the wagon roll away. My emotions were decimated. All my hopes disintegrated into a welter of despair and futility. There was no point in going on.

Olav found me lying on the ground and carried me to the palanquin. Exhausted from all she'd endured, my new little slave had remained asleep while I was pleading for Rorik's freedom, and now I held her close in my arms. I thought I would hate her for taking the coins that would have bought Rorik's freedom, but I didn't. I should have been holding him in my arms, soothing away the pain, but I would not take out my loss on her.

Once back in my rooms, I fell across the bed weeping. "Oh, Cyri, I've lost Rorik. I found him and then lost him again." I fainted and remembered nothing more of that day.

The hours and days that followed had no meaning. For the second time I had lost Rorik, had seen him wounded, and in the hands of brutal men. For the second time he was taken from me. Over and over I relived our brief moment together, the pain and love in his eyes, the agony of separation. After all the torturous months of not knowing whether he were alive or dead I had found him, only to lose him again.

" 'Twas not your fault, Olav." He had joined me in the garden where I was watching a father bird bring food to the nesting mother bird.

"Ali Habib gave me the money, and I returned as quickly as I could."

"I know," I sighed. "If the women had been sold first—"

"The man was from some distance away. He was in a hurry."

On hearing of our finding Rorik, Ali Habib had immediately given Olav the money, and sped him on his way. Olav would have been able to get back in plenty of time if the streets hadn't been crowded with celebrants after the religious pageant.

Even before we returned to the house, Olav asked everyone at the slave mart the identity of the man who had bought Rorik, but no one knew. The auctioneer simply shrugged his shoulders. The buyer had paid the purchase price; that was all that mattered to him. One slave was no different from another.

"He won't be gone for long, Tara." Olav tried to reassure me. "Ali Habib has sent out word among everyone he knows. We'll find Rorik again."

I was not so certain. When our ship was attacked, some inner sense, some inimitable faith, had told me we would not be separated forever. I tried now to resurrect that same feeling, but it remained dead, at least for the time being.

If it hadn't been for little Inga, I would have had no reason to keep on living. When I first brought her home, I handed her over to Cyri. "Take care of her, Cyri. I'll explain later." It was all I could say before I fainted.

Once bathed and dressed, the tiny slave looked like a little doll. She spoke a language similar to a Norse dialect, but she had no recollection of where she came from, what her name was, or how long she had been away from home. Her only memories were of fear and terror of the people she had recently been with. She often cried for no apparent reason, and she suffered from frequent nightmares. She slept on a pallet near me, but almost every night she woke up screaming and I took her into my bed.

When I brushed her now silken blond hair, it formed tiny ringlets around my finger. I named her Inga, a favorite Norse name, because I was certain she came from that section of the world. She responded to every kindness with a disarming smile that wrung my heart. She loved to stand beside my couch in the garden and run her fingers through my hair. I supposed her mother had long blond hair, and an image of it was lost somewhere in the hidden recesses of her memory. I hoped time would restore enough of her memory for me to find her parents.

Like a butterfly newly emerged from her cocoon, Inga moved within a shining aura of innocence, and like a butterfly she flitted from flower to flower in the garden. She was captivated by the mother birds on their nests. She listened intently while I explained they were sitting on eggs and there would soon be baby birds for her to watch. She picked bouquets and helped me arrange them in my room on a little table I had gotten just for her things: a bracelet, a bright pebble, and a blue enamel cup she drank from at every meal. After our first supper, she cried when Cyri tried to carry away the cup along with the other dishes. She clung to it as one clings to a valuable possession. Something else was coming through from the past. Perhaps she had been surrounded by lovely things at home, had come from a family of some wealth.

In spite of her seeming happiness with me and the many ways I found to keep her busy, I knew she was restless. Cyri brought her clothes borrowed from the harem children, and I knew the answer. Inga was still a child, and she needed children to play with.

I had thought never to return to the harem. I wanted to mourn my loss in private, but Inga changed my mind. She was shy at first, not knowing the language, but children do not need words to communicate. Soon she was splashing in the pool while I held her up. There were other girls roughly her age, all eager to involve her in their games and offering her their dolls to play with. She looked at each toy, smiled, and then turned sadly away. Again I wondered if another dormant memory had been awakened.

Then one day the nurse slaves brought in the four babies. None of the mothers nursed their children for fear of spoiling their figures, but they saw them after each feeding by the wet nurses. Inga's eyes lit up. She ran over and looked intently at each of them and then sat by one, pleading to hold him. The mother, Sarah, a sweet-faced concubine, put the infant in Inga's lap, and the little girl began crooning to Abrim. He grew fussy and Inga immediately checked his wrappings and looked around for dry ones. As expertly as a nurse, she changed him, all the while talking and singing to him.

When it came time for the slaves to take the babies away, Inga clung to Abrim and refused to give him up. Sarah tried gently to take him out of her arms, but Inga began screaming; and holding him to her breast, she ran for the other end of the pavilion.

"No, no! You shan't have him."

Only I could understand her, and I tried to explain the seemingly bizarre situation to the distraught Sarah. "I think she is remembering something from her past. She must have had a baby brother, and I'm wondering now if she just misses him or if she saw something terrible happen to him. Let me talk to her. She'll not harm Abrim, I'm confident of that. I think she is trying to protect him."

I walked over to Inga, who had huddled in one corner as if trying to shield herself and the baby from something or someone. She looked terrified.

"Inga," I said gently, "I know you love him, but you must give him back to his mother."

"No, no! They will hurt him." I was deeply troubled by her fears. I dreaded she had witnessed something like the attack on the abbey. If so, maybe 'twould be better to leave the past in darkness. I sat beside her and put my arms around her. There had to be some way to soothe away whatever it was that tormented her.

"She is his mother, Inga. She'll not hurt him."

"His mother?" Behind the tears in her eyes I could see stark horror and disbelief.

"Yes, dear. She loves him, too. You'd not want to keep him from his mother."

This was an important test. Had I gained her confidence sufficiently for her to trust me and believe me more than she did whatever was haunting her?

She lifted her face and wiped away the tears. "I will give him to his mother. Not to the others. They will hurt him."

I put my arms around Inga and, together, we walked

over to Sarah, who had been wringing her hands while I talked to the little girl.

Inga reluctantly handed Abrim to her. "Tara says you are his mother. You must not let them take him. Are you my mother, too?"

I translated what Inga said, and Sarah looked bewildered. She turned to me for help.

"No, dear," I said. "She is not your mother."

"But my brother. Why does she say she is his mother?"

I told Sarah to take Abrim away, and I led the confused little girl to my rooms. Once there, she crawled into my bed and fell immediately to sleep.

Somehow I had to penetrate Inga's mind and force out all the memories that had been obliterated by more recent events. Some powerful or terrifying experience had forced her mind to forget not only what horrors she had lived through but also earlier, happier times. I was frightened at the thought of probing into something as delicate as a human mind, but she would never be free from fears or nightmares until she could release them and share them with someone.

At the same time I was living through my own nightmare. Ali Habib had been unable to learn who bought Rorik. It was as if he had vanished completely. Faith had not helped, so I turned to superstition. If I woke up in time to see the sun before it rose above the garden wall, I would find Rorik. I laid my toilet articles in a precise arrangement on the table, and I became frantic if anyone moved them. I waited for the fledglings to appear, and then watched anxiously to see if one and then another flew to a branch or hesitated and remained near the nest. If he flew safely, I knew I would find Rorik. If he stayed, I dissolved on the couch in tears. All this kept me so tense, I would have lost my mind if concern over Inga hadn't given me something to occupy my time and drive out my own demons.

With such clues as the blue enamel cup, her frequent habit of touching my hair, and her love for Abrim, it was easy to suppose she had come from a family of some wealth; her mother, or someone she was close to, had long, blond hair; and she had a baby brother she thought was in danger. But these were mere fragments.

At times when she woke up after a bad nightmare, she was calm and almost seemed to have forgotten both the terrors of the night and the inhuman treatment she'd endured before I found her. It was as if her mind had the ability to erase anything unpleasant, at least momentarily. After the incident in the harem, we walked into the garden, and I held her up so she could see the infant fledglings in the nest. Paul was there, weeding the beds. His eyes still had a sad look, and he seldom smiled, so despondent was he at his loss of Irenia. So there were the three of us, each mourning in our own way, each trying to find some stabilizing ingredient in the world to make remaining alive worthwhile. Paul worked with his flowers; I invented crazy superstitions, and Inga clung to me. What a desperate trio we were.

When Inga knelt to smell some of the flowers, Paul came over and picked one of them for her. She put her arms around his neck and kissed him, something she had never done with me. Whoever Paul reminded her of, it was someone she had loved very dearly. Paul took her by the hand and led her all around the garden. It didn't seem to disturb her that Paul could not speak. Somehow he knew exactly what she was asking; and in turn, she understood his sign language.

From then on if I missed Inga, I knew I would find her in the garden with Paul. She dug her little hands in the dirt beside his big ones when he weeded; he showed her how to use the knives to prune the shrubs; and he taught her which flowers to pick for bouquets. One day Paul arrived with a miniature straw basket filled with a little bouquet of rosebuds and gave it to her. She added it to the collection of treasures on her table.

"He made the basket for you, Inga."

"I know. He told me."

There was no explaining this special attachment and understanding between the two; but whatever it was, it was making a different little girl out of her. Several nights went by without nightmares, and she no longer cried easily.

Two of the trio had found that meaning they were searching for. But mine was still missing. I was hollow inside, like a tree that has been blasted by lightning yet somehow remains standing in spite of the winds buffeting it from all directions.

Inga was in the garden helping Paul transplant some seedlings and I was sitting under the pergola, covered now with a sweet-scented vine, when Olav came out to join us. He was deeply involved with locating a ship for us and searching for someone who knew the buyer of Rorik. I was really no longer interested in the ship. Not for the present. I was certain Rorik was still close to me, close enough that we would eventually locate him. My omens had all been lucky ones in the past few days: I had seen the sun rise every morning; no one had touched my dressing table; and the little birds were all flying, none had fallen or returned to the nest.

I did not want to travel North if there were any chance he had been taken eastward to Armenia or Persia or Syria. I had one great fear, and Olav knew what that was —Rorik would be castrated as he himself had been. Many slave owners did it routinely to prevent trouble among their servants, whether they needed the men as eunuchs or not. Others preferred to have their slaves interbreed in order to produce more slaves at no cost to themselves. I knew if Rorik were operated on, he would kill himself. Rorik could never live as less than a man. No matter how I fought to wipe the image from my mind or how hard I tried to think of other things, the vision of him bleeding to death from a self-inflicted wound overshadowed every other thought. I groped for the light as one who has once seen it but is now blind.

Olav sat quietly for a few minutes, his usual habit when he had no news but just wanted to visit with us.

"Inga is doing better," he said.

"Much better." My mind had been journeying deep into the shadows and found it difficult to return.

"Perhaps someday she will be able to tell you what happened."

"I hope so," I answered, "but for now I'm glad she finds some peace."

Olav again became quiet, and I once more retreated into the dark recesses where I did not have to think.

"Ali Habib knows who bought Rorik." His voice was completely devoid of emotion.

"Olav!" The word propelled me from my chair. "And you sit there so calmly. Where is he? How soon?"

I felt so exhilarated, so full of joy I wanted to dance with the butterflies and sing with the birds. I did not wait for Olav's answers, but picked Inga up and swung her around in my arms.

"Calm down, Tara, or you will be overwrought."

"Calm down? How can I? And I am already overwrought with gratitude and anticipation."

"The news is not that good, Tara. He has since sold him."

I fell to my knees beside Olav's chair, took the hand he held out, and crushed it between my own. "No, no!"

"We learned only this morning. The man was at the slave market again."

"Why did he sell him? To whom?" I was on top of a hill screaming with joy. The next moment I was tumbling into the depths of the valley below.

"He owned a fleet of fishing vessels in the Black Sea. He thought Rorik would make a good strong man for his crew. But it seems Rorik gave him only trouble. Refused to obey orders. Always trying to run away. So he sold him."

Trying to return to me. My heart throbbed. Why couldn't he have made it?

"Then he must have told you to whom. And where his new owner has taken him. How long ago? Is he far from here?" He was not dead. We would still find him.

"He did not know the man's name. Someone traveling along the shores of the Black Sea with a caravan. Said he could manage the most willful of slaves, and the fisherman sold him cheap."

"A caravan!" I got up and looked through the latticework of the pergola. Was I inside a prison looking out? Inside a prison within a prison? Or was I outside grappling with the chains of the slavery system that had Rorik hopelessly entrapped? "He could be traveling in any direction. The new owner sounds like a cruel man."

"We have one clue," Olav said, and I knew he was trying to give me all the hope he could muster. " 'Tis a small traveling circus."

"But there are hundreds of those. And they move about constantly. Even if we learned where he was, he would be gone before we got there."

"What do you want to do now, Tara?"

"I know not. I cannot think."

I was too distraught to weep. Tears were not enough. I felt desiccated. Like a plant bereft of water, I had gone too long without any real hope. Whatever will I had to keep fighting, whatever instinct for survival, had at last been

303

completely eroded. There was no longer day or night, only endless time narrowing to oblivion. I did not sleep. I sat by the bed and saw Rorik lying on it dead, and I keened in mourning like the old Celtic women in my village back home, the moaning lamentations shutting my ears to all other sounds. Cyri brought trays of food. They remained untouched. One does not eat while watching over the dead. I tore my hair and rent my clothing, trying through physical acts to find emotional peace. Instead I suffered an interminable pain yielding to no opiate. Exhaustion finally took control of my battered mind, and I slept.

I awoke as despondent as ever but more able to face the truth. I called for Olav.

"If you can find a good ship that will take us even as far as Rome, we will make plans. I don't want to go back by way of Kiev."

Olav's heavy shoulders sagged. I knew he sorrowed for me. He would stay in Constantinople as long as I asked him to, but I also knew he longed to return North. He wanted to see Hordaland again, and once more become a shipbuilder.

"Look for a ship, Olav."

Now Inga was more important to me than ever. I rejoiced to see her playing with the other children of the harem, and I shared her delight as she learned more new words every day. Gradually she lost her fear of Abrim's nurse and allowed the slave to take the baby from her. She still cried occasionally in her sleep, but there were fewer nightmares.

Then suddenly one night she woke up screaming, and nothing I did calmed her. I took her in bed with me. I carried her to the garden. I even went into the pavilion after bidding Cyri light some lamps. Inga remained hysterical, screaming loudly and pummeling me so hard on my chest and shoulders, I could scarce hold her on my lap.

"What is it, Tara? What is wrong?"

Thalia had heard Inga's screams and come down from the second floor.

"I don't know. She has been so much calmer lately."

"She's remembering it all," Thalia said.

"I thought maybe 'twas it. But what can we do?" My heart went out to the child, writhing and moaning in my arms. Her excruciating pain was no less fearful for attacking her mind rather than her body.

We could scarce hear each other above Inga's loud protestations.

"She needs something to quiet her," Thalia said. "See if you can give her this."

Thalia handed me a small vial of amber liquid.

While Thalia held Inga, I managed to pour most of it through her lips. It was some time before the drug took effect, but gradually the tortured little girl quieted down and fell asleep.

"What will happen when she wakes up?" I asked. "Will she have another nightmare?"

"There are usually no dreams with this drug. She may be just the same as she has been recently, or she may revert to the frightened child she was when you found her. She will sleep now for quite a while, and I'll get you more of the drug in case you need it."

Inga awoke late in the morning, surprised to find herself in my bed, but as cheerful as she had been the day before.

"I had another nightmare, didn't I, Tara?"

"You did. A very bad one."

"Shall I tell you about it?"

"If you like." She had never offered to do that before, so I had no way of knowing what she suffered during them.

"I think I would feel better if I did. I dreamed we were being attacked again."

Bit by bit the story came out. Inga remembered me and everyone in the seraglio, but she had no recollection of her memory having been disturbed during all her time with us. She spoke of her home, her parents, and her family as if I had been familiar with them all along. Yet much of her past was still a blur. I never learned how old she was when the attack on their farm took place or how long ago it had been. Nor did I ever learn her true age. She could describe her mother and father and brother, but she could remember none of their names or her own.

Many details of her life were always to remain a mystery. Who the attackers were, she did not know. She saw her parents killed, and her baby brother had been snatched from her arms when she tried to hide with him in the stables. More than that her mind refused to release.

"My mother was very beautiful, Tara."

"I'm certain she was, Inga. And your father, very handsome."

"He was a strong man. He used to carry me all over the farm." She paused and began stroking my hair. "Will you be my mother now?"

" 'Twould please me very much." I held out my arms and she climbed into my lap.

"I wish I had a baby brother, too."

"You have. His name is Eirik. And two sisters, Signe and Asri."

"Where are they?"

"Way up north. But we shall see them soon."

I was still devastated by my own grief. I had tried to divest myself of any thought that I would ever see Rorik again, but a minute crystal of hope, more an irritant than a balm, refused to dissolve. Now I pondered the times I sat next to Rorik on the *Raven*, and I remembered something he said. "The *Raven* always brings me home." He let the ship take the wind in her sails, but he kept his hand on the tiller. Winds of chance could take me where they would, or I could resume control and steer my ship. If I were alone, it would not matter; but there were the children to think about. Having bought Inga, I had assumed responsibility for her. I could not abdicate those obligations, even if I'd wanted to.

Inga's pouring out of her story ended her nightmares and released something in me as well. I was now able to make a positive decision. There was no point in lingering any longer in Constantinople. Rorik was gone from me forever, and it was now time to think about our children. They needed me, and I needed them. He would have loved Inga, but so would Thorne. I told Olav I was ready to leave, even if we had to buy a ship and furnish the crew.

Chapter Twenty

MANY TIMES I WALKED INTO THE PAVILION and the women were subdued and untalkative. I never inquired why, although Irenia usually told me about a foolish argument or a heated feud.

One particular day I shall never forget. The room was more than just quiet. None of the children were there, so Inga returned to the garden to be with Paul. The atmosphere was heavy with tension and an unspoken fear I had never sensed before. The women sat in pairs and small groups, but all were as silent as mutes. The musical instruments lay untouched, and the slaves stood around waiting for orders, but no one moved.

I started to leave, loath to ignite the spark just waiting for the wrong word or action. Then I saw Irenia sitting by herself on a divan. Her pregnancy was well advanced, and usually she was all smiles. Today she seemed very morose. I hesitated, not wanting to intrude, but she motioned me over to her side.

"Is something wrong, Irenia," I asked almost in a whisper.

"With me? Oh, no. I'm feeling very well."

"They why—why are you and everyone so quiet? What has happened?"

Irenia didn't answer but began playing with the ends of a scarf. Something had happened that I, still in many ways a stranger, should not know about. It would be best for me not to become too curious. Casually I walked toward the pool and began to undress. I thought such an action would be less obvious than if I simply walked out, until I saw that no one was paying any attention to me.

I slipped into the cool water and took the bar of soap a slave handed me. Leisurely I lathered my body, and then unhurriedly floated from one end of the pool to the other. Tired, I stepped out and allowed the slave to dry me off and then massage oils into my skin. While she rubbed my back, I dozed off, not waking up until I felt someone covering me with a light shawl.

"Irenia?"

"Yes. I thought you might catch a chill. It has gotten suddenly cold."

"Thank you. I did not intend to fall asleep."

"I thought I—I would tell you what is wrong. I knew you were not going to ask, but it is not fair for you not to know. You are like one of us."

"Only if you really want to, Irenia."

"I do. I have to talk to someone. Everyone is so quiet. I can't stand it. It's Nadia."

"Who?" I couldn't recall the name. "Do I know her?"

"She is a slave. You have seen her in here with the children."

"She is ill?" I asked. "Or been sold again?"

Irenia shook her head, tears glistening in her eyes.

"She has died?" I said more softly.

"No. Oh, Tara, it is so hard to tell you, but I feel I must."

"Slowly then. Do not rush it." I took her hands in mine.

"Nadia has a son. He is six years old. He is a beautiful boy. Pale like you with fair hair and blue eyes. His father was a trader from the Far North. Tall and strong and very handsome. He was a good friend of Ali Habib. Nadia was asked to dance at a dinner for him. The stranger thought her beautiful, so Ali Habib honored him by granting him her favors. Nadia did not—did not take care. She said she wanted a child by her lover. And so she had a boychild, Ahmed."

I had been told the women of the harem had ways to prevent conception or carrying a child full term, ways known since the time of the ancient Egyptians, but usually they were forbidden to slaves. Slaves begot slaves, increasing the wealth of the master.

Irenia paused again, twisting her hands in mine.

"And is it the child, Ahmed, who is ill?" I asked. "Or dying?"

"No, no! It might be better if he were. Oh, Tara, it is too terrible to tell."

"But you must." I knew that whatever was tearing her apart had to come out, had to be released in words. "Tell me now. Tell me everything."

"Ahmed will never be a man. Nadia adores her son. She has been allowed to keep him with her. She hoped he would grow to be tall and strong like his father. Be a good servant. Maybe master of the horses or one of Ali Habib's mounted guards. Now he will not."

"He is already dead then? Or hurt in some way?"

Irenia lowered her eyes. Choking with sobs, she was almost incoherent, but she finally managed to speak again.

"Ahmed was put into a scalding hot bath to help deaden the pain, and—and he was crushed."

"Crushed!" I was horrified at what I thought she was telling me, but the real horror was still to come. "You mean he was drowned?"

"No, his—his parts were crushed."

Now I knew. My body shuddered at the pain he suffered, and I went livid with fury. The abomination! Such brutality by people with twisted minds should never be condoned. His testicles had been crushed. Castrated, he would now be a eunuch, one able to guard a harem because the master would know he could be trusted with the women. Or be trained to sing to entertain the master's guests. It was a vile, dehumanizing practice. I couldn't believe it of Ali Habib, so gentle a man, and yet he had many eunuchs on his staff. I had closed my eyes to what went on around me all the time, and now they had been forced open.

"Why, Irenia? Who ordered such a thing done to a little boy?"

"Ben Hassem, my lord's brother. You know him."

Oh, yes, I knew him. Such a cruel act became him very well. I also knew his unnatural fancies and distorted pleasures.

"But Ahmed is only six years old!" I gasped.

"Ben Hassem likes them young. He takes them and—and trains them to please him."

"But he will do the boy grave injury, will maim him. Maybe even kill him. The child's body is too small for—" I could not go on. The vision that erupted in my mind was too horrible to contemplate.

"Ben Hassem does not care. He thinks only of his own pleasures. If the boy does not please him or his beauty is ruined in some way, he will throw him out or put him to menial tasks."

"Something must be done, Irenia. 'Tis too late to restore the boy's manhood, but we must get him out of Ben Hassem's grasp."

"There is nothing to be done, Tara. It is his will. Nadia is only a slave. It is custom."

Custom, was it! Well, I had defied custom before, and I was not afraid to do it again. We would soon be leaving, and I cared not what opinion Ali Habib had of me. I remembered my vow not to interfere anymore, and then immediately forgot it.

"Nadia is not just a slave," I said. "She is a mother."

"Oh, Tara, if you could only do something, we would all be so grateful. Many of the others have suffered in one way or another because of Ben Hassem's evil ways. When he cannot get boys, he—he makes demands on the slave women that are unspeakable."

"And Ali Habib lets him?"

"We are afraid to tell him. Ben Hassem has great power you do not know of."

No, I thought, but I know his ways, and I'll not be afraid to tell Ali Habib. Ben Hassem could not touch me as long as I remained under Ali Habib's aegis. I would make certain I did not put myself in a vulnerable position until I was safely on a ship.

I jumped up from the divan, forgetting I had not yet dressed. Grabbing the shawl Irenia had put over me, I threw it around my shoulders and rushed to my room. Even before I looked for something to put on, I asked Cyri to find Olav for me.

"Please, Olav, tell Ali Habib I require an audience with him. 'Tis most urgent."

Olav returned in less than half an hour. "Ali Habib said to tell you he is sorry he cannot see you. He is busy overseeing preparations for a feast for several important guests."

I had to think of something. I was not going to be denied. Reason told me that the damage to the boy was permanent, but I could not dismiss a faint hope that with proper care and the right treatment his manhood could be restored. Of one thing I was certain: he had to be gotten away from Ben Hassem.

"Olav, help me. Give me an idea. I have to see him."

I looked at the man who had saved my life when our ship was attacked; who had brought me to this place of safety and become a real friend. Would not he of all people appreciate the desperate plight the boy was in? I decided to tell him. Quickly I related the story Irenia had told me.

" 'Tis very sad, Tara. The boy will suffer more than I. I was a man, and the pain was intense. But no man desired my body, so I was spared that humiliation. I was too old and ugly." He laughed, mocking himself.

"You are not ugly, Olav. You are a very good man."

"Thank you. 'Tis been a long time since anyone called me a man."

I turned back to the main concern. "Now, tell me, what can I do?"

"Nothing. You must not interfere. To do so would be dangerous business and you would put yourself in real jeopardy with Ali Habib as well as Ben Hassem."

"I must, Olav." I could not really believe he didn't want me to help the boy. "I must see Ali Habib. He is a good man. He will listen and do what is right."

"I know better than to argue with you, Tara, when your mind is made up. There is to be a great feast for many merchant traders, who have come from all parts of the world. There will be elaborate entertainment. You might ask to be allowed to dine with them. You are curious to see such a feast, to witness the entertainment. You can then go back North and tell everyone what a powerful, wealthy man Ali Habib is. That would please him."

"Olav, 'tis brilliant. What sort of entertainment? Dancers?"

"Dancers, acrobats, jugglers. 'Twill last all night."

"Then do ask if I may join them."

I had an idea. It was daring but it might just work. I knew better, though, than to tell Olav. He had agreed to my attending the dinner, but he would change his mind and not ask Ali Habib if he knew what I was planning. After dinner was over, I would request permission to dance for his guests. I thought Ali Habib would be pleased, and it would be an excellent way to get his full attention.

This time Olav was gone for more than an hour, and I stalked back and forth along the garden paths, impatient for his return and our host's answer. Paul was there, and he handed me a beautiful deep red rose from which he'd picked all the thorns. It seemed like a good omen.

When I saw the frown on Olav's face, I knew I had

311

been invited. Olav was still wary of my interfering, but I told him not to worry; everything would be all right.

The day of the dinner, I bathed in the pool and allowed Cyri to rub the most fragrant pomades into my skin. As I danced, the increasing warmth of my skin would release the odors and waft them across the room to the guests. I brushed my long hair until it glistened like highly polished silver. Then I put it up in such a way that by removing a few pins while I danced, it would cascade around my shoulders.

I donned trousers of blue silk under a skirt of blue and gold brocade, elaborately re-embroidered with colored silk threads and crystal beads. The blouse was of heavy blue silk, with high collar, and full sleeves caught tightly at the wrists. It was a magnificent yet modest garment. Olav looked askance at my wearing it instead of a tunic and dalmatic, but he said nothing. He often admitted that women's peculiar vanities were beyond his understanding.

The banquet was held in a large reception room walled on one side. The other three sides had pillars to support the roof, and the garden came right up to the marble floor, partially covered with Oriental carpeting. It was as if the vibrant colors of the garden, the very flowers themselves, had been woven among their threads. The carpets encircled an open area of mosaic where the entertainers would perform.

Both low divans and piles of cushions had been placed near low, lacquered and gilded tables on which were ewers of wine, jewel-encrusted goblets, silver and gold dishes of sweetmeats, and bowls of clear water for washing the fingers.

I was the last to arrive, and Ali Habib rose from his divan to escort me to a seat.

"Welcome, Tara. We are pleased you wanted to join us tonight."

I looked around the room. He did, indeed, have a motley assortment of guests. There were tall, blond men from the North in sleeveless leather jerkins and woolen trousers; and brown-haired, fair-skinned men who could have come from the continent or from Britain. My heart turned over when I thought I might meet someone from home. Hope rose in me that more than the rescue of Ahmed from Ben Hassem's vile treatment might result from this dinner. I had been right to insist on coming. At first opportunity I would ask Ali Habib about these men. There were slant-eyed Orientals in embroidered silk robes and swarthy Slavs or Bulgars wearing embroidered lambswool coats. There were also a few merchants from Constantinople, easily recognizable by their lightweight tunics, dalmatics, and be-jeweled pelliums.

There was also Ben Hassem. Fortunately he sat on the other side of Ali Habib, and I was spared having to look at him. As far as I knew, he had not tried to seek vengeance against me after my flight from Polybus. For a time, after waiting apprehensively for him to make a move or threat of some kind, I was mystified. Then I realized that this was Ali Habib's house, and Ben Hassem lived in it by invitation. He could well fear reprisals against himself if he harmed me in any way. Yet, I didn't underestimate his cunning, and I knew that after tonight, I would be in far greater danger from him. It was more imperative than ever that Olav find a ship as soon as possible.

The banquet progressed leisurely, course after course of small broiled birds, roasted meats, a great variety of cooked and raw vegetables, all passed on huge silver salvers decorated with plumes and flowers. Between courses, the slaves moved among the guests with small towels and fresh bowls of water.

According to custom, Ali Habib had not introduced me to the guests, but during the course of the meal he turned to me.

"Tara, there are merchants here from your homeland and from Fyn, near Jutland."

My heart leaped. I had not been mistaken.

"Maybe one of them will consent to take you back with him. Would you like me to ask?"

"Please, sire. You have been most generous, and I am not ungrateful, but—"

"I understand." He patted my hand. "I, too, would like to see you returned to Britain or to Rorik's people."

"You have heard nothing, have you?"

"No. I'm sorry."

The unspoken words lay between us. He had given up hope that we would ever learn where Rorik was. It would be futile for me to remain in Constantinople.

"I will introduce you to three of the merchants after dinner," he said. "We will speak to them together."

313

Now came the moment for me to make my request to dance. I should have brought up the subject of Ahmed quietly, while I was sitting next to Ali Habib, but my intuition—or female conceit—played me false. I thought he would be more amenable if I entertained his guests; my having learned to dance in the Eastern style would be like a gift to him.

He looked surprised at my suggestion, but he seemed pleased, and I breathed a sigh of relief. If he had not approved, I felt sure he would have forbidden it. I retired while the jugglers and acrobats performed their astounding feats. When my turn came, I wondered why I had dared to think I could dance well enough to please my host and his guests. My palms were sweaty, and I felt a nervous fluttering in my stomach. I had danced often with the women, but never among a group of strangers.

Three slave girls had already begun playing the haunting melody on stringed instruments, and one beat out a steady rhythm on a small drum. It was that beat, slow at first and then increasing in tempo, that would guide my feet through the intricate steps of the dance. I had to pause a few moments to control my heavy breathing and the rise and fall of my breasts. Then I remembered why I was doing this, and I was ready.

Adjusting the cymbals between my fingers and the palms of my hands, I glided gracefully across the floor on my toes. First I made a low bow of obeisance to Ali Habib, my arms outstretched, my forehead touching the carpet at his feet. Once I had done that, the mood of the music enthralled me, and I thought only of the dance. Moving always on the balls of my feet, I whirled around the room, smiling at each of the guests. Most of the men returned my smile, obviously delighted with my dancing, but those from Britain and Jutland were frowning with disapproval. I could only surmise that Ali Habib had told them something about me after I left the table. Maybe already mentioned I was looking for a way to return to the North. Daughter of one country, wife to another, I should not have been performing thus before strangers. Suddenly I realized I had made a mistake. I was wrong not to be myself and try to act like one from a strange culture.

I had an inspiration. Without breaking rhythm from that of the music, I moved across the floor to where the musicians sat. I took a lute from the hands of one, and sitting down among them, I began to play and sing a ballad well known in Britain. For the next few minutes, I entertained with poignant love songs and lilting ballads of my homeland. The frowns of displeasure on the men from the North turned to smiles, especially when I concluded with one of the rousing tunes which we had danced to in Hordaland.

The applause that followed told me I'd not been wrong to change my program. With a nod to each of the guests, I ended as I had begun, in low obeisance before Ali Habib. Being a guest, I was not showered with coins as the jugglers and acrobats had been, and indeed I was seeking a far greater, more valuable reward.

"Tara, we are most pleased," Ali Habib smiled. "Your performance was charming."

I looked from his pleasantly lined face to the snarling, cynical features of Ben Hassem. The black hatred in his eyes made me more determined than ever to try to free Ahmed from his clutches.

In an ebullient mood of largess—and no doubt to impress his guests with his wealth—Ali Habib asked, "What would you like as a gift? This perhaps?" He removed an enormous emerald from his finger and laid it on the table. "Or this?" He touched the large amethyst encased in a pendant and hanging from his neck on a gold chain.

"Thank you, no," I said quietly. "Your speaking to the men from the North about my wish to return home is enough of a gift." Then I lowered my voice to just above a whisper so no one else in the room could hear. "I crave only one other thing. That you ask your brother to return the boy Ahmed to his mother."

Ben Hassem's face contorted with rage, and he leapt up from the cushions where he'd been lounging. He immediately sat down again, aware of the startled expressions on the guests' faces. Ali Habib only scowled and remained seated, but I knew his silence was more ominous than his younger brother's rantings.

"You trespass too far, Tara, and you presume too much on my friendship."

He was furious. Not so much at my request, but at the fact he had to acknowledge he knew about and tolerated Ben Hassem's warped nature. If I had seen him alone, away from his brother, and been able to communicate

Nadia's despair, I might have succeeded in my request. As it was, I knew I had failed.

"Do not interfere with what does not concern you," he said in a steady, even voice, "or ask for what is not ours to give."

With that I was dismissed. I had failed in my plan to free Ahmed from a life of degradation. More, I had lost all chance to meet the travelers from home. I could only hope that, in spite of his disapproval of what I had done, he would still talk to them. Unable to sleep, I walked the garden paths all night, finding some surcease from pain among the flowers and the night birds.

In the morning, Irenia came to my room more distressed than ever. During the night Nadia had slit her wrists. Before the sun rose, she had bled to death.

Chapter Twenty-one

FOR TWO DAYS I WAITED ANXIOUSLY to learn what would be the result of this second interference of mine into the affairs of the house. Ali Habib must really consider me a thorn in his side now. He would have every right to refuse me permission to go into the seraglio.

I had responded to his kindness and generosity by flaunting custom, by charming myself into his presence with a lie, and then turning on him with a request he could not possibly grant. Would he punish me by not speaking to the Norse or British merchants?

All the while I worried about what my host would do, I was forgetting my real foe. Twice I had put Ben Hassem in a most ignominious position. I knew not what my flight from Polybus had cost him in either gold or influence; this time only his power had been challenged, and unsuccessfully at that, and I hoped that his brother's refusal to grant the request would suffice as revenge.

On the third day, Olav came rushing into the garden where I was sitting in the pergola enjoying the noonday warmth. His body was covered with sweat from running, and his face was contorted with fury.

"Sit down, Olav. You look as if you will have an attack."

He collapsed on the bench beside me. "They have gone!"

"Who?"

"The merchants from Britain and Jutland. They sailed yesterday."

I sighed. It was as I expected. It was my punishment for behaving as I had. "Then Ali Habib did not speak to them." I was heartbroken. After all this time, we had come so close to being able to leave. And I had ruined everything. " 'Tis almost summer. There will be others," I tried to console him.

"You don't understand. Ali Habib did talk to them, and several offered to transport us."

I was stunned and dismayed.

"Then why—do you know what happened?"

" 'Twas Ben Hassem."

He was still furious for my having thwarted his first evil scheme and was no doubt fuming over my attempt to take Ahmed away from him. This was his revenge.

"How was he able to change their minds?"

"I learned that from another sailor. He said the merchants sailed away as fast as they could after talking with Ben Hassem. Somehow he managed to convince them his brother had tricked them by saying you were a guest and needed transportation. He told them you were really a member of the harem, and if they took you, Ali Habib would accuse them of kidnapping, confiscate their ships and goods, and probably have them slain. He was speaking to them as a friend. This was the merchants' first voyage to Constantinople, and they probably came with all sorts of misconceptions about the wily Moslems, and so they believed him."

I felt completely deflated. There seemed no way out of our dilemma, no solution to our problem. We were being frustrated at every turn.

"So that is the threat we face," I said. "How will Ben Hassem explain it to his brother?"

"He had the merchants simply send word they had changed their minds. By the time Ali Habib received it, they were gone and he could not question them."

"And we do not tell him the truth."

"No, we stay out of it and bide our time. We have no proof, and Ali Habib would not take kindly to another accusation against Ben Hassem."

I lapsed into silence for a moment. I had been dealt one blow after another, and I did not see how I could stand much more. If it had not been for Olav—

"Why are you so wise, Olav?"

"Not wise, Tara, experienced."

"Have you—have you known any real happiness since—"

"Since I became a eunuch? I know not. What is happiness? A moment when I forget what I am and just before I remember. I do not think there's any such thing as total happiness. But even in the most desperate of situations, I think there are high peaks or bright days that stand out in relief against the flat, somber ones. In the long run, that is happiness. A bit of mica among diamonds is nothing. But among drab grains of sand, it shines with its own brilliance."

"And so you are a philosopher, too."

Olav made no comment, but returned to the practical concerns of the moment. "Do we again look for a ship of our own?"

"We do." I liked his use of the plural "we" as if we were a strong, enduring partnership. I loved Olav as a friend. If he at any time had acted the part of the humble sycophant, the beholden servant, I could not have stood it. We were equals. I doubted if he had felt any differently when he was a shipbuilder and a member of Thorne's crew. I wondered that he had ever been able to adapt himself to the role of eunuch-slave. The position did not become him at all.

"Then I think I might have found one already."

"Do you really, or are you just trying to cheer me up?" I wanted to believe him, but I was afraid. I had been disappointed too often.

"I would not lie, even to cheer you up. It is a merchant from Jutland who sailed as far as Athens last summer. He spent the winter there, then sailed across the Aegean and Sea of Marmara to trade here in the bazaars. He will be ready to leave in little more than a week."

Once again I suffered from the ambivalent feelings of wanting to go yet yearning to stay. I wanted more than anything to return home, but I feared that with every league we sailed westward and northward, I would be leaving Rorik farther and farther behind. Someday, I knew, the traveling circus would return to the Golden Horn, and I would not be there to see it. That someday, however, could be many years away. Many caravans traveled as far east as Cathay and as far south as Egypt. I could no longer continue to accept Ali Habib's hospitality nor did I want to buy a home in this alien land. I thought constantly of Signe and Eirik and how desperately I longed to see them. It was a very strange feeling to pack with tears in my eyes while my heart swelled with joy at the thought I would soon see them.

Olav, Inga, and I went to the bazaars almost daily for the treasures we wanted to take back with us: icons, carved ivory statues and triptychs, filigree jewelry, fine leather goods, enamel ware, cloisonné, and lengths of silk and brocade. How Astrid would smile when I draped her in silk and bedazzled her with gifts of jewelry. And for Thorne, soft leather slippers and a finely carved ivory-handled knife of the finest Damascus steel. For the table in the long hall, silver forks and gold-etched bowls of glass.

Inga wanted almost everything we saw, not for herself but for her newly acquired brother and sisters. She was satisfied with a second blue cup and a carved ivory icon of the Madonna and Child for herself. She was attracted first to the scene of a mother holding her baby; but once I told her the story of the nativity, she wanted to hear it every night before we went to sleep.

Through the weeks, Inga had blossomed and filled out to become a very beautiful girl. I had thought her to be about ten years old when I took her from the slave mart. Short and scrawny, with skin clinging to her bones, she had seemed no more than a child. Good food and care brought the dimples back into her cheeks and the sheen into her golden hair. Her slim body began to fill out, and it was no longer the figure of a child. Not knowing the real date of her birth, we choose the first day of May, and Cyri and I surprised her with a party to celebrate the beginning of a new way of life. It would be the beginning of a new life for me, as well. One without Rorik and completely centered around the children.

I went with Olav to the ship to see if it would be suitable for a long voyage, and I was pleased. The serpent ship was nearly as long as the *Raven* and as well accoutered as the *Albatross*. The merchant had agreed to build a small enclosure for Inga and me. It would assure some privacy for us. All of the crew were interested in our return to the North and could not assure me enough they would do all they could to make our journey comfortable.

Inga was with us, and she examined every aspect of the ship from prow to stern. She exclaimed over the magnificent dragon head, bounced on the soft pallet we would share, and had the crew explaining each new item that caught her eye. Olav and I might be hard put to keep her from falling overboard if I were not certain the crew would also be keeping an eye on her. They had all fallen in love with her. When she was around, they were very tender and watched their language. They had heard her

320

story, and I imagined many of them thought about a little girl back home and what it would be like to think of her in the hands of slavers.

Two days before we were to sail, Ali Habib sent word he would like me to dine with him at the home of a friend. I was completely taken aback. We had heard no word from him except that he was happy we had found a ship. I thought of the last feast I'd attended away from the house and started to refuse. Then good sense told me that Ali Habib was not Ben Hassem. He might also be trying to make amends for the way he'd had to speak to me at his banquet, and it would be rude of me to hurt his feelings.

As we rode together in the car, the subject of the fatal dinner party did not come up. Instead the conversation remained light and pleasant.

"Moussaud is another wealthy merchant with a well-deserved reputation for his banquets. It should be one you will remember for a long time. He is a Christian, which is why I am able to bring you, and I want you to take with you a pleasant memory of Constantinople."

Had he learned somehow about the evening at Polybus' home? Or was he merely, as I first thought, trying to make up to me for what he'd had to do about Ahmed and for the merchants sailing away without me. Once I might have questioned him. I had learned from Olav to hold my peace.

"I am sorry," he said, "we have not been able to learn anything about Rorik before you leave. I shall continue to seek word about him. We may yet be able to free him and return him to his homeland."

"Thank you, sire, you are most thoughtful." But I would no longer dwell on the hope that he would be successful. Hope can be a blessing when there is still something tangible to support it; after that it becomes an agony that slowly erodes one's emotions.

Because the evening was warm, we dined on a broad loggia overlooking a garden which sloped down to one of the harbors on the Sea of Marmara. Domed balconies projected above us; on one of them sat musicians who played throughout the meal. As Ali Habib had said, Moussaud was a Christian from Damascus, who had been violently antislavery until he moved his base of operations to Constantinople. Like so many others, he had fallen under the spell of the magnificent but malevolent city, which often reminded me of the courtesans it was famous for; like whited sepulchres, they were beautiful on the surface, but rotten and deadly within their hollow core. Yet, I could not deny he was a charming, gracious host.

With the sherbet and cakes, we were entertained by jugglers and eloquent dancers, whose performances were as innocent as those at the earlier feast had been suggestive. Ali Habib had been correct: It was the kind of leave-taking I needed to carry away a good impression of the city.

Once the meal was completed, Moussaud invited us to accompany him to his private arena for a surprise entertainment. We walked through the garden, now lighted with candles and flambeaux, to a game yard, a small, circular arena surrounded by shoulder-high stone walls. On one side were several tiers of raised, upholstered seats under a scarlet and gold canopy. The ground of the arena was covered with sand. For the first time that evening, I was disturbed. I knew what the sand was for. It provided a better footing for contestants. It also absorbed blood. My earlier opinion of our host was slowly changing, and I wondered exactly what sort of entertainment was in store for us. Hundreds of torches lighted up the arena as bright as day, yet at the same time cast an eerie, blood-red glow over the entire scene. It was a perfect setting for death. I was aware of what took place in such arenas.

Although a major, vital center of Christianity, Constantinople had its afficionados of the most barbaric entertainments: cock fighting; bull- and bear-baiting, pitting ferocious, trained dogs against larger animals; and "pit" wrestling—or the fight to the death. Several men, wearing only loincloths, were put into the pit. They battled bare-handed, with no weapons, until all but one were dead.

The action in "pit" fighting was not haphazard. There was a system. All would gang up on the weakest until he was dead. The survivors then turned on the next victim. This continued until there were four left who then fought in pairs. The two victors—the only two still alive—battled to the death amidst the bodies of those who had fallen earlier. There were no restrictions. The combatants could do anything they wanted to do in order to win: gouge out the opponent's eyes, punch the most vulnerable areas, or stomp on his head, chest, and genitals. Before it was over, the pit was flooded with blood and echoing with the groans of the dying. Usually each spectator brought his own slave, and heavy wagers were laid on the outcome.

I sat on my upholstered chair under the canopy, and as if in a trance, I held the goblet of wine I'd been handed. I dreaded what I might be forced to witness during the next hour. I knew not which would be worse to endure, watching men fight each other or seeing poor, innocent animals slash themselves to pieces. Certainly human beings had more worth, and I felt a deep compassion for them, but I could not help but reserve a large store of pity for the animals. My stomach had already become queasy, and I was afraid I would be really ill once the combat began.

Which would it be this night? I'd not seen any of these spectacles, only heard about them, but it did not take a vivid imagination to realize what they were like. I could always close my eyes to the sights, but there would be no way to shut out the screams of the men or the howls of the animals who were being tortured and killed for sport. I clutched the goblet so tightly, I bent the silver stem. To close my mind to what was coming, I concentrated on our sailing on the morrow and how happy I was going to be once we were at sea.

Everyone had settled down, and our host gave a signal. A black bear was brought in on a chain. Growling and tugging on his leash, he looked ferocious. With every step he reared up and released his long, scimitar claws.

"He hasn't been fed for three days," I heard Moussaud inform Ali Habib. "So it should be a real battle, one well worth your coming over here to see. It will be a novelty, too. There's never been an act quite like it here in the city. I have seen it done only once before—in Odessa."

I scarcely heard anything beyond the information that the bear had been starved to make him more violent. I waited to see them lead in the dog or bull, favorite opponents for bears. More afraid than ever I was going to be sick, I tried to think of an excuse to leave. Before I could do so, a cry went up, and I knew the bear's adversary was being brought in. I closed my eyes and forced myself to swallow hard.

The first cry was followed by a low murmur and then several shouts.

"It's a man!" Oh, God. No. There must be a way to leave. I could never sit through it. There was not a chance in the world for the man to survive. I could only pray he would die quickly.

"You mean he's going to fight the bear?" There was actually a note of exultation in the spectator's voice!

"Look at him. He'll not last five minutes. We'll see plenty of blood tonight."

I was feeling ill, but it was nothing compared to the sickness that infected these people. It was more obscene than the erotic dancing and vile mosaics I had seen. These were not human beings talking this way. They were monsters of the most evil kind. I tried to shut out the voices around me, but I could not.

"He's big, but he doesn't look too strong."

"What are the odds? I'll put my gold on the bear, no matter."

"Anybody would be a fool to bet on the man."

"No, he looks like he's been starved longer than the bear."

It was more horrifying than anything I'd ever imagined. If I had not felt the seat beneath me I might have thought I was in the midst of a terrifying nightmare. They were betting on a man's life. They were looking forward eagerly to blood and mutilation and killing.

There were sounds of scuffling. The battle had begun. The spectators were screaming, urging on first the bear and then the man. It was only a game, a lottery. They were thinking of the money they would win or lose, with no concern for a human life.

"He's drawn blood!"

"The man is down!"

Now the screaming increased, their appetites whetted, like those of voracious animals, at the first smell of blood.

Try as hard as I would I could not keep my eyes closed. I opened them just in time to see the bear, between me and the man, grab his adversary with his huge forelegs. I saw the man manage to get one foot around the bear's hind leg and pull him down. He was fighting for his life with every ounce of strength he had. I did not scream, but I prayed. Together they grappled across the sand. Once again the man freed himself and began crawling across the ground. Blood dripping from him dyed the sand a brilliant scarlet. The bear lunged, falling on top of him, squeezing the breath out of him. I stopped breathing. This had to be the end. The man was slowly being crushed to death.

I could not stand to watch anymore. I closed my eyes and waited for the shouts of those who had won their bets to tell me it was all over. But there were still only screams, urging the two on. I opened my eyes again. The man was free once more, but only for a second. He turned, and the bear slashed him across the face.

I screamed.

It was all I could do to keep from fainting, but I had to remain awake. Too dizzy to stand I clutched the ledge in front of me, dropping the goblet and spilling wine on the sand, dark red like the blood already there. In a panic I found my mouth was too dry to speak, but I had to. I had to stop the fight. I had to let someone know it was Rorik out there fighting for his life. Was I going to be forced to watch him die?

I grabbed Ali Habib's arm. "Make them stop!" I finally got the words out. " 'Tis Rorik. Make them stop!"

I dared not call out to Rorik, afraid of distracting his attention from the bear. Time enough once he was safe to let him know I was there.

"Are you sure?" Ali Habib asked. "You can scarcely see what he looks like."

I had to make him understand. He must insist the fight be stopped. And immediately, or it would be too late. Rorik was down again and the bear was clawing his shoulder.

"I know 'tis him. Please!"

Rorik had once more broken free and was standing up, blood streaming down his face. How much longer could he go on? He was swaying on his feet. The bear was on his hind legs again. They were circling round and round, each taking the measure of the other.

Ali Habib turned to Moussaud. "The lady Tara begs you to stop the combat. She cannot watch anymore." Why was he so calm? Why didn't he tell them who Rorik was? It was all I could do to keep from screaming at everyone.

"Then bid the lady Tara close her eyes or leave. She has my permission to retire."

Oh, no. Why couldn't he understand? Rorik had fallen again. The bear was still circling and howling. Rorik made no move to get up. The final, fatal attack would come at any moment.

"You will not stop the fight?" Ali Habib's voice was urgent now, yet for some reason he was moving cautiously.

"No."

Why, in God's name, didn't Ali Habib tell Moussaud that Rorik was my husband? I was becoming weaker and weaker. My legs refused to hold me up, no matter how hard I tried to steady myself against the ledge. I collapsed into the seat. From a distance I heard Ali Habib's voice.

"Then sell the man to me so I can stop it."

"He cost me dearly. Many pieces of gold. I bought him thinking I was getting a strong worker. But he is sullen and obstinate. At least I can be entertained by him."

Why didn't they stop talking? Each second was precious. Rorik lay like one dead. The bear had not yet moved in, but he was sniffing the air, growling, and nudging Rorik's inert body with his paws.

"Tell me the cost," Ali Habib said. "I will pay double—triple."

I grew more and more terrified during this dialogue. The bear had rolled Rorik over and was going for his eyes with his claws. Each time Rorik managed weakly to turn his head. He took the long slashes across his head and neck. His left arm hung limp and lifeless. Suddenly the bear fell on top of him. I could not move. My whole body had gone numb. I began gagging, but I swallowed hard several times and managed to control the nausea. My eyes were frozen open. I could not have closed them now if I wanted to. I was going to watch Rorik die.

"You will pay triple?"

"I will give you three times what you paid."

"And the bear?"

"And for the bear."

I covered my ears. I could not listen to this senseless, inhumane bartering for life. I had never endured such misery. The pain of it was suffocating me, and I found myself gasping for breath.

Then a great shout went up. Guards stationed around the arena ran forward and killed the bear with their spears. His claws, still outstretched, were filled with blood, and from them hung shreds of flesh. I had been so near to fainting, I had not heard Moussaud give the order.

Suddenly I felt the blood rushing through me and I came alive again. Oblivious to everyone around me, I ran down the short steps in front of the stand and across the bloodied sand to where Rorik lay. Attendants were already bathing his wounds while others dragged the carcass of the bear away. I flung myself on my knees beside Rorik. He was still breathing. I looked at his wounds. His arm was mangled, and one leg lay twisted under him. His chest and thighs as well as his head were covered with claw marks.

From the stands, I heard the guests yelling and pounding their seats, demanding to know why the combat had been stopped and who was declared the winner. If I had not been so concerned about Rorik I might have been disgusted by it. As it was, their actions no longer fazed me. They were no longer a part of my life.

I also heard Ali Habib talking to Moussaud. "He is her husband, the son of my great friend Thorne, Jarl of Hordaland. He was enslaved some months ago."

"Had I known that, I should have demanded four, maybe five times the price."

"I know, Moussaud. I know you too well to have made that mistake."

The love for bargaining! And a man's life had depended on it. At least I understood why Ali Habib had not immediately let Moussaud know Rorik was my husband.

Ali Habib ordered a litter. "Take him to my home as quickly as possible. But gently, gently."

Through the fog of despair that Rorik might yet be dying, I heard people talking.

"You should take him to hospital."

"He will have better care at my home."

"They have good surgeons there."

"He does not need a surgeon as much as the attention we can give him."

Constantinople was proud of its several hospitals and the surgery performed in them. I had been amazed and impressed to learn they operated for growths in the breast and rectum and stomach, that they even dared cut open the skull and enter the brain. But Rorik did not need any of that, and I was glad Ali Habib chose not to send Rorik to a hospital. He had been among strangers too long. He needed more than anything else my love and devotion. Only I could give him that in full measure.

A runner had been sent ahead to alert Olav, and Ali Habib honored my request to have Rorik put in my rooms.

Both Olav and a Greek physician of excellent repute were waiting for us when we arrived. Rorik had not moved nor made a sound on the litter during the entire trip. I had seen the amount of blood in the sand, and I feared he had lost too much to survive.

Olav led the way to my rooms. Then the physician took over. Without saying a word, he took command of the situation, and no one disputed his orders. Ali Habib obeyed as much as Olav and I did. And the orders came, fast and imperative. Rorik had broken both his left shoulder and left thigh, and the physician called on Olav to exert pressure while he set and strapped them.

The ordeal of pulling and readjusting the bones opened some of the wounds, and now everyone was busy doing what was needed to stanch the blood. Cyri and I folded strips of linen into pads, passing them immediately to Olav and the physician who kept all their four hands moving from one wound to another. Ali Habib—used to ordering hundreds of slaves and crews around—stood quietly by holding the basin of warm water. Gradually the flow of blood ceased, and the physician smeared salves on each wound and placed a clean cloth over them.

"Do not worry about the bleeding," he said. "It has washed out all the impurities. If the wounds are clean, they will heal. Good food and wine will restore what he has lost. He will need plenty of undisturbed rest to assure the wounds do not break open again. When he awakens, even slightly, put some of the powders I give you in a glass of wine and make certain he drinks all of it."

My heart swelled and pounded in my chest. My hands had remained absolutely steady while we worked on Rorik. Now they were shaking so violently I dropped the piece of linen I was holding. Rorik has to live. This man, this physician says he will. Therefore I must believe it.

"And how long should he sleep?" I asked.

"At least forty-eight hours. That will be time enough for him to begin taking food. The wine will provide what nourishment he needs meanwhile."

I feared to have him remain asleep so long, feared he would slip away unless we woke him.

"How will we know the wounds are healing? Should he not be roused from time to time?" There were so many more questions I wanted to ask, to have each answer reassure me that Rorik would live.

"There will be some drainage, so do not be alarmed if you see matter oozing from them. I have shown Olav what to look for. He will change the dressings. Send for me anytime if something does not look right. I will stay here until morning and see him before I leave."

Rorik's head was wrapped to below his eyes in bandages that looked like a turban that had slipped. The claw slashes on his forehead and cheek were the worst. Those on his chest and legs looked bad, and there were a lot of them, but they were more superficial. The physician assured me again that the greatest danger was past once the wounds were cleaned out. The salve was a mixture of properties that would deaden pain, prevent infection, and speed the healing process. He had perfected the substance after several years of study in both Egypt and Athens.

For the next two days neither Olav nor I left Rorik's side. Sometime during that interim, I thought about the ship we were to have boarded for Jutland, and I shuddered to think what might have been. One more day and we would have been gone, never knowing that we were leaving Rorik within a few leagues of us in Constantinople. Or I might have refused Ali Habib's invitation to attend the dinner. Or I might have left the arena before the combat began as I had wanted to do. I had come too close—much too close to losing him again. Now he had to live. I would not let him die.

At the first change in Rorik's breathing or the first sound from his lips, Olav and I were at his side, forcing the wine between his lips and checking the wounds. Olav changed the dressings regularly, always looking for signs of putrefaction, and I kept reminding myself of what the physician had said: once they were cleansed of the filth from the bear's claws, they would heal.

When the forty-eight hours had passed, I moved my chair nearer the head of the bed. I wanted my face to be the first thing Rorik saw. We had been separated almost exactly a year. His eyes were no longer covered, although his head was still wrapped, and there was a great patch above one eye where his eyebrow had been nearly ripped off. In several places the slashes were too deep or wide to be held together only by the binding, and the physician had stitched them together. Never having heard of such a procedure, I started to protest when he took out a fine needle and a long strand of silk thread. Ali Habib assured me 'twas done all the time. I watched, fascinated yet scared, as he brought the two edges of flesh together and joined them with quick, deft stitches. There would be scars, but thin ones, not livid, unsightly gashes.

The drugs had done their work well, and Rorik continued to sleep, breathing naturally, undisturbed by spasms of pain. Olav went to bring food. I looked at Rorik. This was the man I had hated and then learned to love. How I had fought against loving him! And how foolish I had been to deny that love during the first year. Stupid and proud. Or maybe pride is the child of stupidity. We had many months to make up for. I wondered if there were any way I could show him just how much I really loved him, how dear he was to me.

I could no longer resist the temptation. Leaving the chair, I lay on the bed beside Rorik, putting one arm across his chest. I looked at his left leg, splinted from hip to ankle, and his arm and left shoulder, tightly bound and strapped to his chest to assure proper mending. It would be some time before that arm could hold me, but I had him back, and that was all that mattered.

Becoming restless, Rorik tried to move from side to side but succeeded only in flinging his right arm between us. I raised up gently and moved it so I could rest my head on his good shoulder. In a moment I felt the arm go around me, pulling me closer to him, as he had done so often just before we both woke up.

I could not stop the tears flowing down my cheeks and onto his chest.

"Tara? Is that you?" he whispered softly.

"It is, my love." I could not stop weeping. I had thought never to hear his voice again.

"Why are you crying?" He pulled me more tightly against his chest.

"Because—because I thought I'd never see you again. I thought I had lost you."

He tried to move his left arm and cringed involuntarily from the pain. "You very nearly did, Seabird."

I sat up so I could look into his eyes, and he tried to smile when I ran my hand over his battered face. He would have at least two long scars to remind him of his almost fatal battle with the bear—one through an eyebrow and the other the length of his left cheek.

"Rorik, hold me very close. Promise we'll never be

separated again. I know now how unbearable life is without you. When I lost you at the slave market, I wanted to die. Now I really have you with me, and I'll never let you out of my sight again."

Not until this moment, not until I was quite certain he was going to recover could I relax in the belief that we were together and everything was going to be all right. I had been so afraid I was going to lose him again, as I had at the slave market. And this time would have been, if possible, even worse. I knew I would never get over the horror of thinking I was going to watch him die before my eyes.

"I love you, Tara." In spite of the apparent agony it caused him, he seemed determined to speak. "The thought of someday seeing you again was all that kept me going. No slaver, no butcher of a master ever broke my determination to live and find you."

"Please, love, don't try to talk," I sobbed.

"I must. Have to tell you—" He was breathing hard and running his tongue around his bruised mouth.

"Rest now. We have plenty of time to talk." He was already sleeping again, his breathing returning to normal.

Olav came in with the food. "Not awake yet?"

"He was, but he fell asleep again."

"Best thing for him."

So it went for several hours. He would waken for a few minutes, smile at me, and then doze off. I could wait now. I was no longer tormented by the need to hear his voice, to let him know I was with him.

Once the drug wore off, he was fully awake, and he motioned me back to the bed. I started to sit on the edge, fearful of hurting him, but he insisted I lie beside him.

"Do you have any idea, Tara, what it means to me to have you here beside me?"

"I think I do. Remember, I thought I was going to see you killed right before my eyes."

He drew his arm tighter around me, and I felt the warmth spreading through my whole body. It was the warmth of love I thought would be denied me forever.

"Not until I saw the bear facing me in the arena did I think of dying. I knew then I had little hope of coming out alive, but my thoughts were of you the whole time I fought him. If at all possible, I was going to kill him and then find a way to escape. I know now I would have died if

331

you'd not been there. I can vaguely remember hearing you scream out my name. I wish I had known you were watching. 'Twould have given me added strength."

"No, my love, you could not have fought harder. You— you were almost dead when the fight was stopped."

"By Thor! When I'm up off this bed, I mean to return to Moussaud's house and kill him for what he put me through."

"No, Rorik. Don't think of revenge. 'Tis not as important as you imagine. Being alive and together is. Remember, I once swore to return to Britain and avenge the raid on the abbey. No more. Sad as those memories are, I've learned 'tis better to let go of the past and cling tightly to what life offers each day. Loving you has done that for me. If you had not shown me how wonderful it is to be loved, I might have sought revenge, but no longer. So— we'll just think about returning home."

"Tara, you are a wonder. Warm and tender and amazingly wise. Also the most delightful wench in bed a man could want. Come closer. I have a most powerful yearning to feel you under me and hear you squealing with delight."

It made my heart rejoice to hear him speak like that. He loved me and he was recovering.

"There, there, my love, take it easy," I said. "We don't want to reopen your wounds. Time enough for all that when you're completely healed. 'Twill do neither of us any good for you to start bleeding all over the bed."

"Have your way now if you will." He tried to smile. "But I heal quickly and then—"

When I moved slightly, I saw him grimace with pain, and I knew he was suffering far more than he wanted me to know. Best, I thought, to keep the conversation light.

"What did you think, Rorik, when you felt me lying beside you? And how," I frowned, "did you know 'twas me?"

"I thought I was dreaming again. The dream that has constantly tormented me. I'd find you only to lose you immediately. The way it was at the slave market. When I felt you on my shoulder and I put my arm around you, I dared not believe I had really found you after all the months of wandering and looking."

"But 'twas I who found you." I leaned over to kiss him gently, fearful of causing him pain again. I need not have worried. His good arm tightened around me, and all the months of loneliness and aching fear receded into the past with that one kiss. How long we lay thus I do not know. Together at last, time and place had no meaning for us.

We were finally brought back to the present by Olav's deep cough at the door.

"Sorry to intrude, but I think, Rorik, you will have need of this food. If you're to have the strength to—to carry on."

His laughter broke the spell, but I knew Rorik had to eat well if he were to heal rapidly. He looked quizzically at Olav, as if trying to probe his memory.

"Are you not—? Wait a minute. You *are* Olav, the shipbuilder!"

"I am and mighty glad to see you again, sire. 'Tis been many a year since I lifted you aboard your father's ship."

"And saved me when I jumped overboard thinking I'd know how to swim as soon as I hit the water. How did you get here?" He paused. "Where in the name of Thor are we?"

Olav and I began talking at once.

"Please! One at a time."

Preferring to concentrate on looking at Rorik and assuring myself he was really lying there beside me, I let Olav do the talking.

"You are in the home of Ali Habib, a very close friend of your father. He took Tara and me in when we arrived in Constantinople. I'll let her tell you how she got here. Once you were separated after the attack on your ship, her only thought was to learn where you were. We thought the search was over when we saw you at the slave market."

I felt Rorik clutching me. That memory was opening wounds too painful for us to talk about.

"After—after we lost you again," Olav continued, " 'twas a very sad time for all of us. We finally learned who purchased you, only to be told you had thence been sold to a traveling circus."

"And that was an experience I'll not soon forget." I could see Rorik gritting his teeth.

"Not until then did Tara consider returning North. She had the children to think of. Both Ali Habib and I were looking for a suitable ship to make the voyage. Fortunately, Ali Habib and Tara had been invited to Moussaud's house. And that is about it."

While I fed Rorik so he could keep his arm around me, he started to tell us all he had been through during those long, agonizing months. He'd gotten no farther than the surprise attack on the *Albatross* when Cyri appeared at the door.

"My lady, there is someone here who wishes to come in."

Inga appeared beside her, looked straight at Rorik, and then ran to the bed.

"Jarl! Oh, Jarl, I missed you so."

"Little Blue Eyes! How did you get here?"

Their actions so stunned me I could not think for a minute.

"Where have you been, Jarl? You promised to come find me as soon as I was sold."

"I tried to, Blue Eyes, but I could not, I looked and looked all over. And now here we are back together again."

I had forgotten she was among the same group of slaves as Rorik. They must have been together long enough to become very close.

"I purchased her, Rorik, before I saw you. So I had to send back to Ali Habib and ask him to purchase you. I had spent all my coins on Inga. 'Tis why I could not bid for you that day."

"Inga?"

"My name for her. She has never remembered her own."

"No, she did not know it when we were together. That is why I called her Blue Eyes."

I relinquished my place on the bed to her, and she clung to her Jarl as if afraid she would lose him again. How well did I understand her fears. I knew then I had been right to buy her even if it did delay my finding Rorik and put us both through such interminable misery.

Through the following weeks Rorik recovered rapidly, his scars the only visible reminder of our months apart and his close encounters with death. They in no way detracted from his looks. They only made him appear more like the fierce Viking warrior he really was. It would be years—if ever—before the internal scars of fear and loneliness disappeared.

At night as I lay beside him, I awoke often just to reassure myself he was really there. The slightest movement on my part and he was awake, too. When we renewed our lovemaking with a hunger nurtured by pain and longing, I ceased to feel empty inside. His love pulsated through me, filling the hollows and making me feel like a complete woman again.

While Inga played in the garden or worked with Paul, whose greatest happiness was showing her how to care for the flowers, Rorik and I sat in the pergola or on the loggia recounting all we had been through during the past months. I listened to him with awe and trepidation, almost unable to believe that he had managed to live through it. I said little, but I never took my eyes off him. At times I reached over and touched him, just to make certain he was really there.

"On the night the *Albatross* was attacked," he said, "I was told the two ships had been sent out to escort us home. It seemed a strange maneuver, but I had no reason to doubt their word. The leader told me King Torvald had learned about a group of raiders in the Noric Channel just after we left and sent the ships out immediately. Having gone after raiders myself, it didn't take much to convince me. So—he was able to throw me and my men off guard. By the time we became suspicious, it was too late. Our ship was in the hands of the two crews."

"Did you recognize any of them?" I asked. "Olav said he thought that was the reason he was included."

"Some of the men looked familiar, but there was no one I could say I really knew. I don't remember seeing Olav. But it all happened so fast, it would be hard for me to swear to anything."

"Do you remember seeing me come on deck?"

"Just barely, as if through a haze."

"I wonder you saw me at all. I could not keep from crying out when I saw how badly you were wounded. And in such pain. It was agony to watch you."

"My men put up a tremendous fight in spite of the odds."

"And they'd have kept on fighting if you'd not been tied to the mast and threatened with immediate death if any of them so much as lifted a hand."

"Did any of them live?" he asked. "Do you know what happened to them?"

I didn't want to tell him. It would hurt him so very much to know what had been done to his faithful crew,

335 –

but I knew he'd not be satisfied with anything less than the truth.

"The *Albatross* was set afire. They all went down with the ship."

"By the gods, no! That is one act I will avenge, and do not say me no."

"The gods have done it for you, Rorik. Gunner and all his men were killed coming south on the Dnieper. Our boat was crushed going through the cataracts. That is when Olav saved my life."

"Then even if he was one of them, I owe him a real debt of gratitude."

"He was not there by his own wish. But that is another story. We'll tell you that later. I want to hear all that happened to you."

"It was a good thing I was unconscious, or I would have fought to the death to keep my men from dying like that. I thought all along they'd been enslaved or been able to escape. For a long time I was in too much pain to know where I was going. I only knew we were at sea. After we landed, I learned I was being held prisoner at Helgo on Lake Malar. I was in agony wondering what had happened to you. Then I was told I was being held for ransom, and I assumed you had been taken home. If I had thought otherwise—I don't know what I might have done. Then I was informed there was no ransom forthcoming. My father refused to pay it."

"Thorne! No, he would never have refused. I'll not believe that."

"Nor did I," he said vehemently. "I could only conclude the messenger had turned around before he reached Hordaland or had been persuaded by someone not to contact Thorne. The second seemed more probable. Then the question was: Who? Who wanted to prevent my return? Ruskil or someone else?"

"Ruskil has been a real threat. He has known for a long time he was someday going to have to kill you first. Do you think we will ever know?"

"If we get home. There are a great many questions I would like answers to. We may find them in Hordaland—or in Zealand."

"You suspect Torvald? Your cousin's husband?" I found this hard to believe.

"The relationship means nothing to one as ambitious

336

and greedy as he. He has never been one I would trust, and he seemed a bit overly friendly when we were there. And remember, we showed him that the Three Shires are getting stronger all the time."

"Olav has always said he knew nothing of the plans, and I believe him," I said. "God knows I'd not be alive today if it weren't for him. But—"

"But he might remember something he didn't think was important at the time."

I asked Cyri to find Olav, and he came immediately.

"Glad to see you looking so well, sire."

"Thanks to your good care. Sit down a minute, Olav. Tara and I were talking about the night of the abduction. We thought you could shed some light on it."

"If I can, sire."

"What exactly did you know?"

"As I told Tara, I did not know what we were doing or where we were going until we came up beside your ship. Then I heard someone say we were to escort you. I wondered at that, but, to be honest, all I was thinking about was that would mean sailing to Hordaland and a chance for me to escape."

I listened intently to their conversation, with no desire to interrupt them.

"Your ships sailed from Zealand?" Rorik asked.

"No, we had put out from Svealand some days earlier. We never touched at Zealand."

"You did not leave Zealand soon after we sailed from there?"

"No, sire."

"Do you remember hearing the leader tell me King Torvald had learned of renegades in the Noric Channel and they were to protect us?"

"Not that I recall." Olav shook his head. "I am sure I would have, because it was not true. I was stunned when I saw what was really happening, but remember, I was a slave. All I could do was obey orders. Nor could I alone have prevented their taking you."

"We know that, Olav, and we are in no way suggesting you were a part of the treachery. In fact, we are most grateful for what you have done for us."

"Thank you, sire. Not until Tara was put aboard our ship did I realize there was a way I could do something to help her and save myself as well."

337

"Thank you, Olav. You've answered one question; and as I said, we will always be grateful."

"So," I said, "that means Torvald did not order the abduction."

" 'Twould seem so," Rorik agreed. "But we cannot be sure. He could have planned it all before we arrived. I'll not discount anything until I learn the truth."

"What happened after the ransom was not forthcoming?"

"I was transported to Kiev. Just think, you and I traversed the same route, only several weeks apart."

"I remember Kiev well," I sighed. "I watched every slave auction, waiting and hoping to see your face."

" 'Tis not a place one forgets easily." He said nothing more for a moment or two. When he spoke it was an acknowledgment of brutal memories. "So many thousands pass through there every year. And each one tortured and humiliated in ways you would not believe."

"I know," I said quietly. "I saw it."

"You did not see it all, Tara." Those were his final words on the subject, and certain he had wounds he could not bear to have reopened, I never questioned him about many things that happened while we were apart. But I was left to wonder what could be done to a man that would be as debasing and painful as what I saw done to the women slaves.

"I was sold to a buyer of slaves from Syria," he continued. "We went down the Dnieper as you did, but we wisely portaged around the cataracts. We crossed the Black Sea to Anatolia and thence by caravan to Damascus. I was sold there to a Syrian stonemason.

"More than once I tried to escape. Several of us tried it during one of the portages, but we were caught and chained together. I tried again as we sailed across the Black Sea. We had been unchained briefly in order to change rowing positions after one of them died. I made it to land, but a guard captured me. All my attempts failed."

If I had known during all those months where he was and what he was going through, would it have been easier or worse for me to endure? I would never know the answer, but it no longer mattered.

"The stonemason was a tyrant to work for," he said, "demanding we work during every hour of sunlight with no letup for rest or meals. I finally struck at him with a mallet. I was sure it would mean my death, but I couldn't take it any longer. He had his guards beat me until I was almost dead. When I revived he took me once more to Damascus to sell me. I should have known he would not lose money on me. On the way, we passed a little girl standing by the roadside. She was weeping beside the dead body of an old Syrian woman and begging from all who passed.

"I was ordered to pick up the child and we continued on our way, leaving the old woman, still unattended by the roadside. My owner lost money on me, but he made up for it by selling the child as well."

"That was Inga, wasn't it?" What torments had the child been forced to endure? It was no wonder her mind had forced her to forget much of it.

"It was Blue Eyes. I protected her as much as I could. With other slaves we were taken to the port of Beirut and put aboard a galley. The men did the rowing, chained to our benches during the entire voyage. There was no shelter from either the blazing sun or the fierce storms. When two of the slaves died, they were merely thrown overboard, and the others required to row harder.

"The ship was a small one, so the women had to find space where they could, huddled beneath the benches or curled up among the meager sacks of supplies. Blue Eyes —or Inga—stayed at my feet the entire voyage, leaning against my legs and humming the same mournful song over and over. We finally got to Constantinople. I went wild when I heard her screaming after being sold. I could not see who had bought her, but I knew by her screams it was someone who terrified her."

"Poor lamb," I sighed. "And now she adores Olav."

"Then I was put on the block and sold."

"Ahead of two of the women, and while I waited with such anxiety for Olav to arrive with the money from Ali Habib."

"The man was impatient. He had a long distance to travel."

"If only he had waited. If only the women had been put up first. So many *if*'s and so few minutes kept us from setting you free."

We could not speak of those agonizing moments of discovery and separation. We had endured them once. To talk about them was to live through them again.

"My new master was a fisherman. He was not a cruel man, and he had a certain amount of compassion. But having seen you, having felt you snatched from my arms, my only thought was to get back to Constantinople."

"You tried again to escape?" I should have known during all those weeks of despair that he would do everything in his power to find his way back to me.

"I was caught and sold to the owner of the traveling circus. I thought I had seen cruelty before, but none to compare to the degrading, dehumanizing acts I witnessed with him. Fear of punishments too terrible to mention and threats of starvation kept the few pitiful performers in line. The animals were treated even worse, if possible. I was part of a two-man gladiator act. We were ordered to go at each other with short swords, slashing and hitting until we drew blood. There had to be blood so the people would get their money's worth, and then one of us was to pretend to die with a mortal wound. We took turns dying, staying on the ground and bleeding until the audience left. We were always the last act, the grand finale. And we played it for real, both of us covered with blood before the act was over."

"So that was how you were able to fight off the bear for as long as you did."

"It was good training for it. The only trouble was, I knew the day was coming when I was no longer going to have to feign my death. My opponent was going to make it real. He had taken a rather uncomfortable liking to me and was most unhappy when I rebuffed his advances and told him to go and sleep alone. I knew he had 'accidentally' killed the man I replaced, and I did not intend to die the same way."

I was weak listening to all he'd had to suffer. My troubles had been nothing compared to his. It was almost impossible to believe he was really alive and sitting beside me.

"How did you prevent it?"

"I killed him first. I saw the look in his eye when he slashed out at me the first time in our final match. I parried and then jabbed. The only complaint the spectators had was that the combat ended too soon. They wanted their money back. That was the end of the gladiator act, and I was sold to Moussaud. By that time I was through with being pushed around and simply refused to do anything

340

I was told. But I was back in Constantinople! I didn't know where you were, but I knew I could find you. I had worked out a plan of escape, and I did not intend to get caught this time. Only a few hours until dark, and I would be free and able to search for you. I had seen the palanquin and the clothes you wore, so that would limit my search to the wealthier sections of the city. My only fear was that you were also a slave or—or a concubine. But I knew that once I found you, we would get away together. Then Moussaud decided to pit me against the bear and he kept me chained up for two days. I fought as hard against those chains as I did the bear. But they would not yield."

"Oh, Rorik, what if I'd not gone with Ali Habib that night? What if I'd stayed here and finished getting ready to leave? I can't even bear to think about it."

"I would have been dead, my love, and you would be on your way to Hordaland."

"Hold me close." I felt his arm go around me. I wanted him to crush me. I wanted to feel the pain in my chest, the gasping for breath. "Hold me very close and tell me everything is going to be all right now."

"It is, my love. I promise you that."

Chapter Twenty-two

"BY ALL THE GODS, TARA, I want to go home! I want to command my own ship again. What kind of a Viking am I to sit in a perfumed garden and wear a long dress?"

I laughed. How joyous it was to be able to laugh again after the months of anguish and the days I feared he might still die of his wounds.

"Not a dress, my love, a tunic."

"Dress, tunic—I still have to pull up the skirt before I can—"

"Sssh! Inga is listening."

"Eirik and Signe! I want to see them. And Asri. Damn, Tara, 'tis been more than a year. What am I doing lounging here like one of Ben Hassem's pretty boys."

"Don't jest, Rorik. Never say that." I had told him about the boy Ahmed but not about the night at the home of Polybus. "I cannot bear to be reminded of him and his foul, brutal habits." I wept each time I thought of the little boy. No word about him came to the seraglio, so I could only assume he was still in Ben Hassem's clutches.

"When a man has come as close as I to being a victim of such sordid practices, he does not speak in jest."

I held my breath. He had not been maimed, but how he must have suffered at even the threat of it. "What are you saying?"

"I came within a knife's edge of being like Olav or the boy Ahmed. My first owner, a slave trader from Svealand, to whom I was solid in lieu of the ransom not received, planned to sell me as a eunuch in Kiev. I was strong and powerfully built, just the type needed to guard a harem or a queen. Particularly if that queen had eyes for some man in the court other than her husband. Such a king had sent an emissary to Kiev, and he thought me to be just the man his master sought. Just a matter of castration, and that a very minor matter in the eyes of slave traders."

"How—how did you prevent it?"

"The emissary would purchase me only if the operation was a success. He did not want to pay the money and then have a dead slave on his hands. I knew 'twould do no good to resist. The chains were strong and so were the men who led me to the bench and threw me down on it. Knowing how much the king was paying for me, there was only one threat I could use to prevent the operation. Once the butcher had the knife out and was testing it on a sheep's bladder, I very calmly told the buyer, 'I will kill myself as soon as my hands are free. You cannot prevent it. I have methods you cannot possibly know about.' The knife never touched me, and I was not sold to that particular buyer."

"What methods? You were bluffing, weren't you?"

"I'm not much of a gambler, but my hours with my father were not wasted ones."

"Would you," I asked hesitatingly, "have killed yourself if they had gone ahead with the operation?"

"I'd not have lived as half a man," he said with unshakable conviction. Then he pounded his fist into the palm of his other hand. "And now I want to go home! Why are we delaying?"

"You've been ill. Remember? Also we must find a ship."

"Find a ship! By Thor, we'll buy and outfit one. Where's Olav? He'll know what we need. Also," he looked down at his tunic with disgust, "some decent clothes for me."

That evening Ali Habib asked us to dine with him. 'Twas Rorik's first attempt to walk any distance, and he navigated the tiled floors with help from Olav and me. He limped, favoring the injured leg, but other than that was as strong as ever.

"You look well, my son," Ali Habib said by way of greeting. "You have recovered rapidly."

"Because of the good care I received in your house."

"No, because of Tara. If she were not here, you would have had no desire to live."

"I would not be alive if it were not for your concern and generosity. Tara and I can never repay you. In gold, perhaps, but not in kind."

"You owe me nothing, Rorik. I speak thus because of my friendship for your father and the debt I have been

343

burdened with all these years. And—I have grown fond of Tara."

We were seated around the table before Ali Habib spoke again.

"You have a long journey ahead of you. I know you are all most anxious to get back to Hordaland. Do you feel ready to command a ship again, Rorik?"

"Indeed I do, sire!"

"I know Tara and Olav have thought about purchasing a ship and outfitting it themselves. Perhaps you have the same idea. I would like to make a suggestion. I have a commander in Venice who has long been wanting to sail to the North Sea by way of the Great World Ocean. He is a good mariner, but I am a cautious person, and I have hesitated to send the orders. I hope you will agree to what I propose. You will command one of my ships from here to Venice and then act as guide from there to Jutland, where a merchant awaits my goods, and then to Hordaland to trade for furs."

"Agreed, sire!" Rorik answered almost before Ali Habib finished speaking.

"Good. My best ship is in the harbor now. I want you and Olav to check it over completely, prow to stern, to make certain it is seaworthy for the waters of the North. I will provide anything you need for safety and comfort."

I looked at Rorik. He had risen from his seat and walked over to the archway opening onto the garden. He stood there silently for a long time, his eyes facing due north. In that moment he appeared to grow several inches taller, and I thought his tunic would burst at the seams as he squared his shoulders and expanded his chest. He would be a Viking again, commanding a ship, wooing her to do his bidding whether on calm or rough seas. He had been a slave. Now he was once more a man. He would be giving orders, not taking them. I did not realize until that moment how close Rorik had come to being destroyed. Not the quick destruction of a stab from an enemy's dagger or the slash of a bear's claws, but the slow, eroding attrition of helpless defeat. Death comes in many guises, but not always does it deal a mortal blow.

"Olav and I will go to the ship tomorrow," Rorik said. His always powerful voice acquired a new timbre— deeper, stronger, more masterful. "It should not take us long to look her over. Are all the crew at hand?"

"All are on call." I saw the smile beneath Ali Habib's serious mien.

"Good. I would like to have them meet me there tomorrow. The sooner they know who is master, the easier it will be for us to work together."

"How soon do you think you will want to sail?" Ali Habib asked.

"That will depend, sire, on the ship and the crew."

"Then I had best be alerting my managers to get the cargo ready that I intend to trade in both Venice and Jutland."

" 'Twould seem wise, sire. I have never handled a ship yet that I could not get readied for the sea in less than a week's time."

As quickly as that their positions were reversed. As commander of the ship, Rorik would establish the procedure for loading the cargo and set the date for sailing. Ali Habib might own the ship and the goods to be taken aboard, but Rorik was now the captain.

I, too, had my orders. Not only must I purchase everything we would need for such a long voyage, but I must organize them so they could be stowed away securely and yet be available when the time came for warmer clothing, more bedcovers, or dried food when fresh was not available. My precious treasures, so joyfully purchased, could be taken only—only, Rorik repeated—if there was room. There *will* be room, I said to myself, if I have to wrap each one in a piece of clothing. Rorik will be too busy to notice how I unpack once we are aboard ship and out at sea.

I had another task as well: find materials and make him clothes so he would look like a man again. Like a Viking, not a perfumed seeker of pleasure.

"No more tunics!" he raged. "I want trousers and boots and a leather jerkin."

"I'll do my best, but so much shopping to do and not much time."

"Trousers and boots and vest! Surely you can find those in the bazaars."

I grew miffed at his tone. I was not one of his crew members. I was his wife. "As you command, sire."

"I am not commanding, Tara. Just asking. But if you think 'tis more than you can do—"

"I'm sorry, Rorik. Of course I'll find them for you."

"And a cape, too? A long, double-pointed one?"

"A cape, too."

I knew then what he was feeling. He wanted to stand before his crew, all strangers to him and he to them, as a true lord of the seas. He could do that only in the full dress of a Viking warrior. Once I found the materials and the colored threads, Cyri and I worked for several days, almost without rest, on the trousers and embroidered cape. I had been fortunate to find boots and a leather jerkin, traded by some previous traveler from the North, at a booth dealing in secondhand articles. Something more, however, was needed, and I scoured the bazaar until I found a silver buckle for the cape and some other items I wanted as a special surprise. When all were ready I laid them out on the bed, awaiting Rorik's return from the ship.

He strode in, as best he could stride wearing the long tunic and with his leg still tightly bound though no longer splinted.

" 'Tis time you came to see the ship," he announced. "She's not much like the *Raven*, but she's sturdy and should serve us well."

"And the crew?"

"Good men, all of them. Ready to do my bidding. But I'll feel more like their chieftain when I get out of this damned dress."

"Go look on the bed." I smiled to myself. He had to be pleased.

I waited for the shouts I expected to hear. None came. Had I made them the wrong size? Was he displeased with something? The boots were of Persian leather, beautifully tooled in red and black. Were they too gaudy?

Within five minutes he appeared, stood in the doorway for a second, and then came forward with the long strides so familiar to me from the days on the *Raven*. Picking me up and twirling me around, he then held me close in a bearish grip.

"Now I really feel like a man again. Thank you, Seabird, thank you."

"They all fit?"

"Perfectly." He let go of me and stepped back so I could see. "Where did you find the *hlad* and the armbands?"

"I made them. There are ribbon merchants in the bazaars, so I was able to buy all I needed, and I made the armbands from scraps. I wanted you to be dressed completely as a Viking, nothing lacking."

"And nothing is." If there had been a long mirror, I think he would have spent the rest of the afternoon in front of it, admiring himself. As it was he stared into the small hand mirror and grinned like a child with a new toy.

I was proud of what I had done. The *hlad* and the armbands were covered with gold and colored embroidery, and from the *hlad* hung ribbons of several different colors and designs. The cape was trimmed with braid in an entwined motif.

We rode to the ship in the horse-drawn car Rorik preferred to the palanquin. With his left leg still wrapped, he could not yet ride a horse. Olav had remained at the ship, supervising the changes Rorik ordered. Inga rode between us, jumping like a child in her eargerness to see the ship that was finally to take us north. Sometimes she was very much the young lady, walking sedately in her long tunic. At other times she romped in the garden or hoisted up her skirt to help Paul with the flowers. I caught her once in front of the mirror trying to put her hair up as I sometimes wore mine.

"Would you like me to show you how?" I picked up the brush she had dropped in her embarrassment at being found out.

"No, thank you. It just makes me look silly."

"Not for long. Pretty soon you'll want to wear it that way, and I'll do it the first time for you. In a very short time we will be with Astrid, and she will do beautiful things with your hair."

On this day, however, she was a child again. I shall never forget the look on her face when she first saw Rorik in his Viking raiment. Her first instinct, I could tell, had been to scream and run. Instead she clung tightly to my hand, her small fingers nearly crushing mine. I felt her body trembling with fear. Her blue eyes widened to twice their size, and she bit her lips until she drew blood.

"Well, Blue Eyes, how do you like me now?" Rorik grinned at her. "Am I not the handsomest creature you've ever seen?"

Inga said nothing, but moved closer to me.

"She's frightened, Rorik. It must have been Vikings, the

347

only Vikings she's ever seen, who raided her home. Remember, she saw her parents and brother killed, and then she was carried off."

Rorik came closer and got down on one knee. " 'Tis me. Blue Eyes, your jarl. Come give me a hug and tell me you love me. I'll not hurt you. You know that."

Hesitant at first, she finally reached out and grabbed him around the neck. "I do love you, Jarl, but you looked so mean."

"Did I now. Well, I promise, I shall never scowl at you again. Always smiles for my Blue Eyes." He lifted her up on his shoulders and carried her, laughing finally, to the car.

We had another clue. Her family had not been Vikings nor had they lived in an area where Vikings were frequently seen. Either that, or Rorik had reminded her for just a moment of one man in particular who had been a part of the raid. I wondered, as always, if we would ever know.

Our ship, the *Theos,* was like many I had seen in the harbors, but as Rorik said, quite different from the *Raven* and *Albatross.* A round Mediterranean ship, it carried no banks of oars, depending entirely on sails and rudder for navigating. Some two hundred feet long, it was proportionately wider than the dragon ships, whose slim lines were easily recognizable on all seas. It had a rounded rather than pointed bow and a strangely shaped, elongated stern which looked like a long triangle with its tip squared off or flattened. The *Theos* carried one huge mainsail crisscrossed with lines to shorten it in heavy weather. She also had twin topsails for added power, and a sail at the bow, called an *artemon.* There were lines on pulleys attached to the arm from which the *artemon* hung and which could be adjusted to keep the ship always sailing before the wind.

The entire ship was decked. A second raised deck, the height of a tall man, ran the width of the stern and was reached by rope steps. Beneath this were sleeping quarters for the commander and storage areas. Running out from this in the center of the ship and approximately one-third the width of the beam, was the flat-roofed structure Rorik had ordered built. A good sixteen by twenty feet in size, it provided comfortable sleeping quarters for several people and would be a retreat for Inga and me when the weather was bad.

With the entire ship covered with planking, the hold could be filled with all the cargo Ali Habib was sending to Venice and Jutland. Much of this had already been loaded, and I saw below great amphorae of wine and olive oil, huge, well-wrapped bundles of silk goods, and casks of sugar. I breathed in the odors of spices and perfumes. Ours would be a fragrant voyage if nothing else.

Olav took great pride in showing us over all the *Theos*. As second-in-command until we reached Venice, he, like Rorik, now bore the look of a man who had finally been restored to his rightful place in society. He had been a seaman all his life; and the humiliating years as a eunuch, thought to be only good enough to guard female slaves, were quickly receding. He walked about the deck with a pride and self-assurance not evident even when he was sailing the Black Sea or dining with Ali Habib as a friend. He took Inga's hand and explained to her the workings of every sail, showed her how the mainmast was braced with shrouds of cordage, and took her to the small boat lashed to the deck. We would put it over the side and row to land if there were not a good harbor and we had to anchor out from shore.

I looked for Rorik and saw him where I knew he would be. He stood on the stern deck by the tiller, his hand running back and forth along the sweat-smoothed wood. He was getting the feel of it, learning every quirk of the rudder, and how best to make it obey his touch. He had thrown his cape back over his shoulder, and now it billowed in the wind. With his long hair blowing, and his mustaches and well-trimmmed beard making him look like a young Thorne, he was again a Viking ready to challenge the seas. I might not have been anywhere near him. He stood alone, daring the wind and waves to do their worst and looking eager to conquer all. He looked at the sky to get his bearings, and I knew he wanted only to shout the orders that would release all ties to land and send the *Theos* forward, her sails filled with wind and her bow riding the crests.

When we returned to Ali Habib's, the physician was there to remove the wrappings on Rorik's leg and make his last examination. The news was good. The leg had mended well, although Rorik might always walk with something

349

of a limp. The break had been in the thigh. In spite of the strong pull Olav had exerted on the leg when it was set, the two ends of bone had not joined smoothly but had remained slightly overlapped. The shorter leg should not hinder Rorik in riding or walking, but at first he might tire easily and there would always be some aching when he stood for too long a time.

There were some difficulties in sleeping arrangements right after we found Rorik and brought him to my rooms. Inga had been sleeping on a pallet by my bed or with me when tortured by nightmares. She saw no reason to change her habits, and she made it quite clear she intended to remain nearby to help take care of her jarl. I was at a loss how to explain that I would share the bed with him and she would need to sleep elsewhere. Cyri very quickly and diplomatically whisked Inga away to her room in the seraglio. Evidently Inga was immediately fascinated at being allowed to share the slave's quarters. She put up no fuss.

While Rorik was wrapped in bandages, he depended on me for many things. As a Viking, he looked with scorn on the idea of bathing regularly, and he laughed at me for having picked up the habit since coming to Constantinople. However, once Cyri prepared my bath and I dismissed her, he sat in a chair beside the small pool, his eyes sparkling with envy.

" 'Tis not so much I want to get in the bath," he vowed, "as I want to *be* in it with you."

His comments about what he would do and how he would behave had me blushing. With one arm and leg tightly bound, he was a somewhat awkward if no less ardent lover, and he kept saying over and over, "Just wait, Seabird," and grinning at me as he had the night he tricked me into marriage.

After he had his bindings removed, we ecstatically shared what became a nightly ritual. Together we undressed and slipped into my pool, which Cyri had filled with fragrant water. We lathered each other and rinsed off by ducking and splashing. We laughed and squealed, touched and caressed. Suddenly we were in each other's arms, frantically clinging, searching, and finally finding ourselves joined while the warm water flowed around us. Sated with love and overcome by a luxurious lethargy, we lay on the divan beside the bath and massaged each other with oils. To feel Rorik's fingers running over my skin was exquisite torture, a tantalizing anticipation of more caresses to come. In another moment he was kissing my body, his mouth sought mine, and my whole being opened up to let him enter. Never in all our times together had I so completely given myself to him with nothing held back. I was lifted up, floating in a euphoria of such complete love I felt as if I were no longer earthbound.

On some nights we walked sedately to the bed before reaching for each other. More often we got no farther than the divan or one of the thick carpets. Wrapped in one huge towel, our bodies molded together like a single carved statue.

On another night we ran to the fountain and rinsed under the plashing water. Hidden by the veil of fine spray, serenaded by a pair of nightingales, we stood in the moonlight and made love. Never had the flowers smelled more sweet or the fountain appeared more beautiful.

"Rorik, we have a problem." We had returned from the ship one afternoon and were checking what I had already packed.

"Name it and I'll solve it."

" 'Twill not be that easy. 'Tis Paul."

"Paul? The deaf-mute gardener?"

"Yes. Inga has grown so attached to him 'twill break her heart to leave him behind."

He looked quizzical but knowing at the same time. "Are you suggesting what I think you have in mind?"

"We could buy him from Ali Habib and take him with us." I spoke rapidly, before he could think of any arguments to put me off. "You know Paul would be a real asset on the farm, and I would like to get him away from here and everything that reminds him of Irenia. So 'tis not just for Inga's sake."

"One of these days, my love, you are going to find yourself in real trouble if you do not learn to mind your own business."

"But it turned out happily for Irenia. Ali Habib is pleased about the child."

Rorik shook his finger at me. "You were lucky. Just as you were lucky when I let Thyri and Adair go without

351

following them. If Ali Habib knew the truth, you'd not be smiling so smugly."

I nodded. He was right as always.

"So now," he frowned, "you want to do what you can to make Paul happy."

"Yes. At least give him a chance to meet someone else who will love him."

"Oh, Tara," he laughed. "I do believe your head is filled with nothing but romance."

"I just want everyone to be as happy as we are."

"You win. We shall buy Paul and take him with us. Who do you have in mind for him?" he teased.

"No one. I just want to get him back into the world, a free man."

"Free!" he gasped. "You want me to buy him and then set him free?"

"Certainly. Just as I intend to free Astrid as soon as we get home. Then they can stay with us or leave. I hope they will stay, but the choice will be theirs."

"As you wish. I'm too content to argue with you. Also I know what it means to be enslaved."

"You're a good man, my love." I stood behind him and massaged his shoulders. The one he'd broken still ached at the end of a long day, and only my fingers could soothe the soreness away. I wondered if I dared mention something else to him. No use putting it off, so I plunged right in.

"Cyri wants to go with us, too."

"Oh, no," he huffed, "I'm not going to buy all of Ali Habib's slaves."

"Not all, Rorik. Just Cyri. She and I have gotten very close, and she's such a help with Inga."

"Another one for Inga, eh? You do know how to work on my sympathy."

"No, for me. She will be of real assistance on the voyage. I cannot bear to leave her behind. We'll be at sea a long time, and she can help with the clothes and the cooking."

"We have a cook among the crew, and you will scarcely have to worry about how you look."

"She can sleep with Inga. Being at sea is sure to frighten her. But then," I said wickedly, "Inga can sleep with me, and you can bunk in with Olav."

" 'Tis not fair!" he roared. "You're hitting me where it hurts."

"Yes," I sighed, "a long, long voyage. Nights under the stars, and then I shall go to bed with Inga."

"Come here, you wench." He pulled me down on his lap and smothered my face with kisses. His hands were moving beneath my tunic and caressing my breasts. "Why do I always give in to you?"

"Because you love me."

"Indeed I do. More than I should."

"Never too much, because I love you more than life itself." I turned my face to his, and nothing more was said for the moment about Cyri.

We sailed with the morning tide, crossing the chain that lay deep in the waters of the Golden Horn and which could be raised in time of siege to prevent the entrance of ships. Inga and I stood by the stern rail and took our last look at Constantinople as it receded in the distance. The view of the city was the same one I'd had when Olav and I first approached through the Bosporus: the walls. Now I recognized the dome of the Hagia Sophia and the oval of the Hippodrome. The last object to remain visible was the Tower of Galata, across the Golden Horn from the main part of the city. I might forget many of the sights, but I would always remember the walls.

Cyri was in our cabin making up the swinging bed for Rorik and me in one section and the built-in beds for herself and Inga. Rorik had relented and Ali Habib had been most generous in the small amount he asked for her. She had served his mother, and I think it was his way of rewarding her constancy. Both she and Inga were ecstatic over the news they would not be separated. Cyri cried and hugged my knees and then ran off to get all her things ready.

"I would go naked, my lady."

Not on the ship you won't, I thought, but I didn't say it. She'd not understand my humor. "No need for that, Cyri. Ali Habib has said you may choose whatever you need from among your things in the seraglio. Be sure to get some warm clothes. 'Twill be cold long before we reach the North Sea."

Paul was under the tutelege of Olav, learning the hand signals our second-in-command would use to transmit orders. He surprised us by knowing much more about ships than we expected. He was quick on his feet and agile with his hands when it came to moving about the ship and handling the lines. Like Cyri, he was overcome when he learned he was to go with us. His eyes lit up, and then he immediately went around the garden with Inga, making certain he was leaving everything in perfect order.

Cyri came out to take Inga into the cabin for some rest. The little girl was looking a little queasy from the motion of the ship, so I told Cyri to give her some wine and try to get her to sleep.

"Put her in my bed, Cyri, for a little while. Until she gets used to the motion of the ship. She will be all right in a few hours."

I walked to where Rorik was standing at the tiller, his legs apart and shoulders braced against the wind. I put my arm around his waist, taking my strength from him. The wind increased, and wordlessly he wrapped his long cloak around me. We needed no words to communicate our love. The silence was like a second, invisible cloak that enveloped me in comfort and security.

Chapter Twenty-three

WE SAILED ACROSS THE SEA OF MARMARA, through the Dardanelles, and into the Aegean Sea. Staying within sight of the coast, we anchored each night in a sheltered bay or near the shore. Rorik would have preferred sailing all night, but with a crew accustomed to stopping at sunset, he thought it best to follow their tradition.

So our voyage was slow and peaceful. We were blessed with favorable and steady winds, smooth seas, placid skies, and a warm sun. Within forty-eight hours all of us became accustomed to the gentle rhythmic rise and fall of the ship as she breasted each wave. Our cabin was small but compact, with shuttered windows that could be opened when we wanted fresh air at night and closed for privacy or protection against rough weather. Draperies divided it into three compartments, two sleeping areas and a combination sitting-dining room for the times we preferred not to be on deck. Those times were rare, however, for there was something both peaceful and exhilarating about standing with the wind at our backs and feeling the ship move effortlessly over the water. My favorite place was not the raised deck of the bow, but aft, at the farthermost rail of the stern, where I could watch all the activity on the *Theos* as well as the ever-changing coastline we passed and the variety of ships among which we sailed.

Olav and Rorik alternated at the tiller, and when Rorik took his turn, I stood beside him as I had on the *Raven of the Wind*. At other times we stood together by the rail, and he explained the workings of our ship's unusual four-sail rigging as well as the mechanics of other ships that passed. Over the past months he had been exposed to many new vessels and methods of navigation, and he was already planning on incorporating facets of them into the serpent ships. Boats like the *Raven* had been perfected for swift raids and for going into battle, but if the Three

Shires were to concentrate more on trade than on fighting, he saw many ways the ships could be modified.

"I have other plans, too, Tara. Remember the day on the *Raven* I talked about sailing west."

"Toward the end of the world?"

"Toward the other lands I know are out there. I mean to find them. Will you go with me?" he asked seriously.

"I said then that I would." I smiled, but I was serious.

"When I asked you then, I wasn't thinking of the islands."

"I know you weren't, and neither was I when I answered."

"We should have spoken what was deep inside," he mused, "rather than in riddles. Things might have been different."

"It would not have been such a long, cold winter."

"No, indeed," he laughed. "That it would not. Speaking of winter, I hope we reach the North Sea early in autumn." With that he walked to the tiller, as if by taking over he could hurry us along.

We were sailing by the rocky coast of Macedonia when Paul began gesturing toward a small bay and then to a village of bone-white cottages clinging precariously to the edge of the cliff above. Remembering that Paul had come from Macedonia, I realized he was seeing his homeland for the first time since being captured as a slave. With Cyri and Inga on either side of him, he pointed toward a path cut into the side of the cliff and leading from the bay toward the village. He then pointed beyond to some place we could not see.

"Rorik, we have to stop," I said. " 'Tis Paul's home, and we can't go past without letting him visit it."

"No reason not to. We're within two hours of sunset. I'll not mind getting off and stretching my legs on land."

He gave the order to change direction and sail for the bay. The harbor was not suitable for the *Theos*, so we dropped anchor some two hundred feet from shore. By this time people in the village were aware of our approach and were standing on the cliff edge waving to us. We put the small boat over the side for the first time. Rorik and Olav manned the oars while Paul sat in the stern and directed with hand signals. None of our newly acquired family would agree to being left behind, so while the men worked at getting us there, Cyri, Inga, and I looked eagerly toward shore.

With no beach to haul the boat up onto, Paul jumped overboard and pulled us the last few yards before securing the bowline around a boulder jutting out from the cliff. Inga went ashore on Olav's shoulders; Paul and Rorik made a crossed-arm seat to transport Cyri and me over the short space of open water. In close single file we followed Paul up the steep, narrow path formed by years of peasants' walking between the rocks. The rocks themselves provided surprisingly secure handholds. Inga clung to the hem of Paul's short tunic, and Cyri kept one hand on the middle of the little girl's back. Rorik was a single step behind her, and I followed close on his heels. Even with Olav bringing up the rear, I was afraid to look down at the bay receding farther below with each step I took. I steadfastly refused to think about the return trip.

Once we reached the top, Paul helped each of us navigate the last step and then guided us to the equally narrow, winding mule path leading to the village of tightly clustered, flat-roofed houses. A small herd of skinny goats looked up from the short grass they were cropping, stared idly for a minute, and went back to their meal. Thinking we had come to milk them, three nannies bleated plaintively as their swollen udders brushed against the stiff stalks.

An old woman, dressed and shawled in dusty black, came tottering along the path toward us. Clutching a long pole in one hand for support and balancing a large clay bowl on her head with the other, she left the path and walked toward one of the goats. She ignored us as if seeing such an odd assortment of strangers were an everyday event.

I was surprised she did not greet Paul in some way. Then I looked at him. Pointing to her, he covered his eyes with his hands and stumbled around blindly.

The old woman amazed me. She was blind, and yet she made her way steadily along the scrubby path that curved frighteningly in and out near the edge of the cliff. She walked directly to the one goat she planned to milk, squatted down, and immediately went about her work. Feet and fingers had been trained to carry on the function of eyes blinded by age or disease.

We continued along the path toward the houses that

seemed to grow out of the solid stone on which they sat. Now some of the villagers were approaching hesitantly. Suddenly a shout went up from one of them. A young man raced toward Paul, throwing his arms around him and kissing him on both cheeks. There was nothing to do for the moment but stand there and wait. Finally the young man broke away.

"My name is Clisthenes. Paul and I have been friends since childhood. How very good it is to see him again." With the Greek I learned in the seraglio, I had no trouble understanding him. "Come, we go to my house. You eat with us."

With their arms around each other's waist and talking frantically in sign language, Paul and Clisthenes led us into the village and soon we were meeting members of Clisthenes' family as well as all of the villagers.

No room in the house was large enough to accommodate all of us, so tables were placed in a small, barren yard. Clisthenes' mother, dressed all in black like the old woman, smiled broadly as she brought out cheese and fruit, loaves of hard bread and cups of sour wine. It was not the most elegant feast I had ever attended but it was one of the gayest. Paul was greeted like the prodigal son, and we found ourselves constantly being blessed for bringing him back home. Only one thing was strange. There was no sign of Paul's own family.

As soon as we finished eating, three older men appeared with stringed instruments. Immediately everyone was on their feet and urging us to dance with them. Paul reached for my arm and I grabbed Rorik with the other. In a minute we picked up the steps of the simple folk dance, and before long we were winding in and out among the houses, stamping our feet and yelling with the best of them. At each pause there was more wine, and I looked at Inga to see how she was holding up. When her feet gave out, Olav hoisted her up on his shoulders, and there she sat, singing and clapping while her mount leapt and twirled in time to the music.

Finally I could take no more and had to sit down at the first table I came to. Clisthenes joined me there.

"It is great happiness for us to see Paul again," he said.

"It has given us real joy to see him with his friends."

"We wish—we wish for you to spend the night with us."

"Thank you. It will be no trouble?"

"Oh, no, it is our pleasure. It will be too late to return to the ship."

"Yes," I said, thinking about the treacherous descent to the bay. "Unless we leave very soon."

"No, you must not. Paul wishes to show you his home."

"His home is not here in the village?" I asked.

"His home is on a farm. We go there soon. It is not far from here."

But why, if not far, had not someone run to tell his family that Paul had returned?

Again the five of us, with a sleepy Inga still on Olav's shoulders, followed Paul and Clisthenes along a well-worn path between squat bushes and stiff grasses. The sun was very close to setting, and I hoped Clisthenes' idea of "not far" was the same as mine. Sooner than I expected, we came upon the remains of Paul's home. It was a small farm, a few plots of plowed earth around the broken walls of what had been a house and some outbuildings.

While Paul walked ahead alone to look through the house, Clisthenes explained. "Raiders came down from the north—through the mountains, not up from the sea. We did not know until all was over. Paul's mother and father were killed. He along with his brothers and sisters was carried off. We did not know who did it, but we thought it was the Bulgars. They had not raided in many years, but we always feared them.

"So Paul has no family left," I said, saddened at the thought that Paul had had much to worry about besides his own enslavement.

"None."

"But why does no one live here now? Why has it remained empty?" I asked.

"We waited for them to return. The land is used. We cannot waste good land, but no one will live here."

"A pity. It looks like it was a very fine house."

"It was." Clisthenes remained silent a minute, and then looked me straight in the face. "Paul will be going with you?"

It was an honest question, and I knew he wanted the truth. "I—I think so, yes."

"He told me you purchased him. That was good thing for you to do. He is happy with you. He would also be happy here."

359

Before I could sort out the thoughts that came unbidden at this remark, Paul stepped from the house and motioned for us to join him. He proudly showed us through every room. It was a large house, much more pretentious than any in the village, and it could so easily be beautiful again. Did Paul wish to be allowed to remain? This was his home, and he must yearn to be free again and work the land as his father had done. It was not something I wanted to consider at the moment, nor was it my decision alone.

It was growing dark and time to return to the village. Clisthenes and Paul might know their way at night, but I wanted some light to show me what I was stepping on. Again I saw the two young men busily engaged in hand signals.

"Paul says for us to return to the village. He wishes to spend the night here. Cyri will stay with him."

I started to say something, but I did not. I should not have been surprised. More than one night I had come out from the cabin for some air. Each time I saw the two of them together. At first they were merely standing side by side, looking at the stars or staring into the water. As time went on, they stood closer together, his arm around her waist and her head on his chest. I had no thought of their being attracted to each other when I suggested we take them with us. I should have guessed such would happen. With her jet black hair, sparkling eyes, and petite figure, Cyri closely resembled Irenia. Both had a shy manner that hid a delightfully exuberant personality. And both were traveling to a new land which would be a far less frightening experience if they faced it together.

When Clisthenes said Cyri was staying with Paul in his partially destroyed house, Rorik raised one eyebrow quizzically, but I just nodded my head and began walking back toward the village. It would be easier for Paul to banish sad ghosts with Cyri by his side.

Clisthenes' mother had prepared sleeping quarters for us, and before we retired for the night, she offered us a second supper. The musicians picked up their instruments again and played by the light of torches as long as someone wanted to dance. And as long as the wineglasses were kept full.

While resting between dances, Clisthenes told us more about Paul's family and the raid. "His mother and father were brutally killed. We found them dead in the yard. We knew the rest of the family would be sold into slavery. That was bad enough for Paul's two brothers, but I worried very much about Paul and his sisters. I knew what would happen to the girls. As for Paul, I was sure he would be killed when they learned he could not hear or speak. You cannot know what it meant to me to see him again."

"I think I can," I said. "My husband and I were attacked and separated for a year. I found him being sold as a slave, and I had to ask a friend to purchase him so he could be free again."

"Paul has been gone for more than four years. It would be good if he were free."

I knew what Clisthenes was asking me in an indirect way. I did not want to lose Paul and Cyri. Yet I had promised myself I would free them when we arrived home. Now I knew I was being selfish. I planned to free them only after I made certain they would not—nor could not—leave me. Once they were in Hordaland, it would be almost impossible for them to return to the South.

After only a few hours of sleep, we awoke to a brilliantly sunny day, and I knew it was not only time to get on our way but also the moment when I had to make a decision and then try to persuade Rorik to agree with me.

Paul and Cyri had already walked down from the farm and were waiting for us when we appeared for breakfast. They sat side by side on a bench just outside the door, holding hands and smiling in the way two lovers should smile just after they discover how wonderful it is to belong to each other.

Cyri walked over to where Rorik and I were eating, he with great gusto and me with absolutely no appetite at all. Here it comes, I thought, and I still do not know what I am going to say. No, 'twas not true. I knew what my response would be. I was not so sure about Rorik's.

"My lady," Cyri asked, "may I speak to you and your lord?"

"Indeed you may, Cyri. Would you like to sit down?"

"Thank you, no. We have already eaten. I hope you will understand what I want to say." Her hands were shaking, and I could see she was close to tears.

Trying to soothe her fears and put her at ease, I said, "You know we will. What is it?"

Her request was so completely different from what I had expected, I am certain the shock showed on my face.

"Paul and I wish to marry. We know we need your permission. We not know if you let slaves marry."

"Oh, yes, Cyri, of course you may." I was so relieved, I did not think to ask Rorik if he had any objections. When I looked at him, he was trying to look stern and forbidding, but underneath I could see he was hiding a grin. I knew all too well what he was thinking. I also knew the real question of allowing them to stay behind in Macedonia had only been postponed, not forgotten.

"In church in the village." Cyri's voice brought me back to the immediate situation. "It is Paul's church."

I was ashamed of myself. In all the months I had known Paul I had never thought to ask if he were a Christian. I should have realized that coming from Macedonia he probably would be.

"Certainly in the church, Cyri, if 'tis what you want."

"But—but," she stammered, "we wait two days. It is the law." She looked down at her feet as if certain I would say we could not possibly delay our voyage that long. I, too, wanted to look down, to avoid seeing Rorik's face. I had done it again. I had gone ahead and agreed to something he might disapprove of.

"If it takes two days," I heard him shout, "then let's enjoy them. Olav, go down to the ship and tell the crew. Then bring up enough gold for us to reward these people for their wonderful hospitality. Bring some of our wine, too. Clisthenes, where are the musicians? Tell them we're staying here, and we want the greatest celebration this village has ever seen."

I ran over and threw my arms around his neck. He teased me about being an incurable romantic and then looked embarrassed. "By Thor, if we're going to do something, we might as well do it right," he growled and then strode off.

Since the small church had no priest of its own, a boy was sent running to a larger village to fetch one back. The women fell to work baking and cooking up a feast I would remember for many, many years. Olav brought the wine, the musicians began to play, and no one did any work during those two exciting days. Before Olav left for the ship, I whispered some orders in his ear. When he returned, I handed Cyri the pale pink silk tunic and embroidered dalmatic he brought with him. There were few flowers in this arid land, but Paul and Inga found enough to fashion the ceremonial crowns and a small bouquet for the bridal table at the wedding feast.

Late in the evening, while guests were still dancing and feasting, Cyri called me to one side. "Paul and I leave now for farm. We spend the night there. We be here in morning when you ready to leave."

"To bid us good-bye?" She would ask me now for permission to stay. How could I tell her no? My heart ached for her, and yet I did not feel I should ask this of Rorik, too. Not after I had persuaded him to buy them for Inga's and my sake. I could not look her in the eye while waiting for her answer, and I was filled with a burning shame for being such a coward.

"Oh, no, my lady. To go with you. We not want to stay here. We belong to you."

I had to ask her. I had to give her the chance to tell me how they really felt. "Cyri, tell me honestly. Is Paul hoping he can remain?"

"No. He very happy to see home again. He love farm. But he want to go with you. He wanted to see farm and friends, but he not want to stay."

"Thank you, Cyri. I am very, very happy you want to go with us. We would have missed you very much."

The next morning, there was just time for a quick breakfast if we were to make the treacherous descent along the rocky path to the bay in time to catch the tide. The crew had taken advantage of the two-day layover to sail farther along the coast to a larger town that provided what sailors are always looking for: plenty of available women and strong drink. 'Twas evident they had had even fewer hours of sleep than we, but they evinced little reluctance to get right to work once they saw the stern look on Rorik's face. He might permit a little relaxation and levity on special occasions, but when it was time to get back to work, he brooked no laxness. We were on our way within the hour.

From Macedonia we sailed south through the Aegean, along the eastern coast of Thessaly, around the southern tip of Peloponnese, and then north past Corfu, Epirus, and Dyrrachium into the Adriatic. At long last we arrived at Venice, the famous city of islands ruled by doges or dukes.

The location of these islands, formed by the mingling of the Piave and Adige rivers, made the city almost totally invulnerable to attack from any direction. As a result, Venice had become a thriving commercial clearinghouse between Europe and the Near East. Its ties were stronger with Byzantium than with the western empire, and therefore it acknowledged Constantinople rather than Rome as its overlord.

We had no trouble locating Zenos, the commander of Ali Habib's Adriatic trade route, but he greeted us with disappointing news. Because of Moorish raiders attacking from both the Iberian peninsula and the African coast, it would be too dangerous to attempt the passage through the straits of Hercules between the Mediterranean and the great World Ocean. He decided against making the voyage to the Northlands.

We were disheartened at the thought of abandoning plans so carefully made. The *Theos* had been rebuilt and strengthened to fit all our needs, and we were comfortably settled in. Rorik was the most downcast of all. He had finally gotten a ship to command; he was not going to give it up without an argument.

"Are you saying, Zenos, we have not enough manpower to ward off a few wild raiders? I thought the Iberian and African coasts were within the Byzantine empire, under control of Constantinople. If so, we should be protected, not attacked. Also, we're a Moslem ship, not Christian. That should make a difference."

"Rorik," Zenos said, "listen to me. Those Moors are pirates. Outlaws. In the second place, they do not stop to ask our religion. They see only the size of our hold and estimate the amount of cargo it carries."

"Our ship can't outsail them?"

"Never. The *Theos* was not built for speed. Theirs are faster and they attack too swiftly to be outmaneuvered. We've too few men to fight off a boarding attack."

"If we mounted guns? The Greek fire I saw in Constantinople?"

My heart went out to him. I knew he was trying desperately to find a way to keep from aborting our plans. I was impatient, too, but I had never discounted the possibility of our having to take an overland route across Western Europe. Rorik would be satisfied only if he could sail.

"Impossible." Zenos shook his head. "No, Rorik, I want to sail North, but not under present conditions."

Rorik returned to the ship, where we continued to stay while we made plans.

"By the gods, Tara, there has to be a way!"

"Can we not buy the ship and sail her north ourselves? You once said there was no sea you could not sail. I'd not be afraid to go with you. Nor would Olav or Paul or Cyri. And Inga would sail over the edge or be captured by monsters if she were with you."

"Thank you, Seabird, I know you would. I suggested that to Zenos, but he said we will never find a crew to go with us except from among the desperate and the dregs. If we had only men on board, I might attempt it. Never with you and Cyri and Inga."

"We'll don men's clothes. They'll not know the difference."

"Don't be foolish, Tara. 'Tis not just that they'd discover it immediately. 'Tis what you would be subjected to. Their talk, their habits."

"So we don't sail, is that it?" Try as hard as I would I could not keep my own disappointment from my voice.

"I need some time. Zenos might be wrong and we could find a ship and crew."

Days went by while Olav and Rorik scoured the city for trustworthy men who would dare first the Moors and then the unknown waters of the World Ocean. Meanwhile, Cyri, Inga, and I explored the ancient city. Traveling the canals in small boats, we visited the many Venetian islands. We gazed in awe at the shrine containing the bones of St. Mark, stolen in 828 by Venetian merchants from a church in Alexandria. It seemed strange to move about by boat rather than on foot or in carts. The wealthy traveled past us in elaborate, curtained barges, rowed by two or four oarsmen, much as I had gone about Constantinople in a palanquin.

Finally Rorik came by information that made us decide to take the overland route home.

"There have been a number of special pilgrimages to Rome. Our journey north will be safer if we travel with such a group."

"You are giving up the idea of sailing?" I was stunned, but he didn't seem too disappointed.

"I am. Zenos was right. We'll not find a crew I would

trust. Only those who have urgent reasons to leave Venice will go with us. Such a crew would murder us before we left the Mediterranean. We will travel overland to Genoa and from there sail to the mouth of the Rhone. We can follow the Rhone Valley, then across to the Rhine, and sail north on the Rhine to Frisia."

I was finding it hard to follow his words. "It sounds complicated."

"Not really. Many pilgrims have made it more than once, and we may be fortunate enough to join up with an emissary of the Church who has traveled the route several times."

"So," I asked, "what do we do now?"

"Olav and I will see to purchasing wagons, donkeys, and horses. You and Cyri will repack. If you want to take everything you—"

"I do."

"Then force two boxes into one. We will have far less room in the wagon than on the ship. And don't leave such necessities as food and warm clothes behind! I know your propensity for rationalizing. We cannot eat blue glass vases, even ones encrusted with gold filigree."

"Why do we need to take food if we are going to travel on land?"

"Because, my love, we have no idea how many leagues between one hospice and another. There will not be inns stationed conveniently at the end of each day's travel."

Cyri and I set to with a will. Each day's delay was one day longer before seeing Signe and Eirik. My head was filled with thoughts of them as we packed and repacked. We had many weeks of travel ahead, but we were on our way toward them, and soon I would see my precious babies.

Clothes and food had to be easily accessible. No crate or bundle could be too heavy. Instead of folding my Byzantine garments and laying them flat, I wrapped them around the breakable items. We took only one change of warm clothing instead of three or four. Unlike at sea, we would surely be passing through towns where they could be replaced.

Rorik planned to buy horses only for Olav and himself. Paul would drive the wagon.

"And where do I ride?" I asked.

"In the wagon, of course."

"Oh, no," I insisted. "I'd much rather sit astride a horse than bounce around in a wagon."

"It wouldn't be ladylike."

"I want to be comfortable," I argued, "not play the part of a lady."

"You'll not be *playing* a part. You are a lady. You will behave like the wife of a Viking."

"And they never ride horses?" I had him there, and he knew it.

"All right, but sidesaddle, not astride."

"Dear God in Heaven! All right, if 'tis the only way."

Once on the road I'd manage someway to change saddles. Or lose mine and ride bareback with only a blanket. I'd done that many times, much to my mother's chagrin.

We encountered no problems while making our way by land from Venice to Genoa. There we were able to sell the horses to a local priest and two pilgrims on their way to Rome, and the donkey cart to a fisherman. We received what we thought was more than enough to pay our passage to the Rhone.

Chapter Twenty-four

WE HAD A WAIT OF ALMOST A WEEK before we found a galley sailing to Cartegena whose captain agreed to transport us along the coast. While I supervised the loading of our bundles and crates—and tried to keep track of Inga, who had become fascinated by the Genovese fishermen—I overheard a heated discussion between the ship's captain and an old woman. She stood beside a small barrow in which a young man lay curled up among a scattering of rags.

"What is it, Granny," I asked her. Her dry, weather-beaten face was spider webbed with fine wrinkles. Wisps of dusty white hair fell out from under a sun-bleached green kerchief. Her voice cracked from exhaustion or age.

"He wants me to pay twice what I did on the way over. And he'll not take the barrow." Her downcast eyes had a desperate look in them. With her hunched shoulders and back bent almost double, she looked as if she would break in two if touched. Why was she on this road? She should be by a fire knitting, not traveling.

"You sailed with him before?"

"No, but the fee should be the same," she said.

The captain glowered at me for interfering, but I refused to be intimidated.

"Why are you charging her so much?"

" 'Tis a nuisance, she is. Her and that idiot in the barrow. I've no room for 'em."

His greed and lack of compassion made me fiery mad. "But you would if she paid the price!"

" 'Tis worth it. All the trouble we'd have with 'em."

I'd not heard Rorik walk up behind me. "They will be no trouble at all compared to what I'll cause if you do not take them—at the regular price." His tone implied he had no intention of arguing the point.

"See here!" the captain bellowed. "You can't be telling me who to take. 'Tis my ship."

"And a pretty copper you charge to sail on her. I believe you regularly transport goods for the merchants of Constantinople. One, Ali Habib, is a close personal friend. 'Twould be very simple for me to suggest he spread the word you are no longer to be trusted. So I advise you to take the woman and the boy at the lower price—which I will pay—and put the barrow aboard at no extra charge."

The man had gone white at the mention of Ali Habib, and all the bluster went out of his voice. I smiled smugly at the man's discomfiture. Rorik's threat had reached its mark.

Fraida, the old woman, was overcome with gratitude. Her grandson Horst, she assured us, was not an idiot but suffered from a crippling disease that caused every part of his body to jerk convulsively whenever he moved. His face contorted with spasms when he tried to talk, and only his grandmother understood the seeming gibberish that issued from his mouth.

Fraida and Horst were returning from a pilgrimage to Rome to a small village on the Rhine. They had hoped their piety and faith would be rewarded by a miraculous cure for the boy. In this they were not unique. The roads were thronged with the lame and the blind, who believed such a journey would bring the desired cure, especially if they were among the fortunate to be blessed by the Pope. They traveled in rich conveyances or on the backs of donkeys. They were led or carried by loved ones. Many made the journey only by begging from village to village. Some died along the roadside.

"I don't know how many months we've traveled," Fraida said, as we settled ourselves into the galley. "I've pushed Horst the entire distance."

I looked at her, slumped now among some bundles after making certain Horst was comfortably braced between two crates. I did not see how she'd had the strength to walk, let alone push the barrow and care for him. Horst was in his early twenties, but he lay curled up like a child, and he could have weighed no more than a young boy.

"There was no cure in Rome," Fraida said, "but I've not lost faith. Any moment now he'll sit without jerking and I'll hear him speak normally." All the while, her face

369

glowed with happiness that her faith would yet be rewarded.

What a pity! How outrageous it was that the destitute and incurable should be encouraged to make such a hopeless journey.

"Our family is poor," Fraida continued, "with many children. Horst was rejected by my son and his wife. They thought him a changeling, an evil creature of the devil." She spoke calmly as if changelings were common occurrences. "But I knew he was not, I was there when he was born. He was no changeling." Now her voice became stronger, and I saw the determination that moved her. "When they put him in with the chickens—pecking for grain and drops of water—in hopes he would die, I took over his care. I refused to let him die."

She was amazing. She had spent countless hours trying to teach him to walk. She allowed no one to mock him when he uttered only guttural sounds. He was hers. Her love for him and her faith he would ultimately were normal were boundless. This old woman, clad only in rags, was an example of pure, unselfish love.

The voyage to the mouth of the Rhone was crowded and uncomfortable, with all of us and our goods packed fore and aft the rowers. Every meal was the same, half-raw fish and stale bread. For all that, we paid out most of what we got for the animals and cart. After the second meal, I found it impossible to keep the food down. During the ride from Venice to Genoa, I suspected I was pregnant, and now I was certain of it. For the time being, I let Rorik think I was seasick. He had enough on his mind without worrying about me. The others tolerated the scanty fare and crowded conditions without complaint, but we were all overjoyed to leave the boat when we reached the mouth of the Rhone.

For a few small coins, a villager allowed us to sleep in his cattle barn, a stone lean-to attached to his small house, and we were enjoying our first comfortable night ashore. After the rolling and heaving of the ship, none of us objected to bedding down on soft piles of straw. Although he said little, I knew Rorik was concerned about getting our small group safely overland to some port on the Northern Sea. Such a journey was dangerous for even large, well-armed parties. Bands of brigands waited to ambush the unwary traveler, and barbarians still made sporadic raids. I knew he was hesitant to reveal his fears, but I saw no point in keeping the others completely ignorant of the dangers. So I took it upon myself to broach the subject.

" 'Tis not going to be an easy journey, is it?" I asked.

"No, but we'll take it slowly. We've no need to hurry now that we're well on our way."

"Nor safe," I said quietly, as if 'twere an afterthought.

"There will be some dangers, but none for you to be concerned about."

"No, just let you do all the worrying."

Rorik said nothing for the moment, only tightened his hold around me. "I should have known better than to think you blind to my feelings. The route is dangerous. I'd feel safer if we were going by water. My wits are honed to deal with seaborne threats, but I've little knowledge of the land and its perils."

"But you have a plan." I knew him too well to think he had not carefully thought everything out. "Your mind has not been idle."

"I do," he laughed, "and I think it's one you'll approve of highly. We can't fend off any kind of highway attack with force. Olav, Paul, and I will be no match against even a small band of highwaymen. So we must use strategy to prevent being set upon. Thieves are most likely to be on the lookout for signs of wealth and for women. If I can find a wagon, we'll put our bundles in the bottom and cover them with straw. We'll ride donkeys instead of horses. Fraida and Horst will, of course, travel in the wagon, but the rest of us will take turns riding and walking. All of us will dress like peasants, as ragged and poor-looking as possible. That should keep away anyone looking to rob us for gold or valuables."

"And if they're looking for women?"

"They will see only Fraida in the wagon. You and Cyri will dress like men and Inga like a farm boy. It'll not guarantee we aren't set upon, but it should lessen the chances. So, my love, you will get to ride a donkey, if not a horse, like a man."

He was so pleased with his plan, I still didn't tell him I was pregnant. If I had no problem riding and walking, he need not know until it was impossible to conceal my condition.

"Will we be armed?"

"All of us. Knives for the women, swords and knives

371

for the men. Olav and I will train you in the most effective way to use them. Will you be frightened?"

"Yes, but not nearly so much as if you'd not trusted me enough to include me in your planning."

The third day after our arrival, however, brought an unexpected development. While Rorik and Olav searched the countryside for the sturdy wagon and animals we needed, a ship arrived in the harbor. Cyri and I were making final alterations on the clothes Rorik told us we needed. She and I went through the bundles for goods to trade for the rough garb we would wear during the remainder of the journey. The local peasants were dumbfounded but more than willing when we offered them silk and fine linen in exchange for well-worn, crudely made trousers and blouses. Inga was delighted at the thought of masquerading as a boy. After what she suffered during enslavement, our hardships seemed like a lark to her. She danced off to show her costume to Paul, who was repairing Fraida's barrow. Although she and Horst would ride in the wagon, the barrow was to be taken along. There might be need for it.

Cyri demurred at wearing the rough, scratchy garments next to her skin. "Outside, yes," she said, "but no one know what I have under. I wear silk so I feel like a lady if I must look like a man."

I heartily agreed with her, and we set about making silk trousers and long-sleeved chemises. With hems to be taken up and tucks put in the peasants' clothes, we had a busy two days.

Our first response when we saw the ship sail into the harbor was fear. We remembered what Zenos had told us in Venice about Moorish pirates roaming this section of the Mediterranean, and we were not many leagues distant from Moslem strongholds on the Iberian Peninsula. 'Twould not be unusual for them to enter the Rhone for fresh water. Paul and Inga were nowhere in sight. All Cyri and I could do was gather up what we'd been working on and hide behind some bushes.

In another minute we jumped up in amazement, awestruck by what we saw. The first man to step off the ship was dressed in full bishop's regalia, a tall mitre on his head and a crossier in one hand. He was followed immediately by four uniformed, armed men. A few other travelers straggled off the ship behind them, but we paid scant attention. Our gaze remained on the regal-looking churchman.

I ran forward, Cyri following a few steps behind. "Your Holiness," I whispered, as I went down on one knee and kissed the ring on his outstretched hand.

His only response was a deep growl of either disgust or disapproval. I looked up and was even more bewildered by the shocked look on his face. Only then did I realize I had not donned the peasant garb I was working on when he arrived, and I was wearing only the silk undergarments Cyri and I had been sewing in.

I turned to see Cyri with hands over her face to hide her amusement, and I ran as fast as I could to the bushes where we'd first concealed ourselves.

In spite of the humiliation at having to approach the bishop again, my interest in him and his company forced me to go back once I was properly dressed. It scarcely helped that he obviously disapproved of the male garb as much as he did the more intimate garments. His supercilious attitude, however, did not bother me in the least when I learned who he was and where he was going.

Bishop Roden, having recently been elevated to the position of Papal legate to London, was bound for the British capital. With some condescension he deigned to allow our group to join his entourage. Horses, not donkeys! I thought. We could all ride horses and not have to take turns walking. I could hardly wait for Rorik to return. With the four Papal guards, we would be perfectly safe.

"No, Tara, no horses," Rorik announced after he met the bishop and learned of the new plans.

"Please, Rorik. Who wants to jog along on a donkey? Why should we when we could ride comfortably on a horse?"

"Because I battled the forces of Hel to get what we have."

I looked at the stubby but sturdy animals and counted them. "Can we at least have enough so we need not take turns walking?"

"Everyone will have a mount. I realize 'twill delay us if some are walking."

"Well, thank you for that small consideration!" A donkey! I felt insulted. Although it was unlike him, I thought maybe he was doing it to shame me for some reason.

"Tara, look at me. Do you have any idea how much of the money we received for the jewels has been spent?"

"No." We had received so many pouches of gold that, at the time, I didn't see how we could ever spend it all. The very idea of having so much gold dazzled me.

"Much more than I figured on when we first made plans to return home. Remember, we'd not counted on buying Cyri's and Paul's freedom or bringing them along. Since then Fraida and Horst have joined us. And we know not what expenses we face ahead of us before we reach the northern coast. Or passage on a ship to Hordaland."

"I am sorry, Rorik. I'd not been thinking."

"You are a spendthrift, my love. The sight of gold carries you away. You are also most generous and I love you for it. But we have to be more careful. When we get home, you can spend all the money you want."

Home. Once that meant Britain, the land I thought I would never see again. Now it meant Hordaland. How much I had changed in so few years!

" 'Twill be safer though, traveling with the bishop?"

"I think so. If only he'd not wear his jeweled cross and all those expensive robes."

"Speaking of clothes—" I began.

"You will still be more comfortable in peasant garb."

"They're so old and smelly." I made a horrible face and shuddered.

"Just good farm smells, my love."

"Ugh, like cow dung and musty straw."

"Just pretend they came from tumbling in the hay," he laughed.

"Very romantic!"

"You thought so the night we landed." He whacked me solidly on the rump and then took me in his arms in front of an astonished audience of the bishop and his entire following.

" 'Twas different," I mumbled. "I was not bouncing along on a stupid donkey."

It did not take long for Rorik and Bishop Roden to reach a mutual agreement as to route, the distance to be covered each day, and—most important—who was authority as to final decisions once on the journey. Bishop Roden's arrogant manner and tall, imposing figure might have cowed a lesser man, but Rorik was a true leader. His assumption that he was the logical one to guide the group was not challenged by the bishop. In fact, the churchman was relieved to relinquish his authority to one more able and experienced. A native of Lombardy, he had never traveled any farther than Rome, and he realized there was a difference between being the spiritual leader of a quiet community and the commander of a group traveling through potentially dangerous countryside.

So our ranks were suddenly doubled by an interesting and diverse collection of humanity. Rorik, in his new position as leader of this motley cavalcade, had gotten himself a horse. He rode in the vanguard followed immediately by two of the Papal guards. Like their bishop, they recognized and acknowledged his authority. They were strong, taciturn men who followed orders without argument and remained alert to any signs of danger. At the rear rode Olav with the other two, equally silent guards. Throughout the weeks that followed, we gradually broke down their reserve, and they sang or joked with us to relieve the monotony of the journey.

The rest of us jogged along in between. Accompanying the bishop as clerk and general servant was a young priest. Father Utrillo was a pudgy, good-natured, awkward stumblebum. Although he bounced uncomfortably on the meanest donkey I ever saw, he never complained. His puffy cheeks merely reddened, and his chest heaved from the exertion. If we crossed a stream on a log, he was certain to fall off. When we forded one, his mount headed for the deepest pools, and he emerged sopping wet. But he just grinned and kept on going. At each stop, he hurried to the side of the bishop, tripping over the hem of his dusty brown robe, and waited for orders.

Father Utrillo left no doubt that he considered being chosen to serve his Holiness the greatest accolade he could ever hope to win. So eager was he to please, he was usually trying to do more than one task at a time only to foul all of them up—spilling the bishop's supper plate as he made a detour to smooth the older man's sleeping pallet over a thick, protruding root. For all his arrogance, the bishop was amazingly patient with the young man, who was so likable no one could stay upset with him for long.

Three other travelers on the ship from Rome joined our entourage. The first was Andrew, an itinerant tinker, who had taken to the road many years earlier when he discovered that a life on the move was more exciting than one confined to a few villages. A short, jolly man, he said he never knew from one day to the next which direction he would take. He joined us just because we looked like the kind of people he would enjoy being with. A man of many talents, he mended saddles, took charge of caring for the animals, and did whatever carpentry work we needed. Except for one fault, he was a real asset.

The second was John, currently a spice merchant after having failed at every trade or job he tried. Once apprenticed to a stonemason, he found the labor too arduous and ran away. He spent the intervening years trying to find some way to make a fortune without having to do any hard work. Failure and disappointment had given him a perpetually dour mien. Because his conversation consisted entirely of self-pitying, hard-luck stories, no one stayed near him for long, and he usually rode alone like an outcast. Having purchased several sacks of spices, he hoped to make enough profit to open a grog shop along the banks of the Thames. He might finally have been successful except for one failing: he loved to gamble. Unfortunately, so did Andrew the tinker, though he was both luckier and cleverer than John.

The last was a gaunt, ascetic friar who kept to himself and seldom spoke except to chide the rest of us for indulging in the various sins of the flesh. He was the only one who did not avoid riding beside John, but his response to the merchant's complaints gave no comfort. He merely quoted long, sonorous passages from St. Augustine. His one meal a day, eaten late in the evening, consisted of bread and wine—the latter for his stomach's sake—and occasionally some fruit. He rode a nag as bony and spare as himself, and I heard Andrew and John laying macabre odds as to which would expire first.

Cyri and I usually rode side by side while Paul and Inga explored the countryside for unfamiliar plants and herbs. Whenever we had the opportunity, we asked the local people what each was good for and conveyed the answers to Paul. With the patient help of Cyri, he was slowly learning to read lips, making communication with him much easier. He collected and dried the plants, having a fantastic ability to commit to memory what he learned. The straw piled thick atop our belongings in the wagon made comfortable seats for Fraida and Horst, and she expressed to us every day her gratitude for no longer having to push the barrow, now tied on behind.

Slowly but steadily we traveled the length of the lush Rhone Valley. Sometimes we arrived late in the afternoon at one of the hostelries established to serve the many pilgrims journeying to Rome. When they were comparatively clean, we minded not the crowded conditions that had us all packed together with other travelers in one low-ceilinged, second-floor loft. At least we were sheltered from the weather, and there were steaming meat pasties and rich, dark ale for supper. Before we set off in the morning, we sat down to a stomach-filling bowl of hot porridge.

When we found ourselves in a hostel with vermin-filled pallets and a common room reeking of stale cabbage and rancid grease, I would have preferred sleeping under a tree after cooking on an open fire. And in fact, we often did make camp in the beautiful valley, stopping within a protective grove of trees or beside a clear stream.

Whatever the hardships, my heart sang as we rode along, for we were at last traveling north, and each day brought us that much closer to Signe, Eirik, and Asri. Nearly a year and a half had passed since we left home, and I tried to imagine how they looked. The closer we got, the more anxious I was to see them, but I had to curb my impatience while we still had many weeks of travel ahead of us.

The best nights were those we spent in an abbey or monastery. The friars and monks welcomed us warmly, and there were always clean sleeping quarters. Whenever we approached one of these communities, Bishop Roden moved to the head of our train and donned his finest robes. As Papal legate, he was always greeted with great ceremony and accorded the special perquisites his position entitled him to. Such stops also gave us an extra day of rest. The communities did not often play host to such an exalted personage, one who had touched hands with the Pope, and they wanted him to hear confessions and say mass. It took little urging on their part for him to agree. Nor were any of us averse to breaking the journey with a day of rest.

Several times we were bogged down in muddy roads and had to wait out a storm and then the time it took for the roads to dry to hard-packed clay before we could go on. If we were lucky, we had arrived at a hostel or monastery. When we had to camp by the roadside in whatever shelter available, life was miserable.

All of these delays slowed our progress considerably, and it was November before we left the Rhone Valley. When we reached the point near the head of the river where we would turn east and take an old Roman highway to the Rhine, I was still feeling no discomfort from my pregnancy. Rorik remarked a few times he thought the journey must be doing me good the way I was putting on weight.

"I'll soon be calling you my plump partridge," he laughed, "instead of Seabird."

"You like it not?" He must not guess. I feared he would insist on stopping at some place where we could stay until the baby was born.

"Indeed I do. It becomes you. You were always too skinny. Now I've something I can really squeeze."

Fortunately—or unfortunately—I was one of those who put on weight all over. Arms, legs, and face filled out before my belly began to swell, so attention was drawn away from there. I really wanted to tell him, to share the excitement with him that I felt over having another child. But even if it did not mean delaying the journey, I knew what his response would be. Off the donkey and into the wagon! As long as I felt well I saw no harm in continuing to ride.

"I think 'tis because I'm happy," I said. "I know we'll soon be home with the children."

"They'll not recognize us, will they?" Rorik said wistfully.

"No, but Thorne and Astrid will not have let them forget about us. Remember how your father played with them on the floor, riding them around on his back."

"I'll bet he has them on a real horse now."

I tried to imagine my plump little cherubs on a horse, and I knew I would be seeing children, not babies, when we arrived.

The days on the road were not always trouble-free. One night in camp, Rorik stormed into our tent.

" 'Tis got to stop or one of them will be killed."

"What? And who?" Seldom had I seen him so angry.

"The gambling between John and Andrew."

" 'Tis still bad?"

378

"Very bad," he said. "I should send them off on their own. But Andrew is valuable to us, and I feel sorry for John. Andrew has won every copper John had with him, and now they play for the bags of spices. John will end with nothing, and his trip will have been for naught."

"If John is fool enough to play when Andrew wins all the time," I asked, "why bother with them?"

"Because John is getting riled, and I've seen him fingering his knife. I don't like it."

"Do you think Andrew cheats?" I could not believe it of him, but it seemed the only answer.

"No, I know he doesn't. I watch him closely. He just has all the luck on his side, and John has none. Never has had, from the way he talks."

"So what do you plan to do?"

"I don't know. I've told them to stop, but John as much as told me to mind my own business and Andrew just laughed."

"Have you thought of confiscating the spice sacks until the journey is over?" It seemed to me the only sensible thing to do.

"I have. I think John would steal them back. After all, they are his. About the only thing I can do is warn Andrew to be on his guard. If John pulls his knife, there may be no one around to stop him."

Rorik was right in saying we could not get along without Andrew. He had already made a new wagon wheel, mended two of our cooking pots, and fashioned a kind of seat with a harness for Horst so he could view the passing scene without falling out of the wagon. He'd also taken it upon himself to assist Fraida in lifting Horst in and out of the wagon whenever we stopped. Nobody really liked John with all his whining, but we did feel sorry for him. Also, he kept the mournful friar from commiserating with the rest of us about the erring world we lived in and our sins in particular.

The problem of Andrew and John was solved shortly after this, but not in any way we had anticipated.

Late one afrtenoon, as we rode a narrow trail between densly forested hills, we were caught by a sudden storm of rain mixed with sleet. While trying to pull the hood of my cloak over my head, I let go the reins and my donkey stumbled in a rut. Sliding in the mud, his feet went out from under him, and the next thing I knew, I was lying in a puddle with the rump of the animal on top of me.

The first knifing pain startled me; the second shook my whole body, and I heard myself screaming in agony. I remember thinking that no one knew what had happened, because it took so long for them to come help me. Finally, I saw Rorik and Olav running toward me, and I watched, hardly able to breathe, while they lifted the animal off me. Inga began to cry, and Paul carried her to the wagon where she lay under the blankets with Fraida and Horst. I heard voices, but I had no idea what anyone was doing. At last Rorik lifted me up, and I was soon lying on a pallet of blankets near a large fire. I wondered how the other men had gotten one started so quickly as I drifted off into a restless sleep filled with strange nightmares.

The storm increased in intensity. I woke once to see that someone had erected a rude shelter above and around the three sides of me away from the fire. Another time I felt Fraida putting extra blankets on me. Next I was awakened by a series of wild yells and Rorik shouting orders. Then Cyri aroused me to insist I eat some of the stew she had prepared. Yes, she said, the storm had abated and she had been able to cook a hot meal. In spite of that, her face looked taut and drawn, as if she were very upset about something. I had not seen Rorik since he first carried me to the fire.

Not until I waked two or three times to darkness did he come.

"Why did you not tell me, Tara?" His face was white and haggard.

"Tell you what?" I had no idea how weak I was until I found it difficult to get breath to speak.

"That you were expecting a child." How had he found out? Had I cried out in my sleep?

"I thought 'twould worry you."

"And you think I am not worried now? Fraida says you are in danger of losing the baby."

No, I couldn't lose the child. I had not hurt for long after I fell, and there was no pain now. Not much anyway. And that, surely, came from falling under the donkey. I would be fine. I could ride in the wagon until the soreness passed.

"I'm sorry. I didn't want to hold us up."

"There was room in the wagon." There was no smile on

380

his face, but I could sense the concern beneath his stern words.

"I know," I said, and I couldn't hold back the tears. " 'Tis all my fault for insisting I ride instead."

"There, there, you were doing fine until the donkey stumbled. You could not have prevented that." He was trying to comfort me when he should have been scolding me for being so stupid. I wanted to hold him and beg his forgiveness, but I couldn't lift my arms.

"I don't want to lose the baby, Rorik."

"Fraida says with rest, there is a good chance you'll not." Was he telling me the truth or trying to reassure me while keeping the truth from me? "She is a midwife and will care for you."

"I can't rest here. 'Twill hold us up too long. I can ride in the wagon. See, I feel much better." I tried to sit up, but a pain stabbed through my belly and I had to fall back down on the blankets.

"No, no riding in the wagon now. We are going to have to stop anyway. The weather is getting worse, and we should not try to travel for the next three months at least. I have sent Olav, Bishop Roden, and Father Utrillo on ahead to find someplace where we can spend the winter. Meanwhile you will rest here until you can be moved."

The words "until you can be moved" sounded ominous. I knew there was some bleeding, but I tried to hide my fears from both Rorik and myself. The sharp pains had subsided to a dull ache, and when morning came, I was able to watch the activity of the others while I slowly recovered my strength. I was certain, as each hour passed with no further problems, that I would keep the baby.

Inga sat by me and kept me entertained. Paul had taken it upon himself to gather wood and keep the fire going. Andrew used the opportunity to make needed repairs and strengthen the wagon and harnesses. Two of the guards went in search of farms where they could buy fodder for the animals. The other two stood watch. Cyri kept busy spreading out rain-soaked clothes and blankets to dry. She assisted Fraida with the cooking, watching the pot when the midwife was busy with me. In spite of my pleading, she would not tell me what she thought the chances were for saving the baby. When the bleeding did not stop, I became less optimistic.

"I haven't seen John," I said when Rorik came to sit beside me.

"He is no longer with us." His tone was very curt, as though chiding me for my curiosity.

"He left?" He proffered no answer. "You sent him away?" I couldn't believe it of him. "In this weather!"

"No. He is dead."

Dead! It was what we'd feared. "He and Andrew had a fight, didn't they?"

"No, it never came to that. We were set upon by highwaymen after your accident. He was the first to see them, and he alerted us by running out to intercept them. He fought valiantly until we got ourselves together enough to repel them. He killed one man, but was finally brought down from behind as he attacked a second."

"So," I said quietly, "I was really the cause of his death. 'Tis not something to be proud of."

"On the contrary. If we had continued on, we would have been ambushed where the road narrows less than a league ahead. Here we were in open country. Up there is a heavy growth of trees where they would be hidden until we were trapped between them. Being forced to move in single file, we could have been wiped out."

"John saved our lives." It was the last thing I would have expected of the man who thought the fates and all the world were against him.

"He did that," Rorik said. "I'm sure he knew it was one way to make up for the trouble he'd caused."

"Or he thought, having lost everything, there was no point in going on."

"Actually, Tara, I doubt if he thought at all. In an attack like that, men don't think; they just act. At least he'll be remembered as a hero rather than a ne'er-do-well."

Rorik moved so I could lay my head in his lap, and he ran his fingers through my hair. "How are you feeling now?"

"Fair." No point in denying I still felt too weak to move.

"You still have a fever. I don't like that."

"Fraida says 'tis natural. She'll not tell me anything more."

"We'll not take any more chances than we have to. If necessary we'll stay in one place until the baby comes."

It was what I had feared. "No! We have to get home."

"A few months will make no difference if it means your

life." He turned his head away as if he had said too much or didn't want me to see his face.

It was the first time I realized I was in any danger. I had been thinking only about the baby. I would do whatever Rorik said to stay alive.

Bishop Roden and Olav returned to say there was a monastery two days' journey ahead which would take us in until spring made travel possible again. Father Utrillo had stayed there to help prepare for our arrival. Rorik carried me to a bed made for me in the wagon. To make room for it, some of the sacks under the straw were strapped onto my donkey and John's horse.

As I jounced along in the wagon, unable to find a comfortable position, I became more and more miserable. But I said nothing to Rorik. I knew he wanted to get me to the monastery as quickly as possible. When we stopped for the night, I remained in the wagon rather than incur any risks by being moved. During the night the pain became more intense and I knew labor had begun. I thought I was nearly five months along, and the birth would be as involved as if I had gone full term. I did not know when I felt the first pangs that it would continue for many hours. After one severe contraction, I heard Fraida tell Rorik the baby was dead. But I was too weak to cry. I closed my eyes. All I wanted to do was sleep.

"I was afraid of that, sire," she said.

"How long?"

"Since she fell, I think. 'Tis good she is getting rid of it now. The dead baby was putting a poison in her system. She would not have lived much longer."

"And now?" I could hear the desperation in his voice.

"We must get it out soon. She will have to do all the work."

Hours went by. I pushed when I was told, but the baby refused to descend to a position where Fraida could pull it out. I knew I was losing a great deal of blood by the number of times she replaced the blankets under me, and finally the time came when I had no more strength to push. I heard voices, but they were very faint. I was traveling further and further away from them. It took all my strength just to remain focused enough to hear a few snatches of the conversation.

"She is getting very weak, sire."

"There must be something you can do! We can't just

stand here and let her die." When he was at the tiller he could bring a ship through the worst storms. He could command men. But he was helpless in the face of this kind of death that he could not fight. These thoughts swirled through my head. There was no more pain, but I felt suffocated by a heavy fog that pressed on my chest and muffled their voices.

"Call Cyri," Fraida said. "She can do what Tara cannot."

I felt Cyri massaging my belly as she would knead dough. The contractions increased in frequency and duration. At last I felt hands reach in and pull something out. The baby or all of my insides? The searing pain of tearing flesh was as nothing to the relief at knowing the worst was over. While Fraida kept working frantically to complete all that had to be done, I wondered if in fact the danger were past or if I were going to die. 'Tis a strange feeling, that of considering one's own death. I was not afraid to die; I was just angry. I wanted to see Signe and Eirik again. More than that, I wanted to watch them grow up. It was not fair! I had endured being captured, enslaved, nearly drowned in the rapids, and forced to travel the rugged distance to Constantinople. Now that Rorik and I were at last on our way home after being separated for so long, I was not going to be denied the pleasure of getting there.

"I am not going to die!" I thought I said it to myself, but Rorik was immediately at my side.

"No, my love, no one thinks that."

"Fraida does." I could barely get the words out. "Tell her I intend to live."

"She knows that. You said it loud enough."

"Ask—ask Bishop Roden to pray for me, and—and pray to your gods, too."

"You want him to say a mass for your recovery?"

"Yes."

"Do you think it will help to say I will become a Christian if God allows you to live?" As sick as I was, I knew what it cost him to say that.

"You would do that for me?" I had to stop and find breath to go on. "No, Rorik, you cannot make deals with God. A—a conversion can be true only if you come to it by faith. But—thank you."

I fell asleep after Rorik told me we had lost a little boy.

I was more determined than ever to live and give him another son, one who would live.

The good monks had everything ready for us when we arrived at the monastery. Olav and two guards rode on ahead to apprise them of my condition while the bishop remained with us in case his services were needed. The clergyman's presence did little to ease my fears, nor the fact he donned robes appropriate for administering the last rites and wore them during the entire ride.

The monastery was a large one, rebuilt on the site of one destroyed many years earlier by barbarians. Well able to take us all in, they were delighted to have with them for the winter a man of such importance as a Papal legate; in every way they made us feel equally as welcome. Accustomed to having pilgrims stay with them for long periods of time, they had more than adequate facilities and our stay was comfortable. The simple food was well prepared, and there was plenty of it. The sleeping quarters were sparsely furnished but clean. The months passed in the monastery were a hiatus we most sorely needed before continuing our trek to Frisia on the Northern Sea. For several weeks I remained in bed until midday and then sat in the cloistered garden to allow my strength to return.

Each of us made a place for himself within the community. Bishop Roden acted as titular head of the monastery and advised the monks who were making plans to establish a monastery school. Rorik, Olav, and the Papal guards carried and laid stones with those who were building an addition to the chapel. Father Utrillo secluded himself in the library with those monks who were copying or translating manuscripts. Occupied by the task he loved most, he was no longer the awkward young man who dropped or stumbled over everything he touched. Slowly and patiently he covered sheet after sheet of parchment with delicately flowing script.

Andrew and Paul showed the monks how to have an herb garden the year round. The tinker built oblong wooden boxes small enough to be carried into the kitchen from a sunny corner just outside when the weather became harsh. Paul filled them with dirt, then carefully planted a variety of herbs. He nurtured them as tenderly as he had the flowers in Ali Habib's garden. Cyri and Fraida assumed many of the housekeeping tasks, about which none of the monks complained. The cook, however, refused any offer of help in his bailiwick, much to the women's disgust.

For the first time in his life, Horst was neither scorned as an idiot nor pitied as a cripple, but simply accepted as a human being. He was left free to move in his awkward gait through all the buildings and the surrounding yard. Like a child just learning to walk he fell often, but no one humiliated him by rushing to his aid. His favorite spot was the chapel, where he spent hours gazing at the statues. The large one of Mary, whose silk robes were changed with the seasons and for holy days, was his favorite. As for Inga, whether helping Paul with the herb gardens, learning to copy manuscripts in the library, or assisting Fraida and Cyri with housekeeping chores, she was the darling of everyone. In the eyes of the monks, she could do no wrong.

By midspring, after a time of heavy rains that changed the winter-frozen roads into morasses of thick mud, the sun finally shone hot and bright for several days and we were at last able to go on our way.

We would always be grateful to the monks, but the last few weeks had seemed endless. It would be good to get on the road and be moving again.

Chapter Twenty-five

OUR GROUP WAS BECOMING SMALLER. It had been decreased by one with the death of John. Now it was diminished by two more. The monks invited Horst to remain with them. The serenity of the monastery and his acceptance by the community had done much to alleviate his condition. He would never be completely cured of the spasms that racked his body, nor would he ever speak clearly, but he was made to feel useful through his ability to perform a few simple tasks. One was to keep the chapel clean. It took him most of the day to attend to this simple job, but there was no need to hurry. More important, he was happy in the monastery, especially during the hours spent in the chapel adoring his favorite statue of the Virgin.

Fraida could not remain in the monastery, but a position was found for her in the nearby château of the duke whose lands adjoined those of the church.

She bid us a farewell compounded of both smiles and tears. "Sorry I am to see you go, but 'tis a real miracle I've seen. I knew there would be a miracle if I did not lose faith. To think my Horst has at last found others who love him like I do."

"We shall miss you, Fraida," I said, returning her embrace, "but we are happy for both of you."

"He's to be a monk, you know. To think I would live to see him become a holy man. I always knew he had a good heart; now others know it, too."

Through the weeks we were there, Horst had shown that though he might be enfeebled physically, he was not dim-witted. He had a good mind that needed only to be taught. Before we left, he had learned from Paul the rudiments of herb culture and managed slowly to help him plant a small flower garden. The patient monks spent long hours in the library with Horst, and they were surprised at how rapidly he was learning to read. He could never write the fine script needed to copy documents, but he was to be the first student in the school they were opening the following autumn.

So we bid them good-bye with conflicting emotions. We were happy for Fraida and Horst, but I would never forget what she had done to save my life.

When we reached the Rhine, Andrew announced he preferred to continue roaming the land rather than sail on the river.

"No one on a ship needs a tinker," he said just before we embarked. "The women in farmhouses and villages do, and I should hate to deprive them of my superior services. I've also a mind to settle down and work out of one place." I knew he was referring to the home of the buxom, red-faced widow in a village we'd recently passed through.

When Andrew caught up with us at the river's edge, he was even more jolly and expansive than usual. "Good-bye, Andrew, and good luck," we all said.

Rorik clapped him on the shoulder. "We'd not have made it without you, tinker."

When we walked aboard the barge whose owner agreed to take us all the way to the mouth of the Rhine, we were once more reduced to our original party: Paul, Cyri, Olav, Inga, Rorik, and myself. The barge Rorik found for us was built much like the *Theos,* broad-beamed and sturdy, with a shallow draft for river travel. It also had a cabin on deck, divided into two compartments. Olav said he preferred sleeping on deck during the pleasant spring nights. Inga, who had adopted Olav after Paul and Cyri married, announced she would place her pallet next to his.

The leisurely sail on the Rhine was the most pleasant part of our entire journey. We enjoyed warm, sunny days, cool breezes at night, and delightful vistas along the shores we passed. We sailed by uninhabited wooded islands and others scarce large enough to hold the massive castles dominating them. These lofty structures also clung to the edge of the high banks we glided between, some with towers flying gaily colored flags, though a few showed signs of decay. Flowers bloomed everywhere.

The most satisfying thing about the journey was being able to discard our peasant garb and don the soft, delicate garments brought from Constantinople. Paul and Olav returned to tunics, but they persuaded Cyri to make new pants and blouses. Rorik proudly strode the deck in his Viking garb.

We reached Frisia and the coast of the Northern Sea in good time. I could hardly believe I was at last looking across the final expanse of water that separated us from Hordaland—from Signe, Eirik, Thorne, and Astrid. Now I could begin to count off days instead of months and weeks.

The port, long an important center of trade with all Norseland, was a busy one. Rorik anticipated no problems in finding a ship to take us home. We located a public house to stay in for the few days until we set sail for the last time before stepping onto our homeland.

Olav was sent to locate a ship bound for Norvegia. He returned within two hours to say he had talked with a Viking ship captain; when he finished repeating the conversation, we were aghast with disbelief.

"I saw the man giving orders on board his serpent ship, and when he came ashore, I approached him eagerly. I could scarce believe it when he said he was indeed bound for Hordaland. 'My master,' I told him, 'is Rorik the Jarl, son of Thorne, King of the Three Shires.'

" 'Your master lies,' he responded. 'Rorik is dead, and Ruskil is King of the Three Shires.'

" 'But what of Thorne?' I asked.

" 'He, too, is dead.' "

"I'll not hear such words!" Rorik stormed. " 'Tis your informant who lies."

Nor could I believe what Olav said. I would not believe it. Thorne had to be alive.

"Did you tell him Rorik is right here?" I asked.

"No, I thought it best to keep that news secret for the time being. I checked with other Vikings in the harbor, and all told me the same story. 'Tis truly believed that Rorik died when his ship was attacked, and Thorne died within the past few months."

"My father dead. I cannot believe it." Rorik turned away so I could not see his tears.

"Had they any word of the children?" I was desperate for news of Signe, Eirik, and Asri. I would mourn Thorne's death, but I had to know if the children were safe.

"I dared not ask direct questions, but no one mentioned any other deaths. We must assume, Tara, they are still alive and safe."

389

Would they be safe now that Ruskil was king? As beloved as Rorik was in the shires, Ruskil might see his brother's son as a threat. We dared not waste time in getting home.

"We needs must return immediately," Rorik said. It was as if he had been reading my mind. "We will find another ship."

"No, sire," Olav warned. "I am certain the first I talked to is one of Ruskil's men. He will report what he heard, and Ruskil will await you in a murderous mood. Or he will have the ship we sail on scuttled."

"We cannot stay here forever!" Rorik raged. "I cannot hide like a coward, not knowing if my children are safe or how my father died."

"There is no need to," Olav calmed him. "We merely bide our time. I'm as anxious to return home as you, but we must not be hasty."

"You have suggestions?" Rorik asked. He had learned to trust Olav as much as I did. "I think you have already put your wits to work."

"I have. We go to your cousin by marriage, King Torvald of the Dani."

"Do we dare?" Rorik asked cautiously. "Remember, we're not yet sure he wasn't behind the plan to attack me."

" 'Tis a chance we will have to take, but with Ruskil in power, I think not. No mention was made of his being under Torvald's thumb. If the king plotted to rid Hordaland of both you and Thorne, 'twould be to take control himself. No, from what I heard, Ruskil is no puppet ruler."

So began our despondent detour through seas that should have been carrying us home. On the *Seafarer*, a long ship bound for Zealand, we sailed around the northern tip of Jutland, entered the Noric Channel, and came within sight of Scandia. We looked with despair on shores we dared not touch.

Rorik's mood vacillated between hatred for Ruskil and sorrow over loss of his father. There seemed to be no way I could reach him. Our ecstatic resumption of lovemaking after my recovery from the loss of the baby came to an abrupt halt. We shared a bed for sleeping but for naught else. Nor did Rorik sleep much. He thrashed about restlessly the few times he came to bed. More often he paced the deck. His face was drawn, and he was in far worse condition than when I first saw him at the slave market. He and Olav were often deep in conversation, but the shipbuilder was the only person he spoke to.

My own worry was intensified by his refusal to confide in me, either his feelings or his plans. Never before had I felt so completely shut out of his life. Neither my months of denial in Hordaland nor our long separation had made me feel so completely lost as I was during these last days at sea. Paul and Cyri knew something was amiss and were disappointed at not going straight to the home I had described, but they had no idea of the depths of our tragedy.

Signe and Eirik might still be alive, but we had no assurance. Certainly Ruskil would not let them remain alive long enough to challenge his position or his son's. More than ever I was overwhelmed by the loss of my baby. I feared, though I dared not tell Rorik, that I would be unable to bear any more children. My stupidity and selfishness had cost the life of the son who might have been Rorik's only heir. Comfort me as he had, I knew it was my fault. I was too good to ride in a wagon. I had to have my own way. If I had ridden in the wagon, there would have been no donkey to stumble, and I wouldn't have been thrown. Fraida never came right out and said I'd now be barren, but she cautioned me against sleeping with Rorik until I was completely healed. In fact, my system had never really returned to normal. I was not yet well nor might I ever be.

I longed to pour all this out to Rorik and have him confide his feelings to me in turn. Instead I waited until he left the bed, or I knew he was not coming at all, to cry into my pillow.

We came in sight of Zealand late in the day, and the Viking captain chose to wait until the morning tide to enter the harbor. Suddenly Rorik's taciturn moroseness changed to self-assured exuberance. Once more he was not to be daunted by whatever lay ahead. King Torvald represented a challenge, and Rorik approached a challenge in only one way: with the knowledge he would win. Whether his cousin by marriage had been in on the original attack plot or not, Rorik intended acquiring from him the necessary ships and forces to return to Hordaland, overthrow Ruskil, and take control of the Three Shires which he considered rightfully his.

When I retired for the night, I left Rorik standing at

the rail. He gazed not at the shore before us but out to sea, toward the land he was determined to return to. Sometime later I felt him slide into the pallet next to me.

"Tara, my love, hold me close. I need you."

"And I've needed you all these nights."

"I could not come to you. I knew if once we spoke, I would break down and not be able to go on."

His face was pressed against mine, and I felt his tears. He cried as I had cried into my pillow when he was gone. We wept for his father, but he would not weep for Signe and Eirik.

"They are alive, Tara. They have to be. I will not believe Ruskil is that cruel."

"We will know soon, love," I whispered. "Of a certain, Torvald must know what is going on at home."

We clung to each other that night with a spiritual rapture, a special passion born of need, and an awareness that whatever awaited us in the days ahead, our strength lay in facing it together.

The *Seafarer* would be staying in the harbor for several days. Rorik was urged to remain on board while Olav went ashore to learn what he could about the situation in Hordaland, and to ascertain if Torvald had a part in any plot against Rorik. Olav was gone the entire day, and we feared the worst: he had revealed himself as our friend and been taken prisoner. Near sundown, however, we saw him striding along the harbor, and he came aboard with the first cheering news we'd heard in some time.

"From all I could hear, and believe me I listened in every likely place where the truth is revealed—market, tavern, dockside—I learned that Torvald was genuinely distressed at hearing of your disappearance and probable death. As your host, he held himself responsible for your well-being until you sailed safely through the Vik. It must be true if people remember after all this time. Some spoke of seeing him ride by, his face shadowed by gloom. He offered a reward to learn if the sinking was accidental or planned. Some said he paid it but never moved against the culprits. The rumor is they were too powerful and important. When he learned of your father's death, he went into mourning, for the sake of Thorne as much as for your cousin, his wife."

"So you think 'tis safe to go ashore?" Rorik asked.

"I do, sire. If you permit it, I will go ahead and tell them you are here. I do not think it would do to surprise them. Once I would have suggested it, to test for shock on seeing you alive. I'm certain 'tis no longer necessary."

Through all our misadventures, Olav had managed to keep the armband given him by Thorne. When he left the ship in the morning for his audience with Torvald, he was an imposing figure, proud to be a Viking serving his jarl once again. We were to give him from morning tide to the sun's zenith to meet and talk to Torvald before we left the ship.

Once Olav left, Rorik gave me special orders. "Get out your finest garments. It is imperative we make a striking appearance. No groveling like poor relatives. I am still a powerful Viking jarl, and you are my wife. We have been the guests of an important Byzantine merchant."

With all our worry about the children, I had given no thought to my appearance. Now, while Cyri sorted through our garments to look for something presentable, I brushed Rorik's vest and trousers, located his armbands and *hlad,* and polished his boots. Cyri found a long, pale blue tunic, embroidered dalmatic, and jeweled pellium, which I donned. No matter how often we'd had to consolidate our packing, I refused to relinquish any of my beautiful garments or art objects. Now, Rorik admitted, I had been right.

When we stepped onto the wharf, we anticipated walking to the austere castle we'd visited previously. To our surprise, two horses awaited us, held by guards who were to escort us. A magnificently embossed, silver-inlaid sidesaddle rested on the back of a handsome white stallion for me. But I was no longer swayed into complacency by such courtesies. Was Torvald really our friend, or were we riding into a trap as we had sailed into one when we left his castle two years before? I knew Rorik was as wary as I.

There was no formal greeting of king and jarl. We no sooner dismounted than Rorik's cousin, Esrig, ran forward and threw her arms around him.

"My beloved cousin! We thought never to see you again. We thought you dead."

Torvald's greeting was more staid but no less welcoming. "We are indeed pleased to see you alive and well. There is much to talk about. Your man Olav has told us

393

some of the past two years, but there are many questions and details to discuss."

We followed them into the dining hall where a feast was laid such as I had not seen since leaving Constantinople. In every way, Torvald was making us feel welcome. He was either very cunning or genuinely happy to see us alive.

"No one was more distressed than I," Torvald said, "when we heard your ship had gone down. Our first thought, of course, was that it was a simple shipwreck, especially since it was reported lost near the treacherous skerries. Then we began to hear rumors. Some fishermen had seen the ship on fire. Others reported hearing talk about a planned attack and scuttling of a ship belonging to a person of importance. Many rumors were bruited about. I offered a reward of gold for real news. The result was most unexpected."

"You learned who was behind it?" Rorik asked, moving to the edge of his chair.

"I think so. But 'twas not information I could act on. Not at that time."

"You were too close to the bastard!" Rorik knew who Torvald was going to name.

"I was and am. All I learned pointed to your brother Ruskil with a confidante here in Zealand, who got word to the ships the exact time you left. Thorne was still alive. 'Twas not my place to move against his son. You were dead—or so we believed—and we were on good terms with the Three Shires. We would gain nothing by moving against them. We felt certain your father would learn the truth and administer whatever punishment he deemed proper."

"But somehow he didn't," Rorik mused. "Ruskil would be too shrewd for that. Right at home by my father's side, he could deny any rumors that reached them. And the spy here?"

"A woman. Does the name Raghild mean anything to you?"

Rorik's face reflected my own amazement.

"Indeed it does. She was my first wife. She was very bitter when I—I sent her away for personal reasons."

"I would say she got the revenge she sought," Torvald nodded.

"Did you do anything with her?"

"No, by that time she had fled from here."

"To her father in Frisia, I've no doubt," Rorik said. "So you learned nothing more?"

"On the contrary. Through the succeeding months more information filtered in. Some of it you've also revealed yourself when you described your experiences. We can reconstruct the rest. We can assume, I think, it was intended for you to be sunk with the ship. The renegades decided to get more than the original amount agreed on for the sinking by taking you and holding you for ransom.

"I'm sure," he continued, "the demand was sent to Thorne. He would have paid it. So Ruskil must have learned of the failure to kill you and managed to intercept the messenger. He knew, too, your father would pay it, and that did not suit his purpose at all. Instead of feeling thwarted by the failure, your abductors got the additional money by selling you into slavery."

"I thought much the same thing," Rorik agreed. "What about my father? Do you think Ruskil had anything to do with his death?"

"No, I do not. He'd not dare go that far. Thorne died a natural death less than three months ago. Ruskil merely took advantage of the people's love for your father to assume control."

Less than three months. I was torn by guilt. It was my fault we had not arrived in Hordaland before then. Thorne was dead and Ruskil was king because of me. I had no doubt Thorne's death could be partially attributed to a broken heart, grieving over Rorik who he assumed must be dead. He would be alive or at least Rorik would have been there to challenge Ruskil if I had not acted like a spoiled child instead of a woman.

"What do you suggest I do now?" Rorik shifted in his chair, eager for some positive word. Knowing his whole future depended on the action he took, Rorik—for the moment—deferred to the wisdom and experience of the older man; but I also knew caution would make him reserve final judgment of the elder man's advice.

"You are welcome to stay with us as long as necessary. Olav told me you have others with you."

"Yes, two slaves purchased in Constantinople. They are, however, more like friends than servants. We have traveled far together. Also a child we rescued. We think she was

395

originally stolen from somewhere in the Northland, but she cannot remember. She is like our own daughter."

"We will make arrangements for all of them. Accommodations will be ready when they get here. Now, as to the suggestions you requested. I will send a man to Hordaland to study the situation, to learn the best way for you to return."

"And the children," I interrupted. "Please have him find out about Signe, Eirik, and Asri."

"If I may suggest something," Rorik said. "Have your man contact either Sven, the weaver, or Haki, the woodcarver. Both can be trusted. Haki is a former slave my father freed during the spring festival. They will be best able to tell your man how things stand. And I would like exact details of my father's death."

"I will summon Halfdan tomorrow," Torvald said, "and you can tell him all this yourself. He, too, will be one you can trust."

We spent the next few days waiting in our various ways for Halfdan to return from Hordaland. Olav watched the ships and fishing boats swarming the harbor. Rorik stayed closeted with Torvald much of the time, studying the older man's ruling methods. Inga, Paul, and Cyri explored the town. I remained by the tower-room window, my eyes seldom moving from the horizon, the invisible line that separated us from home.

Torvald sent word the minute Halfdan returned to the castle, and I rushed down to the audience chamber. He would surely have news of the children.

The information he had was reassuring in some ways and frightening in others.

"Your father died a natural death, sire," Halfdan said. "He took to his bed with pains in his chest. He had suffered from them for some time. There is no thought of foul play. His wives were by his side the whole time."

"Did he die with a sword in his hand, Halfdan?" I knew the importance of this to him. It would mean his father was in Valhalla, the last resting place of Viking warriors.

"He did, sire. One of the slaves—a young man named Nels—put it there himself. I know this to be true because I talked to him. Your father was given a Viking chieftain's funeral, and is now in Valhalla."

"The children?" I asked. I was aching to hear about

396

them, yet was almost unable to breathe with the fear of what I might learn. "What about the children?"

"They are alive and safe." Thank God! I all but collapsed with relief. "But," he hesitated too long, "I know not for how long."

"What say you!" Rorik leapt up from his chair and I could not stop the long moan that came from my lips.

"I went to the shops of the weaver and wood-carver as you bid me. 'Twas at the weaver's I met the slave Nels. After the death of the Jarl Thorne, there were those who feared for your children's lives when Ruskil took over his father's position. I'll tell you about that next. Nels and another slave named Astrid fled with Signe and Eirik and sought refuge with the weaver. They are there now. Only those who can be trusted know where they are hiding, living in a back room where no one but the weaver goes."

May all the saints bless Astrid; I knew she would let no harm come to Signe and Eirik. And Nels, too. There would never be a way to repay them for their love and loyalty. I remembered that back room where I had first seen the beautiful *Tiald* I bought for the *skaalen*. Now Thorne was dead and Rorik an exile. Worse, the children were threatened and had to live in hiding. We had to get them with us.

"You think they are in peril?" I asked, my voice trembling.

"I do. I think they should be removed from Hordaland as soon as possible. There are rumors Ruskil intends to get them out of his way when he finds them."

"Then 'tis imperative we return immediately!" Rorik pounded his fist on the table. "We dare not wait any longer."

"Wait, sire," Halfdan said, "until I tell you all. Ruskil is a tyrant. He took over immediately on your father's death. He did not wait for a meeting of the Thing and an election. He has put his own men in power. There are signs the jarls of Sogn and the Fjords are planning an uprising, but 'tis not yet time. Ruskil has spies everywhere. You would not reach Hordaland alive."

"If I led a powerful force from here?" Rorik was not a patient man, and word of our children's danger had him wrought up to a murderous passion.

"Listen to me, my son." Torvald had waited a long time before he spoke. "I cannot send that number of men with you. I cannot afford to lose them in a fight that is not mine. I know how anxious you are about your children and your people, but you must be patient."

"Patient! When my children live under a daily threat of death?"

"I did not say do nothing, but for you to haste over there and get yourself killed will not save them. This is what I propose. I will send a trading ship with Halfdan aboard. While the others are dealing with the merchants, he will see the children again and get them on board ship. All of this will be accomplished as swiftly as possible. Signe and Eirik will be here with you before Ruskil knows they are gone."

"And Astrid?" I said. She must not be left behind to suffer Ruskil's wrath.

"Astrid?" Torvald asked.

"She is the nurse who has cared for them since they were born and is in hiding with them now. She would not be safe if left behind."

"I will bring her, too," Halfdan said. "I met her, and would not think of leaving her."

"How about Asri?" I asked. Halfdan had not mentioned her as being with the twins.

"She is under the protection of Thorne's wives."

"Nevertheless," Rorik said, "she must come, too. With the others gone, Ruskil would turn on her. 'Twill be dangerous to send someone to the farm, but I want her with me."

"Halfdan," I said, "when you go to the farm, seek out Ruskil's wife named Helga. I did a great favor for her once. She'll not have forgotten. I trust not the others, but Helga will help you get Asri out of the house. Merely tell her that Tara asks about her son."

" 'Twill be done," Halfdan said. "I have a man I would trust with my own child."

"Now then," Torvald said, "once this is accomplished, we will talk about your return. Agreed?"

"Agreed," Rorik said. "Hard as it is, we will wait."

During the following days I could do little more than pace the courtyard. Occasionally I visited the harbor with Inga, who loved to watch the fishermen come in and to explore their boats. But the ship I waited for did not appear. If the true reason for Torvald's men being in Hordaland were discovered, they could be detained and the hiding place of the children discovered.

Cyri insisted I try to rest every afternoon, but I usually ended up standing at the window of the tower room, looking down at the harbor. It was from there I spotted what I thought never to see again: the golden dragon head of the *Raven*. I was so elated and relieved, I was too excited to think. Were the children on it? One moment I was buoyed up at the thought of seeing them; the next second found me in the depths of misery at the thought they might not be aboard. Why the *Raven*? It should be a good omen, but I was shaken by the mystery of it.

When I dashed down the stone steps to tell Rorik, he had already seen it. Torvald had horses ready, and together we galloped to the wharf. Apprehension, fear, and joy had me in turmoil as I spurred my horse on.

Chapter Twenty-six

THE FIRST SMILING FACE I SAW WAS ASTRID's, and I clung to her, weeping with gladness and relief. Then out from behind her skirts came the two I had ached to see over the many long months. Eirik stood back shyly, his fingers in his mouth, but Signe laughed and flung herself at me. Not to miss out on the kisses and attention his sister was getting, Eirik edged slowly forward and hugged me around the legs. While I held him close, crying and laughing, Rorik gathered up Asri, who immediately began covering his face with kisses. It was a long time before we could say anything. I had feared the children would be shy, but Astrid had not let any of them forget us. I could not believe I finally had them with me. I held them away to look at them, and then clutched them to me.

At three, Signe was slim and slightly taller than her brother, with pale blond hair and fair skin. She looked like her father, but with my coloring. She was truly our child. Eirik, on the other hand, was Thorne's grandson, with his plump figure, ruddy complexion, and reddish-gold hair. Asri, at six, was a delicate, beguiling miniature of Thyri, already hinting at the beauty she would become.

The hours were not long enough for me. I wanted just to sit and drink in the nearness of my children. I needed to know everything about their lives during the years we were apart. Astrid and I alternated talking at the same time and sitting quietly while Signe and Eirik grew accustomed to being with me. As for Asri, she never let her father out of her sight.

"I never let them forget you, my lady," Astrid said.

"I knew you would not."

"Always we talk about you when we sit around the fire at night. The Jarl Thorne loved to play with them and tell how their handsome father brought their beautiful mother to Hordaland."

"We were so afraid for them," I said, "and for you when we learned about Thorne's death and Ruskil's threats."

" 'Twas Nels who saved them. When their grandfather died, Nels was certain they were in danger, and he whisked us away to the shop of Sven, the weaver."

"You took good care of them, Astrid."

" 'Twas a trust you bestowed on me. Loving them like my own, I could do naught else. 'Twas a joy to watch them grow up strong and healthy. Our one sorrow was that you were not there. Lord Thorne mourned the loss every day. The children were his only consolation."

I watched them now, running around the courtyard, chasing Paul and Olav, or being shepherded by Inga to the harbor where she had made friends with all the fishermen. Her joy at finally being with her new brother and sisters was boundless, and she watched over them like a little mother.

"I bring you something else," Astrid said. She reached into the deep pocket of her gown and brought out two flat stones. "I find only these among your things. I think others were thrown away."

I looked at the rune stones in my palm. Of what value were they now? Or had they ever been more than just two flat stones with strange inscriptions carved into them?

"Thank you, Astrid. I have wondered if things might have been different for me if I'd had them with me. But then, had I not gone to Constantinople—" I could not finish the sentence. The nightmare of what might have been still haunted me. "I'll put them among my things to save for the children, but I'll not be reading the future again with only two. That is just as well. There are certain things one is not meant to know."

"Guard them well though, my lady. They are still very valuable."

I put the stones away and immediately forgot about them.

Rorik spent his days on the *Raven*. Unbeknownst to us, Torvald had sent a large enough crew to bring back the *Raven of the Wind* if she were still afloat and ready to sail. She had evidently remained in the harbor all the time we were gone, and there was much work to be done before she was really seaworthy again. Rorik and Olav were once more blissfully engaged in doing what they liked best, repairing and repainting a serpent ship. The magnificent dragon head needed to be completely repainted, and Rorik toiled for hours over every individual feature and scale. Always Asri sat on the floor right beside the long table where he worked.

"Do you want to help me?" I heard him ask her one day.

"Oh, Papa, may I?"

He handed her one of the smaller brushes, and I watched, delighted and amused, as she carefully imitated his strokes in outlining the purple scales with gold. If Rorik's marriage to Thyri had been a mistake, it had produced one good result. Asri would be a joy to her father for the rest of his life. She made me think again of Thyri and Adair. Like them, we were now exiles with the future a frightening unknown.

Others besides Astrid and the children returned on the *Raven*. In fact, Torvald need not have sent extra men. Sven, the weaver, Haki, the wood-carver, and Nels had all begged to be brought along. They knew their lives were in jeopardy once Ruskil learned of the children's flight. In addition, several from Rorik's crew on the *Raven* insisted they would sail again only under their former chieftain.

Rorik had been right to insist we spend our money wisely. Torvald was a more than generous host, but Rorik felt bound to assume the responsibility for his own men. He had no wish to be beholden to the king for any more than he was already.

Many hours were spent in discussing when and how we should return to Hordaland. Ruskil's grip on the shires was a strong one. To try attacking his power with a single shipload of men would be like one man facing a pack of hungry wolves with no more than a knife. We had one advantage now that the children were with us. We could wait for a propitious moment. With spies in the other two shires, news of an uprising would reach us in time for all to move together. Torvald would take no part, but he agreed to harbor ships from the Fjords and Sogn so it would be a well-armed armada that bore down on Ruskil from the sea while other forces attacked from land.

" 'Tis a good plan," Torvald said one night at dinner. It was now late in the summer, and we had to move soon or be forced to wait until the following spring. " 'Tis a plan that might work, but do you honestly want to follow through with it?"

"I don't understand," Rorik said. "Why do we talk strategy if we mean not to carry it out?"

"Many men will die. Is the overthrow of Ruskil worth that price?"

"Those are strange words for a Viking!" Rorik pushed himself away from the table and stood up. "Do you think I would falter during a moment of danger?" He glared at his cousin by marriage, and one hand went to the knife at his belt. "For if you do—"

No, I wanted to scream. Don't anger him. Rorik's patience was nearly at an end, and I feared he would say something he'd regret.

"Sit down, Rorik!" Torvald spoke sternly but without raising his voice. "I am your elder by both age and experience. I will excuse your insolence because I know of your anxiety. Now—to get back to the point I was trying to make. All my men returning from Vestfold, Jaeder, and as far north as Trondelag tell me the same thing. The rebellion of the two shires against Hordaland and Ruskil is now thought doomed to fail. There are not enough who actively disapprove of Ruskil, and he is gradually winning the others over to his side."

Torvald paused to study Rorik's reaction to his words. I was puzzled by my own response. Had we been lulled into complacency by Torvald's hospitality and seeming concern for us and the children? Why didn't he want Rorik to return home?

"Your brother is a tyrant," he continued, "but it is a tyranny that has benefited the jarls while keeping the free men and serfs more downtrodden. 'Twill be a rabble you lead against a powerful force of well-armed men. Thorne was dearly loved, and you were popular. If you had remained in Hordaland, you would be King of the Three Shires. But you have been away, and people forget quickly."

"By Odin! I was not away by choice. Does that not count for something? Surely those jarls who loved my father will shift to my side."

"What have you to offer them that Ruskil does not? You are wrong if you think compassion for what you suffered is as powerful a persuader as increased income from higher taxes."

403

"If they know Ruskil is a traitor?"

I listened fearfully to this dialogue. It did not bode well for our cause; of that I was sure. But did it bode real disaster?

"A traitor? Because he took over when his beloved father died? No, they will not see it that way. They accept him as a tyrant. 'Tis easy to ignore what one does not wish to hear."

Rorik listened intently, but his body had not relaxed, and he continued to scowl at Torvald. "I am to creep away into some corner like a frightened mouse and forget I was ever a Viking, is that it?"

"Your wife and your children are here. You will always be a Viking. Why do you really want to return? To help your people or to become king?"

"I want revenge!" Rorik clenched and unclenched his fists. "Ruskil has much to answer for. I was beaten up and my ship burned. Tara and I were separated and enslaved. Do you expect me to forget that? I do not intend that Ruskil will either. He will learn how I, Rorik, avenge the treatment meted out to my wife and children. Then I will kill him—slowly—to avenge what I suffered. Once I am king, I will take care of my people."

"Revenge is a most selfish reason for such an undertaking. I had thought you would say to help your people. I was prepared to proffer an alternate plan by which you might yet be king without having to kill any of your countrymen."

During all this I remained silent. I was mystified. Rorik was right. Torvald did not speak like a Viking. To a true Viking justice was an obligatory and often personal undertaking. Treachery could not go unpunished, and had to be adjudicated either under Thing law or in hand-to-hand combat. From the time we learned of Thorne's death and Ruskil's treason, I thought only of returning to Hordaland, of seeing Rorik vanquish his brother and become king. I had the feeling Torvald was thinking along different lines, and I was uneasy.

"Many from Daneland and Norvegia have left these lands to settle new colonies on Iceland," he said. "They are beginning a new life, but they lack one thing—a strong, experienced leader. The colonies are scattered, and there are troubles between them because each has its own Thing with its own Thing law. They need someone they will all listen to, someone who can bring them together at a Gulathing where a single code can be worked out and agreed upon. I think you are such a man. If you take your people along with some of mine, I will provide whatever extra ships and goods are needed. Word will soon spread. Those in Hordaland who wish to be with you will hear of it and follow."

"By the gods, Torvald!" Rorik shouted. "I'm thinking you have been in league with my brother all along. All the fancy words and fine-sounding plans are playacting to cover up your true allegiance. Suggesting I go to Iceland is naught but a ruse to keep me away from Hordaland."

"Rorik, I do not take kindly to having my words disbelieved or my actions questioned." His cheeks were flaming. He was not used to being challenged by one he considered an underling and I sensed that one more ill-chosen word from Rorik could put us in a dangerous situation. Somewhat calmed, Torvald went on, "I was happy to give you refuge, but you trespass too far on my good nature."

"For my wife and children, I thank you for your generosity. We will not impose on you much longer. There should be word soon from the leaders of the uprising."

Torvald flared up again. "You are a rash young man, Rorik. You have dared to question my integrity with no fear of incurring my wrath. Do you know what I do to my jarls who challenge my authority?"

"No, sire." Rorik continued to stand tall and unflinching, his eyes focused on Torvald.

"You have already experienced slavery. You might prefer the alternative of death."

"And my family?"

"Tara can remain here or be returned to Britain, whichever she chooses."

I wanted to protest, to convince Torvald that Rorik was indeed rash to accuse him of treachery, but that was scarcely reason enough to threaten such dire punishments. But I was in no position to speak. I had to sit still and listen as all our dreams evaporated in a welter of harsh words. I could only hope something would happen to make Torvald relent. If only Rorik had been less hasty in speaking. I refused to visualize a future without him in either Zealand or Britain.

"However," Torvald continued, "out of respect for your

father, I will accept your apology. I think 'twould be a mistake for you to count on any real help if you continue with your plans to invade Hordaland. I will send no men with you, but you may stay here until you sail. Do not think I am doing this to prove my loyalty. I have no need to do that."

"I apologize for questioning your motives," Rorik said, but there was nothing of the humble supplicant in his pose or voice. "Only one thing matters to me—destroying Ruskil. I will challenge anything that stands in my way. You think I should consider taking my family and friends to Iceland. I do not. So we will accept your offer to stay here until our plans are complete and we can return home."

"I still don't trust him," Rorik said when we had returned to our room high in the tower.

"I know. What do you think his reasons are for not wanting you to return?"

"I think he is a thorough scoundrel, an unmitigated blackguard and hypocrite. His evident interest in our future is an incidious mask to cover either hatred of me or overweening ambition."

"If you think he allies himself with Ruskil for his own grandiose aims, why is your brother so obviously still in control?"

"Because my father has not been long dead. Nor am I convinced his death was a natural one, in spite of the attempts to make me believe it. I think Torvald is giving Ruskil a long leash. But soon he will reel it in. We know the Three Shires are divided. How easy for Torvald to move in, the benevolent ruler who has the strength to unite them under his dragon. Or simply to take over through superior strength. He knows that if I overthrow Ruskil, the shires will unite under me. He is strong, but he fears my strength would prove invincible."

Rorik walked over to the slit window and looked down toward the harbor. Already three ships from Hordaland and one from Sogn had appeared to follow him when he invaded.

"Remember," he said, "Torvald already controls land on each side of the Noric Channel, and he is not without allies in Svealand."

"So you believe Torvald was involved in the treacherous attack on our ship?"

"I do. His acquisitive fingers reach as far as Malar where I was taken."

And we were in his clutches again. If all that Rorik feared were true, we were not safe for a moment as long as we remained in the castle. I wanted to convince myself that Rorik's hatred for Ruskil and his lust for vengeance were swelling Torvald's words all out of proportion.

"But he seemed sincerely overjoyed to see you alive," I said, "and he has been the most generous of hosts."

"He could not very well do elsewise. 'Twould be fatal to his plans to have his part in my abduction suspected."

"You did not suspect him at first."

"Not until he said he learned of Ruskil's part in the plot but did not make it known. If Torvald learned, why did not my father? Or why did he not tell my father, who would surely have punished my brother? Because he did not dare. He spoke as if Ruskil were too powerful a person. No, I'll not swallow that."

"Then why is he letting us stay here while plans go forward for the invasion? Do you think he means to kill us here?"

"No, I don't fear that. It would be too dangerous for him. But how better to know exactly what is going on and warn Ruskil, then let Ruskil do the slaying for him."

I nodded. It was dreadful if Rorik were right, and I feared he was. "I'd not thought of that. Does that mean you have to give up the idea?"

"No, we'll have two plans, one Torvald knows about, the other a secret between me and Olav."

"And the other ships?"

"We will meet at a place Torvald will know about; then we proceed with an alternate move. No one must know I do not trust him."

"If he warns Ruskil?"

"There is no way my brother will not be aware of what is going on. But our strength will be that he will not know when to expect the attack."

So began the days of preparation. Twice Olav slipped away and ventured into the enemy stronghold. Once his home, he had been away so many years, he could now come and go as he pleased without being recognized. Only one of his family remained, a daughter married and with children of her own. His wife was dead, and his two sons lost at sea. Though he longed to reveal himself to his daughter, he refrained from doing more than watching her from a distance.

"Why, Olav?" I asked. "There is no reason she cannot know you're alive. What a wonderful reunion it would be."

"There is time enough for that when we have subdued Ruskil. Right now we can trust no one. Not that I think she would purposely tell about my return, but she might let something slip. Then, too, I have been away many years. Her loyalties might already lie elsewhere."

"Oh, Olav, she will be happy to see you again."

"I think so. I think she will remember the games we played and the miniature ship I built for her."

Olav brought back word of which islands at the entrance to the fjord Rorik could safely sail between on the way to the mainland without Ruskil being alerted. There were a few islands inhabited by people still intensely loyal to Rorik and ready to fight with him on learning he was alive. Their ships would be ready to sail with ours under his command.

The ships that arrived in the harbor at Zealand from the other shires brought word of which jarls were ready to attack by land at the same time Rorik led the ships up the fjord. Timing was vital. Now that Rorik no longer trusted Torvald, no final decision on when to move could be made until after all the ships left Zealand and met at Tunsberg in Vestfold, on the western shore of the Vik. Rorik would leave first and wait there for each ship to arrive. Only then would he reveal the day of the attack. From there the Vikings would go to various ports to await their individual sailing dates, carefully calculated so that all the vessels would arrive at the first loyal island of the Hordaland archipelago at the same time.

Not until every Viking chieftain who would attack from the sea was informed of the invasion day could word be sent to those jarls planning to attack by land.

"Who will be responsible for contacting them?" I asked.

Rorik was working with a map roughly drawn by Olav. Vikings used no maps when they sailed the various seas, relying solely on their knowledge of solar and stellar movements and wind direction to plot their courses. They knew the coasts of the Northlands and those to the west as well as they knew the inside of their homes. This time, however, Rorik used a map to chart time and distance from each of the bays where the ships would moor before setting out for Hordaland. Using small pebbles, he located every ship exactly where he wanted it before the final move.

"This one, the ship of Eynstein, a jarl from Sogn. He can sail up this fjord without suspicion. A messenger will be waiting for him. We are allowing for plenty of time to inform our allies, but not enough time to warn Ruskil."

" 'Twill succeed, won't it, Rorik?" I asked anxiously.

"It has to."

"I can see you now, standing on the stern of the *Raven* as she sails right up to the mole where Thorne waited for us that day you brought me to Hordaland."

"Not the *Raven*, Tara. She will remain at Tunsberg with you, Cyri, Astrid, and the children on board.'

"No! You have to go in with the *Raven*."

"Two reasons why not. She would be immediately recognized and an alarm sent to Ruskil. The islands we have chosen to pass are said to be friendly to our cause, but that might not include everyone on them. More to the point, I want to be sure you and the children are safe. You cannot stay here, and of course you cannot sail with us."

"What do you mean 'of course'?" The delay was making me irritable.

"We go in as a fighting force. There can be no women aboard."

"No, I'll not be separated from you again."

"Tara, I cannot endanger your life. Nor the children's. I could never keep my mind on fighting if I were worried about you."

"We can stay in the outer harbor, near one of the islands, while you sail up the fjord. Put us on a small boat. No one will pay any mind to us. But I will not be left heaven knows how many leagues away. Worrying while not knowing."

"Listen to me, Tara, and look at this map. Those pebbles are ships, and each ship will have at least thirty men aboard. I have to concentrate on one thing—getting them all to Hordaland at the same time. None will question my commands because to do so would endanger all our lives. I ask only one thing of you—follow orders with the same trust in me those men have."

"I am sorry, Rorik, but I'm afraid. I'm afraid of losing you again."

"Tara, my love, I make two promises. I will return for you the minute Ruskil is overthrown and Hordaland secured. Some of my best men will be on board with you. We will sail the *Raven* in together."

"And the second promise?"

"We will travel to Britain for that long-overdue visit just as soon as I am named King of the Three Shires." I wanted to smile at his indomitable spirit—and his pride. It never occurred to him someone else might be elected king.

"How—how long will we be apart?" I wanted to sound more mollified than I really was. I would obey his commands, and trust him, but I was not happy about it.

"I know not. I will be the last to leave Tunsberg, after I know the messenger from the loyal land jarls has been alerted. All the ships should be at the outer isles within hours of my arrival. I don't want to tell you how long I think I will be gone. If it takes longer, you will worry. Better you be surprised at seeing me return so soon."

He was trying to keep it light, but I was worried. The *Raven* carried his luck. The last time Rorik sailed on another ship—the *Albatross*—we were attacked. Although I knew his reasons for not taking her up the fjord, I wanted to tell him he was wrong. He had to sail on the *Raven* if he wanted the invasion to succeed. But he would not understand. He would think I was being foolish.

Before we sailed, I had some serious thinking of my own to do. There were promises I had made to myself when I thought we would be sailing directly to Hordaland. Now was the time to fulfill them.

I found Astrid putting the twins down for their nap. As usual they were postponing it as long as possible.

"Signe," I said, trying to be stern in the face of her laughing eyes. "Get under those covers and do not tease Astrid anymore. And Eirik, there will be no more visits to the fishing boats if you don't close your eyes this minute. Inga and Asri will be waiting for you when you wake up."

"Promise?" He grinned as he always did when he thought he had gotten his own way.

"I promise, love."

Astrid returned to the sewing she had laid aside when the children came in from their noon meal. I sat down beside her and gazed out the window for a minute. The harbor shimmered a deep blue under a brilliant, warm sun. Fishing boats sailed around the serpent ships floating easily at their moorings. There were not many days left prior to our departure from Zealand, and certain important decisions had to be made before we knew whether the invasion of Hordaland had succeeded and Ruskil been overthrown.

"Astrid, if all goes well, we will soon be returning to Hordaland. If it does not—well, I really know not what we will do. After the twins were born, I promised myself I would free you when they were grown. I think 'tis time to talk about it now."

"No, no, I wish not to leave you and the children." She put her hands over her ears to shut out whatever I had to say. Quietly I leaned over, took them down, and held them between my own.

"Astrid, listen to me. We know not what is ahead." I did not want to put into words my fear that Rorik might be killed. Or that we might all have to flee to Britain. "You have earned your freedom with your care of Signe and Eirik. Here in Zealand we can find a ship sailing for Norrland, and you can return to your family's farm."

"You are kind, but you don't understand. I could not bear to be separated from the children. Nor do I wish to return to Norrland. It has been too long. You are my family now. You will need me."

"Yes, we will always need you," I assured her, "and the children would miss you. But take your time about a final decision. As of this moment you are free, whichever you choose to do."

"Thank you, my lady. I have not thought of myself as a slave since I began serving you. Not, that is, until the jarl Ruskil took over. Then I feared for what might happen to me." Her eyes opened wide with shame that I might misunderstand her last remark. "I assure you, my first thoughts were always for the children—"

"I know that, Astrid."

"But I was relieved for myself as well when Nels suggested we flee to Sven in the village. As a free woman, 'tis my wish to continue serving you. If you remember, I told you how hard life was on the farm. 'Twould be no easier now."

"I do remember. I only thought—"

"I know, and I thank you for it. Today, a week from now, my decision will be the same. I remain with you."

I had prayed that would be her answer. I didn't know what I would do without my faithful Astrid, but I could not have lived with myself if I had not made the offer.

411

Paul and Cyri made the same response when I approached them.

"No, no," Cyri insisted. "We go with you. We came North to this strange land to be with all of you. It matters not where that be."

"We could find a way to get you back to Macedonia," I suggested. I looked at Paul. He had read my lips when I sounded out the name of his homeland. Slowly he shook his head.

"If Paul wanted to be there," Cyri said, "we would ask before. We decided then to stay with you. We feel the same way now."

"I am grateful and pleased. One thing remains the same, though. As of now, you and Paul are free."

The *Raven* sailed from the harbor of Zealand on a gloomy overcast morning that suited my mood perfectly. I'd not become reconciled to Rorik's belief that he should not go in on the *Raven*, but I was managing to keep my fears to myself. I would not add that burden to the ones he'd already shouldered.

From the moment we sailed, all Rorik's thoughts were focused on invading Hordaland. He was a man dedicated to one purpose—the destruction of Ruskil and his own restoration to power. Hour after hour he strode the deck with Olav beside him as they plotted the strategy of attack. It must not fail. Nothing must go wrong. Speaking to none save his chieftains, he was no longer husband and father, only a Viking warrior. In his intense concentration on what lay ahead, the children and I might not have existed. He came neither to lie beside me at night nor to seek me out to talk during the day. He spent his nights on the stern deck, conferring with the helmsman and sleeping fitfully, wrapped in his cloak.

We sailed along the eastern coast of the Vestfold, at the northern tip of the Vik, for a fortnight. To allay suspicion, we stopped at Borre, Oseberg, Tunsberg, and Gikstad. From time to time we returned to Tunsbergsfjord to rendezvous with some of our chieftains. Rorik either met with them at an ale shop in the market town for, ostensibly, an evening of drinking and recounting stories or they visited each other's ships. Such conviviality was natural when Vikings met after being at sea, so Rorik was certain no one troubled to question their meetings.

After settling all details with the last ship, we set out to sail south and then west to Jaeder. The gloomy weather that accompanied our departure from Zealand had not improved. The sun had been covered by heavy, dark clouds during our stay at Vestfold, and now they began to descend. By midafternoon, we were mired in a suffocatingly thick gray fog. We dared not move. Rorik ordered the sails furled and rowing to cease. All we could do was drift aimlessly, shunted helplessly about by wind and current. Without sun or stars to steer by, there was no way to follow our proposed route. We would be certain to founder on shoals or crash into a headland.

I started aft to the stern where Rorik was slumped over the tiller. Was nature to be our enemy as well as Ruskil? 'Twas not unusual for these fogs to last several days. Rorik vacillated between despondency and fury.

"By Odin! The gods can't do this to me. If we do not arrive as scheduled, the others will think I've abandoned them or scrapped the plans. They'll wait one, maybe two, days, but no more."

There was nothing I could say, and I returned to where Astrid and Cyri were preparing a light meal.

"My lady," Astrid said, "is the jarl worried about the fog?"

"Yes, dreadfully worried. We dare not continue sailing, but we cannot miss assembling with the other ships. This fog is fatal to all our plans."

"But you have the stones."

"The rune stones?" I asked. "What good are they now?"

"Use their magic to guide us."

"What are you saying, Astrid?" Was there something more to the stones than the meaning of the inscriptions, something I'd never been told? I was ready to believe anything now, even magic.

"No one told you? The stones were born in the land from seeds dropped by the Great Star of the North. Always they seek to return to their father in the sky. Get the stones. I will show you."

I hastened to where I'd put them among my things. When I returned, she tore a thread from a seam and looped one end around a stone. Then she held it out at arm's length by the other end. Slowly the stone twisted and turned as if it were seeking the path it wished to follow. Then it stopped and remained immobile.

413

"Note how it hangs," she said. "Now try it yourself."

I lifted the string and spun the stone around. When it stabilized, the tip was pointing in exactly the same direction as before. I turned around. No matter which way I faced or now much I twisted the string, the rune stone returned to its original position.

"You see," she said, "it never shifts. Now take it to the jarl. The magic will guide us to Jaeder."

At sea level, we were completely enveloped by the fog; but above us, the mist thinned to a smoky haze for a moment, and the sun burned a brilliant red like a ball of fire. I shivered in the icy wind blowing down on us from the north. Fire and ice! "Remember the runes when the Raven flies through fire and ice." Had old Signe really been able to see this far into the future? It mattered not. This was an omen, an omen for good. I hastened back to Rorik.

He scoffed when I explained the power of the runes. "I've not heard of such power. 'Tis coincidence," he snorted, "or the wind."

"The wind keeps changing," I said. "You doubt the runes?"

"I doubt they know their way to Jaeder."

"No, but to the North Star. Can't you steer if you locate the position of the star?"

"And if they lead us straight into shoals or south to Jutland?"

"Is that worse than remaining becalmed here? Losing our only chance to invade Hordaland?" I had been turning the stone around. "See, always it points the same way."

"Fasten it to the tiller. The men will have to row." He called for one man to climb the mast. "If you see anything —anything at all—shout it out immediately."

Slowly we moved across the water. Astrid had to be right. Rorik was trusting me, going against his own best judgment. If this failed—I would not think about failure. The men were silent; the only sounds, the lapping of oars against the waves. For the rest of the day the fog was a pale, ghostly gray. As night came on, it was a dense, black curtain. For two days we moved thus, never unfurling the sail. Rorik remained at the tiller, his eyes on the rune stone, his voice urging the men not to be afraid.

Sometime during the early hours of the second night, the wind freshened. As quickly as the fog had enveloped us, it was dispersed by a stiff breeze from the east. One by one the stars appeared above us, and the moon shone full. When Rorik saw the North Star to the right of the dragon head, he said quietly, "We are still on course." With that he turned the tiller over to Olav and fell into an exhausted sleep on the stern deck.

In the large harbor at Jaeder, all the ships were waiting for us. We moored among them, and now began the second part of the carefully designed plot. Rorik was under no illusion that Ruskil was unaware of the move against him. But we had one advantage: Ruskil did not know when.

A skeleton crew remained on board each ship to protect it, but the rest followed Rorik a half-day's forced march inland. In addition to their own weapons, the men carried extra tools, kettles of pitch, food, and anything else they would need to exist independently. They were all seasoned Viking warriors; but like any good military commander on the eve of battle, Rorik put them through a concentrated period of intense training to make them even better fighters. Their reflexes became quicker and their eyes keener. No enemy would sneak up on them. They became accustomed to going two days without food with no loss of strength or agility.

They constructed a solid, hard-packed earthen wall and practiced throwing axes at it at steplike intervals and then climbing up hand over hand by holding onto the ax handles. They had no gate to break in, but they cut down a tall, sturdy tree and stripped the branches. Then they lined up on either side, put the trunk on their shoulders, and walked with it until Rorik told them they could put it down. After a short rest, they picked it up again. Over and over they repeated the exercise until they could lift the huge trunk as easily as they would an armload of kindling. Next they grasped it with both hands, and while Rorik shouted out the command, they swung it at a large pine in the rhythm they would use to ram a gate until the tree came crashing down.

In the evenings they celebrated the end of the training sessions by downing horns of mead or ale and howling wildly as they romped through the violent spears and axe games I had first seen the day I was captured. By the end of the week, the men were hungry for blood. As planned earlier, half the forces were to sail up to the town and attack from the fjord. The rest would debark below the town, meet up with the other land forces, breach the wall from the rear, and attack Ruskil first—to draw his main body away from the waterfront.

In the morning, Rorik and Olav would transfer to the *Sharkfin*, the smaller ship now stripped for battle. In spite of our protests that they had no part in our quarrel with Ruskil, Nels and Paul insisted on accompanying Rorik into the fray. They would go in with the land forces. Past the age of fighting, Sven and Haki remained on the *Raven* with us.

Neither Rorik nor I were able to sleep the night before his final departure for Hordaland. We stood at the prow, guarded by the magnificently fierce dragon head that loomed above us, and I remembered the night he first carried me there, screaming and protesting. I had been tricked into marriage, and for a long time had fought against falling in love with him. Not because I did not find him the most forceful and attractive man I'd ever known, but because I feared the consequences of succumbing to him completely. Now we were about to be separated for a second time, and I knew not how I would endure the ensuing days and nights without him. I had been tortured the first time we were apart by not knowing what had really happened or why. 'Twas no easier now, aware as I was of the dangers he faced.

"Hold me, close, Rorik. Tell me you'll be back soon."

"Before you miss me, Seabird.'

"No, I'll long for you every minute you are gone. Please, my love, let me go with you. I can't bear the thought of being separated again. I'm afraid for you."

"No reason to be. We will be attacking from land and the fjord at the same time. Ruskil will be caught in a wolf trap from which there is no escape. I will return for you the minute Hordaland is secured and 'tis safe for me to leave."

"Then sail on the *Raven*," I urged again. "I'll not be so fearful if you have the dragon head to guide you. You know what happened when we traveled to Zealand on the *Albatross*."

"I never thought you to be superstitious, Tara. No, my love, 'tis the chieftain commanding and the men pulling the oars who make the luck, not the ship. There are too many of you to be comfortable on the smaller ship, and the *Raven* is not fitted for battle."

"At least let us sail part of the way with you and moor near one of the outer isles. We'll not be in danger there, and not so far for you to come when 'tis over."

He gave me no answer, but he held me so close our hearts beat as one while we stood there, enveloped in each other's arms.

As dawn lightened the eastern sky, Rorik donned his thick, protective leather jerkin, his woolen trousers tightly wrapped to his legs with leather thongs, and the twin-pointed cape I made for him in Constantinople. For the first time since the day of the raid on the abbey, he was also wearing the bronze helmet with the twin horns of Odin. Only then did it really hit me that he was truly armed for battle.

The *Raven* was now commanded by the Jarl Hardred, an elderly but shrewd Viking who knew the waters between Jaeder and Hordaland as well as any man alive. With the first threat of danger, he could sail into seldom-traveled fjords and through inland waterways few dared to navigate.

"And will we be sailing rather than remaining moored?" I asked Rorik just before he left to board the *Sharkfin*.

"I'm granting one of your requests. Hardred has orders to follow tomorrow."

I reached up and brought his face close to mine. "Thank you, my love. You'll not be sorry."

"But you are to stay in the outer isles, away from all danger."

Rorik sailed with the tides. Twenty-four hours later we followed. Mooring at one of the islands friendly to Rorik's cause, we spent most of each day on land and returned to the ship only to sleep. There were three small farms where we bartered for milk and fresh vegetables. Without the children, who took me by the hands and insisted on exploring all of the island, I know not how I would have endured the long days of waiting. Although we were less than four leagues from the mainland now, no word came to us about any confrontation between Rorik and Ruskil or any battles being waged.

During the day, I was all right, walking the island, picking flowers with the children, eating a simple lunch by the stream. With sunset, however, the nightmares began. No matter how often Astrid assured me the passage of time must mean the victory was going to Rorik, I envisioned him and all our men lying dead.

"As long as we remain here undisturbed," Astrid said, "our men are succeeding. If not, Ruskil's men would have pounced on us and carried us off by now."

"They might not know we are here."

"Do not be mistaken, my lady. They would know. They are too busy to bother with us."

"Oh, Astrid, I hope so. I desperately hope you are right."

Still I could not sleep. I curled up on the pallet in the prow, trying to pretend that Rorik lay next to me, his strength sheltering me against all illusionary fears and ephemeral terrors.

Near the middle of the second day after we moored at the island, I saw a prow swiftly cutting the channel of the fjord, aided by the outgoing tide. I did not recognize the ship. I saw only the tattered sail hanging from a broken mast; and when it came closer, I counted the number of empty oar locks. Calling for Astrid to watch the children, I hastened down from my hilltop lookout to shore. Then I waited frantically for the ship to reach land. Be it Rorik's or Ruskil's ship, I knew the suspense would soon be over. If Rorik had won, I would be overjoyed. If Ruskil, I would no longer care what happened to me.

Some twenty Vikings manned the oars and nearly that many lay deadly still or moaning in agony on the battered planks of the hull. Most were covered with blood. A few had ben hurriedly wrapped in makeshift bandages. None of the faces was familiar to me, and my breathing returned to normal with the hope the ship was one of Ruskil's. If so, Rorik was victorious and the enemy were fleeing.

All too soon my nightmares became reality. One of the rowers, his head swathed in dirty linen, turned his face to me. It was a chieftain who had gone in with our ships. I stood there unable to breathe, bereft of all hope.

Chapter Twenty-seven

PULLING AN OAR, but so begrimed with dirt and blood I scarce recognized him, was Paul. Near him was Sigurd, one of the men who first captured me outside the abbey. Since then I had come to know him as a stalwart friend of Rorik and a fierce warrior. If he had fled from the battle, the situation was desperate. I indicated to Paul where Cyri and the children were and hastened to Sigurd's side. I had to know the truth, devastating as it might be.

"Where is Rorik? Tell me, Sigurd, where is he?"

"It was a fierce battle, Tara. I've never seen such slaughter."

"Later! What has happened to Rorik?"

"It was a rout, a complete rout!" I expected him to be wailing rather than shouting like he'd lost his mind.

As cold as it was for early autumn, Sigurd was covered with sweat, and blood streamed from a wound in his arm. I shivered and then broke out in a nauseated cold sweat.

"He is dead, isn't he?"

"No, no, Tara. 'Tis true that those of us who breached the walls were too busy with our own fight to know how those from the other ships were faring. We met up with the land forces opposed to Ruskil and attacked as planned. It was finally by Rorik's order I sailed down the fjord on the *Seahawk* with some of the wounded. He wanted to trick Ruskil into thinking many of our men were fleeing."

"But who—who, Sigurd—is winning?" I gritted my teeth to keep from shaking the information out of him.

"We are! Once we breached the wall—"

Merciful heavens! At last I could breathe again.

"No more now. That's all I wanted to know." In the distance I saw Cyri and Astrid coming with Paul to care for the wounded. Meanwhile Hardred had left the *Raven* and was also hastening toward us. After weighing the odds, I made a decision.

"Hardred," I asked, "is the *Raven* ready to sail?"

"She is always ready."

"Summon the crew. We're sailing up the fjord. If Rorik is still alive, I want to be with him. If he is slain, I must see he has a Viking chieftain's burial."

"No, my lady," Sigurd intervened. " 'Tis not safe. We might never make it back through the village."

"Are you afraid for me or for yourself, Sigurd?" I was determined to go in and furious with him for wanting to delay me.

"I am no coward, Tara. And I know too well your lack of fear. If you choose to return, I'll be the sword at your right hand."

"Thank you, Sigurd. See to the laying out of the dead on the *Seahawk* while I confer with Hardred about sailing in. I need also to make arrangements as well for Astrid, Cyri, and the children to stay here on the island."

All this took no more than a few minutes. A farm family agreed to take care of the wounded who remained behind. Meanwhile the crew from the *Raven* had honored the dead by laying them out in the *Seahawk* with their weapons beside them. Within the prow and the stern, they piled dry faggots and straw and fashioned torches from branches and torn garments. A free man from the island who was caulking his boat gave us the pitch to smear on the torches.

The red-and-white-embroidered sail on the *Raven* was unfurled and the ship guided around the *Seahawk* so that, once set on fire, the latter could be sent to sea on the outgoing tide.

While this was being done, Sigurd and I were engaged in another argument.

"Not the dragon head," Sigurd insisted.

"I'll not go in without it. 'Tis Rorik's insignia."

"Yes, and will be recognized while we're yet sailing up the fjord. 'Twill be dangerous enough trying to land and get into the village. Why announce our coming in time for Ruskil to get prepared and ready for us?"

"You can stay here and nurse the wounded," I fumed.

"By Thor, Tara, I'm no nursemaid, and you know it. 'Tis foolhardly, but I'll argue no more."

At that same moment I saw something that chilled my blood more than my fear of meeting up with Ruskil. Approaching the strait from the sea was a new ship. I had seen it in the harbor at Zealand. It was one of Torvald's. Rorik had been right. Now the Dani were coming either to assist Ruskil in the battle or to block our escape route. No matter how quickly we prepared to sail, they would soon be upon us and catch us long before we reached the town. Even should they let us sail clear up the fjord, they would be a fearsome foe at our back, dividing our forces, while we tried to make our way into the village. Yet, if we remained on the island, they would attack us there.

Hardred looked as worried as I felt. "What say you, my lady?"

What we needed in order to escape was a diversion. My mind reverted to the day I watched as wolves circled around me, waiting for the fire to die down so they could approach. Then suddenly they turned on my defenseless horse and slashed him to pieces.

I looked at the *Seahawk*, ready to be fired and sent to sea.

"We use the dead to save the living," I said.

The crew of the *Raven* were seated at the oars to augment the power of the sail. The golden dragon head glinted in the sun. Five of the less seriously wounded were ready to fire and launch the *Seahawk*. Hardred, following my suggestion, was standing on the stern deck of the *Raven* waiting for the most advantageous moment to give the signal.

Torvald's ship continued to sail up the strait, increasing its speed as it saw what seemed to be easy prey just waiting to be snared. To my surprise, I saw the king himself standing in the prow. For a frightening second, I thought I might have been wrong, that he was coming to our aid. Then I saw both Torvald and his warriors draw their swords and pick up their shields. At this close distance, there was no doubt they had recognized the *Raven*. They were coming as foes, not friends.

Suddenly Hardred dropped his sword arm. Too late for the Dani to see what was happening and to slow their rate of approach, the *Seahawk* was fired and launched into the outgoing tide, amid wild entreaties to Thor and Odin. Just as the burning *Seahawk* reached the channel, Torvald's longboat crashed into it amidships. Flaring timbers and flaming tar-covered masses of cloth were sent flying through the air. The enemy sail caught fire; then the mast flared up and crashed down in flames amid the frantic, bewildered crew. The screams of the men mingled with the roar of the flames, the sounds of exploding pitch, and the hissing of burning wood as it hit the waterline. Before we were out of sight, the two ships melded into one tremendous inferno as the tide carried them out to sea. Until the last, until he was engulfed by heavy smoke and falling timbers, Torvald remained standing at the prow, his sword held aloft as if in a final challenge to the gods. He was no coward, but he was a traitor; and I rejoiced to see him meet a traitor's death.

In spite of my words to Sigurd, I was still desperately afraid. I had no idea what I would do when we reached the town. My thoughts were concentrated on finding Rorik. Sigurd's assurances that our men were winning did not dispel my fears that Rorik could have since been slain and Ruskil was still in control of the town.

As we sailed up the fjord, I moved to the prow to stand under the dragon head. Audacity might prove a stronger shield than fear or temerity. Sigurd came to stand beside me. I needed something to take my mind off the battle raging in the town and my fears for Rorik.

"Tell me, Sigurd, how went the fighting when you attacked?" I forced myself to concentrate on his description of the ploy to distract Ruskil's attention from Rorik's landing on shore. As he related the vicious turmoil of the previous days, I found it harder and harder to listen. Our men had fought valiantly, many of them to the death.

Sigurd and other chieftains had sailed their flotilla to a landing site a league below the town. A deserted bay, used only during the summer fishing season, its few inhabitants offered no threat. The fighting ships moored to a natural breakwater, they marched by night, without flares or torches, to the fields beyond the walls of the town. The men followed a stream to a forest, went through the forest and past a scattering of farms. Only the sheep, aroused by a group of strange men sneaking past their byre, disturbed the stillness of the night. In sight of the town, they joined up with the allies from Sogn and the Fjords.

The men from the northern shires had met little resistance on their way to and through Hordaland. Then they learned that Ruskil had ordered a convening of the Thing with only his own followers to make new laws. It was being held in the town. At dawn our forces attacked first the hirdmen bivouacked outside the walls. The fighting was fierce but erratic. Since Ruskil's men had been taken by surprise, they had no time to organize a unified plan of defense. No Viking sleeping in the open, however, ever lies down without sword and spear, so once roused by the attack, they were ready to fight.

Within an hour, the air above the battleground was noisy with whirring, screeching hawks and ravens that came to gorge on the slain. Greedy dogs, hungry for fresh meat after a meager diet of scraps, skulked over from nearby farms.

By evening of the second day, the perimeter of the town was secured by our forces, but with a heavy toll of men. Heavier yet were the losses among Ruskil's allies. Those not dead or mortally wounded were captured and tied to the trees in full view of anyone observing from inside the town. If Ruskil looked out, he would see a strange phalanx of warriors, all standing straight and tall, all facing the town as if ready to attack. But all were bound and helpless.

The one sad note for me was the death of Nels. I knew then why Paul had seemed particularly distraught when I saw him on the *Seahawk*.

"Yes," Sigurd said, "Nels saved his life. Paul fought as valiantly as any of the Vikings. When one of Ruskil's men attacked him from the rear, Paul could not hear a warning shout. Nels dashed between them, and the blade meant for Paul slashed his skull. Paul will always feel he should be the one lying on the field, not Nels."

Among Ruskil's men attacked in the camp were no jarls and few chieftains. They had spent the night within the town, carousing and celebrating after the day's formal meeting. When they did not come to the assistance of their men outside the walls, Sigurd knew Rorik's ships had attacked from the fjord as planned.

Once the area around the town was secured, Sigurd's forces laid siege to the walls. While some moved the dead to be buried later and tended to the wounded, others set about chopping down a tall, straight, sturdy pine and cut off the branches. The sound of axes rang like a clarion through the now deathly still air.

The heavy wooden gates of the tunnel through the earthwork walls had been bolted from the inside. Twenty of the strongest men heaved the tree trunk to their shoulders and marched to the gates. While one chieftain shouted out the command, the men began a steady pounding of the solid gates with the battering ram. The hard days of training were now being put to the test. Over and over they thrust forward and pulled back until it seemed they would drop from exhaustion. But these were men who manned the oars of their serpent ships for as many as eight hours at a stretch without breaking stroke. Again they struck, and again.

When the gate still did not give, Sigurd led a group to the walls. First one and then another threw his axe, each higher than the last, until they had formed foot- and hand-holds by which they could scale the hard-packed earthwork. Now came the time to use the tree's branches, which had been laid aside but not discarded. They were covered with pitch, which the men had lugged from the ships, and set afire. Each man scaling the wall carried his sword in his right hand and a flaming weapon in his left. In spite of being so encumbered, they clambered from axe to axe like cats scurrying up a tree. But the descent down the other side was halted by forces waiting below for the invaders. The first man flung his flaming torch among those guarding the tunnel entrance, setting several men afire and dispersing the others long enough for more men to mount the wall and send their torches flying toward the enemy. Soon the rough grass on the inside of the barricades caught fire, and the entire area was aflame.

In the midst of this searing holocaust, Sigurd and his men were fighting hand to hand with the enemy forces not rolling on the ground to put out the flames burning their clothes. During a lull in the skirmish, Sigurd's forces managed to open the gate to allow the mass of men still outside to enter and assist Rorik in taking the town.

Sigurd found Rorik and a small force fighting along the stream that runs through the middle of town. Rorik was slashing out and disarming every man who approached him.

"At that point, he was winning," Sigurd said, "but Ruskil and his jarls had pulled back to regroup their forces and plan a new strategy. Our men were piling into town by way of the gate, and Rorik's forces were being strengthened with more of his followers coming by way of the beach. However, we didn't know how many free men were in town or their loyalties. Would they come to the aid of Ruskil or us? It was then Rorik saw I was wounded.

He suggested the feint of getting a ship and making it look like we were fleeing. I chose among the wounded those who, at a distance, still looked hearty enough to fight. If the ruse were to succeed, we must not look like casualties. On the beach, we picked up a few who were more seriously wounded or dying to save them from mutilation by any free men opposed to us."

We were now approaching the town. When Sigurd left, Rorik was winning; but we knew not what had occurred during the succeeding hours. They could have given Rorik the opportunity to secure the town, or they might have afforded Ruskil the time to reorganize his forces and prepare for a new counterattack. There were few people along the waterfront, so I knew whatever fighting was still going on was taking place elsewhere. I was apprehensive about those watching us approach, not knowing their feelings. I was going in as their jarl's wife and I ordered the crew to raise their oars in salute before furling the sail. Then the men rowed in swift, steady rhythm toward shore. Once tied up to the mole, they raced off the ship, banging spears against shields and raising their voices in wild yells to Odin.

If nothing else, our actions might dumbfound the enemy long enough for us to appraise the situation. Cautiously I left the ship and walked the long, solitary distance of the mole, remembering the warm, bear-hug greeting I had received there from Thorne. Now he was dead, and Rorik was trying to re-establish his rightful place among his people. Had they welcomed him ashore with joyful shouts or had they challenged him? Looking on the faces of those waiting along the beach, I could find no answer.

Suddenly I was surrounded by a frantic group, clutching at my arms, grabbing my clothes. There was no way to to escape them. I was terrified and bewildered. When had their love turned to hate? Then I saw the smiles. In my fear, I had forgotten that such an exuberant greeting was typical of the Vikings. They were not attacking me; they were welcoming me home! It had to mean the free men were on Rorik's side and he was winning. I was still shaking, but now I could return their greetings.

I noticed a woman pushing her way through the crowd. Her skin was pale and her face drawn and grief-stricken. "Welcome, my lady. I am Greta, daughter of Olav."

How very glad I was to see her! I recognized her as one I

had seen often when I rode in from the farm. And to think I had not known then who she was.

"How goes the fighting, Greta?" I needed her assurance that I was right to be optimistic. "I have come to be near Rorik."

'They have been fighting near the breastworks, but our men are winning. I think it safe for you to approach."

"Is Olav with them?"

"My father is dead." No, he couldn't be. Not after all we had been through together. Not after what he had come to mean to me. Greta maintained a stoic calm, but I was shattered by grief. "Come," she said, "I will go with you. We will speak of my father later." She meant it would not do to weep in front of the others.

Half the crew remained near the ship; Sigurd and the rest formed a protective guard around us.

As I followed Greta through the streets, I mourned the death of my good and faithful friend, the stalwart companion who had saved my life so many times and made endurable my days in Constantinople. I loved him much as I had loved Thorne; both had filled the role of the gentle, supportive father I'd never known. I lost much with their deaths. There would be time later to cry and berate the gods for the unfairness of it all.

Nearing the stream where Sigurd said Rorik had first done battle with Ruskil's men, we passed many dead, their flesh already being attacked and pulled apart by ravenous hawks and other scavengers. Gagging, I turned away as a wild dog tore open a man's belly and ripped out the intestines. The animal ran away with the mangled remains wrapped around his body.

Some men lay alone: a spear had pierced the eye of one; a double-bladed ax lay embedded in the skull of another. Many had fallen with their arms around their opponents after both had sustained mortal wounds in hand-to-hand combat. We had to pick our way carefully through the morbid scene, willing our senses not to react to what the mind could scarcely tolerate.

I dreaded what I would see when we reached the earthenworks. Greta said our men were winning, but what of Rorik? Instead of the sounds of battle I expected to hear, there was an ominous silence ahead of us. We seemed to be walking toward a land of the dead.

We crossed the stream that bisected the town and

neared the inner entrance to the tunnel. A number of our men sat leaning against the wall and the neighboring buildings. They were slumped in every conceivable posture of exhaustion, but not defeat. I prayed it meant the battle was over, the town secured. One raised his hand and silently pointed. We turned and hastened toward an area of open land within the town walls, the burial ground. It was immediately apparent that there among the boat-shaped mounds an especially fierce battle had been waged. Many of the mounds were trampled down, and there were torch-seared patches of grass. Men lay between the mounds or propped against them, those still alive as quietly inert as their dead allies and foes. There were few untouched by sword or ax blade.

Amidst the slaughter and carnage I saw the one face I had been seeking. Towering above them all like a protective guardian was the figure of Rorik, and I began trembling with relief. His long cape hung limp in the still air, and his face was lined with fatigue; but there was a new assertive power in his stance. With his sword, he was directing the activities of those still on their feet.

Immediately I saw him, I picked up my skirts and ran toward him, heedless of the men and bodies I had to pass.

"Tara! What in the name of Hel are you doing here?" Let him shout and scold. I was too joyful to care.

"I had to come. I had to know if you were safe."

"You could have been killed, you little fool." But he was smiling and reaching for me.

"Twould not have mattered what happened to me if you were dead." I was out of breath from exhaustion and fear.

All the while scolding me for having disobeyed him, he gathered me up in his arms and held me close. Under the cloak I felt his heart beating as fast as mine, and I knew it was not from the exertion of battle.

"Is it over, Rorik?"

"Almost. Just one more bit of business to attend to. During the night, Ruskil and four of his jarls managed to get past the walls and barricade themselves in a farmhouse just outside."

It was just the sort of thing a blackguard like Ruskil would do—leave his men to fend for themselves while saving his own skin.

"And his other chieftains?" I asked.

"Dead or captured."

"Then surely 'twill not be hard to attack and put an end to him."

" 'Tis not as easy as that. They are holding the family hostage. An attack would mean innocent deaths. There've already been enough of those."

The bastard! I thought. His heart was as warped as his evil visage. "What then do you plan?"

"I have sent a challenge to Ruskil to meet in hand-to-hand combat. He was much too cowardly to face me during battle, but he'll not dare to refuse such a challenge."

My heart sank, but I could say nothing. If that was Rorik's wish, so be it. I had seen them fight before—wrestling without swords, to be sure—and they were as equally matched as any two men could be. It would be impossible to forecast the outcome. Luck would play the most important part in deciding the winner. It would be two strong, invincible men—each hating the other, each determined to be King of the Three Shires—who would meet face to face. I could not bear the thought of watching it, but neither could I leave Rorik's side. Somehow I had to find the strength to remain.

While we waited for Ruskil's response, Rorik and I sat on one of the burial mounds, and he told me of Olav's death.

"Olav was wounded more than a dozen times, I warrant, before he finally fell. Even then he still breathed, and I hoped to save him. We found his daughter and carried him to her house in the town. Her weeping was most pitiful. 'Why,' she asked, 'do you make me mourn twice? As a child I cried when told he was dead. Now I must weep anew.'

"I tried to assure her there was a chance he would recover, but she saw better than I the signs of mortality upon his face and body. 'He will have a warrior's death,' she said. He'd not loosed his grip on his sword, so we knew he would go to Valhalla."

"Did she know of her father's—his condition?"

"Not at first. I returned later in the day. Olav was gone by then, having roused up only long enough one time to know he was with her and that she knew him as her father. When she cleansed his body for burial, she learned the truth."

"It must have been a hard moment for her," I sighed.

"It was, but she said it consoled her for his death. She could remember he died a man even if forced to live so many years as less than one."

I wept quietly, thinking of all Olav had meant to me. "I never thought him to be anything but a man, a true Viking in all he did and was."

"She was right though, Tara. We never really knew what he suffered during these past years. He would want to die a warrior, not an enfeebled old eunuch. Once I have seen Ruskil die, we will prepare Olav's ship for his final voyage."

In midafternoon, Ruskil walked through the tunnel. Behind him strode his four cohorts, armed and wary. At his side, her hand lightly but possessively touching his cape, walked Raghild, as haughty and sullen as ever. I gasped involuntarily, but there was no change of expression on Rorik's face. He merely raised one eyebrow and nodded to some of his hirdmen, who sauntered over and casually grouped themselves near her. Then he turned his back for a moment, as if this fight were of no more consequence than a hunting expedition.

From the smirk on Ruskil's face, I knew he was either certain of an easy victory or he had some evil ruse within his grasp. Sword in hand, he marched straight up to Rorik, who kept his back toward his brother just long enough to show his contempt. Then he turned around slowly. During the long, terrible minutes that followed, I remained frozen in one place. Nor did I take a single easy breath. I marshaled all my inner resources to control my fear and watch in silence.

"So, Ruskil, you are at last ready to meet me face to face."

"I did not wish to spill your blood, dear brother."

"No, you sniveling coward, you would pay others to do it for you."

Ruskil's expression of proud self-confidence changed to rage and hatred. "By Thor, I *will* kill you for that."

"Only if you are also prepared to die."

With that Rorik clapped his helmet more securely on his head and threw off his cloak. Under it he wore a jerkin of leather thick enough to ward off the heavy blows of a double-edged broadsword. A high leather collar protected his throat as well, but his arms were bare.

Now all attention was focused on the two brothers. Those who were in a condition to stand—jarls, chieftains, and free men—formed a circle around the combatants. None made any move to stop the fight. Nor would any come to the aid of either man. This was a fight to the death between the two brothers. The wounded anxiously propped themselves against the burial mounds. Only the dead were oblivious to the drama unfolding before them. As I stood with the rest, my eyes never moved from Rorik's face and my heart beat in the steady, heavy rhythm of a death knell.

Rorik's shield already bore scars from warding off many a powerful blow. Sigurd moved to stand beside me, and I was fearful lest I should need his strong arm before the deadly combat was over.

For a long moment Rorik and Ruskil made no move; and the air was heavy with the stillness of unexpelled breath. Each stared, eyes filled with venomous hatred, into the face of the other.

Suddenly Ruskil raised his arm, and Rorik parried the blow aimed at his head. From then on there was no cessation of the battle. Broadsword fighting is all whacking and slashing; seldom do the combatants jab point first, as with a spear. Rorik struck Ruskil a solid blow to one shoulder. Ruskil returned with a resounding smash on Rorik's helmet, and I wrung my hands as he staggered back, stunned and reeling from the impact. Undaunted he began raining blows on Ruskil's left arm and shoulder while Ruskil protected his sword arm with his shield. First blood had been drawn.

So it went, it seemed for hours—attack and parry, attack and parry. Ruskil appeared always to aim for Rorik's head whereas Rorik strove to disable his brother's arms. Neither showed any signs of weakening.

Then, without any break in rhythm, Ruskil changed tactics and hit Rorik twice, first in the chest and then on his right arm. Horrified, I saw Rorik's sword go spinning out of his hand and land in front of Ruskil. He immediately put his foot on it, so that if Rorik attempted to retrieve it, he must come close enough for Ruskil to strike a mortal blow.

For a second Rorik stood bewildered. A new fear engulfed me. I was certain I was watching the end, and I was not prepared for it. I wanted to clutch Sigurd's arm, but I dared not show any alarm. According to Thing law, a man could fight only with his own sword which must be left lying where and as it fell. Although Rorik still had his knife, and his shield was within reach, these were no defense against Ruskil's strong arm and deadly blade. Rorik would have to approach carefully and then bend down to retrieve his weapon.

However, instead of edging forward cautiously, a step at a time, Rorik lunged toward his brother fearlessly, too swiftly for Ruskil to react immediately. But Rorik was finally thwarted by two sudden movements by Ruskil. Ruskil pressed his boot down hard on the sword, snapping the blade from the handle. In the next second, his own sword struck ruthlessly against the side of Rorik's head, missing the exposed back of his neck only because Rorik saw the blow coming in time to shift position.

Rorik was stunned but not finished. How he did it, I'll never know, but he managed to crawl safely away from his brother. I yearned to aid him in some way. It was agony to stand by helplessly, and it took all my strength to keep from rushing to him. Beside me, Sigurd seemed as restless as I. Unable to stand still, he kept pushing against me. Rorik raised up on one knee, shook his head as if to clear it, then stood up, still wavering. Then he was backing slowly in our direction, never taking his eyes off Ruskil's face. Sigurd nudged me again, and I felt my hand grasping cold steel. I was momentarily stunned to realize he was handing me his own sword. Rorik was almost close enough now to touch, and I saw his hand reaching back toward us. Then it dawned on me. He was relying on Sigurd to interpret the Thing law of "as it lay" in the same way he had. Ruskil had defied that law by breaking Rorik's sword. Now Rorik was free to use any sword offered him. And Sigurd wanted me to be the one to aid Rorik, to be my husband's true helpmate. In another second I had placed the sword in his hand. Still keeping the weapon concealed behind his back, he once more advanced slowly toward Ruskil.

Unaware that Rorik had a second weapon, Ruskil relaxed his vigilance and prepared to attack. Then, seeing Rorik coming toward him, once again with sword in hand, he flung his shield up to protect his head from the blows he anticipated. Rorik took two steps, raised his sword, then unexpectedly lunged and jabbed Ruskil in the belly with a single, slashing thrust. At the first impact, Ruskil fell back, dropping sword and shield. The look on his face registered his shock at realizing he was mortally wounded.

With blood pouring from his mouth, and a gory mass bulging through the jagged wound, Ruskil crouched at Rorik's feet. Each breath was agony; each word a desperate effort.

"Kill me, Rorik," he panted. "I can't live. Get it over with."

"No!" Rorik's voice was completely devoid of emotion.

I looked at Rorik's icy blue eyes. Never before had I seen such hatred and contempt as glared from them at that moment.

"Would I could force you to live hour for hour as I did while a slave. But you will suffer before you die."

"Let him die!" I screamed. "For God's sake, Rorik, end his suffering."

"Quiet, Tara. You are a Christian. I am a Viking, and I always will be. Watch how a Viking kills. This is the revenge I sought."

Slowly, painfully, Ruskil began struggling toward his sword. If he had to suffer, he would at least go to Valhalla as a warrior. Now he was hemorrhaging profusely from both the mouth and the rectum. He tried to contain his entrails with one hand while he reached desperately for the handle of his sword with the other. I felt as if I were suffering with him every agonizing movement, every painful, gasping breath. I hated Ruskil, yet I was sickened by his horrible situation. Just as his fingers touched the blade and his face relaxed, Rorik strode over and kicked the sword out of reach. Ruskil's face went ashen. Greater than his fear of death or suffering was his terror at being denied entrance to Valhalla. As one, the onlookers gasped in disbelief. Slowly, deliberately, Rorik looked at each of the jarls. Shocked and incredulous at this display of cruelty and power none moved to touch the sword or hand it to Ruskil.

"No, Ruskil, you'll not die like a Viking. You'll suffer eternally in the dark regions of Hel. 'Tis my final act of revenge. Think on it as you draw your last breath."

Then Rorik flung his own sword in the air with a wild yell to Odin. "Oh, mighty Odin, look on me and approve what I have done in your name!"

After that Ruskil collapsed completely, but he was not yet dead. Nor was anyone allowed to go near him.

"Let him lie there," Rorik commanded. "Odin's ravens will make short work of his body. See, they come now and hover over us, just waiting to feed on his corpse and pull out his hair to line their nests. 'Tis a fitting end for such a traitor as he."

I looked at Rorik. He was more than the forceful warrior who had carried me off or the dominating lover I had married. He was the vengeful king who had reclaimed his rightful position as ruler over the jarls, who now stood amazed and awestruck before him. He frightened me, yet I knew I could never have respected him had he acted otherwise.

As one, Ruskil's followers went down on their knees to pledge fealty and swear their allegiance to Rorik as their king. Our men stood to one side, confused about how to respond. Their loyalty was not in question, but they knew somehow this was not the proper course to take.

"Get up!" Rorik demanded. "What makes you think this play-acting will atone for such treachery as you displayed these past months?"

"Forgive us, Rorik. We intended no treachery. Your father died, and we thought you dead. Who but Ruskil was the rightful leader?"

"More fool you. Did you think my father died a natural death?"

"So we were told."

"So you were told," he mimicked. "And when you learned I was returning, did you think it a ghost come to claim what was his by rightful succession?" Once more his ice-blue eyes shot fire at the astonished men.

"What would you have us do?" they asked. "Do you plan to kill us as slowly as you did Ruskil?"

Rorik did not relieve their fears by answering directly. "First you will prepare all the dead for burial. You—not your serfs of hirdmen—will carry out this chore to honor the men who fought with or against you. Then we will hold a Gulathing of the Three Shires to elect me king in the proper manner." He left no question that there would be no one to challenge his position.

"I have one more command." His autocratic tone indicated he expected it to be carried out with no argument. "Word is to be issued immediately that I now proclaim myself King of Zealand and ruler of all lands along the Noric Channel formerly controlled by Torvald."

The defeated jarls accepted the announcement with equanimity. Since the question of their future had not yet been decided, they were not ready to dispute his will. Their punishments would have to await the deliberation of free men and other jarls at the Gulathing. Our men surrounded Rorik, clapping him on the shoulder and proclaiming him the greatest Viking ever to rule in Hordaland.

At that moment Raghild wrenched herself away from the hirdmen who had moved in and made her captive the moment Ruskil was defeated. She flung herself at Rorik's feet.

"Forgive me, Rorik. I was out of my mind with jealousy. I knew not what I was doing."

Without looking at her, Rorik ordered, "Take her away! Put her aboard a boat—alone—and send her out to sea. Let her pray to Odin for her life."

As I watched Rorik issue commands and direct the action, I knew that for the moment I had no place in his thoughts. But I could be patient. I was wife to a Viking. When the brutal, masculine business of the day was finished, he would seek me out; and I would be waiting to give him the comfort and love he needed.

I did not have to wait long. Rorik walked slowly over to where I'd stood unmoving since the fatal duel began. His face was lined with fatigue; but his eyes, no longer aflame with hate and vengeance, shone with the glory of victory. Enveloped in his strong arms, my face against his broad chest, I listened to the steady beating of his heart. And I wept. I could not have gone on living if he'd been slain.

"Is it over now?" I asked.

"It is over, Seabird." He tipped my head up. The hands that had ruthlessly killed Ruskil were now surprisingly gentle against my skin. "I love you, Tara. I could not have done this without you."

"I did nothing but hand you a sword."

"You were near when I needed you. I ordered you to stay on the island because I feared for you here, but I desperately wanted you with me."

"And now?" I ran my fingers along the scar on his cheek.

"We go home at last."

Home. The word was sweet to hear. "And when you're proclaimed King of Zealand and the Three Shires?"

"I'll rule from the farm until I locate the best site on the coast for a massive round tower. I intend for it to proclaim my strength to all Norseland. Will you like being a queen?"

"Only if I can always stay by your side. Being your wife means much more to me."

He lifted me up and carried me to the cart one of his men had procured. The sun had dropped behind the mountains. When I shivered in the cold air, he wrapped us both securely in his cloak.

"Forever, Seabird. I'll go to Zealand to establish my claim, but you'll be with me."

The cart rode easily along the road to the farm. What would we find there? Astrid said Ruskil had destroyed everything I left behind after we embarked on our ill-fated voyage.

" 'Tis a pity," I said, "that I no longer have all the rune stones. I could read our future."

"We've no need of them now. Those Astrid saved came to our aid when we needed them most. If 'twas your fate to possess them for that one time only, they served their purpose."

He was right. Snuggled close to him, I cared not what the future held for us as long as we were together. I no longer had any desire to return to Britain. When we saw the farm lights in the distance, Rorik tightened his hold around my waist and brushed his lips across my hair.

"By all the gods, Tara, 'tis good to be coming home with you." His face broke into the smile that set my heart pounding and my blood racing. "A bit of supper and then —oh god, Seabird, you'll never know how much I need you."

With those words that he needed me, the last of my fears that he might someday put me aside disappeared.

"Who do you love?" I asked, burying my face against his neck and then biting the tip of his ear.

"Ow!" he shrieked. "You, you little minx." He reached under the robe and tickled me until I laughed so hard I fell off the seat and pulled him with me onto the floor of the cart.

No longer urged to step lively, the horse slowed to an ambling, leisurely pace. Rorik and I, lying wrapped in each other's arms on the soft straw and out of sight of the whole world, were in no hurry to reach the farm. Nor did I need the rune stones to show me what wonderful years with him and the children awaited me in the future.

AUTHOR'S NOTE

Throughout the book I have used some names and terms that are familiar to modern readers but which were not in existence in the tenth century. For example, *Byzantine* and *Byzantium* were not applied to that great empire until just before it ceased to exist. Nor was the city of Venice called by that name until the thirteenth century. There are some less important examples, but in all cases the modern names were used for the convenience of readers.

**THE HISTORY-MAKING
#1 BESTSELLER
ONE YEAR ON
THE NEW YORK TIMES LIST!**

THE THORN BIRDS

COLLEEN McCULLOUGH

"A heart-rending epic of violence, love, piety, family roots, passion, pain, triumph, tragedy, roses, thorns....The plot sweeps on in truly marvelous fashion to its tragic but triumphant conclusion."
<u>Chicago Tribune</u>

"A perfect read...the kind of book the word blockbuster was made for."
<u>Boston Globe</u>

AVON 35741 $2.50

TTB 6—78